VI

The ropes were flung over a beam, well apart, and tied off leaving Mary dangling upside down, her inverted skirt obscuring everything but her hair and her hands, both of which barely touched the ground. From belly to knees she was bare, her plump, well-furred quim clearly on display between open thighs.

'I do apologise, my dear,' Snapes stated. 'You must understand that it is entirely for your own benefit, and that if it obliges you to adopt a somewhat ridiculous posture, then that is but a small price to pay for the benefits. Sale, perhaps you could usher the next of our subjects in.'

Sale nodded and ushered in the tall blonde girl, whose face briefly registered surprise at the sight of Mary hanging upside down from the beam, before she too was grabbed, upended and suspended by her ankles. One by one they were given the same treatment, until all fifteen hung upside down, with fifteen plump young quims spread bare and ready for Luke Hurdon's attention.

Snapes contemplated the line of girls with his hand on his podgy chin before addressing Hurdon. 'Splendid, splendid, to work then. Here are the syringes, here the goose fat with which we shall ease their passages – a job, I think, best suited to myself.'

VELVET SKIN

Aishling Morgan

This book is a work of fiction.
In real life, make sure you practise safe sex.

First published in 2001 by
Nexus
Thames Wharf Studios
Rainville Road
London W6 9HA

www.nexus-books.co.uk

Typeset by TW Typesetting, Plymouth, Devon

Printed and bound by
Clays Ltd, St Ives PLC

ISBN 0 352 33660 9

To the Usual Suspects

Glossary

Barkers – pistols.

Bewray – to foul, to soil oneself.

Bitch booby – a military or town term for a country wench, implying both naivety and slovenliness.

Biter – in full – a wench whose cunt is ready to bite her arse – meaning a rampantly lascivious girl. 'Biter' might be deemed complimentary in some circumstances; 'bitch' biter definitely would not, much as a highly sexed modern girl might enjoy being called dirty, but not a dirty dog.

Black fly – a priest, because of their black robes. So called by farmers after paying tithes on a harvest, who might say that they have lost as much to the black fly as to the rain or frost.

Bobtail – any willing girl, but especially one who wiggles her bottom to excite male admiration.

Bull – one crown.

Cab – a brothel as well as a public conveyance.

Carib – a member of a cannibalistic tribe originally from South America, and from whom the word cannibal derives. When discovered by Europeans, they were eating their way slowly up the chain of the Antilles islands, devouring the local Arawaks. They were extremely warlike and resisted both Spanish and British for over two hundred years before being pacified.

Cove – another man of the crew, or the criminal fraternity in general.

Crew – a gang, or any association working together, be they the men on a ship or those intent on criminal exploits. One of the period slang words that has survived to this day.

Crop – to hang someone, or to break their neck.

Cull – any potential victim or person not of the criminal fraternity.

Darkmans – night-time, the time for thieves.

Dell – a young, but ripe girl, in some contexts a virgin. 'No deeper than a dell's doodle sack' – the depth of a vagina with hymen intact, i.e. very shallow.

Douser – a boxer, literally someone who puts their opponent's lights out.

Dust – money, especially in the form of winnings.

Flashman – a generic term for a madam's bully, hence the name of the notorious bully from *Tom Brown's Schooldays* and the modern *Flashman* series.

Feak – the anus.

Green gown – a dress smeared green at the back from its wearer having been mounted while lying on grass.

Hangallus – the shortened form of 'hanggallows', technically a criminal likely to end up on a gibbet, but more usually used as a general insult. Also a 'hanggallows look', meaning having a long face.

Hog – one shilling.

Lascar – an Indian, especially an Indian sailor, but often used as a wider term for non-white foreigners.

Leak – to reveal information, usually used in the sense of breaking a criminal code of silence.

Maid – a female servant, but also a young girl. In the

west-country, 'the maids' would be the daughters of the house and not servants for all but the gentry.

Miss Laycock – the vagina.

Mort – a woman, and generally a woman of the lower classes.

Prigging – thieving, especially as a profession. Usually qualified, such as 'priggers of prancers' meaning horse-thieves. The word was also slang for riding and having sex.

Rum – fine or valuable, much like 'wicked' in more recent slang. In the late eighteenth century 'rum' was also used to mean peculiar, which became the primary meaning, only to die out almost entirely.

Saunt – flat or smooth, when referring to a road or field, also smooth motion. Devon.

Sirreverence – faeces, a word said to derive from 'Sir, Reverence', an apology demanded of those caught relieving themselves at the roadside.

Smelt – a half-guinea.

Toad-eater – a dependant relative, and thus one who must put up with being the butt of jokes or taking on menial tasks. Later any person fawning on richer friends or those higher in status or rank.

Traps – watchmen and thief-takers in general. The term 'pigs' was also in use at the time, but later disappeared from common slang, only to re-emerge after about a century.

Upright man – the leader of a criminal gang, also a thief who preys on other, weaker thieves.

For a more detailed study of period slang see *A Classical Dictionary Of The Vulgar Tongue* (Captain Francis Grose, 1785, 2nd Ed, 1788) and *1811 Dictionary of the Vulgar Tongue* (Various inc. 'Hell Fire Dick', 1811, unabridged reprint 1984, Bibliophile Books).

One

As he lifted his claret glass, Henry Truscott's eyes followed the sway of Suki's hips beneath her dress. There was something taunting about the way she walked, either an indifference to what others might think or simple insolence. In any case, it was all too easy to imagine the full, dark-skinned bottom which swelled out the seat of her skirts, not covered, but spread bare for his attention, as she had been on numerous occasions. Even as she had passed he had caught her rich, distinctive scent, causing his cock to twitch in his breeches.

Sipping from his glass, he let the cold wine fill his mouth, then slide down his throat. His eyes left Suki's rump as she drew away from the table, turning to his wife, Eloise. She was in a cheerful mood, chattering happily to Charles Finch, who sat beside her, her face framed with red-gold hair set in an elaborate confection of ringlets. Her cheeks were flushed with wine, perhaps enough to mean she could be drawn into some erotic amusement, if only the opportunity could be had. At the least he could find an excuse to thrash Suki's delectable black backside, and from there ...

'Iced claret in July. I must say you do yourself well, Mr Truscott,' a voice broke in on Henry's thoughts.

Henry turned, smiling at Lewis Stukely, who had spoken.

1

'Our ice house[1] is across the stream,' Henry answered, gesturing vaguely to the far side of the valley. 'The north slope gets little enough sunlight, and once the lake is finished we expect to have ice the year round.'

'Quite the thing,' Stukely replied, following Henry's gesture to the steep, wooded slope, still partly in shade despite the height of the sun. 'You are on slate, I imagine?'

'In the main,' Henry replied.

'My own estate is much the same,' Stukely went on, 'although, of course, more mature. Still, the old ice house is quite inadequate, as are the cellars. There are many disadvantages to old-established land. I plan to have both renovated.'

Henry nodded, ignoring the implied insult to his new-found wealth and letting his thoughts return to Suki as she emerged from the house with a tray. From the front she was no less appealing than from the rear. Large breasts pushed out her bodice above a tight waist and wide hips, while her full lips and huge, dark eyes added not only to her exotic appeal, but to the same impudence conveyed by her walk. Again wondering if the luncheon party might not be followed by some more sensual amusement, he glanced around the table.

Eloise could usually be relied on, once sufficiently drunk. Failing that, she could always be aroused by the firm application of his hand to her naked rump, although the spanking process risked scratches. Charles Finch would certainly be keen; Judith Cates also, Charles's mistress and lacking any pretension to modesty. Stukely was hard to judge: boastful, yet occasionally priggish. Alone, Caroline Cunningham would have feigned shock and resistance, briefly. In company her refusal would be adamant, while the

2

presence of Mrs Aldgrave as her chaperone made matters yet more difficult. He sighed to himself, reflecting that he would have to wait until the evening and the pleasures of Eloise's warm curves.

'The estate is no more than ten years old, is it not?' Stukely asked, pressing his point.

'Nine,' Henry answered. 'The land was enclosed in 'eighty-four, but old Driscoll spent so much getting the act through that he ended up a bankrupt. I had the land from Child's Bank.'

'A common enough story, both in Devon and elsewhere,' Stukely went on. 'Enclosure² is to the good, of course, yet I do feel it important that the land remains in the hands of the old families. We alone understand our obligations.'

'My brother Stephen was saying much the same when he called on Miss Cunningham the other day,' Henry answered, knowing full well of the rivalry that existed between the two men.

Stukely didn't reply, and was blocked off from Henry's sight as Suki bent to serve. The curve of one breast pressed to his arm and once again he caught the scent of her body, rich and musky, very different from that of Eloise. His cock stiffened in response and he determined to find some excuse for a visit to the kitchens once luncheon was done. With luck Mrs Orcombe, the housekeeper, would be distracted – also Joanna, the girl they hired from the village when they had guests. Then he would be able to have Suki alone. A few kisses and she would go down across a table, or into the pantry, gripping a shelf while he turned up her skirts. He would expose her magnificent black bottom, the cheeks wide to show off the thick tangle of dark hair between them and the bright pink mouth of her sex. With no time for ceremony, he would put his cock straight to her, wetting the

3

head with spittle in case she was not ready. A few firm thrusts and he would come in her, or across her naked buttocks, leaving her to use her fingers for her own pleasure, as she always did after a fucking.

Henry shook himself as Suki moved away, trying to clear his head of lust. It didn't work, and even the normally satisfying combination of cold pigeon and claret failed to take his mind away from thoughts of ripe female bodies and his now hard cock. With house guests it had been hard to do more than enjoy Eloise at night, and he cursed himself for inviting Caroline Cunningham, who, for all her sweet curves and willing nature meant the presence of Mrs Aldgrave and Stukely.

His intention had been a few days of unbridled debauchery, with Eloise standing in as chaperone to Caroline. With enough drink and the wanton skills of Judith, it should have been possible to have all three girls out of their clothes at once. It might have been four girls, even five, if Caroline and Eloise could be persuaded to overcome their social concerns as well as their modesty and play with the maids. Unfortunately, the Cunninghams knew Henry's reputation and had sent Mrs Aldgrave along, following which Stukely had managed to attach himself to the party.

As Suki walked back towards the house, Joanna emerged, carrying a fresh jug of claret. For a moment they were side by side, Suki's dark skin brought into contrast with the pale cream of Joanna's. Joanna was taller, with abundant tawny-blonde curls, her figure promisingly full beneath her clothes. As she approached, Henry wondered how she would look stripped down, preferably beside Suki, cream against ebony, heavy breasts, gently swelling stomachs, chubby bottoms . . .

It was too much; he had to do something, even if only to relieve himself into Eloise's mouth once

4

luncheon was done with and he could get a moment of privacy. Unfortunately a trip was planned to nearby Meldon Pool, which made even that unlikely. The occasional snort or chink of harness from the direction of the stable signalled that Mr Orcombe was already putting the horses into their gear.

The rest of the meal passed in growing frustration, Henry doing his best to concentrate on anything but his need for sex and failing miserably. Only afterwards, with Eloise insisting on changing for the short journey, did his chance come. Excusing himself as quickly as he could, he followed his wife upstairs. She was at her dressing table, with Suki working on the buttons of her dress. Henry's hand was already going to the flap of his breeches as he came up behind her, his fingers fumbling at the buttons. As she turned he squatted down, catching her breasts in his hands.

'Harry!' Eloise squeaked as her breasts popped free of her bodice. 'Not in front of the servants!'

Suki giggled, stepping back as Henry's fingers found Eloise's nipples. His cock was free, pressing into the groove of her buttocks through her dress. She struggled, trying to get his hands away from her chest.

'Dammit, she's seen it before,' Henry growled, 'and more besides.'

'No, not . . .' Eloise began, stopping as Henry's mouth found hers. Her resistance went, her hands relaxing as her mouth opened under his.

He continued to fondle her, wondering if he had time to make Suki more than just a spectator. Eloise would do it, he knew, if allowed to retain the pretence of being pushed, yet there would be objections first, even if all three of them knew it was no more than a ritual. Deciding that there really was no time, Henry broke off the kiss, standing to prod his erection at Eloise's mouth.

'Is that all you want, you beast?' she said, but her mouth came open as he pressed his cock to her lips.

It went in, and he sighed as the warm, wet flesh of her mouth folded around his penis. Suki was watching her mistress suck, eyes twinkling, a sharp tongue flicking out to moisten her full lips. Henry took Eloise by the scruff of her neck, feeding his cock deep in and out of her mouth and trying to concentrate only on the pleasure of what he was doing. His orgasm was already approaching, his muscles tensing even as his eyes closed in bliss and came abruptly open at the sound of a timid knock at the door.

Eloise drew back hastily, Henry trying to keep his cock in but failing as she pushed him away. The door was opening and he turned to the window, pretending to admire the sunlit Devon countryside as he hid his erection.

'What is it, girl?' Eloise demanded, hastily returning her breasts to her bodice as Joanna stepped into the room.

'Beg pardon, ma'am,' Joanna replied, 'but Mrs Orcombe asked as to whether you'd be needing Suki or me up along Meldon way.'

'Certainly we shall need maids, both of you,' Eloise answered. 'You may ride behind the carriage.'

'Yes, ma'am,' Joanna replied.

Henry was forced to wait until the door had clicked shut behind Joanna, but Eloise had already risen. She threw him an arch look as she left the room, Suki following. Henry cursed, but followed, determined to make Eloise pay for her teasing in due time.

In the yard, both the carriage and Charles's high-perch phaeton were ready. Who was to travel in which had already been decided, leaving Henry in the company of Caroline Cunningham and the chaperone, depriving him of the chance either to discipline his wife or finish off what he had been doing. Sitting opposite Caroline, he was unable to ignore the way the uneven motion of the carriage made her breasts bounce; his frustration grew during the journey. By the time they reached the little village of Meldon it had reached a level which was close to unbearable.

Only then did his hopes rise. The track up to the moor and Meldon Pool proved too narrow for the carriage and too rough for the phaeton. Henry suggested that those who were able should continue to the pool on foot, knowing full well that this would exclude Mrs Aldgrave. Sure enough, she declined not to come, obliging Caroline to stay with her. Stukely quickly declared his intention of remaining. Eloise hesitated, glancing between the rough, water-worn track and Henry before her mouth took on a determined set and she agreed to come. Leaving Joanna to tend to the rest of the party and loading Suki with what provisions they needed, they set off.

Suki followed the others up the track. It was steep, running between stone walls and quickly moving into a wood of stunted trees, each hung with grey-green lichen, some with rough bark, others with clusters of orange berries. The path was rocky, and it was hard to move in the clumsy dress and petticoats, making her wish she could take them off to go naked in the warm sun. Both Judith and Eloise were also clearly uncomfortable, hot and struggling with their skirts. Yet Suki knew that neither woman would remove her dress, and that if she did so herself she was likely to have her bottom whipped for her trouble.

Eloise was cruel and liked to use the whip, which left her aroused, often enough to want Suki to use her tongue if they were in private. It was a pleasure Suki would have given gladly, yet Eloise seemed to need to find an excuse before she demanded it, as if overcoming some invisible barrier. That Eloise never returned the pleasure she could understand, it being a simple matter of status as to who was licking who. It had been the same in the longhouse, with the older girls often demanding their genitals licked by the younger, both for simple pleasure and as a mark of respect.

It was one of the few things she did understand about the culture, or at least that seemed to make any kind of sense. In the five years since being taken from the Benin coast, she had come to understand the English language – more than she ever admitted – but not the culture. For one thing they claimed to worship a single god, but had feast days for many. Then there were the strange clothes and the taboos attached to them, the slow and elaborate courtship, the formal titles and address, the way emotions were hidden or subtly revealed, and much, much more.

The Truscotts at least expected nothing abnormal, only service and sexual pleasures. The man who had taken her from her home, Snapes, had demanded things that went against nature, breaking the taboos of both her culture and his own. Nor had he given her any coin, which she now knew she was entitled to, and which she received each week from Mrs Orcombe.

Still wishing that she could take her dress off, but knowing better than to do so, she pushed on. Ahead of her, both Eloise and Judith were struggling, holding up skirts and petticoats to avoid tripping on the loose stones and roots which marred the path. Eloise was determined but silent, Judith gay, laughing over her difficulties and making sure to allow the men plenty of glimpses of her petticoats and calves.

Eventually they stopped, looking down over a pool, an expanse of perfectly still water between the wooded slope and a cliff. Sunlight reflected from the

8

surface, except in the shade of the rock, where it was so clear that the bottom could be seen as a jumble of pale shapes and shadows. The air was hot and still, making the water seem cool and inviting. They descended the slope, stopping on an area of soft, flat grass beside the pool.

'Quite beautiful,' Henry remarked, 'and, now that we are among old friends, I propose a swim. No doubt you are all as hot as I?'

'Here?' Eloise questioned. 'Might we not be over-looked?'

'By whom?' Henry answered. 'Certainly by nobody of consequence.'

'Well, I shall swim,' Judith declared, 'and I do not care in the least for who sees me.'

Suki gave a doubtful glance towards Eloise as Judith began to undress. Eloise ignored her, fiddling uncomfortably with a ribbon. Both Henry and Charles had also begun to undress, both watching Judith as they did so. Already Judith's bodice was open, her firm white breasts showing bare, a choice obviously made to excite the men as she then set to work on the ribbons which held her stockings at the knee. That in turn provided plenty of glimpses of soft, pale thighs and even a hint of dark red pubic hair, a display which put an expression of mingled jealousy and doubt on Eloise's face.

'Come, Eloise, nobody shall see,' Judith said brightly, tugging off a stocking. 'Suki, would you do my buttons?'

Suki nodded as Judith gestured to the back of her dress. Walking across, Suki began to undo the buttons, tugging at each until Judith's dress fell open.

'You will swim too?' Judith asked, pointing at the water. 'Swim?'

'Yes, I shall, Miss Judith,' Suki answered.

As Judith shrugged her dress from her shoulders Suki stood back, starting on her own clothes. They were simpler, unfastening at the front; and, as Judith began to push her dress down off her hips, Suki's chest was already bare. Both men had paused to watch the girls strip. Judith, tugging open her drawstrings, made a deliberate show of her bottom as she pushed her petticoats down, drawing another jealous look from Eloise. Mindful of Eloise's disciplinary habits, Suki contented herself with letting her dress and single petticoat fall to the ground, then bending to pick them up so that her bottom was towards the two men. With both Suki and Judith nude, Henry stood, pushing down his breeches, to reveal a half-stiff cock.

'I'll not waste this a second time,' he said, addressing Eloise. 'Come girl, strip off; you know what cold water will do to me.'

'Henry, I really do think . . .' Eloise began.

'Come,' Henry declared. 'You've nothing Judith hasn't, nor yet Suki. Off with them, or by God I'll do it for you.'

'You wouldn't dare!' Eloise answered, taking a step backwards.

'By God, but wouldn't I?' Henry answered.

'No, Henry!' Eloise squeaked, putting her arms out in defence as he closed with her. 'No!'

Henry feinted at her wrists, then ducked low, catching the hem of his wife's skirt and hoisting it high over her head. Eloise squealed in outrage, kicking out, only to fall backwards onto the grass. Her petticoats went up, revealing her stockings, then everything as Henry jerked them high and pinned her to the ground. Eloise was protesting furiously, her outcries muffled by her skirts. Her legs were kicking frantically, making a far better display of the ginger

10

curls and pink crevices between her thighs than she would have given if she'd stayed still. Henry only laughed at her efforts, holding her down with one hand as he tried to get a grip on her legs. One shoe came off, then the other, kicked into the water. Henry caught a leg and they came apart, giving a fine view of Eloise's sex, with the pink of her open vulva showing. Fresh outrage filled Eloise's cries as she realised what she was showing, but she went on struggling, keeping the display as rude as ever.

Suki giggled, understanding the feigned reluctance and admiring her mistress's naked quim. Eloise was kicking frantically, showing everything as first one stocking and then the next came off. Henry grabbed her knees, suddenly, pulling up her legs to leave her sex-lips peeping out from between her thighs and her buttocks parted, the puckered ring of her anus showing, a tone darker than the pale flesh around it.

'I can't wait,' Henry growled. 'It's time I split your beard.'

Eloise gave a final, choking protest as Henry moved on top of her, then went quiet, making no effort to resist as he began to rub his cock in the wet flesh of her sex. Suki watched as Eloise spread her thighs in submission and Henry pushed in, letting go of Eloise's dress as he entered her. The dress came down, revealing Eloise's face, her eyes shut in shame and ecstasy. Henry was moving fast, his buttocks bobbing frantically up and down, making Eloise gasp, then grunt as he rapidly approached climax.

To one side, both Charles and Judith were watching, both naked, his arm curled around her waist. As Suki watched, Judith's hand moved down, taking hold of her lover's cock and beginning to tug at it. Their eyes met and Judith smiled. Together they watched Henry fuck Eloise, his rhythm growing faster

11

and faster, her grunts growing louder and more urgent, then turning to little, ecstatic cries. Henry also called out, gave one last powerful push and stopped, holding himself deep inside her until at last he had finished. He rolled to the side, leaving her vagina gaping for one instant, his semen dribbling from the open hole, before she hastily closed her legs and pulled down her skirts.

'You are a bastard, Henry Truscott!' she declared.

'Such language, from the daughter of a Count,' Henry answered. 'My apologies, Charles, Judith, if I became a trifle overexcited.'

'Pray don't mention it,' Judith answered.

Henry rose, stretched, took a single breath and dived into the water. Eloise sat up, her face flushed as she tried to poke a loose curl back into place. Judith was going to her knees, taking Charles's cock in her mouth, indifferent to Eloise's chagrin as she began to suck. Suki hesitated, wondering if Eloise wanted to be helped to dress, to undress, or even to be licked.

'Help me with my dress then, stupid girl!' Eloise snapped suddenly.

Suki hastened to obey, kneeling down beside Eloise. The top two buttons had come undone, and Suki began to redo them.

'What are you doing?' Eloise demanded.

'Buttoning,' Suki answered.

'I wish to swim, stupid child!' Eloise snapped. 'Unbutton, do you understand?'

'Yes, ma'am,' Suki replied quickly.

'You shall learn,' Eloise stormed. 'Stupid, disobedient brat! Come here!'

Eloise's hand snatched out, grabbing Suki's wrist and pulling her sharply down across her lap. Suki yelped in surprise, then pain as Eloise's hand smacked hard down on her bare bottom.

The spanking was frantic, delivered in a cascade of furious, stinging slaps. Each one expressed Eloise's impotent rage at the way she had been so casually exposed and mounted in front of her friends, and also at her response to the treatment. Suki knew that she was being punished more to soothe Eloise's injured pride than as a punishment. That didn't stop it hurting, and she let her feelings go, kicking her legs and bawling freely as her bottom was brought up to a smarting, burning ball of pain. Her face was in the grass, her breasts hanging down, wobbling as she was beaten, her hips kicked high across Eloise's raised knee. She heard Charles laugh at the sight she made, a sound that somehow annoyed Eloise and made her spank harder still.

'Leave poor Suki be, or you'll get the same yourself,' Henry's voice sounded suddenly.

'How dare you? She is my maid and I shall punish her as I please,' Eloise stormed, but the spanking had stopped.

Suki rolled gratefully off Eloise's lap. Her bottom was smarting, and she could feel the warm, ready sensation the beating had brought to her sex, making her eager for a cock. Charles was erect, Judith still sucking on his penis, but turned, showing that she too had watched the spanking. Throwing a cautious glance towards Eloise, Suki found her mistress's face a storm of emotions, anger, petulance and cruelty, but also arousal.

'Make her lick your cunt, my little puppy!' Henry called from where he was standing in the water. 'It will soothe your feelings, as it always does!'

Eloise threw him a look of pure fury, but her hands were already going to her skirts. They came up with her knees, once more exposing the soft white flesh of her thighs and the plump swell of her sex. Her eyes closed in shame as she showed herself, but her legs were coming apart, leaving herself open for Suki's attention. Charles swore softly at the sight of Eloise's open sex and Judith began to suck harder, watching all the while as Suki crawled in between her mistress's thighs. Eloise was wet, her hole still dribbling Henry's semen. Suki poked out her tongue, tasting the salty flavour. Slowly, she began to lap, working on the fleshy pink folds of Eloise's sex, along each lip, slowly upwards towards the clitoris, then on it, dabbing at the little bud with firm, rhythmic flicks.

In no time Eloise was moaning in bliss, the last of her reserve forgotten in the pleasure of being licked. Suki responded, lapping more firmly still, pressing the little bud of flesh down under her tongue harder, then harder still. She felt Eloise's thighs tighten around her head, muscles squeezing, then jumping. Eloise cried out in ecstasy, calling Henry a bastard once more before going limp on the ground. Suki pulled back, her mouth full of the taste of quim and Henry's semen. Her own sex needed filling, badly, but as she turned she found Judith, still kneeling, with a broad smile on her face and a thick trail of white running from a corner of her mouth. She had been masturbating, and her fingers glistened with her own juice.

Suki wished she had done the same. Eloise had pulled herself up into a sitting position, resting on one arm, her expression more chagrined than ever. Hesitating, Suki knelt up, folding her hands in her lap.

'My dress, girl,' Eloise snapped. 'Do you never learn?'

Hastening to obey, Suki crawled over and worked quickly on Eloise's buttons. As Eloise was undressing, Charles plunged into the water, followed by Judith, more timidly, testing the water with her toe first, only to be grabbed by the legs and pulled in.

14

When Eloise was naked she followed, carefully avoiding Henry so that she could get in without being molested. Suki hesitated, unsure if it was her place to swim as well and also badly in need of attention to her body.

With the others ignoring her completely, she moved to the edge of the wooded slope, finding a flat area of grass between two spiked bushes. She lay back, spreading her thighs, one hand going to the soft swell of her sex, the other to her breasts. With one hard nipple between her fingers, she began to stroke herself, teasing her outer lips and only occasionally letting a finger wander to the wet centre of her quim.

She had been punished and it had made her bottom smart – now it was a warm, glowing sensation. It always did, and she had lost count of the number of times she had come under her fingers after having her bottom smacked. The spanking had warmed her, but it was not what she wanted to think about when she came. There had been hard cocks, but not for her – even if she did have the taste of semen in her mouth – and they weren't right either.

There were other things, many memories: cocks, dark and pale; male buttocks; female breasts. What Snapes had put her through felt wrong, and she had too much pride to come to climax over it. The same was true of the spankings, despite the pleasure they gave her, and of being made to lick at Eloise's sex and suck Henry's cock. Revenge was never an option, not directly; yet sometimes it amused Henry to punish Eloise in front of her, and that was good.

Eloise hated it, and fought crazily to stop it happening, but in the end was always betrayed by her feelings. Having her bottom beaten aroused Suki, but Eloise craved it for its own sake. The spankings would always come after an argument, or when

15

Eloise was being particularly difficult. Henry would warn her, bait to which Eloise almost always rose.

Suki was rubbing herself, eyes closed in bliss, her mind focused on the last time she had seen her mistress punished. It had been in the drawing room, with Eloise thrown kicking and struggling across Henry's knee. She'd been cursing, in French, which she always spoke when she lost control. She'd been trying to scratch, and hammering her fists on Henry's legs futilely. He'd responded by twisting both her arms high into the small of her back, then started to turn up her skirts. She'd been spitting with fury as it was done but, with her skirt up, her angry demands had turned to pleas not to be done in front of Suki. Henry had ignored her, whistling an air as he'd lifted her petticoats, exposing chubby white buttocks with a puff of red-gold hair visible between them.

With her bottom bare the fight had gone out of Eloise. She had lain limp over Henry's lap, whimpering slightly as he fondled her buttocks. The spanking had started, firm, slow swats that had made Eloise's buttocks bounce and quiver, parting to show more of her quim and the tight spot of her anus. She had been silent at first, then begun to squeal as it got harder and faster, pleading for mercy; then snivelling; and finally giving way to a full-throated blubbering as the punishment reached a furious crescendo with her buttocks dancing to the slaps and her legs kicking wildly to show every detail of her quim.

Suki had watched it all, delighted by her mistress's pain and distress, and still more delighted by the reaction. Once soundly spanked, Eloise had gone down on her knees to suck Henry's cock and then been fucked across the same chair, all modesty gone, no longer caring that Suki was watching. Afterwards Suki had masturbated, in her attic room, legs spread

16

wide with her fingers in her quim, just as she was now, masturbating in delight over her mistress's punishment.

With a little cry, Suki came. Her thighs were cocked wide and high, her sex gaping to the warm sun. Every muscle in her body was tense, her back arched, her buttocks clenching over and over. Her eyes were tight shut, her head full of her picture: Eloise, bare-bottomed and kicking, pale skin flushed pink, thighs wide to show the quim Suki was so often made to lick. It lasted beautifully, her thoughts fixed on Eloise's bare red bottom, her fingers dabbing at her clit. Even as she came down she stayed still, letting the pleasure fade slowly, until finally she opened her eyes.

She lay staring upwards at the sky and the leaves of a tree. As she blew her cheeks out a movement caught her eyes and she sat up at the sound of a gasp. There was a horse beyond the bush, its rider looking down on her – Lewis Stukely, his eyes wide in surprise. Beyond him two other riders sat, female, in still shock on their side-saddles: Caroline Cunningham, her cheeks pink with blushes, and Mrs Aldgrave, her face set in amazement.

'A pox on Stukely, and that old ape-leader Aldgrave to boot,' Henry said as the carriage with Caroline Cunningham and Mrs Aldgrave vanished from view, Stukely's horse following immediately behind.

'Really, Henry, you think nothing of our social position!' Eloise chided.

'Social position be damned,' Henry answered. 'The mine's producing well, ain't it? The rents still come in for the estate, don't they? I've no time for such company in any case; they're as bad as Quakers. I'm for rakes and biters on all occasions.'

'You can be most coarse,' Eloise rejoined.

'I can indeed, and the better for it,' Henry said. 'Come, Charles, what of some sport? Shall we race the girls? A guinea to the winner and the loser's cunt?'

'Henry!'

'You may drive, if you're scared of Charles's cock – but naked, for the sport.'

'I shall do no such thing!'

'Come, come, puppy, or do you need my belt taken to your arse before you'll play?'

'You need do no such thing,' Eloise answered. 'As you force me, I shall take part.'

Henry laughed, surprised by how easily Eloise had given in. At Meldon Pool she had been in a playful mood, as she always was after surrendering her normal dignity. At least she had been until the unexpected arrival of the remainder of the party on horseback, the side-saddles having been hired at one of the farms in the village.

They had returned to the estate in an embarrassed silence, with Mrs Aldgrave sitting in frozen immobility in the carriage. Henry had made no effort to make amends, well aware that the departure of Mrs Aldgrave and therefore Caroline Cunningham would also mean the departure of Lewis Stukely. Without them he would be able to indulge himself in the sort of entertainment originally planned.

'Suki is to be whipped,' Eloise remarked.

'As you see fit,' Henry answered, 'but after the race: a sore backside is sure to put her off her stride. No, let us be fair. If she wins we'll spare her arse!'

'A fine motive to make her run!' Charles called, 'but what of Judith? She's likely to lose to spare Suki's hide.'

'Then she too may be whipped, should she lose,' Eloise suggested.

'She takes it too easily,' Henry objected. 'That is not the answer. No, she is much of a weight with you, so she shall ride. We shall put Joanna in harness. I'll warrant a bull will be enough to buy her modesty, the prospect of another enough to make her run well.'

'She is tall, but a touch fleshy,' Charles pondered, 'while Suki is strong. I don't fancy Joanna's chances.'

'I'll lay a guinea on her to win,' Henry responded, 'with Eloise's whip at her tail and ten shillings before her eyes.'

'I also,' Eloise added. 'A guinea.'

'Taken, both,' Charles answered. 'There's too much cream gone into the making of Joanna for her to be a good runner.'

They had turned to walk towards the house, where the two maids were helping to clear the remains of the outdoor lunch. Mrs Orcombe was also there. The afternoon had begun to cool towards evening, with the shadows lengthening on the lawn.

'Fetch the shooting gigs, if you would, Charles,' Henry remarked. 'And send the boy on some errand. I'll join you presently. Ah, Joanna, my dear – a word, if I may.'

'The rest of the day is your own, Mrs Orcombe,' Eloise added, nodding towards the housekeeper. 'Little John is asleep?'

'Very well, ma'am. Sound asleep, ma'am,' Mrs Orcombe answered, her face held carefully expressionless, as it always was in the face of anything she considered improper.

Henry struggled to hide a smile, amused by her blend of disapproval and loyalty. How much she knew he was uncertain, but he suspected that she would have reacted with the same stoic acceptance more or less regardless of his behaviour. She curtsied and left, taking the last of the silverware with her. Judith emerged from the same door a moment later.

'Ah, Judith, my dear,' Charles said. 'We're going to race and we want you to drive. I trust you're game?'

'I am game,' Judith answered immediately. 'What is the course and what the stakes?'

'The stakes are a whipping for Suki if you lose,' Henry explained. 'That's if we have a filly for my dear wife. For the course, we've yet to decide. Now, Joanna.'

Joanna had stepped forwards, looking worried.

'What does Mrs Orcombe give you each week?' Henry asked.

'Four shillings, sir,' Joanna answered. 'That and what I care to eat.'

'Your husband – William, is it not? He is a day labourer, I believe. How much does he earn?'

'Eight shillings, sir, maybe; sometimes six or not that.'

'Ten shillings then, in a poor week. How would you care to make that in an hour, over and above your normal pay?'

Joanna shot him a doubtful glance, looked at Eloise, then back.

'What would that be to do, sir?' Joanna asked.

'To race,' Henry answered. 'In a shooting gig: you know the ones.'

'Drive a gig for ten shillings? Certain sure I can.'

'Not drive, exactly; Mrs Truscott will be driving. You would be pulling.'

'Pulling, sir? Like a horse?'

'Exactly like a horse.'

'Well, sir, I hope you're not expecting me to be as fast . . .'

'Good girl, that's the spirit. You'll be naked, of course.'

'Naked, sir?'

'Naked, naturally. Did you ever hear of a horse wearing clothes?'

'Well, no, sir, but . . .'

'Then you shall be naked, save for your shoes. Now go to the stable, along with Suki, who has done this before.'

Joanna hesitated, shuffling her feet. Henry put his hand into his pocket, feeling out the shape of two crown pieces. He drew them out, showing them to the girl in the palm of his hand before offering one. Joanna bit her lip, then quickly reached out and took the money.

'Good girl,' Henry declared, 'now we shall have some fine sport. Come, to the stables.'

Joanna followed Henry and Eloise as they made for the stables. She felt uncertain, and embarrassed by the thought of taking her clothes off. Yet ten shillings was ten shillings. It could mean a new bonnet. More than one; in fact, a new dress. Yes, it would be shameful to be bare, but for ten shillings a little shame could be borne. Besides, Suki would be bare too, so she wouldn't be alone, and Mrs Truscott would be there, and Miss Cates, so it wasn't even improper – not really.

In the stable yard, Mr Finch was wheeling out the second of the two light shooting gigs which Mr Truscott had ordered that winter. Joanna's cousin was the blacksmith, and there had been no shortage of business since the Truscott's had bought the Driscoll estate. One of her brothers worked in the mine he owned across the Tamar, Wheal Purity, and her husband worked the estate land as often as not. What Mr Truscott wanted might be strange, but then who was she to judge such a fine gentleman?

He was handsome too, which made it a great deal easier as she began to work on the fastenings of her dress. With the bodice and waistband loose it fell

21

away, revealing her naked body beneath. Her exposure brought a hot flush to her face, which she tried to hide while glancing sidelong to see if either Mr Truscott or Mr Finch were paying her any attention. Both were, to her and also to Suki, who had stripped without any show of modesty at all.

Folding her dress, Joanna carried it to a rail, placing it carefully to avoid soiling the cloth on the ground. In nothing but shoes and stockings, she folded her arms demurely across her breasts and belly, waiting to be told what to do. Suki was nearby, not troubling to conceal anything, her bottom turned towards Joanna. The dark skin showed a purple flush, and Joanna realised that her fellow maid had been spanked, an idea which amused her, but also made her concerned in case she was to be given the same treatment.

'Very well,' Henry declared, rubbing his hands together. 'For the course we shall use the path around the house, down by the sundial to where the lake is being dug, and back around the house. Three laps should do, I would imagine, unless either filly should collapse before completing the course, in which case the race is forfeit to the one standing.'

'Are there wagers other than Suki's whipping?' Judith enquired.

'Whipping, Miss Judith?' Suki said quietly.

'Yes, whipping,' Henry said. 'Mrs Truscott feels you should be punished for your behaviour by the pool, but I thought it sport to give you a chance. You must beat Joanna here to avoid a bottom-tickling.'

Suki looked blank, then worried.

'Race,' Henry explained, 'as before. Lose and . . .'

He took up a dog-whip from one of the gigs and flicked it at Suki's buttocks, drawing a yelp of surprise and pain as it caught her skin. She nodded and Henry turned back to Judith.

'A guinea against Charles says Joanna wins,' he said, 'and the like for Eloise. D'you care to bet on yourself and Suki?'

Judith nodded thoughtfully and stepped over to where Suki was rubbing at the fresh welt on her left buttock and looking back in an effort to inspect the damage. She straightened up as Judith approached and put her hands on her head at a gesture. Joanna watched as Judith squeezed the muscles of the black girl's thighs and calves, then patted one dark buttock. The leisurely, intimate way in which it was done set Joanna's stomach fluttering, increasing her sense of uncertainty and bringing a new feeling of shame at the way she and Suki were being treated as animals. Even worse, what Henry had said implied that if Suki won, then it would be Joanna who was whipped.

Judith straightened up, walking to Joanna, who shut her eyes in embarrassment as the red-haired girl gave her thigh a squeeze. She held them closed, struggling with her emotions as her legs were felt, until an unexpected pinch of her bottom made her open them again.

'A bull says we win,' Judith stated, stepping away.

'Cautious,' Henry said. 'So, then . . .'

'Begging your pardon, sir,' Joanna broke in, unable to hold back any more. 'I am to be whipped if I lose?'

'No, no, not at all,' Henry answered, laughing. 'You have one crown piece, and you shall have another if you win, but we'll spare you the whip.'

'Thank you, sir,' Joanna answered gratefully, biting back a twinge of annoyance at the way ten shillings had been promised and then half withheld.

'We must set the harness low,' Henry remarked, turning to Eloise. 'Our filly's strength is in the breadth of her hips, we must be sure she pulls with them. Come, Joanna, step between the shafts, thus.'

Henry had taken Joanna's hand, leading her to stand between the shafts of one of the shooting gigs. It was small, designed to be pulled by a pony on the estate, with the shafts at the level of her waist as he lifted them. There was a pile of tack in the gig, straps with brass buckles and rings. She took hold of the shafts, supporting the gig.

Joanna found herself wondering how he was going to fit her into a harness designed for a pony. Looking back, she saw that Henry had already begun to sort pieces out, working with an air of confidence which suggested it was not the first time he'd done it. He took out an old girth strap, winding it around her waist. Traces followed, Henry whistling as he worked, apparently indifferent to where his fingers touched on her body. With her waist wrapped tightly in the thick leather strap, traces were led around each shaft, supporting them on her hips. More straps followed, led back between her breasts and over her shoulders, through a ring at the centre of her back and down again to the girth, transferring some of the weight to her upper body.

Her feelings of shame grew as she was put into harness; also helplessness as each of her wrists was taken in turn and bound with leather, wound around several times and lashed off on to the shafts. She could do nothing, but only stand there with everything showing, unable to hide her breasts or the thick growth of dark gold hair which hid her lower belly. Nor did having Suki nearby in the same condition make it any better. To look at Suki's naked body wrapped tight in leather was to know how she was herself.

Not that anybody seemed to care, discussing the coming race and the harness as if her nudity was not important at all. Even Henry, whose fingers had more

24

than once brushed her breasts and buttocks, seemed indifferent. With her body strapped up, he turned her attention to her head, making her open her mouth to take a twist of sour leather between her teeth for a bit and fastening it behind her head. Reins followed, tied at the sides and led back to the gig, after which he stood away to admire his handiwork, his smile growing to a broad grin. A hand came out, taking one of Joanna's breasts and weighing it thoughtfully before brushing his thumb over her nipple, which came immediately to erection.

She let out a little sob, unable to do more, and wondering what he would have done if they had been alone. To make her kneel would have been easy, after which he could have enjoyed her from the rear, the way animals did it. It was also the way her husband liked her when he was drunk, buttocks high and wide with his cock inside her and his pot rested on her back in between draughts. Half in relief for the presence of the other women, half in regret, she shut her eyes while Henry finished exploring her breasts.

Eloise ignored Henry's casual interference with Joanna's body, even when his fingers went lower, to burrow into the warm, wet cleft between her thighs. Only when he had finished and Joanna had opened her eyes again did she turn from where she had been testing a dog-whip against a post. Joanna looked down in alarm at the long lash of braided leather, dark and glossy with oil and use. Eloise smiled, stepping close and ordering Joanna to kneel.

Joanna immediately went to her knees, fearful of the whip and wondering if the experience was really worth five shillings, or even ten if it was going to include having such a vicious implement taken to her body. She was trembling and trying not to stick her bottom out too obviously, sure that it looked huge and would provide an irresistible target. There was also the question of not revealing too much of herself, and just how wet her quim had become.

With the shafts low to the ground, Eloise stepped over them, pulling her skirts up as she seated herself primly in the gig. Joanna stayed still, acutely aware of what she was showing behind but not daring to move until she was told to do so. In front of her, Suki was already standing. Judith was taking the reins from Charles, also a whip, a long switch of plaited twigs like the ones used for pigs. The sight of the black girl naked but for the system of leather straps made Joanna swallow and glance down at her own body, even as Eloise ordered her to rise.

Again she obeyed without hesitation, finding the gig lighter than she had expected. She jumped at a sudden sharp pain across her bottom and the smack of leather on her skin, then moved forwards, walking carefully. The rein at her right cheek tightened and she turned without hesitation, eager to follow orders and so avoid her mistress's lash. Her stomach was knotting as she walked across the yard, pulling the gig behind her. She felt fear of the whip, and shame for her exposure; confusion, too, from her sudden excitement. There was a determination to win as well, so that if she had to endure the pain and indignity of being raced like an animal, at least it would be for ten shillings and not five. It was a pity it meant that Suki had to be whipped, yet it was impossible to deny that it would be really rather fun to see her friend made to dance under a cane or dog-whip, or maybe the pig-quirt.

'Steady then,' Henry declared, stepping back as the knot in Joanna's stomach tightened yet harder, 'and run!'

Joanna started forwards as fast as she was able, then stumbled as the dog-whip smacked down across her bottom. It was a hard cut, stinging, and she found herself dashing for the gate, her breath already coming fast as she reached it. Eloise caught her with the whip again, screaming for speed as Suki and Judith turned around the side of the house. Suki was ahead, and getting further ahead; Judith was laughing. Joanna struggled to go faster, only to find herself on a path of pressed gravel, too narrow for her to overtake even if she had been able to.

Again the whip cut down across Joanna's bottom, sideways, catching both cheeks and making her jump and bite hard on her gag. Eloise swore at her, calling her lazy and stupid, demanding more effort. Joanna tried, straining, but reaching the sundial twenty yards behind Judith's gig. At the bottom of the slope it was thirty, then forty as they rounded the wide pit which was to become the lake. Then it was uphill, the extra strain coming on to Joanna's hips and shoulders as she started on the gentle slope.

She was sweating, her skin prickling, especially on the welts that decorated her bottom. Her limbs were burning, hot with the strain as she struggled to pull Eloise up towards the house. It was harder than on the flat, far harder, but Eloise showed no mercy, cursing and applying the whip to Joanna's bottom over and over, until both her cheeks seemed to be burning. By halfway she was on the edge of collapse, only keeping on in a senseless effort to escape the stinging cuts of the dog-whip. Eloise was yelling, the words lost on Joanna, until she shook her sweat-sodden hair out of her eyes and looked up.

Suki was having more trouble than she was, struggling to pull the gig at all, only thirty yards ahead, while Eloise's words were not curses, but encouragement. Joanna bit hard into her gag, straining to pull on. Judith looked back, her pig-quirt raised above Suki's haunches, her expression worried. They reached the sundial, speeding up on the flatter ground, leaving Joanna behind, but still trying.

Joanna's every muscle was burning, her vision blurred, her skin dripping sweat as she reached the top, staggering on and gaining speed. Eloise gave her another cut across her buttocks, urging her on. Suki and Judith had disappeared, around the corner of the house. Joanna followed, running as hard as she could, panting rhythmically now, the pain in her bottom and limbs dulled, her mind hazy.

The stable yard was empty, and she passed the two men as she came out again. Henry waved his hat, cheering mockingly; Charles was taking a sip from a flask. Still Suki was invisible; then the gig came into view again as Joanna reached the front of the house. They were going down the slope fast, Judith's bonnet gone and her red curls in disarray. Joanna followed, losing ground, then holding it and at last gaining as Suki once more started up the slope.

Eloise was urging her on, but the whip-cuts no longer really hurt. She was twenty yards behind again, then ten, only to fall back once more as Suki again reached the crest of the rise. She pressed on, forcing herself to plant one leg in front of the other, trying to ignore the pain and exhaustion, thinking of the pretty dress she would buy. The other gig was ahead, not far, disappearing around a corner, appearing again, stopped.

Suki was on her knees, head bowed to the ground, Judith standing over her, holding the pig-quirt in hesitation. Joanna staggered on, bumping the gig over the edge of the lawn, dragging it past the other. Charles appeared, running.

'Come on, dammit!' he urged.

'She's spent,' Judith answered. 'It's no good.'

'Come on, girl!' Charles exclaimed. 'Up, up. Judith, put the quirt across her arse.'

'It's no good,' Judith answered. 'She's all in.'

Joanna lurched on without looking back, still running, determined that if Suki did manage to carry on she would have as much lead as possible, only to stop as Eloise drew back on the reins and called a halt. Joanna turned to find Suki collapsed, lying on the gravel of the path, a bedraggled, sweat-soaked mess, her hair plastered to her face and her chest heaving.

'Damn!' Charles swore as Henry appeared from the stable yard, his face breaking into a grin as he saw what had happened.

'My call, I believe!' he shouted.

'Your call indeed,' Judith answered. 'She needs water.'

'I shall fetch some,' Henry said. 'Give the poor girl some brandy, Charles.'

Charles bent down, pressing his flask to the black girl's lips. She took it, swallowing, her eyes shut, her whole body trembling as she drank. Joanna sank to her knees, then forwards in exhaustion, indifferent to the display it made of her naked bottom. Behind her she heard Eloise dismount without a word. Joanna had won, and she knew she could have completed another lap. Not fast, but she could have done it, a knowledge that gave her pride despite all her aches and even the shame of what she had done. Rolling to her side, as comfortable a position as she could manage with her wrists strapped, she watched as Eloise walked across to the others.

Henry filled a bucket at the pump, feeling both amused and aroused at the race, with just a little sympathy for Suki's condition. The same was true for what Eloise was going to do to the maid, and he determined not to allow it to go too far, despite the pleasure he knew he would get from watching the girl whipped. The art would be to allow Eloise some expression of her anger, but to stop it soon enough for Suki to feel grateful to him.

There was also Joanna, whose body had been everything Henry had anticipated: full, pale curves, firm flesh but plenty of it. Also, the ease with which she had abandoned her modesty in return for a crown had suggested she would be game for more. Letting her watch Suki be punished could only heighten their intimacy, but it was important not to scare her, and Henry knew full well how far Eloise could go if she lost her temper.

Nodding thoughtfully to himself, he returned to the others. Joanna was kneeling, watching, still bound to the gig and apparently resigned to her nudity. Charles was kneeling beside Suki, working on the straps that held her wrists to the shafts. Eloise was standing face to face with Judith, both women's faces set in anger.

'I'll whip my servants as I please!' Eloise was saying as Henry approached.

'She is in exhaustion!' Judith protested. 'Can you not see that?'

'All the better for handling her,' Eloise answered. 'Charles, leave the straps on her wrists; we shall need them to hang her from a tree.'

'She'll not be whipped! Not now!' Judith stated.

'Ladies, please,' Charles cut in. 'There is no need for unpleasantness.'

'No need at all,' Henry added. 'Come, my dear, allow the poor girl to recover a little, at the least.'

'I . . .' Eloise began, only to stop short as Henry threw the bucket of water over Suki, forcing Eloise to jump back.

30

'It is my intention . . .' Eloise stated hotly, only to stop again.

A man had appeared around the corner of the house and halted, staring in astonishment at the scene before him. Joanna squeaked in alarm, getting quickly to her feet and disappearing into the stable yard.

'Ah, Rector,' Henry managed. 'You must excuse us. A little matter of domestic discipline. I don't believe you have met Miss Cates or Mr Finch, who is my partner at Wheal Purity. Judith, Charles, the Reverend Gould, who is parson to the village.'

'Delighted,' Gould answered, throwing a worried look at Suki's naked body. 'Mr Truscott, Mrs Truscott, while I would not wish to interfere in any way with your domestic arrangements, I do think that it is incumbent upon me to stress the impropriety of this. It is indecent, Mr Truscott.'

'We intend to whip her,' Eloise stated. 'There is no indecency.'

'Proverbs, chapter twenty-three, verse fourteen,' Henry added, ' "Thou shalt beat him with the rod, and shalt deliver his soul from hell." A verse which was drummed into me at school.'

'Just so, Mr Truscott,' he answered, 'and yet naked? Between the shafts of a cart?'

'Whipping at the tail of a cart is common enough,' Henry said with a shrug.

'At the tail, yes,' Gould replied. 'Not between the shafts, and seldom naked – at least not in a woman's case.'

'It is a French thing,' Henry extemporised. 'My wife, as you know, is French.'

'Young Joanna Pearse also?' the parson demanded. 'She is a wife of the village. Surely it is her husband's duty to correct her?'

'For the present she is my maid,' Eloise said firmly.

31

'Well, no matter, perhaps. I feel sure you know what you are about,' he answered, shaking his head. 'I have no doubt you acted with good reason, yet I do feel I must plead for both clemency and decency, whatever the custom across the Channel.'

'We were discussing the matter as you arrived,' Henry put in, 'but, in any event, how may I help you?'

'My call in fact concerns this girl,' Gould answered, once more glancing at Suki's naked body as she pulled herself up into a kneeling position. 'Might we speak in private?'

'Certainly,' Henry said. 'My dear, I think Suki has perhaps learned her lesson, Joanna also. Both may, I feel, return to their duties.'

Eloise gave him a single hot look, but said nothing as Charles once more went to work on the straps securing Suki's wrists. Henry joined Gould, who gave one last nervous glance at the naked black girl and then set his face firmly away.

'You are concerned for Suki's welfare?' Henry asked. 'Let me assure you . . .'

'Her physical welfare, no,' Gould interrupted. 'You hold good repute among those who work on your estate, and I have no doubt that this is reflected among your domestic staff. Certainly Mrs Orcombe speaks well of you.'

'She does?' Henry queried.

'Most highly,' Gould assured him. 'No, it is not a physical matter that concerns me, but a spiritual one, a moral one also. Your maid, Susan . . .'

'Suki,' Henry corrected him. 'Her real name is something entirely unpronounceable, but Suki is close enough. She's from the Benin coast, don't you know?'

'Precisely, Mr Truscott, and it is this which concerns me. The moral matter is trivial; indeed, I am embarrassed to have to bring it up, yet it is my duty.'

'The matter being?' Henry asked, wondering if Gould had heard about the incident at Meldon Pool.

'She is . . . she is free, I trust?' Gould asked. 'Not in slavery?'[3]

'Free?' Henry laughed. 'As free as the next, I dare say. She's in my service.'

'She is paid?' Gould persisted.

'So I would suppose. Mrs Orcombe deals with such matters.'

'Ha, hum, very well. The other matter, Mr Truscott. She does not attend church . . .'

'She's not a Christian, I don't suppose.'

'Should she not be, Mr Truscott? Do you not think it our duty to bring to her the benefits of the faith? There are, I have heard, terrible heathen practices in her country: cannibalism, idolatry?'

'She barely speaks English, Mr Gould. I confess that my natural inclination is to let matters be. As to being a Carib, you have my word she's not eaten a single person. Nor does she keep an idol in her room.'

'Nevertheless, Mr Truscott – her soul. We must consider the poor girl's immortal soul. It is kind of you to give her a place, savage that she is, and to bring civilised values to her, yet there is more than this.'

Henry didn't reply, wondering if Gould genuinely considered harnessing Suki to a cart and whipping her to represent civilised values or whether he was simply trying to be tactful in a difficult situation. If either case it was clearly best to agree to whatever the man said and get rid of him as soon as possible.

'Doubtless you are right,' he declared suddenly. 'It has been remiss of me, my wife also, and I shall give the matter my immediate attention. Be assured, Mr Gould, of Suki's attendance at divine service this coming Sunday.'

Two

As he stepped from the porch, Henry Truscott drew in a breath of fresh air, glad to be free of the stifling confines of the church. The day was hot, hotter than any so far that year, and the long service had left him both uncomfortable and bored. Beside him, Eloise's reaction was very different, her mouth curved up into the same serene, satisfied smile she always wore after taking communion. He would, he reflected, never understand the workings of her mind. She was ardent in her belief, yet she had converted from Rome in order to be able to marry him without hesitation. Again, she could be coy, even cold, yet when aroused he had seen her on her knees with her face buried in the quim of her own cousin. She now held his arm, nodding politely to the wife of one of the wealthier yeoman farmers, a woman for whom she wouldn't have spared a glance before the revolution in France and the collapse of the social order into which she had been brought up.

He steered her away, gently but firmly, determined to escape the churchyard before the Reverend Gould could detach himself from the other worshippers. Suki had attended, sitting in a pew with an expression of patient bafflement on her face. How much she understood, Henry was unsure, but he was certain that the moral implications of Gould's sermon would have been completely meaningless to her, and that the same was true for the psalms and hymns. As far as he was concerned, the less she understood the better, as it would be a great shame for her to lose the innocent enthusiasm she brought to sex.

Pulling Eloise through the lich-gate, he paused in its shadow, waiting only long enough for the servants to catch up before starting for the house. Gould was in earnest conversation with another parishioner, allowing him to reach the horses without interference. Mounted, they set off up the lane towards the estate, quickly leaving the servants behind.

Gould, he hoped, would now be placated, and leave him in peace. The rector had been a problem since Henry bought the estate, expecting Eloise and he to take a leading role in local affairs. Henry's own preference was to allow the Orcombes to run the house and estate, and to let the fields to villagers. Gould disapproved of the practice, saying it led to the indolence which he felt had prevailed before the enclosure act had come into force. Gossip, of which there was far too much for Henry's taste, had then led him to discover that Suki had not been brought into the church. Given that the Orcombes had proved so loyal, it seemed likely that Joanna Pearse was responsible for Gould's discovery. After all, it had happened shortly after they had taken Joanna on.

Thinking of Joanna turned his thoughts to his plans for her seduction. She'd be game, he was sure, especially in return for a few extra shillings. Her husband, William Pearse, was more the problem: a big, rough man who liked to drink. Given the difference in their status, he was unlikely to actually confront Henry, even if he did discover infidelity; yet it was not impossible, and by all accounts he had a hot temper. Visiting Joanna's cottage while William was at work was clearly unwise, with sharp-eyed neighbours eager for any scandal. There was also the problem that, as a day labourer, it was hard to predict when William Pearse would not be at home. Nor was his own house easy, even though it would not be difficult to find a pretext for hiring Joanna. While Eloise was of sufficiently debauched character to enjoy the maid, it was unlikely that the reverse was true.

What he needed was a little time alone with the girl, enough to persuade her, and if necessary pay her. Certainly she was not to be missed. Dressed, she had been tempting enough, with her abundant golden hair and half-shy, half-knowing smile. Naked, with her breasts and buttocks jiggling to the motion of her running and her pale skin glossy with sweat, she had been simply too fine to resist.

Joanna Pearse pushed her plate away, sitting back as she watched her husband finish his meal of boiled mutton and mashed turnips. A quart pot of cider stood at his elbow, the third he had taken with his lunch, drinking more or less steadily since they had returned from church. She knew what was coming, as it did every Sunday. Once replete he would sit back in the corner of the settle beside the chimney, spread his legs and pull open the flap of his breeches, freeing his penis. He would nod to it and she would go down, on her knees, taking it in her mouth and sucking while he sipped his cider.

Sometimes he would come in her mouth, or across her face, which he always enjoyed, rubbing the thick come in across her cheeks and nose with the head of his cock. More often, he would tell her to turn around, presenting him with her bottom. Her skirts

36

would come up under his hands and he would kneel behind her, still with the pot of cider in one hand. A big, rough hand would pull one of her buttocks aside and his cock would go in, pushed into her body until his balls pressed to her flesh. She would be wet after sucking cock – even before, knowing what was to come. With his cock well in, he would fuck her, holding her dress in one hand and drinking with the other, occasionally using her bottom or back to rest his pot. He would come in her, deep in, often stating the hope that she would be pregnant soon after. Four months after marriage, she was surprised that it had not already happened.

Being fucked after the Sunday lunch had become routine, and there was no reason to think it would not happen again. The trouble was that this time her bottom was marked with welts, which he could hardly fail to notice, even drunk. During the week she had managed to keep her secret, with William returning from work tired and hungry, uninterested in sex until they had found the darkness of their bed. Now it was not going to be so easy, with her whole rear on plain view. He liked her bottom and was unlikely to allow her to go on her back for entry. Her sole chance of evading detection seemed to be to mount herself on his lap before she was ordered to present herself.

Failing that, she would have to explain – not the truth, or even close to it, as she knew that the very idea of other men seeing her naked would drive him into a blind fury. Instead she would have to confess to being whipped, and it would have to have been by Mrs Truscott, as William was quite capable of confronting Mrs Orcombe. Even so, Joanna could not be sure of his reaction, and it was with considerable trepidation that she cleared the table.

37

Sure enough, after taking a slice of pie, he refilled his pot and went to sit in the chimney corner, spreading his thick legs with a contented sigh. Joanna smiled nervously, watching as he pulled up his smock and fumbled open the flap of his breeches. His cock came out, a thick, dark shaft, the wet pink head already showing where his foreskin had begun to peel back. Joanna knelt as he took up his pot, gulping his cock into her mouth as he took a swallow of cider.

He tasted strong, of man and earth, making her gag briefly until her saliva had overcome the flavour. She began to suck, the way he liked it, drawing her mouth up and down on his cock as it stiffened, so that the sensitive flesh of his foreskin rubbed on her lips. He hardened quickly, his cock growing in her mouth until the tip began to nudge the back of her throat each time she took it in. In the hope of making him come in her mouth she began to suck harder, squeezing her tongue around his cock and pressing the head to the roof of her mouth. She took his balls in her hand, tickling beneath them with two fingers. He had started to groan, and she thought he was going to come in her mouth, only to feel his hand lock in her hair.

Joanna tried to rise, intent on mounting herself on his erection. He held her down by the hair, pulling her off his penis as he put down his pot of cider. She went back, giving in to the discovery of her beaten bottom, only to have him grab the shaft of his erection, jerk it hard a couple of times and spray come into her face.

She shut her eyes in time, her mouth an instant too late. His semen was inside, coating her tongue and hanging from her lips, but if one eye was closed beneath a thick blob of come, at least she had stopped it going in. He held her tight by the hair, emptying himself into her face, over her nose and the other eye, before pressing his cock to her skin as he rubbed the semen over her features, smearing it over her screwed-up eyes. The last of the slimy mess he spread across her nose before prodding his cock at her lips to make her take it back in her mouth. He sighed in contentment as she sucked the last of his come from his cock. Joanna swallowed, her arousal blending with disgust at the salty taste and the slimy feel of the mess he had plastered across her face. It was in her hair too, and she dared not open either eye.

Whatever he had done to her face, and however much her instincts regretted not having taken his cock in her quim, she felt mainly relief. She had kept her bottom hidden, and now that he'd come he was sure to sleep for a while, leaving her to her own devices.

Sure enough, he had gone upstairs before she had finished cleaning the semen from her face. No sooner had he gone than she was in the chimney corner herself, well out of sight of the window. Her skirt came up high, a thick fold jammed into her mouth to stop the screams she knew would shortly be inevitable. Ready, she set her thighs apart, her hand going to the plump swell of her quim and delving between the lips. She was wet, and her fingers went up easily: two, then three. With her thumb on her clitoris she began to masturbate, thinking of her husband's thick cock and the way he took her so casually, kneeling, bottom high – so immodest a pose, so lovely a pose.

She was rubbing hard, her mind concentrated on the joy of offering herself to be mounted from behind, of her quim filling with hard cock, of his hands on her buttocks, parting them so that he could watch himself go in . . .

Joanna Pearse came, biting at the cloth in her mouth, struggling to control both her body and mind, and failing. Her mouth came open in a scream and her thoughts slipped to herself in the same rude, open pose – not in front of her husband but Henry Truscott. The scream she stifled, turning it to a gasp; the image she could not. It was Henry, about to enter her from behind: but, more, her wrists strapped to the shafts of a cart so that she could do nothing whatever to stop him mounting her.

Henry Truscott stepped out on to the terrace, placing both hands on the balustrade to look out over the estate with a satisfied smile on his face. Below him, beside the sundial, Eloise was instructing Suki as the maid set up an easel to overlook the valley, with a set of watercolours on a low table beside her. Beyond, a group of men were visible in the lake excavation, working with shovels.

During the night he had taken full advantage of Eloise, visiting her and staying until shortly before dawn. She had been asleep when he entered, and he had begun by lowering the bedclothes and lifting her nightgown, stroking her body with one hand while he readied his cock with the other. He had mounted her before she was really awake, and her protests had quickly turned to sighs once he had opened her thighs and put his cock to her quim.

Despite employing a wet-nurse for their son, she was still in milk. He had suckled her as they fucked, a practice they both enjoyed, and which he suspected was what kept her milk flowing. After his first orgasm they had held tight to one another, becoming playful, until Eloise had eventually managed to tease him back to erection. Using oil from the bedside lamp to grease her anus, he had sodomised her, taking his

40

second climax up her bottom as she lay grunting and panting beneath him. The third had come in her quim again, much later, after a long session of rubbing his cock between her buttocks, leaving him sore and sleepy to retire to his own bed.

Despite the night's lovemaking he had not cleared his thoughts of Joanna Pearse. When he had woken with the sun already high in the sky he had masturbated over the thought of her broad white buttocks, thinking of her kneeling in long, sweet grass and bright sunlight. Having come, he had decided it would in fact be the best way to have her: outdoors, well away from both house and village. Catching her was unlikely to present much difficulty, leaving only the problem of her husband.

It was a satisfying thought, which kept him in a buoyant mood as he breakfasted. Now replete, he looked out over his estate, wondering what could be made of the day. Eloise turned, waving to him, and he started down the steps.

'I had hoped to paint the lake this summer,' Eloise remarked as he joined her. 'These little fellows are forever at their work, yet no progress seems to be made.'

'The sides are nothing but gravel and sand,' Henry answered. 'The men are lining the excavation with clay in order to prevent the lake from drying out in warm weather. It is tedious work, no doubt.'

'That is really something of a nuisance. Can they work no faster?'

'No doubt, but we'd be better to hire more men.'

'If you might, my dear. I had so hoped for it to be down by the time the leaves start to turn.'

'I shall see to it, puppy, rest assured,' Henry answered, and started down the slope, the idea which had come to him at Eloise's remarks maturing rapidly in his head.

Mr Orcombe was easy to pick out, with his grey hair and drab brown coat, holding the plans Henry had had drawn up for the estate. Crossing the path, Henry jumped down to the flat expanse of raw slate which was to be the bottom of the lake.

'Good morning, Mr Orcombe,' Henry greeted him. 'All goes well, I trust?'

'Well enough, Mr Truscott, sir,' Orcombe answered.

'Mrs Truscott is concerned by the pace of the work,' Henry continued. 'She hopes you will be able to complete matters by the autumn.'

'No difficulty there, sir. We should be able to fill in two weeks, three at most.'

'Splendid, Mr Orcombe. Yet no doubt you would benefit from a few more hands?'

'Certain sure, sir. There'll be idle hands enough with the hay in – not that they're really needed.'

'As the rector says, we must discourage indolence,' Henry said. 'Use two or three of the day labourers. That fellow . . . Pearse, is it? Well-made lad. Him, for instance.'

'William Pearse, sir? Strong enough, I dare say.'

'Perfect,' Henry declared, 'and a couple more.'

After a few more general remarks, Henry left, turning back up the slope towards where Eloise had now begun to paint. He reached her to find that she had already applied the wash and was frowning at the paper, as if hoping the painting would appear of its own accord.

'It is done,' Henry remarked. 'Mr Orcombe now hopes to be able to fill the lake in two to three weeks.'

'You were a beast, last night,' she remarked. 'I am quite uncomfortable.'

'Your arse invites sodomy,' he replied, 'besides which, I recall you requesting me to do so. Pleading might not be too strong a word, even.'

'Do not be so coarse, Harry,' she answered.

Henry laughed, remembering her words as his penis had pushed past the tight ring of her anus – in French, and coarse in the extreme.

Listening carefully, Joanna Pearse tried to make out what Mr Orcombe was saying to her husband outside the door, her hope rising as it became plain that the estate manager had come with an offer of work. Presently she heard them take farewells, and William came back into the cottage.

'I've work to Squire Truscott's,' he announced. 'On the ornamental lake.'

'That'll be a few shillings more,' Joanna answered, thinking of the two crown pieces carefully hidden among her things.

'One and three a day, good wages for plain labour,' William answered. 'You'll save on my meal besides, Master says, as it'll be provided, cider too. Now, I'd best be along.'

He kissed her and went to the door, from where she watched until he had disappeared behind the church-yard wall. She stepped inside, thinking of the possibilities of her day. Okehampton was seven miles, and seven miles back, but it was a market day, which meant ribbons and cloth in pretty colours and all sorts of things. It would have to be explained, but she could say she'd had a bargain. If she bought something for him as well he wouldn't be too cross, at least for no longer than it took her to get his cock free of his breeches.

After a hasty trip upstairs to fetch her money and put her bonnet and boots on, she left, trying not to draw attention as she walked through the village and up the lane that led towards the town. The day was hot, and before long she had loosened her bonnet strings and was shaking her skirt as she walked, wafting cool air over her legs. High banks shut off her view to both sides, until she reached the crest of a low hill and came into view of the great dull green sweep of Dartmoor and Burley Down behind her. The Truscotts' house was visible, standing in brilliant sunlight opposite the wooded slope of the down, and she smiled to herself, then blushed at her own thoughts, turning her eyes away, then as quickly back.

A figure was visible, on horseback, moving slowly across one of the fields between her and the down. It was tiny in the distance, but the brilliant scarlet of the rider's coat was unmistakable, and she was sure only one man locally wore such a colour: Henry Truscott. She bit her lip, at once feeling guilty and wondering whether he was likely to meet her in the lane if she turned right at Knole Cross. He was, there could be no doubt about it, or at least they would pass close.

Reasoning that there was no harm in just bidding him good morning, she hurried on, only to stop in indecision as she reached the crossroads. To the left was to reach the Okehampton road, to go right to risk meeting Henry Truscott: both decisions that made her feel guilty and excited, but one much more so than the other.

Taking one of the precious crowns, she glanced quickly to see that she was alone and flicked it into the air. As she caught it she decided that the King would signify Okehampton, St George Henry Truscott. Raising her hand, she found a picture of George III's[4] head and her face set into a frown. Again she threw the coin, securing the saint and the dragon, and a third time, with the same result. Her frown changed to a smile as she turned to the right.

Both her guilt and her excitement rose as she walked, occasionally scrambling up the bank to peer out across the fields. He was not visible, and she began to hope he had not turned back. He had seen her naked, after which it was hard to imagine that he would not want to take advantage of her if they did meet, alone and over a mile from the village. She knew it would have been better if it had happened while she was harnessed to the cart, when her inability to resist would have reduced her guilt, while her vulnerability would have added to the excitement.

As it was, she knew she was likely to have to show willing in some way, and that her feelings were going to make it difficult to flirt, however much she wanted the outcome. There was another reason too, at the back of her mind, making her more eager – the four months of daily sex and her obstinately flat stomach.

She heard his horse before she saw him, giving her time to slow her walk and adjust the curls that hung down from her bonnet. With artless care, she waited until horse and rider appeared around the corner of the lane, then stepped to one side, giving him a coy smile before turning her head to the ground.

'Joanna,' Henry greeted her, immediately reining his horse in. 'What brings you here?'

With no answer she found herself blushing, which Henry ignored, dismounting and taking the horse by the reins.

'I'd thought to ride up to the moor and take a gallop,' he went on, 'but, finding you here, I'm not so certain. I trust you've recovered from the other day? Quite a cut to that dog-whip, I would imagine?'

'Quite recovered, thanking you, sir,' Joanna answered, now blushing furiously at the thought of the welts which still decorated her bottom.

'Not as easy a ten shillings as you had imagined, I judge,' he laughed. 'I don't suppose you'd care to earn some more?'

'On the cart, sir?'

'We might race you again, if you've a mind to be discreet. I was thinking more that Miss Laycock might care for half-a-crown, here and now.'

Joanna found herself unable to answer. Her face was red with blushes but her mind was calculating that if he was offering to pay for what she would have given freely, then it would be foolish to decline. Not that it was so easy to give her acceptance, especially when what she wanted to say was that it would be nicer if she was tied, as she had imagined herself.

'I . . . I'm sure no married woman'd do any such thing,' she managed. 'Not if she could help herself.'

'And if she couldn't?'

'She'd have no say in the thing, I don't suppose, no more than I had a say in what was done to my arse on the cart, tied fast as I was.'

Henry paused, then laughed. Joanna responded with a smile.

'That's the girl,' Henry said, 'to work, then. Well, not in the lane perhaps, and I've no mind to give you a green gown and have that husband of yours angry with you.'

'Down by the stream perhaps, a little way along,' Joanna suggested.

Henry nodded, smiling and taking her hand. She followed, her heart hammering and her belly fluttering, both from the prospect of what she was going to do and the casual way he had suggested it. Where a shallow stream crossed the lane they turned into a sparse copse, Henry leading the horse in a little way before looping the reins around a tree. A few paces further and they were screened both from the lane and the fields, where Henry put his back to a tree and drew her in.

Joanna let him lead, opening her mouth under his and folding her arms around him. A hand curled

46

around her waist, then down, cupping a buttock even as the other found her chest, kneading one breast through her dress. She could feel him inching her dress up, and knew her bottom would soon be bare to the wood. He tugged at her bodice, pulling one breast free and ducking down to take the nipple in his mouth, sucking as if trying to get milk. Joanna giggled, holding it up for him and pulling the other free.

As he suckled her both his hands went to her dress, pulling it up, clear of her bottom. Her cheeks were taken, squeezed, opened, then slapped. He went lower, pulling from her breast, lifting the front of her skirt as she took the back. His lips found her belly-button, kissing it, his tongue burrowing in, then lower, licking her belly and kissing the tangle of curls over her quim as she shut her eyes in bliss. William never licked her quim, but she had imagined it while rubbing at herself, and as Henry's mouth found her sex her mouth came wide in ecstasy, greater even than she had imagined.

She began to play with her breasts while he licked her, cupping them and rubbing her fingers over her nipples. His hands were busy too, fondling her bottom, stroking and gently smacking her cheeks, pulling them apart to let the cool air touch her anus. He had found the bud at the centre of her quim, and was flicking it with his tongue, bringing her up towards climax. She was moaning, everything forgotten except the pleasure of her body, her thighs tightening in Henry's face. A finger found her anus, tickling the little hole, which was wet with sweat and her juice, letting him inside as he probed. She gave a little sob, wondering if he was the sort of man who liked to put his cock in the same place.

It didn't matter; she was coming, screaming aloud and pushing herself into his face, then screaming as the climax welled up inside her and broke. Her anus tightened on his finger and her hands squeezed her breasts, pinching the hard nipples. She screamed, unable to bear the sensation as his tongue pressed hard on to her quim, thinking of herself, bare in the woods, as she came, and of what he was certain to do to her at any moment.

She felt weak as the orgasm subsided, vulnerable and ready, with her juice and Henry's spittle running cool down her thighs. Henry rose, his lips wet from her quim, which she tasted as he kissed her again, his hands still holding her bottom.

'Now for my own,' he said, breaking away. 'For one, I'll want to see your arse, and try not to be so damned noisy.'

'I can't stop it, sir,' Joanna panted.

'Then I'd best stop your mouth,' Henry answered. 'Who can say who's in earshot?'

Joanna made no resistance as he turned her with his hands. Still holding her skirt up, she let herself be pushed down, bending to take hold of a low hawthorn branch. It was the position she had imagined: bent, bottom high, her quim open to him from the rear. She turned, biting her lip as she saw the bulge in his breeches.

'By God you're glorious,' Henry remarked, putting a hand to her bottom, 'and none the less for your welts. Now for your bonnet, and I'll be in you soon enough.'

Joanna tugged loose the bow that held her bonnet tight beneath her chin as Henry reached for it. It came away and she opened her mouth, guessing his intention as he balled the soft cloth in his hand.

'Good girl,' Henry said as he wadded the cloth into her open mouth. 'You've been gagged before, if you're a screamer, I'll warrant.'

She managed to shake her head, at which Henry laughed, clearly not believing her. Her hands were close, and she was hoping he would remember to tie her, a need realised as he took hold of the dangling bonnet strings.

'Not much length, but enough,' he said, pulling them to force her head down on to her hands.

She went into the awkward pose, with her bottom higher than ever. Henry looped the strings down around her wrists and the branch, then back behind her neck. He tied them off, leaving her gagged, bound and helpless with her bottom flaunted in a position that she knew was both rude and somewhat ridiculous. Henry laughed as he stepped back, and slapped her hard across her upraised cheeks.

'By God, but my Eloise gave you a drubbing,' he said. 'I'll wager it still smarts to sit. Still, I've a mind to thrash you myself. With an arse so big and white it's hard not to.'

Joanna tried to shake her head, which was hard with her face tied to her hands. Instead she stamped her feet, wriggling her bottom. Henry chuckled, and as she heard the soft rasp of his belt being drawn from his breeches she realised that he had misunderstood her response. She wriggled harder, making her bottom quiver, trying to speak but only managing a muffled mewling sound. Something hard touched her bottom, laid across the upturned cheeks: his belt. She stiffened and felt him press to her; the firm, bulbous head of his penis pressed to her quim, rubbing briefly in the wet mush and she was pushing her bottom back.

He went in, groaning as she felt her hole fill. A hand took her skirt and the belt lifted from her buttocks as he began to fuck her to a slow rhythm. She relaxed, letting the dizzying pleasure of having his cock inside her fill her head and trying to ignore her uncomfortable position. The beating had been abandoned in his urgency, or so she thought until the thick belt smacked down across her buttocks.

Joanna jumped in shock and pain at the blow. Henry laughed and brought the belt down again, increasing his pace. She tried to speak, and kicked one leg out, only to be lifted by her waistband; Henry was grunting with effort, pushing himself deep up her as the belt smacked down hard on her flesh. She went on to the other leg, struggling to dull the pain, only to feel her buttocks bounce once more and cry out into her gag.

'Stay still, damn you!' Henry swore.

She tried, not knowing if she wanted it or not, with her bottom hot and stinging, her quim eager despite her pain and resentment. Henry began to fuck faster, timing deep pushes to smacks of the belt, and she was lost, wiggling herself on his cock, her eyes shut tight, her teeth locked on the wet cloth of her bonnet. Henry began to grunt, his smacks growing clumsy as his excitement rose, striking her hips and the soft flesh of her waist, ever faster, his cock pushing ever harder. Joanna lost the last of her control, bucking and writhing on his cock as she was beaten, her buttocks bouncing, her hanging breasts jiggling to the smacks and thrusts. Her whole body was burning with pain, and all of it focused on the cock inside her, which seemed to fill her middle, even her head as he gave a last strangled grunt and jammed it in to make her gag on her mouthful as he came deep inside her.

Eloise paused, dissatisfied with her efforts at painting the landscape. The reality was beautiful, with the lawn sloping down to what was to be the lake and the high, wooded slope of Burley Down beyond. To her left was a patchwork of fields and woods leading away to the sweep of Dartmoor in the east. To her right the land fell away, to the valleys of the Lew and the Tamar, with Bodmin Moor in the distance.

Despite her efforts at layering the washes and colours, her painting failed to capture the grandeur of the scene. The composition was wrong, she decided. There was too much distance. Dartmoor should have been behind Burley Down, and higher, the round hills and rocky tors taller, more dramatic. The light was wrong too, quite wrong, with the dark greens and shadows of Burley Wood quite out of place when there was so much sunlight beyond. Then the lake should have been finished, and the hard lines of the grey granite miners' cottages softer, less harsh. Finally there was the group of workmen in the lake excavation, whose noise and appearance were both distracting.

Not that watching a dozen burly young men at work was entirely unpleasant. The day was hot, with no more than a light breeze, and many had removed their smocks or shirts to go bare above the waist, showing hard torsos and well-muscled arms. They were hard to ignore, and tempting, especially as she knew that the worst Henry would do if she strayed was take a belt or cane to her bottom.

It was more tempting still because of the way Henry had treated her in the night. Her bottom-hole still felt loose and a little sore, reminding her of how she had been sodomised. Also how she had been told to give herself a climax while he had been up her bottom, so that he could feel the muscle of her anus tighten on his cock. She had done it kneeling, rubbing at herself while he buggered her and coming with his cock so far up her hole that his balls had pressed to her quim. It had been nice, yes, but so dirty. Besides which, it was all very well for him. He had come in her gut and pulled out, none the worse, while she was left smarting and loose. Indeed, her ring had been so open that she'd had to spend a good while seated on her chamber pot before she could be sure that she wouldn't soil her bed.

Her resentment at being sodomised mingled with her annoyance at her inability to capture the scenery in her painting. The temptation was to walk down to the excavation, pick the best of the men, maybe three, even four, and demand that they come up to the house on some pretext. From there it would be into her room and the rest of the afternoon would be spent in a welter of cocks and tongues, with all of them doing just what they were told.

Socially, she knew it was an impossibility; practically as well. It was hard enough to maintain any sort of social respect with Henry's debauchery, never mind if she gained a reputation for indulging herself with the local labourers. In any case, even if the men did obey her at first, once they were erect they were likely to be led by their cocks and lose their awe of her position. Knowing men, she was likely to be sodomised again, or taken with a cock in each orifice, her mouth included, a thought which sent a shiver the length of her spine.

It was tempting, but there were simply too many difficulties. Better, she decided, to rely on the safe and discreet services of her maid. Rising from her seat, she turned for the house, hoping that Suki would be working on her own and not with Mrs Orcombe.

Joanna Pearse walked slowly in the direction of the village, the expression on her face alternating between a satisfied smile and a worried frown. For all the pain and indignity of the way Henry Truscott had taken her, it had been thrilling: not just for the feel of his cock or the orgasms she'd taken before and after being tied, but because it had been illicit. There was pride too, in the attentions of a handsome and wealthy landowner, and satisfaction for the new half-crown that nestled beside the other coins in her pocket.

Against that there was the state she was in. She could feel the persistent throb in her beaten bottom, and knew that her flesh was a mess of welts and bruises. A brief inspection once Henry had untied her had shown just how well-coloured the sides of her cheeks were, and she knew the full view would be worse still.

Her bottom was bad enough, but her bodice was torn and her bonnet was a mess of chewed fabric, and dirty where it had been tied against the rough bark. She wouldn't have to have her skirts lifted for people to realise that something was amiss, and she was pretty sure that the village gossips would come to the right conclusion.

Reaching the crossroads, she stopped, trying to decide on a story for William. For a moment she considered saying she'd been set on and raped, only to abandon the idea. There would be a hue and cry, and in all likelihood her lies would come out. If he did see her bottom, the blame would have to go to Mrs Truscott. For the bonnet, it was best not seen, which in any case would give her an excuse to make her trip to Okehampton and buy a new one.

There was a breeze getting up, and a bank of clouds was visible in the west. Pleased with her decision, she undid the bonnet and threw it high over a hedge, intending to blame the wind. Her bodice she could say had caught on a snag, and if William thought she had been home all day, there would be little reason to doubt her explanation.

She reached the village and their cottage without having to speak to anybody, avoiding a group of women gossiping near the lich-gate by going around behind the churchyard. Once indoors, she set about the day's tasks, working as fast as she could to give the impression of a full day's labour. By the time the church bell tolled six she had the house tidy and was peeling turnips at the table in front of the settle. The crash of the door signalled William's return, making her start.

'I'll have a dish of tea in a moment, love,' she called.

'I'll take cider, that's more the thing,' he answered, pushing the door closed. 'Hard work that, and thirsty, but he's no miser, Squire Truscott. There's all the cider a man could want, in a butt by the workings.'

Joanna turned. William's face was red and streaked with sweat and dirt. He was drunk, staggering slightly as he came into the kitchen. His eyes were bright, and he leered as he came up to her.

'How about a kiss, then?' he asked, putting his arms around her and taking a breast in each hand.

'Mind your filthy hands, you great fool!' she protested.

His mouth stopped hers with a kiss, to which she responded, letting him pull her round on the chair. He was fumbling with her chest, clumsily, but she could feel her nipples going hard. Dropping her knife and the turnip she had been peeling, she put her arms around his neck as one breast then the other was popped free of her dress.

'Not now, lover,' she said as he broke the kiss. 'Take a drink while I make ready your supper. Aren't you tired?'

'Not so tired,' he answered, nuzzling her breasts as she struggled to push him back.

'William, no!' she insisted. 'The window's wide. Someone's sure to see!'

'Then I'll put you in the corner,' he answered, picking her up bodily from the chair.

Joanna relaxed, expecting him to put her on his cock upright, as he sometimes did. He carried her easily, taking three long steps to where the chimney breast hid the view from the street. Her arms were around his neck, her thighs spread around his hips, with the hard bulge of his cock already pressing to her crotch. She was lowered to the settle, hastily pulling up her skirts as he fumbled with his breeches. His cock sprang out, half-stiff, and she was taken by the hair, pulled in and her face rubbed against his genitals until she managed to get her mouth around them. She sucked, quickly bringing him to full erection, still expecting to be put on his cock, only for his powerful hands to grip her by the shoulders and start to twist her around.

'No, not like that!' she protested, quickly pulling back. 'It's . . . it's not decent, William!'

'Don't like your arse up! Since when?' he demanded. 'Now get across.'

'No!' she squealed, but could do nothing as he turned her body, tipping her across the settle and pressing his erection to the seat of her skirts. 'William, please, not that way around!'

'What's the matter with you?' he demanded, tugging her hand away as she tried to hold down her dress. 'Leave go, will you?'

Her hand came loose, pulled roughly away. She tried to defend herself, but he put a knee in her back, pinning her down and wrenching at her skirt. It came up, despite her protests and struggles, over her thighs, then her bottom and William stopped abruptly.

'So that's why you didn't want to show. Who in hell's been at your arse?' he demanded.

'Mrs Truscott,' Joanna sobbed. 'I'm sorry, I didn't want you to see. I dropped a jug, ever so expensive. She took a belt to me.'

'She did, did she?' he growled.

'I deserved it, William,' she answered. 'I did, but I didn't want you to see, for the shame of it.'

'Deserved or otherwise, it's not her place to beat you.'

'I took it willingly, lover, it was that or the end to the work I've had. We need the money, you know we do. She is such a fine lady besides, and I was clumsy, and stupid. How could I say her no?"

'Fine lady or no fine lady, she's no right to thrash my wife. I've half a mind to speak to her. Yes, I shall.'

'No, William, think of the work!' Joanna urged. 'There'll be no more, not with you opening your great mouth over nothing!'

'Nothing! That's not nothing! She's hued your arse like a burst plum! I'm amazed she's the strength in her arm.'

'She was right to do it, William; I was clumsy. The jug cost a guinea piece, to London!'

'No matter. He's a fair man, the squire, by all accounts, and she's a vicious piece. I've a mind to speak to him, and you with me.'

'No, William, let us leave well enough alone. It's no matter. I'm not hurt, I'm not. It looks bad, but it's not . . .'

'Be quiet, will you?' William cut her off as he took his knee off her back. 'We'll go up to the house now, and have done with it.'

He took her arm, pulling her to her feet, his face set in angry determination.

Henry reined his horse in and dismounted. He was grinning, thoroughly pleased with himself as he handed the reins to the stable boy. His plans for Joanna Pearse had come to fruition faster than he had expected, and beautifully. Meeting her in the lane on the very first day her husband was employed on the lake gang had been a fine chance. Her response had been all he had imagined, coy yet wanton, with just enough reluctance at having her bottom whipped to add a touch of spice.

He was also sure he could rely on more of the same in the future. Her kisses had held genuine feeling, not at all like those of a whore, for all that he had paid her. She would be discreet, he was sure of it, and had the wit not to let her husband see the state of her bottom. Not that Pearse was likely to do much if he did come to suspect, not when Henry provided his livelihood. Best of all, being married, he could come inside her with impunity. Since leaving her he had ridden up on to the moor, as he had originally intended. The short turf on the face of Sourton Tors had provided a fine gallop, leaving him exhilarated and entirely satisfied with the world – also hungry.

Allowing the stable boy to take care of the horse, he made his way to the house, finding it quiet except for faint noises coming from the direction of the kitchen. Imagining it to be Mrs Orcombe, and thinking of a slice of the game pie they had started at lunch, he walked quickly towards the sounds, flicking his crop on his boot as he went.

The kitchen was empty, the noises coming from the scullery, and not the sort of sounds Mrs Orcombe might have been expected to make, but low moans and the unmistakable smack of leather on flesh. Grinning, he threw the door open.

As he had suspected, Eloise was there, her back to the scullery table, her skirts lifted high over her belly and her bodice open to liberate her breasts. Suki knelt at his wife's feet, stark naked except for a bonnet, the dark skin of her buttocks and back criss-crossed with purple welts from the dog-whip Eloise held in one hand. The pose also left the black girl's buttocks spread, with her quim showing vivid pink between pouted sex-lips and her anus a dark knot, glistening with sweat.

Both women looked up sharply as Henry entered. Eloise's expression of rapt pleasure barely changed. Suki glanced from his face to his crotch and went back to work. He put his hand down, squeezing his genitals through the front of his breeches. Suki's ripe, welted bottom tempted, both the pink of her quim and the black of her anus. Pulling one side of his breeches flap loose, he freed his cock, moving in close to the girls. Eloise took it in her hand, tugging urgently as she turned her face to kiss him. She was pulling him in, putting his cock to Suki's face, and he felt the warm, wet cavity of the black girl's mouth as she took him in. He put a hand to Eloise's breasts, stroking and fondling them as his cock hardened in Suki's mouth.

Suki stopped sucking him, returning to Eloise as his cock reached erection. He took it in his hand, rubbing the head in Suki's hair and against her face and Eloise's thigh. Moving down, he sucked a nipple into his mouth, drawing hard, until he tasted the sweet sharp tang of her milk. She moaned, her arm tightening across his back, gripping Suki by the hair at the same time.

Eloise had dropped the whip, and as he sucked on his wife's breast Henry began to flick his crop at Suki's out-thrust bottom, watching the chubby black cheeks wobble from the corner of his eye. Eloise moaned again, pulling him in tighter still. Her noises turned to choking sobs, then a long squeal of pleasure, catching in her throat as she came under Suki's tongue. Henry pulled back, his wife's milk dribbling down his chin, the white spots still growing on her taut nipple. Suki kissed his cock, taking it in her mouth again. He pulled away, in no hurry to come, and wondered if she could taste Joanna's quim on his penis.

'Get across the table, the pair of you,' he ordered. 'I've a mind to have you both, side by side.'

'I ...' Eloise managed, still flushed with her orgasm, but Henry was already pulling her around and she went with the pressure, letting out a sob as she was pushed down across the table.

Suki followed, rising to lay herself next to her mistress, both girls looking back over their shoulders as Henry stood back, stroking his cock as he admired their bodies. They were much of a size and shape, black and white, Eloise's bottom pale and unmarked, Suki's dark, her perfect skin ridged purple with whip-marks. Both girls' cheeks were parted, the lips of their quims peeping out behind, Elosie's pale in a tangle of ginger, Suki's dark in a nest of crinkly black. Their bottom-cheeks were open too, flared to show tight little holes, both hairy, save at the actual entrances to their bottoms. Suki had perhaps a little more meat, chubbier, prouder buttocks, if less sweetly tucked under than Eloise's. Both were glorious, and it was hard to know which to fuck first, or indeed if he should push his cock into the tighter ring of an anus.

Henry licked his lips at the sight, then moved forwards, pressing his cock to his wife's quim. It went in easily, deep up her, and he began to fuck. As he did so he put a hand to Suki's bottom, feeling the ripe cheeks, the wonderfully smooth skin, ridged where she had been beaten.

'Kiss each other,' he said, letting his fingers slip down between Suki's buttocks.

Eloise hesitated, but Suki obeyed, turning her head to plant a peck on her mistress's cheek, then on her lips. Henry's finger found Suki's anus, pressed at the little wet hole, then slipped lower and into her quim. Holding Eloise by the back of her dress, he began to fuck her more rapidly, at which she gave in, opening her mouth under Suki's. Henry watched them kiss, his excitement growing until he was forced to pull back or come.

His cock pulled free, slippery and marked white with his wife's juices. Suki was ready, her hole open and moist; and, without giving Eloise a chance to protest, he moved quickly behind the black girl and pulled her buttocks open, slipping his erection into her willing quim. On being entered she became more passionate in her kissing, hugging Eloise to her, their chests pressing together, dark breasts and pale, side by side, soft, female flesh in two colours a sight too glorious for him to hold back and he was coming, jerking his cock free of Suki's quim at the last instant and snatching at it to milk what come he had left over her proud black buttocks.

Spent and gasping, he stepped back and sank into one of the scullery chairs. The girls cuddled closer; Suki pulled Eloise up onto the table. Their limbs tangled around one another, the maid's thighs spread across her mistress's leg, open brown and pink quim pressed tight on white flesh. Suki began to rub on Eloise's leg; Henry stared in delight, wishing he'd held back his orgasm. Always before Suki had stayed servile to Eloise, but now she was rolling on top, her hips bucking faster and faster as she strained to get her clitoris on Eloise's skin.

The jiggling black bottom was too good to resist. Henry pulled himself to his feet, bending for the riding crop. Lifting it, he brought it down hard across Suki's bottom, making her grunt into Eloise's mouth and buck all the faster. Again he hit and again she grunted, rubbing with desperate speed, pushing her bottom up, then down as the crop smacked into her flesh a third time. Suki came, her body crushed to Eloise's, spread thighs locked tight, quim pressed in hard, muscles locked in ecstasy.

Henry stood back as Suki's body went slowly limp. Three new cuts decorated her bottom, purple on rich brown, the flesh already rising in ridges of roughened skin. What had happened earlier Henry had no idea, but Suki's buttocks were covered in weals, both glossy, sweat-slick hemispheres marked a dozen or more times. Her thighs, though, were unmarked, and her back hardly, showing that the whipping had been sexual, doubtless engineered by Eloise as a punishment, but sexual nonetheless.

With Suki finished, Eloise seemed to come to her senses, pulling herself quickly from the table as soon as the black girl had risen and smoothing down her skirts. She was blushing, but smiling too, a reaction he knew well.

'Fine sport,' he remarked. 'So, Suki, you got your whipping after all?'

Suki responded by showing her teeth in a broad grin. She stood up, craning back to inspect her bottom, still entirely unconcerned by her nudity. Her brow furrowed as she stroked a particularly bad welt, but she made no complaint. Eloise said nothing, frowning as she inspected the smeared mess of her make-up reflected in the bottom of a polished copper pan.

Henry stretched, wondering if he could persuade the girls to another bout, and if he wanted to. He was hungry and his cock was sore, making him decide against it, despite the opportunity of taking full advantage of Eloise while her guard was down. It was not the time, and it was also certain that Mrs Orcombe would appear soon to prepare the dinner. Reluctantly, he put his cock away.

'You've work, I suspect, Suki,' he remarked, 'but be a good girl and cut me a slice of pie before you start.'

'Pie, sir,' Suki answered, bobbing her head and making for the pantry.

'Henry, my dear . . .' Eloise began, only to stop at a sudden rapping at the scullery door.

'Mrs Orcombe, I suspect,' Henry said. 'I see you'd the sense to lock the door. Do put some clothes on, Suki; you may fetch my pie presently.'

He went to the door, sliding the bolts back and opening it to find not the bulky figure of Mrs Orcombe, but William Pearse, with Joanna behind him, held firmly by the arm.

'Ah, Pearse,' he said, 'Joanna. What may I do for you?'

'I'd like a word, if I may, Mr Truscott, sir,' William Pearse answered, firmly but with some uncertainty showing in his voice. Henry smelt the wash of alcohol on the man's breath and cast a hasty glance at Joanna.

'Quite,' he answered. 'Quite. Would you come in?'

'Here'll do well enough for what I've got to say,' Pearse went on determinedly.

'As you like,' Henry answered. 'Eloise, my dear, I'll join you in a minute.'

'It concerns the lady and all,' Pearse said. 'Seeing as how it was her who did it.'

'Did what?' Henry demanded.

'Beat my poor wife,' Pearse answered. 'Black and blue, and for no more than breaking some knick-knack.'

'What is this?' Eloise demanded.

'Nothing, really, ma'am,' Joanna put in quickly. 'William's just . . .'

'Just nothing,' William cut her off, rising to his task. 'You've hued her arse good and proper, ma'am, pardoning my speech, and I say it's not right.'

'What right have you to question me!' Eloise snapped.

'A moment, my dear, a moment,' Henry put in. 'This is, I'm sure, easily resolved. You were, perhaps, a little stern with Joanna.'

'A little stern!' Pearse retorted. 'She can hardly sit for the bruises.'

As he said it he wrenched Joanna forwards. She squealed in protest as he bent to grab her skirts, but they were yanked high, with such force that she was forced to turn to keep her balance. The move left her bottom showing, both full cheeks welted and colourful, with little of their surface unmarked.

'This is not my doing,' Eloise said coldly. 'I applied a dog-whip, yes, in order to correct a slovenly maid. That was some days ago. The rest is clearly fresh and, as you well know, she has not been with us this afternoon. Come, Henry, get rid of this beastly fellow. He is probably trying to extract money.'

'Not whipped this afternoon, you say,' Pearse growled.

His eyes had gone past Henry, who glanced back to see the dog-whip and riding crop still lying on the floor, in plain view.

'A moment,' Henry said. 'There is something in what Pearse here has to say. Perhaps a shilling would make amends?'

Pearse appeared not to hear, and was still staring past him, now pop-eyed. Henry turned fully, to find Suki, plainly visible in the pantry doorway, stark naked and holding a plate. She was watching them, the welts on her thighs clearly visible. Too late he realised that she had understood about the pie, but not the clothes.

'I . . . It . . .' he stumbled. 'Er . . . Suki is, er . . . was a savage, Pearse. She has little understanding . . .'

'Certain sure she don't,' Pearse answered and his eyes moved to Henry, first to his face, then lower.

Henry glanced down, immediately realising what Pearse was looking at. The front of his breeches were smeared white with the girls' juices. Rising anger showed in Pearse's face, his mouth working, his fist coming up and tightening.

'Return to your cottage this instant, you beastly little peasant!' Eloise snapped. 'Take your sloven of a wife with you! How dare you . . .?'

She stopped. Pearse was ignoring her, and grinding his teeth as he looked at Henry.

'This . . .' Henry tried. 'I mean to say . . .'

'You've had my Joanna, you hangallus bastard!' Pearse roared.

Henry lurched back as Pearse swung at his face, missing by inches. Eloise screamed. Joanna grabbed her husband's coat. Pearse came forwards, mounting the step up to the scullery and driving a fist at Henry's face. Henry ducked, only to catch Pearse's left in his midriff. He doubled up, lashing out in defence, catching Pearse's arm, only to be knocked aside and sent to the floor by another hard left. Pearse was swearing, over and over, Joanna too, screaming at her husband to stop. On the scullery floor, Henry found himself looking up at Pearse, the big man's face red with rage, one massive fist drawn back. Eloise screamed again and the fist came down, into his jaw, slamming his head against the floor.

His vision went red, his head dizzy, in a tumult of curses and screams. He kicked up, hitting something,

64

then again as another crushing blow drove into his face. The world went black, his hands scrambling at the floor, finding the table leg and pulling himself under. Pearse roared again and a boot struck Henry's hip. Voices called out, male, then fresh female screams and a curse from Pearse. Booted feet were hurrying past as the beating let up and he dragged himself under the table. Suki screamed; a man cursed; Eloise's voice rang out in fury.

Pulling himself up at the far side of the table, Henry stood, dizzy with pain. Pearse was opposite him, with Joanna hanging on to his back. Eloise was pressed against the wall, her face white. Two men in brown were struggling with Suki, one with blood pouring from his hand. Shaking Joanna off to tumble onto the floor, Pearse came at him. Henry dodged, only for Pearse to thrust the table forwards, jamming Henry against the cupboards. Winded, he doubled up, and Pearse's fist lashed out, full into his face.

There was no vision, only light and jumbled noise, jarring pain and a desperate need for air. He felt the next blow through a haze and then was lying on the floor with boots near his face, slim dark ankles and bare feet, another boot.

'Slaving bastard!' a voice shouted and the boot was driven into his face.

Three

Henry Truscott shifted uncomfortably in his chair. His ribs still hurt, although the bruise on his thigh had gone down enough to allow him to walk without a limp. One eye was still more comfortable shut than open, but the cuts on his lips seemed likely to heal without leaving much in the way of scars.

He had come round looking up into Eloise's face. Pearse had been gone, along with Joanna, Suki and the two men who had seemed to appear from nowhere. Eloise had explained that they had taken Suki, dragging her outside, at which point she had fled, scared of suffering the same fate. When she had returned, only Henry had been in the scullery, unconscious on the floor.

Initially his concern had been purely for himself, but as the initial pain and anger subsided the question of what had happened to Suki, and why, had become increasingly important. It had also become increasingly outrageous that his wife's maid should be taken, while his antagonism towards William Pearse had faded with the undeniable certainty that he himself would have reacted in much the same way.

The following day he had sent for the mine captain at Wheal Purity, Todd Gurney, determined to retrieve Suki and exact a revenge which he knew would also soothe his chagrin at being so easily beaten by William Pearse. It was a far more satisfying prospect than attempting to prosecute the case through the law, which in any event might well not yield satisfactory results.[5] Gurney had arrived the next morning, the solid bulk of the ex-soldier doing a great deal to increase Henry's security and confidence, Eloise's also.

'It's this fellow Gould, the parson,' Henry stated, once he had explained what had happened. 'I'm sure of it. Just the other day he was wanting to know if we paid Suki a wage. The fellow seemed to think she might be a slave.'

'Not though, is she?' Gurney answered. 'As I dare say you told him.'

'I did,' Henry answered, 'but who's to say he believed me? I mean, the last thing I heard before I went out was one of them calling me a slaving bastard. I've never slaved in my life, so what other explanation might there be?'

'This is true,' Eloise added, 'and more besides. Even as they manhandled Suki they were seeking to explain that the act was for her own good.'

'So where'd they go?' Gurney asked. 'How, besides. On horses? In a carriage?'

Henry shrugged.

'My concern,' Eloise said, 'was with my own safety.'

'Seems likely they were seen,' Gurney went on. 'Two strangers hereabouts.'

'The hour was near seven,' Eloise replied, 'while it began to rain shortly after they left.'

'Still,' Gurney said, 'could be they were seen. What of this fellow Pearse and his wife?'

'No doubt they'd have seen something,' Henry said. 'I'm in no mind to ask him.'

'You should have him transported,' Eloise cut in, 'or at the very least flogged.'

'I've no concern with Pearse,' Henry answered, drawing an angry snort from Eloise.

'That's as is,' Gurney said, 'but you could if you'd a mind. I'll ask him myself, and say to him you'll not be prosecuting his assault so long as he says what he knows.'

'A useful beginning,' Henry answered. 'As to Gould, there's no sense in asking him. He'll hardly admit to it.'

'I'm not so sure on the parson,' Gurney stated. 'He seems a harmless sort, from all I've seen. Sir Joseph Snapes is the man for me. He's the means, the malice too. Don't suppose he'd forget how we took him and gave him to the enschego.'

Henry grunted, smiling at the memory of the chimpanzee and promptly wishing he hadn't as his split lip twinged in pain.

'Could be,' he admitted, but my money's still on Gould. He saw us after we'd been racing Suki, Joanna Pearse too. It may well be he didn't believe our story about punishing them, and you know how priests can be for morals. So we'll play it like this. Speak to Pearse, and watch his temper. I'll send to London for Charles to see if Snapes might not be our man. As to Gould, see if he's gone anywhere or been seen with strangers.'

Joanna Pearse sat, hunched and miserable, at the kitchen table. William was in the parlour, scowling and silent, as he had been since the fight. They had stayed apart, speaking as little as possible, and she had not admitted to having sex with Henry, but made no attempt to deny it either.

Her own feelings were of guilt and sorrow, partly wishing she had held her feelings back, but more that she hadn't been caught out. Twice she had tried to make up, but William had rejected her efforts, refusing even to eat the meals she put in front of him or to share their bed. His black mood was frightening, but he hadn't lifted a finger to her, or touched her at all, so that part of her was wishing he would, if only things would then return to normal. There was gossip in the village too and, although nobody knew the truth, she was sure the rumours were as bad, if not worse.

Suddenly he grunted and rose from his chair. Joanna started, backing into the chimney corner, scared, only for him to push out into the backhouse after throwing her a scowl. She heard him move something heavy, then other noises and the scrape of metal on stone.

'What are you about, William?' she asked, rising and moving towards the door.

He answered with a grunt and then emerged, holding a length of hemp, coiled in one hand. Sitting, he began to tease the strands of the rope open at one end, ignoring her completely. Splicing the rope's end back on itself, he formed a knob and Joanna's hand went to her mouth, realising what he had made and that it was certainly going to be her it was used on. Yet she made no attempt to run, her fear mingled with relief, if only he would give her the beating she knew she deserved and then make up.

She swallowed as he smacked the rope's end against his hand. She found herself trembling, expecting to be ordered across the table, skirts high, or even taken out into the street and thrashed in public so that William could restore his pride. He did nothing, except turn the piece of rope and begin to tease open the other end. Joanna watched and, when he continued to ignore her, she returned to the settle.

William went on with his work, opening a section of rope at the middle and splicing the loose ends into it to form a loop.

'What are you about?' Joanna asked again when curiosity at last got the better of her.

'Forming a halter,' he said. 'Market to Okehampton today. Cattle and such.'

'Market?' Joanna echoed, hope rising as she wondered if he wasn't trying to smooth things over.

'Market,' he repeated. 'I've some selling to do.'

'A pig?'

'You could say that, yes. A sow.'

'May I come, William?' she asked.

'Oh, you're to come,' he answered. 'Wouldn't be nothing to sell 'less you come.'

'Why's that, William?'

'Why's that? That, is on account of how you're the sow I plan to sell.'[6]

'That's a cruel joke, William!'

'No joke. You're mine, as Parson Gould said when he married us. Now you've made a cuckold of me I've a mind to be rid of you, at the best price.'

'You can't do that, William!'

'Can't I just? So long as you're on a halter there and on a halter away, it's my right.'

'Not to me, William! I thought you'd made the rope's end for my arse, and that'd be the end of it! Wouldn't that be better?'

'I'll not be called cuckold,' he answered. 'Now slip this around your neck and we'll be on our way. Best to be there while there's plenty of folk about.'

He held out the halter to Joanna, loop first. She looked at the thing, agonising humiliation welling up inside her. He was determined, it was obvious, and for the sake of his pride more than anything, a realisation which brought her a flush of anger.

Snatching the halter from his hand, she tugged it down over her head and around her neck.

'Sell me, then!' she spat. 'Sell me like a sow if that's all I'm worth to you!'

'Might not get so much,' he answered. 'James Chillcott had his wife for two shillings and sixpence, to Launceston.'

Joanna spat at him, fury boiling up inside her. He merely laughed, the first humour he had shown since he had seen her smacked buttocks. Jerking the halter, he pulled her towards the door. Joanna hesitated, thinking of begging at least to be spared the indignity of being led through the village on a halter, only to be forced to stumble after him as he tugged on the rope.

'What of my Sunday dress?' she demanded as he pulled her out into the bright sunlight, 'and my sewing tools and such like?'

'You've nought but odds,' he answered. 'Besides, I dare say there'll be another to use them, soon enough.'

'You're . . .' Joanna began, her voice rising, then shutting off abruptly. Two women were looking at her, and a group of the day labourers who were gathered outside the Black Horse in the hope of employment.

She looked away, blood rushing to her face as one of the men jerked a thumb in her direction and passed a remark to his friends. Their answering laughter came clear and she turned away, feeling the tears start in her eyes as William threw the halter across his shoulder and set off towards the church, not troubling to look back.

He walked out of the village and up the hill with Joanna trailing miserably behind. The few people they passed cast them curious glances, some shocked,

71

some amused, but nobody sought to intervene. Until they reached Knole Cross she was still thinking it was being done to torment her, to humiliate her and teach her a lesson, and that he would turn back at the boundary of the parish. William crossed the junction without breaking step, reaching the main road and turning north beneath the loom of the moor.

Past the cross, she realised that he really intended to go through with it, selling her at Okehampton market among the pigs and sheep, bullocks and geese. The tears that had started in the village came again, hot and angry. She began to plead, begging for a beating instead, only to stop, realising that the last thing she wanted was to be taken back by him. Silent, she walked on, only to change her mind again and start to plead, even to be put in the village stocks for public disgrace, or whipped naked at the tail of a cart. William said nothing, but began to whistle a tune, at which Joanna returned to an angry silence.

By the time they reached the gentle hill down into Okehampton town her tears had dried on her cheeks and she was walking numb with shock, indifferent to the curious, intrusive stares of passers-by. The town was crowded, with people, horses, and cattle, the main street half-blocked ahead of them where a heavy dray was unloading outside an inn. William walked patiently on, pushing between a group of bullocks, towing Joanna behind him until they reached the market square.

People were jostling against her, peering into her face, making ribald comments. Somebody squeezed her bottom through her dress, laughing as he stepped away. Another offered William a jar of gin he held swinging from his fingers, also laughing as he was told to wait. Burning with shame, Joanna let herself be led to the centre of the market, among the animals, where men and women were haggling over prices, sellers showing off the qualities of their produce while buyers looked for faults.

'There's William Pearse!' a coarse, loud voice called out. 'Ho, William, not tired of your Joanna already, surely?'

'That's right, Tom,' William answered. 'I didn't get the bargain I supposed I was, and so she's up for sale. You likely to be buying?'

'Not I, what'd my Mary say?' the man answered. 'Still, a shame.'

He leered at Joanna, his round, red face beaming into hers. She looked away, feeling alert, but confused, while William suddenly seemed a different man, a complete stranger. The last few months seemed hazy, unreal, their courtship before that yet more so, and once again she was the young girl who had been frightened of the big, muscular labourer. He climbed on to the side of a broad granite trough, tugging her up behind him. She followed, stepping up and turning to look out over the crowd, a sea of heads, hats and bonnets, many turning as William blew a piercing whistle. Slowly the crowd went quiet as people turned, loud conversation and laughter turning to whispers and grunted remarks, nervous giggles from the women. Beyond, the market was still noisy, leaving them in an island of quiet.

'I'm William Pearse,' William called, 'as a good few of you know, a local, man and boy. Now here's Joanna Pearse, Joanna Hannaford as was, who I took to wife four months past. Now it seems she's not the woman I thought she was, in a way of speaking. I dare say you'll hear the tale in time, and I want none saying they had her false, so I'll say now. She's been with another man, and I want rid of her for what I can get. Try and smile, girl; get that hangallus look off your face.'

Joanna turned him a dirty look, her temper flaring at his words. The tears were threatening to start again, in rage and shame, but she couldn't meet the eyes of the crowd, only look away over their heads.

'Pretty maid she was, when I married her, and still is pretty,' Pearse continued, putting a big hand under her chin and tilting her head up. 'There's not a better head of hair in Devon, they used to say.'

'And more besides, William,' someone called out, drawing laughter from several of the men.

'True enough,' Pearse answered. 'Now, she's a tongue in her head and she's contrary too, as I say. Still, a good drubbing now and again and she'll suit well enough. She's clean and has been maid to a fine gentleman, this being part of the trouble. So who'll have her, then?'

'A peck of cider!' somebody called out.

Pearse nodded.

'Ten shillings, Wheal Joshua token!' another called.

'And spend it in your mine shop?' Pearse answered. 'I'm less of a fool than I might look.'

'Twenty pennies and a quart jar of Plymouth gin,' a man called, close to.

Joanna saw him, a sailor, red-faced and bald with half his teeth gone, the others black. He was drunk, a gin bottle clasped in one rough hand. Her instinctive smile faded as quickly as it had come.

'Could be,' Pearse answered the man.

'Three from my old sow's litter,' another called, a big, fleshy man, as red-faced as the sailor but with a mop of tow-coloured hair.

'What, sell one for three more of the same?' Pearse called back. 'Still, it's the best offer I've yet to hear, Jan Bawden. Who can better him?'

The sailor was pulling a lanyard from around his neck.

'Twenty pennies, the gin and this knife,' he said, holding a heavy folding knife up to Pearse.

'Now he's a fine piece,' Pearse said, reaching out to touch the handle of polished horn. 'You don't see many better than him.'

The sailor nodded, and as he reached up to open the knife Joanna realised that he had only three fingers on his left hand, and those twisted and scarred. She looked around in desperation, catching the eye of Jan Bawden. He at least she knew, a small farmer from Sourton. She smiled at him, and quickly tugged her dress taut to make the best of her chest.

'Five piglets, William!' Bawden called out.

'Well, I don't know,' Pearse answered, glancing to Bawden, then back to the knife. Joanna looked at the farmer, smiling, her eyes wide, genuinely pleading.

'Seven,' he said.

'A middling good offer, Jan,' Pearse said. 'Can you better him, Jack?'

'Reckon I have,' the sailor answered.

'So it may be,' Pearse said. 'Maybe it's a matter of who'll treat her as she deserves.'

'I've eight acres, as you know, William Pearse,' Bawden called, 'and likely to have more. She'll not want, and I'm not at sea half my life.'

'That's not what I meant,' Pearse said, leering at Joanna. 'Let's see your twenty pennies, Jack.'

'For them you'll have to visit my lodgings,' the sailor answered.

'I shall offer a guinea piece, and I have it here.'

It was a new voice, and Joanna turned, finding the speaker almost hidden behind two others. He was short, his face fleshy and wrinkled, with a cheap wig showing beneath his hat and a blue coat open across his ample belly. In one hand he held the golden coin.

'A guinea?' Pearse echoed, turning from the sailor.

'One whole guinea, recent mint,' the man answered, pushing closer. His face, Joanna realised as it broke into a broad grin, reminded her of nothing so much as a toad, loose-fleshed, wide-mouthed, with a lump for a nose and eyes set wide.

'A guinea it is, Master,' Pearse said quickly, reaching out and taking the coin. 'She's yours, Master. Now remember, seeing as you're a gentleman and may not know the way of it. Keep a hold of her halter, all the way to your door. Elsewise the sale isn't proper.'

'I know the form, thanking you, young man.'

'Then here she is.'

Pearse passed the end of Joanna's halter to the man, who took it firmly in one fat hand. She stepped down, and as she left Pearse's side the reality began to sink in. She had been sold at market, like any pig or calf, auctioned on a block to the highest bidder. It was too much to take in, and she stumbled after her new husband, or owner, in a daze.

'Sold to a gentleman, which is better than you deserve!' she heard William's voice behind her. 'Sorry, all, but I've no more to sell.'

Joanna heard him laugh at his own wit and he was gone as he jumped down from the trough. She had turned, but as the halter tugged at her neck she walked on.

'Joanna, you say your name is?' the man said. 'Well, now, I'm Thomas Carew, and you'll be Joanna Carew, just as soon as I get you indoors.'

She didn't answer, following blindly as he led her from the market. The people seemed to have lost interest, and only a few curious stares were turned her way. Beyond the square the crowd thinned quickly, and the little man increased his pace, walking with little, precise steps, no more than a few yards along the main street before turning off and stopping almost immediately. Joanna watched him as he fumbled a key into the lock of a high black door. It was a shop, the window shuttered and dusty within.

'You don't read, I wouldn't imagine?' Carew said as the door came open. 'A pity, no doubt, but you'll be useful just the same.'

He chuckled, leading her inside, to a square room with sloping cases against two walls, each showing books, bound in smart new leather. Carew released the halter and turned to lock the door, still chuckling to himself, as if at some joke that had stuck in his mind. She looked round, bemused, feeling unreal yet acutely aware of the smells of leather, glue and dust.

Carew opened a door, gesturing to a narrow flight of stairs. Joanna went up, catching a glimpse of a long workroom through another door. At the landing she paused, and Carew nodded, indicating the single door. She opened it, finding herself in a bedroom, the furnishings worn and dusty, but finer by far than those she had had in the cottage. He pushed in behind her, rubbing his hands as he crossed to the window. Turning, he grinned at Joanna, more toad-like than ever, then twitched shut the curtains, leaving the room in dim, tallow-coloured light.

'Come then, my dear, no call for shyness, not in front of your husband,' Carew chuckled.

Joanna looked at him, vaguely aware that she was expected to undress. Mechanically, hardly knowing what she was doing, she began to undo her bodice. Carew watched, his eyes fixed on her chest as the laces came loose and Joanna pulled her arms free from the sleeves. As she pushed the front down her breasts swung free, heavy and bare, and his tongue flicked out to moisten his lips. She loosened the drawstring at her waist, letting the dress fall to the floor, and she was naked. Again Carew's tongue darted out.

'You can keep the stockings,' he said. 'Now, you can't read, but see this.'

He waddled quickly to one wall, taking down a picture from above a chest of drawers. Joanna took it, to find it showed a woman, plump and pale, on a bed, her skirts up, her legs high, exposing a plump belly and the open pink groove of her quim.

'Like that,' Carew said, 'for a start, then move about, and jiggle a bit. Make sure I've plenty to see.'

Joanna nodded numbly and climbed on to the bed, spreading herself into the rude position he had demanded. Carew gave his dry, dirty chuckle and began to undress, his eyes fixed to her nude body as he shrugged off his coat.

'Move it about, move it about,' he said.

Unsure what he wanted, she pulled up her legs to her chest, squashing her breasts together between her knees. Carew took off his hat, his wig with it, revealing a bald dome and a thin fringe of grey hair.

'A little buttock, if you please,' he said.

Joanna rolled, showing her bottom sideways. Her senses were coming back, shame and indignity, made worse as Carew gave a little choking sound at the sight of her naked rump.

'Been whacked?' he asked. 'By that husband of yours, I dare say?'

She nodded, disinclined to explain.

'That'll be my task, for now,' he said. 'Not that you need worry, not unless you're bad. Come on, keep on the move, and jiggle.'

Joanna moved to her knees, a position every man she had known liked her in, and one which meant she didn't have to watch Carew. With her bottom stuck high, she wiggled it, feeling a stab of shame even as she followed his lewd instructions. He chuckled and she did it again, her eyes shutting tight even as she set her knees apart to give him a yet more intimate view.

She stayed put, occasionally shaking her hips to make her bottom wobble for him. He said nothing, but she could hear him as he undressed, and imagined his toad-like body, until she was forced to look again. Going up on to her elbows, she looked back between her hanging breasts and parted thighs, framing him. He was naked, or near naked, his breeches lowered but his boots still on. From knees up nothing was covered: spindly legs, a low-slung paunch, narrow chest and thin arms, his flesh pale and loose, hairless except for his groin, where a skinny white cock stuck out among a thick growth of rusty grey pubic hair.

He was hard, the meaty white foreskin rolled back from his glans, shiny red and tipped with fluid. Joanna watched, expecting him to climb up behind her and plunge the ugly thing into her body. Instead he began to look around the room, telling her to hold still. She watched, wondering if he was going to belt her, as William had their first night together, to teach her her place. With her buttocks already a mass of bruises, the thought was unendurable, and for the first time since being sold she found herself wanting to protest.

Carew grunted suddenly and ducked down, drawing a wooden box from beneath the chest of drawers. Joanna felt her stomach tighten as he took up a long wooden brush, only for him to set it aside and pull out a jar of bootblack. He chuckled, rising as he pulled off the top.

'What are you about, sir?' Joanna asked, at last finding her voice.

'I've no wish to hurt you, my dear,' Carew answered. 'I aim to ease your passage.'

'I'm easy enough, I'm sure,' she said, glancing at his skinny cock. 'There's not need for that.'

'Where I'm going there is,' he replied, poking a finger into the jar and pulling it out, filthy with thick black polish. 'I've no need for brats, not at my age.'

'How do . . .' Joanna began, and then realised as the dirty finger was pushed in between her buttocks and she felt the polish squash against her bottom-hole. 'You dirty . . .'

Her mouth came open in shock as his finger found the little hole, poking into the virgin ring and up, delving inside to smear the paste up her bottom while a thumb smeared it around her anus. It felt strange, loose and rude, and she remembered her disgust at a friend's revelation of taking her husband in her bottom to avoid adding to their eight children. What had made it truly shocking was the woman's giggling reaction to what she had done, mixing embarrassment with obvious pleasure. Now, with a finger deep in her bottom-hole, Joanna could no more understand it. It was dirty, disgusting, the rudest thing imaginable, to have a man's cock where her dirt came out.

Her face was screwed up, and as the bed creaked under Carew's weight she felt her stomach knot. It was going up her bottom, the thin pink cock that had become so obscenely erect in reaction to her naked body. The finger pulled from her anus with a sticky sound and she farted, bringing a new flush of shame. Carew chuckled and wiped his dirty finger and thumb on her bottom.

Joanna gritted her teeth as his thumbs took her buttocks and opened them, spreading the target. She expected pain, and could feel her anus tightening. Something touched her, in her crease, the firm meat of Carew's penis, sliding in the mess of boot polish,

80

then prodding, above her hole, then on it. She gave a single choking sob as he pressed the head to her ring. Her muscle gave, greasy and loose, pressing in, pushing up her bowels until with a sudden stab of pain the cock was going in.

She gasped out loud as her anus gave and the full length of his cock slid suddenly up her bottom. Agonising shame filled her head as she realised that her anal virginity was gone: she was being buggered, kneeling and naked, in the light, so that the man could see every rude detail of her bottom. It was up, well up, filling her, making her sob with shame and reaction, and clutch the bedcover from the awful loose feeling in her bowels.

Carew's fat paunch pressed to her buttocks as he pushed himself in. His hand moved higher, gripping her by the hips. He began to move it in her gut, puffing and grunting as he buggered her. Her eyes were wide, her mouth too, drooling on to the bolster beneath her head. His rhythm had begun to make her breasts swing, brushing the nipples against the cover of the bed and bringing them to erection. The pain had gone and, with the most excruciating stab of shame and misery, she realised that she was enjoying it.

Joanna tried to hold back but found herself panting, then moaning. She wanted to put her hand back, to rub at her quim and make herself come while he was up her. It was hard to resist, then impossible. She had done it, burying her face in the bolster as her fingers found the plump, wet swell of her sex and started to fiddle with the soft folds of flesh at the centre. She was sobbing, close to tears, but masturbating, unable to stop herself. Shutting her eyes, she forced the image of the squat, toad-like man who was up her bottom from her mind and thought of Henry.

His big cock would be inside her, from the rear, only not up the soft, wet purse of her quim. Instead he would be in her dirty bottom-hole, greased and juicy, straining with hard, hot penis, slimy and filthy as she was used, deep and hard where her dirt came out . . .

She came, biting the bolster to stop herself screaming, bucking her hips on his cock, thrashing and writhing beneath him, lost to everything except the ecstatic feel of reaching a climax with a cock up her bottom. That it was Carew didn't matter, as long as it was a man, in her body, pushed deep up so that she could feel her sloppy, dirty little ring tighten over and over on his penis.

Only as she came down from the height of her orgasm did she realise that Carew was grunting and panting. He was jamming his cock in, deeper and deeper, and mumbling obscenities, about her breasts, her bottom, her quim, her anus, and how it looked stretched tight on his cock. As he got faster and her pleasure ebbed it began to hurt, a numbing, bruising pain, then sharp, only for him to stop with a last pig-like grunt and she realised that he had come up her bottom.

Suki lay still on the bed, feeling scared and alone, more so than at any time since the first awful night on board Sir Joseph Snapes's ship. She was naked, as she had been when taken, and since. This in itself meant very little to her, but the iron collar and the chain which linked it to a heavy ring set in the solid stone wall meant a great deal. Not even Snapes had chained her, contenting himself with having her hands and feet tied after her first frenzied attempt at escape and once or twice in England.

As if the collar and chain was not enough, the windows of the room were shuttered and barred.

What light there was came from holes in the shutters, too high for her to reach. The door was locked too, and from occasional noises she knew that a man was stationed outside, probably one of the two who had taken her. It was a prison, obviously, and it was equally obvious that it had been prepared in advance.

The motives behind her capture were as puzzling to her as most of the things which had happened since being brought out of Africa. There seemed no sense to it, nor any reason why it should be her rather than another girl, unless it was for her dark skin. As they seemed strange to her, so she knew that she must seem strange to them. Judith had been fascinated by her colour, while Henry liked to see her side by side with Eloise. Snapes had shown less interest, having been to Africa, but since her arrival she had seen only three black people, Snapes's man John and two others, both in London.

Her captors had said nothing, and nor had they forced themselves on to her, which she had expected, especially after being thrown on the bed and held down while the collar was fixed to her neck. Nothing had happened, and she had supposed it was because they were servants and that their master would come for her in the night. He hadn't, nor the night after: only the two silent men, one bearing food while the other stood by with a cudgel.

The food was a surprise, not the scraps Snapes had fed her, nor the pickings of the kitchens she had been used to at the Truscotts'. Instead, no more than an hour after she had been chained up, the men had brought a thick stew of mutton and dumplings with a pudding of steamed suet and treacle. She had made the best of it, eating as much as she wanted, only to be threatened with the cudgel until she had swallowed every last mouthful. The process had been repeated in the morning, with thick slices of white bread spread with jam and cream. Each meal since then had been equally sumptuous, filling her until she felt bloated and sleepy, while the behaviour of her captors seemed more puzzling than ever.

Caroline Cunningham reined her pony in. She was high on the north flank of Kit Hill, looking out across the Tamar valley. Mrs Aldgrave was well down the slope, her mount making heavy going of the furse. Looking down, Caroline frowned, wanting to just ride on, losing her chaperone, but held back by thoughts of the lecture she would face from her brother.

Raising her head, she looked out across the countryside, wishing she could just ride and ride, and knowing perfectly well in which direction she would head. Well out across the valley she could see the ridge of Burley Down, tiny beneath Dartmoor and hazy with heat and distance. Beyond, she knew, was Henry Truscott's estate. There, she could have relied on being teased and cajoled into sex, ending up indulging in the most deliciously rude pleasures without ever once having to abandon her modesty or risk having her virginity taken unexpectedly. Henry understood.

Yet Eloise Truscott was sure to be there, making the prospect less appealing. An alternative was yet further, on land hidden in the purple haze of distance, the older Truscott estate, home to Henry's brother Stephen. He was an admirer, but dry and dull, also unlikely to try for more than a chaste kiss. Rather better, and the nearest, was Lewis Stukely, whose land bordered the ducal estates across the river. His house was even visible, a tiny square of grey among woods where the valley of the Lyd came down from

Dartmoor. He lacked Henry's boldness, but he had more than once taken a squeeze of her bottom through her dress, and there was at least a slight thrill of danger in flirting with him.

'Really, my dear, might we not have remained on the ride?' Mrs Aldgrave remarked as she approached.

'I wanted to admire the view,' Caroline answered. 'Is it not beautiful?'

'Quite so,' Mrs Aldgrave answered, 'but it is hardly suitable to ride in such a manner. You are not a little girl any more, Caroline.'

'Indeed not,' Caroline answered with feeling.

'What, after all, would Mr Stephen Truscott think of such behaviour?'

'I don't care. He's a bore and he's twice my age besides.'

'He has twenty thousand pounds a year, my dear, and is likely to be a member of parliament in due time. He is really quite suitable.'

'I like Stukely better.'

'You are young, Caroline, my dear. Pray take mature advice and chose with your head and not your heart. Mr Stukely is something of a spendthrift, and his family are not of entirely good repute. You would not wish the like of Spanish Stukely[7] for a son.'

'Oh, you do talk nonsense!'

Suddenly determined to be as far from Mrs Aldgrave as possible, Caroline dug her heels in the flank of her pony. In moments she was racing around the side of the hill, and down, laughing at her chaperone's angry remonstrances. As she went she thought of Lewis Stukely, and how obviously he had been excited after they had caught the black girl touching herself by Meldon Pool. Not that it had left her unaffected. It had been such a rude sight: so wild, so unrestrained, beautiful too, with the girl's pretty face set in ecstasy and her smooth dark body taut in a moment of absolute rapture.

She wondered what Stukely would have done if he'd been alone. The girl had little or no English, and obviously no morals. He would probably have had her, then and there, pushing his hard penis up her inviting, wet hole as she lay spread-eagled on the grass. She had thought about what she had seen all the way back to the Truscotts', and afterwards, Mrs Aldgrave's frosty silence making it all the easier to let her thoughts run.

Ever since then she had envied the maid, just for daring to be so rude. To masturbate was one thing, alone in the dark of her room, or even with a candle lit, in front of her tall mirror so that she could watch her body react to her own caresses. Out in the open was another thing all together, wild and dirty, and so tempting to any man who chanced on her. After all, what man could resist pushing his penis up a girl already naked and wet, ready to let him in?

As she slowed her pony to a walk she found herself shivering inside. She knew what she wanted to do, and the idea was alarming, frightening almost, but also so, so tempting. All it needed was somewhere secure, on their own land, where she knew who would be doing what and where she would be safe. Then it would be off with her clothes, until she was naked, not just bare below, but nude, stark naked, out in the warm sunlight. Then she would masturbate, on her back, like the black girl had done, legs wide to the sky without a care in the world.

With a sudden, guilty determination, she decided that she was going to do it. Reining her pony in, she turned to Mrs Aldgrave, signalling that she was heading back for the estate and starting off before the woman was able to remonstrate.

* * *

86

Henry moved carefully in his seat, trying to find a position which best spared his bruises. Eloise was by a window, staring out over the valley. Her mood was angry and petulant, a condition he normally cured by the application of a hand or strap to her bare bottom. Now he shared her feelings, and had neither the ability nor the inclination to deal with her.

All day they had argued over Suki, blaming each other for how easily she had been taken, disagreeing over who had taken her and why it had been done. They agreed only that what had been done was intolerable, and that they would do their utmost to get her back, if mainly to restore hurt pride, then partly for the girl's sake.

'Where the devil's Todd?' Henry demanded, not for the first time.

'He will be here presently, no doubt,' Eloise answered. 'Indeed, he is approaching at this moment.'

Henry sat up, trying to look somewhat less of an invalid as Todd Gurney appeared on the terrace, doffing his hat to Eloise.

'What news?' Henry demanded. 'Did the Pearses see anything?'

'Little enough,' Todd answered, 'though I've had what I can from William. Joanna made to interfere, seems so, and William after. Fellow drew pistols on them and he backed off.'

'Did they have a coach, horses?'

'A gig, sir, drawn by two greys. They bundled Suki in and away; William didn't see which way on account of being preoccupied by his wife.'

'A gig drawn by two greys? Well, that shouldn't be too hard to track down. No more detail? What'd Joanna say?'

'No detail, sir. As to Joanna, I didn't speak with her, on account of William taking her to Okehampton market this morning and selling her.'

'Selling her?'

'That's right, sir, selling her. To a gentleman, so he says, who gave him a guinea.'

'For a guinea!'

'Seems a lot, certain sure. Tilly Chillcott, to Launceston way, was had for two shillings and sixpence. William Pearse was boasting, so I expect.'

'Barbaric!' Eloise exclaimed.

'Common enough, ma'am,' Gurney answered her.

'I don't doubt it,' Eloise sniffed. 'The English!'

Standing absolutely still, Caroline Cunningham listened to the noises of the wood. A jay had called in alarm as she had entered the clearing, vanishing among the trees with a snap of its wings and a flash of vivid blue. Now there was near silence, only faint noises from the distant mines and the steady chop of an axe, equally distant. There was a lump in her throat and she swallowed, glancing around.

The clearing was perfect, or at least it looked perfect. A great beech had fallen in the spring, leaving an open area, down grown up with grass, soft and dry; warm too in the sunlight. Dense undergrowth shielded her on two sides, the slope of the hill on the third, leaving only one direction from which she could possibly be seen, and that protected by a stream and a hundred yards of woodland.

It still felt risky, deliciously risky, and her fingers were trembling as she fumbled with her clothes. Her shoes went first, then her stockings, with her trembling growing as each garment was removed. Her dress was difficult, with no maid to help her, but she managed the catches, her excitement doubling as it came loose and redoubling as she let her bodice fall open and her breasts came bare. Again she swallowed, willing herself not to stop as she opened the drawstrings on her dress and petticoats, pushing it all down as one, over her hips and bottom, to go bare. It was all around her legs, and then she was bare as she stepped out of the puddle of cloth.

Just being nude felt so wonderful, and she forced herself not to hurry, enjoying her own fear. With shaking hands she forced herself to fold her clothes, placing each article neatly on top of the beech trunk with deliberate care. To do so meant walking around the mass of roots, which was important, because it meant that on the little piece of grass she couldn't even see her clothes, but was stark naked in the open air, completely, deliciously vulnerable. It also meant coming in view of her pony, who watched her from big, moist eyes, indifferent to whether she was dressed or not. His gaze made her embarrassed, and she stepped quickly back into the shade of the roots.

She stretched her arms up, feeling the cool air on her body. Her nipples were already hard, her quim wet, and she knew it wouldn't take long, just as soon as she was ready. Squatting down, cross-legged, she put a hand between her thighs, stroking her sex as she let her mind wander. Her first thoughts were of the black maid. The brief glimpse of her masturbating had been such a wonderful shock, and she had been beautiful, her skin a rich, glossy brown, and perfectly smooth. She had been so feminine too, her body all soft curves, of hip and belly and breasts, all of which Caroline would have loved to explore, yet it was hard to imagine the circumstances of their lovemaking.

Abandoning Suki, she let her imagination shift to her sister, Alice, with whom she had shared guilty caresses often enough. Alice was easier to think about, as she only had to remember the feel of her hands and mouth, her silky hair, the gentle touches on her breasts, the sharp little tongue tracing a line down her belly, the soft lips kissing her own, or on her quim, even her bottom, down between the cheeks, puckered to kiss her anus on a dare.

Caroline's fingers were wet, running juice from her quim. She was open, ready, her breath coming fast, her mind filled with the joy of being nude in the open, nude and masturbating over the guilty secret she shared with her sister. Lying back, she spread herself on the grass, in the position she had imagined, legs up and open, quim spread bare to the sky. For a moment she played with her breasts, wishing someone else was there to do it for her.

Thinking of Alice was nice, but Alice wasn't there, and she wanted the experience to be as real as possible. What she wanted was to come over the simple joy of being nude outdoors, and it was that she concentrated on as she continued to stroke herself, teasing her quim to make her muscles jump and shiver in rising pleasure. It was going to be good, she knew it, a truly beautiful climax, taken for its own sake, and without wishing anybody else was there or for an experience she hadn't had.

One finger stole down to the tight hole of her quim, with the taut half-circle of her hymen, ready to be broken when a man finally had her. As she touched she immediately wished she hadn't, her mind filling with uncertainty and the fear of pain. Any man who caught her would be bound to put his cock in her, she was sure, tearing her precious maidenhead. Except Henry Truscott. He had had her, tricked and flattered her into sucking his cock and, worse, surrendering her anal ring to him, taking his cock up her bottom and letting him come in her bowels, all to save her precious virginity.

She was shaking, her thighs opening and closing on her hand at the thought of how she had been

90

sodomised by him, so rudely, so openly, and with Alice and her sister-in-law May looking on, watching her, holding her as she took a cock in her bottom-hole . . .

It was good, too good to stop. Her mouth was open, her eyes closed, her hands between her legs, one to spread her sex, one to rub. She was coming, thinking of the feel of her anus spreading around the firm, thick head of Henry's penis, of her tiny vagina, an inch away, wet, vulnerable, ready to be filled . . .

Caroline screamed out to the empty wood, and as she came her mind filled with regret, not for what she'd done, but that Henry hadn't taken his chance, forcing her, filling her suddenly with cock, tearing her silly, stupid hymen and plunging himself right to the hilt in her body, fucking her and at last coming deep, deep inside her.

Four

'It is not right!' the Reverend Gould thundered. 'It is against scripture and the law! Our duty is to return this poor girl to her rightful place!'

'Your duty, perhaps,' Henry answered. 'Not mine. You forget, this is a yeoman parish, and I've no more duty than giving the odd crust for the poor.'

'Nevertheless, you are an educated man and a Christian,' Gould went on. 'You cannot, surely, stand idly by while this dreadful deed takes place?'

'No?' Henry retorted. 'Well, as I see it, Joanna's well rid of William Pearse, and if this fellow can afford a guinea to buy her, I dare say he'll keep her in better style than she's used to. Better style than William Pearse did, anyhow, and a few less black eyes to boot.'

'They are bound by God, Mr Truscott. Have you no sense of Christian duty?'

'As much as most, I dare say, but in this matter all seems for the best. Besides, how do you figure to set it to rights?'

'By speaking with Pearse, naturally, and whoever the man who bought poor Joanna is. Then she will come back, the money will be returned and it only remains to prosecute a case against this loathsome man.'

'Who is?'

'Pearse does not know him, yet . . .'

'A gentleman, he says, who paid a guinea. Pearse has lived in these parts all his life, and must know everyone of any rank, locally. They're in Exeter now, or towards Bristol, London even.'

'Nevertheless, they must be found!'

'It's not worth the candle for my money, Mr Gould; and, in any case, Joanna may not want to come back. If you find her and she does, then, yes, I'll speak to the fellow, but I'll not lay out on a prosecution. That's my final word.'

'Then I will bid you good day, Mr Truscott, although I leave in the hope that you may yet come to take a more Christian and responsible attitude.'

Gould made a stiff bow, which Henry returned. As the priest left Henry turned to look out over the valley, remembering how content he had felt so short a time before. Now he was not only deprived of Suki, but Joanna too, while Eloise remained short-tempered. His bruises still hurt, too much to face the effort of getting Eloise in trim across his knee, but after three days of abstinence his need was becoming strong.

In the dim warmth of her room, Suki lay prone on her bed. She had been woken not long after dawn, when a breakfast of oats in cream, kippers, sausages and thick slices of fried bread had left her bloated. As always, the men had served her, then watched as she ate, the larger of the two toying with his cudgel. Her initial expectations of beatings and rape had faded, as neither man had so much as touched her, nor even shown interest in her body. Their master had not arrived either, and her confidence had grown, at least in her immediate safety. All they seemed to want of her was that she should eat. If their conduct was strange, it was no stranger than that of Snapes, who had wanted to mate her with a chimpanzee, nor of the Truscotts, who both clearly desired her but seemed to need to punish her before they could express their lust.

With increased confidence had come boredom, and her desire to escape had become methodical. Her chain, she already knew, was strong. A link had been hammered shut to close the collar about her neck, and she had no way of opening it. Nor could she make the wall fixture move more than a fraction. The room was bare, panelled in oak with only the bed and a commode as furnishings. With a man always in the corridor it was pointless to try the lock, but she had investigated both windows, finding the shutters bolted into place. The walls were also solid, with none of the odd compartments and shafts she had found in Snapes's mansion. Her only, tiny success had been to move the commode so that she could reach the holes through which daylight came in. The result had been a view of rolling wooded hills, with the low grey bulk of a moor in the distance, a scene not greatly different from that outside her room at the Truscotts'. It told her only that she had travelled no great distance, which she knew anyway. Now she lay still, thinking of the strangeness of the English and the mild discomfort in her stomach.

At the sound of footsteps outside the door she sat up, pulling the bedcovers over her body from a sense of protection rather than modesty. The door swung back and the two men came in, as grim-faced as ever. The smaller was holding a jar of glazed white china marked with black letters, a pencil and a roll of cloth tape. The other stepped close and jerked down her covers, leaving her curled naked on the bed. Her hands went to her breasts, the knot of fear tightening in her stomach.

'Get them wide,' the smaller man said, the larger making motions that she should spread her legs.

Suki nodded miserably, realising that she had been wrong. They were going to rape her, and the time was now. The larger man had his cudgel, as always, and was tapping it on his open palm, the same menacing gesture he used when she was struggling to eat her food. Knowing that resistance would only mean bruises and that she'd just be held down anyway, she let her thighs come apart. The larger man grinned, glancing at her quim; the smaller merely nodded, but stepped forwards. Suki turned her head to the side and shut her eyes, her legs spread wide. Waiting for his cock to be put in her, she felt strangely numb, but her muscles jumped as a hand touched her inner thigh, then another. Something was pressed to her flesh, sideways across her thigh, then withdrawn. Again it touched, close to her knee, and again, hard knuckles brushing the flesh of her quim.

'She needs four inches, I reckon,' one of the men said.

'Thereabouts,' the other answered.

Again Suki tensed, expecting a cock to be pushed into her. Nothing happened.

'What's she say, Davy?' one asked.

'Doctor Pilgham's Ablution Preparation,' the other answered, 'some old trade. Here, take hold of this you, open your eyes.'

Suki opened her eyes, unsure of their words but not detecting any aggression or even lust. The smaller man was holding out the white jar to her.

'Use this,' he said, pushing the jar towards her.

Suki took the jar and opened it, finding a thick, sweet-smelling cream inside. Hesitantly she dabbed a finger into it, sniffed it and dabbed it onto her tongue. It tasted vile and she made a face at her captors. Both laughed.

'No! Fool girl,' the one called Davy said. 'Rub it in yourself.'

Feeling suddenly stupid, she realised that it was a skin cream, much like those Eloise used. More than once Henry had used them to open her bottom-hole, and she realised that she was to be sodomised. The knot in her stomach became harder.

As she knew, compliance would make it quicker, and mean fewer bruises, while there would be fewer still if she showed enthusiasm. She would be sodomised anyway. Climbing from the bed, she stood naked in front of the men, trying to control the trembling in her hands. They watched, impassive as she dipped her fingers into the jar and reached back behind herself. With her eyes closed, she told herself she would try and imagine that it was Henry and Eloise toying with her, not the two men. Her fingers went down between her buttocks, finding her anus and slipping inside easily, with the cream smearing up between her cheeks and into the little hole.

'Not up there, you dirty bitch booby!' Davy said.

He began to make signs, running the flat of his hand over his legs and belly. Puzzled, Suki pulled her finger out of her bottom. She began to imitate him, smearing the cream on as he indicated. The man nodded, sitting down on the edge of the bed. She rubbed the cream in as they watched, over her thighs, belly and breasts, until the front of her body was glossy and slick. She had been wondering if she was putting on a show, but neither showed interest, and only when she began to do her arms did the smaller man shake his head.

'Turn about,' he ordered, swivelling one finger to show what she should do.

He rose, pulling up his sleeve. Suki found herself swallowing as she turned. It was going to happen, now, a cock pushed up her oily bottom-hole as she bent. She put the cream jar down, closing her eyes and resting her hands on the window ledge, expecting the touch of rough hands on her bottom as she pushed it out in miserable resignation.

'You're the biter and no mistake,' the man said from behind her. 'Look, Nathan, how she wants one up her.'

The other laughed and Suki hung her head, gritting her teeth. The man stooped to pick up the cream jar and a moment later she felt the cold, greasy touch of it, between her shoulder blades. He began to rub it in, over her back, going gradually lower, towards her bottom. Suki stayed still, wishing he would get it over with and bugger her quickly instead of drawing it out. Yet she realised that oiling her was arousing him, as punishing her aroused Henry and Eloise, and that his cock would be slowly hardening in his breeches as he touched her. When she was done it would come out, and up it would go, into her quim or her anus, maybe both, maybe her mouth as well, or between her oily breasts.

As his hands found her buttocks she knew it would not be long. He was stroking them, rubbing the cream in with slow, circular motions that made them spread, showing her anus. She was shivering, but held still, trying hard not to show her feelings, not to give them the pleasure of having her struggle or beg.

His hand left her bottom. The cream jar was placed beside her on the window ledge. He touched her arm, wiping his greasy hand off on her skin. She braced herself for sodomy, screwing her eyes up tight and relaxing her anus so that it wouldn't hurt, stifling a sob.

'Dirty bitch!' he said. 'Like a she-cat on heat, ain't she, Nathan?'

'No more shame than one, Davy,' Nathan agreed. 'Come now, there's beef and pickles to the kitchen. I'll bring up a plate if you've a mind, and ale.'

Davy answered with a grunt and stepped away, talking to Nathan as he left the room. For a moment Suki stayed still, thinking it was a cruel trick. Neither man came back. Slowly her muscles relaxed and the fear and misery drained from her mind. When at last she turned from the window she found herself shaking, astonished that she had been spared.

Joanna shut her eyes, trying to relax, trying to forget the squat form of Thomas Carew watching her as she sat on her chamber pot. He had given her a nightgown, a long, embroidered one which covered her from neck to ankles. She had been grateful at first, only to discover that it had not been done for the sake of her modesty but for the pleasure he took in lifting it.

It was now bunched around her neck, held up over her breasts, as he had instructed, leaving her naked below, with her thighs wide to allow him an unobstructed view of her bare belly and quim. She knew what she was supposed to do and her bladder felt tight; yet it was hard with him watching, almost impossible. Trying to think of anything except his little staring eyes, she struggled to relax. It was hard, with him sitting watching her, his own nightshirt pulled up and resting on his paunch, his hard little cock in one hand as he masturbated slowly over her exposed body. She set her teeth, straining, and was rewarded by the first warm moisture on her quim.

'It's coming,' she said and the slapping sound of the old man tugging at his cock increased in volume.

Her quim twitched, she felt her cheeks flush hot and suddenly it was happening, her pee gushing out into the pot beneath her and splashing against the china. Carew chuckled as Joanna gave a little sob. She let it out, unable to hold back her relief as her bladder emptied, her eyes still shut, only to open at the creak of wood. Carew had risen, his cock in his hand, his face red. He was coming towards her, beating frantically at his erection, his face red with effort, his eyes fixed on the golden stream gushing out from between her thighs. Joanna's mouth came open in protest, even as his cock erupted to fill it with semen, then more, spattering her breasts and belly, the last piece falling into her pubic hair as it came down her front.

'Must you?' she protested, screwing up her face at the salty flavour of the come in her mouth.

'I must indeed,' Carew answered, panting as he sat back heavily on the bed. 'It's not often I get to watch a big, handsome woman like you on her pot, and more normally it comes expensive. Now you're my wife I intend to make the best of matters.'

Joanna didn't answer, balling the sperm in her mouth and then spitting it into the chamber pot as her pee finished. Rising, she began to clean herself up as Carew recovered his breath.

'Now, don't think yourself hard done by,' he was saying, gently now. 'It doesn't cost you to show your fine body, and if you're a touch sore in the behind then that'll soon go. Meanwhile, I've a bit put aside, and I'll be meaning to buy you gowns, and petticoats, and all manner of fine things, rings too. Won't that make you glad?'

She didn't answer, not wanting to admit that it would, nor to seem ungrateful by protesting. After all, she reasoned, William had liked to come in her face, and there had always been more semen. Instead she began to dress.

'You'll be expected to keep house, naturally,' he went on after a while, 'and fetch what I need from the town and such. I've work enough in the shop, and perhaps I can teach you something of my trade, which is the binding of books . . .'

He stopped, breaking off at a sharp knocking sound from the shop below. Walking quickly to the window, he threw open the curtains and opened it. Joanna finished dressing as Carew held a brief conversation with whoever had arrived, then followed him down the stairs. A man pushed into the shop as Carew opened the door, richly dressed, and as he stepped in she recognised him as Lewis Stukely.

'Mr Stukely, sir,' Carew was saying, 'a pleasure, sir. Sorry to have kept you waiting. Now, what may I do for you? The Bible, I trust was to your satisfaction?'

'Quite the thing, thank you,' Stukely replied, glancing at Joanna.

'My wife, Joanna,' Carew said. 'Joanna, I would like you to meet one of my most valued customers, Mr Stukely of Lydford.'

'I've seen you before, I imagine,' Stukely answered. 'Don't you work as a maid for the Truscotts?'

'I did,' Joanna replied.

Stukely responded with a thoughtful nod of his head, glanced at the door, then back to Joanna. Leaning forward, he quickly whispered into Carew's ear, then stood back.

'Quite, I fully understand, sir,' Carew answered. 'Joanna, busy yourself upstairs; Mr Stukely has an important matter to discuss.'

Doing her best to curtsy, Joanna moved back up the stairs, but stopped in the doorway of the bedroom, intrigued by what could be secretive about book-binding.

100

'I wish another book bound,' Stukely was saying, his voice coming clearly to her. 'It is a somewhat delicate matter, and I need not say that I require your absolute discretion.'

'And you shall have it, sir, rest assured,' Carew answered. 'You may rely upon me absolutely. A moment, sir.'

Joanna heard the rasp of a bolt being pushed into place, then Carew's voice once more.

'So how may I assist, sir?'

'I wish this bound,' Stukely went on. 'It is, I believe, an imperial quarto.'

'Imperial quarto, yes indeed,' Carew answered. 'May I suggest calf leather? Perhaps Morocco? Would you care to inspect some skins?'

'No, thank you. I will supply my own leather, of particular quality. Irreplaceable, in fact.'

'A foreign hide?'

'Exactly. Similar to Morocco, in fact. Still, you may charge as if you had supplied the hide. I wish the binding to be immaculate.'

'Immaculate it shall be, sir, rest assured. It is already cut, I see. May I?'

'Doubtless you will anyway, soon enough.'

There was silence, then a soft exclamation of surprise.

'French?' Carew's voice came again.

'Revolutionary matter, caricature and satire against the established order. See, here a monk and a nun compare genitals; and on the subsequent leaf a woman is forced to an act with a prelate.'

'Remarkable, and lewd to say the least. The nature of your interest, naturally, is political in nature?'

'Never mind the nature of my interest, but no, I have little interest in their politics, save to trust that the same never happens here.'

'God forbid, but here, I see, are other matters. This is a Bouchet, is it not?'

'Indeed, I see you have some acquaintance with the erotic motif in art?'

'I confess it, sir. This is a handsome collection. I can see that you would wish it bound well, and with discretion.'

'Absolutely but, as you have an interest, note these engravings, which are Italian, done in Verona.'

'Truly skilled. The detail is remarkable, the anatomy exact.'

'The original drawings are said to have been by a physician. Perhaps less skilled, but more remarkable, are these, from a collection of woodcuts made on an expedition to Africa. See here, these native women, shamelessly bare, or in no more than a loose wrap, and here, more extraordinary still.'

'Gracious! What is this creature?'

'An enschego; I have seen one in London. They are a species of ape.'

'So I see, but why . . .? No matter. Extraordinary, as you say.'

'I had them at considerable expense.'

'So I would imagine.'

On the landing, Joanna's curiosity finally became too strong. Ducking down, she peered between the banisters, and as she saw the illustration on the page open between the two men her hand went to her mouth in horror.

'We'll talk as we ride to the mine,' Henry said.

'You've business at the mine, sir?' Todd Gurney answered. 'All's well enough.'

'That I do not doubt,' Henry replied. 'I'd more of a mind for a round of the buttock ball with Peggy Wray. She's there, I trust?'

'As always,' Gurney laughed, 'and willing enough, no doubt.'

'That's as well,' Henry went on. 'Eloise is out of sorts, and I dare say she will be for a while, at least until she finds a decent maid. We've a girl from the village, but by all accounts she's nothing but fingers and thumbs. So what have you found?'

'Little enough, sir. As you say, a gig drawn by paired greys is like enough to be noticed, but one's not passed a toll house.'

'Well, there are none locally like that. They must have gone around by the lanes.'

'Seems so, and I've a mind where. This is a bonnet I found, in a hedge to Knole Cross way.'

Gurney fished the object from his pocket, leaning across to pass it to Henry. It was a woman's bonnet, cheaply made, smeared with mud and still damp.

'She was wearing one when they took her,' Henry remarked. 'The same, I imagine.'

'Suki could've thrown it out to mark their way,' Todd stated, 'and if they were to have shaved a corner off the moor they'd have missed Okehampton toll. It's saunt enough land for a gallop.'

'Or for a gig, well driven,' Henry added. 'So they went Exeter way. Well, that's no great surprise. I've been thinking on Gould. He's fire in him enough, and no doubt he disapproves of me heartily. What's more, he never batted an eye while on his hobby horse over Joanna Pearse, nor asked after Suki. To my way of thinking that's because he knew full well she's not there.'

'Could be, sir, but he hadn't left the village, nor met with any from outside, so far as I can find. My mind's still more to Snapes. He owes us a grudge, and most men make that a better reason than any amount of morals.'

'True enough, Todd, I for one. Still, in his shoes I'd have given me my drubbing and settled for that. Where's the sense in pinching my wife's maid?'

'Could be he needs her for the enschego, sir. Two birds with one stone, as it were.'

'Could be, but you're forgetting this slaving business. Gould's the only one who said so much as a word on the matter. No, by my reckoning Gould somehow tipped the word to some fellows who've bees in their bonnets over the matter, and they came and took her, post haste.'

Closing the piano, Caroline Cunningham stood to look pensively out across the lawns. The house was quiet. Her brother had retired to the library with a glass of brandy; May and Mrs Aldgrave were in the rose garden; the various servants were going about their tasks. Pleasantly drunk, her mind had turned to what she had done the day before and the prospect of doing it again. Afterwards it had seemed impossibly rude and dangerous. She had ridden back to the house as quickly as possible, flushed with guilt.

Yet that night she had masturbated over what she had done, and thought of being caught. She had imagined it being the keepers, and having to suck their cocks for their silence. As she neared orgasm it had changed to a mine crew, a dozen rough, dirty men, taking her one by one, in her mouth, up her bottom, and at last in her quim, breaking her virginity without caring, without even knowing.

Nobody was visible on the lawns, and she knew the woods beyond would be equally deserted, tempting her to repeat her indulgence. All she needed to do was establish the whereabouts of the two keepers and she would be safe, safe to strip, to go naked in the sunlight, to bring herself to a peak of ecstasy as wonderful as before.

Stepping out from the French window, she felt the familiar thrill, her body responding to her knowledge of how naughty she intended to be. It was nice, and as she walked down on to the lawn the thrill grew stronger with each step. Listening carefully, she caught the throb of the mine engine, then the thud of an axe, as she had the day before. Immediately her mouth pursed in annoyance, realising that the sound came from roughly the direction of her special place.

Still, she reflected, there was no shortage of woodland, and so long as she kept clear of the mine and the keepers there was little chance of disturbance. Best, perhaps, were the woods to either side of the drive, thickly planted to screen the house from the road, but purely ornamental and with no path. Smiling to herself, she set out across the lawns, the delicious knot of anticipation in her stomach tightening as she gave a guilty glance towards the rose garden. Nobody was paying attention, and as she reached the first trees of the avenue her fingers were already twitching nervously at her dress.

The drive stretched arrow-straight before her as she walked, a double row of young elms to either side with the stone arch of the gates in the distance. Twice she glanced back, praying that nobody had seen her, before stepping on to the grass once more and going towards the wood, walking with as much nonchalance as she could manage. Only when she was within a few yards of the sheltering foliage did she see someone, and not towards the house but through the gate, approaching up the long lane that led towards them before turning to the mine.

She paused, watching the two riders approach, with her expression of concern changing to a grin of pure mischief as she realised that one was Henry Truscott. Walking as quickly as seemed decent, she made her way towards the gate. Several times she looked back, praying that her brother would not choose that moment to come to the library window, and when she reached the gate she stepped into the shade of the arch.

'Ah, Caroline, taking the air?' Henry greeted her as he approached. 'How pleasant to chance on you.'

'Indeed, sir,' she answered, curtsying and returning a nod as Todd Gurney touched his hat to her.

'Mrs Aldgrave is with you, I assume?' Henry went on, glancing down the avenue.

'Not at all,' Caroline answered. 'I am quite alone. As you say, I was taking the air and thought to walk a little way down the lane.'

'Then perhaps I might accompany you?' Henry said. 'Todd, ride ahead, I'll join you presently.'

Henry dismounted, throwing his reins to Todd Gurney, who caught them and nodded, grinning as he put his horse into a walk. Caroline felt the blood rise to her face, wondering how much the mine captain knew.

'Saunder is at home?' Henry asked.

'My brother is in the library,' Caroline replied. 'It is, perhaps, a little warm for the lane. The woods are pleasantly shaded.'

'Ideal,' Henry answered, offering his arm, which Caroline took.

Inside the gate, they crossed the avenue as quickly as possible, and as soon as they were in the shelter of the trees Henry grabbed Caroline, pulling her to him. She squeaked in surprise as one breast was popped free of her bodice, then giggled as she tried to pull back.

'Not here!' she urged. 'Further in, where we can't be seen.'

Henry caught her by the arm and she stumbled after him, giggling until he stopped and pulled her in, kissing her and pushing her down at the same time.

His hands were already fumbling for her dress. It came up, her petticoats with it, and his hand closed on her bottom, kneading one fleshy cheek. Her arms were around his back, and she let herself be pressed down, her eyes closed as they kissed. Her other breast was pulled free and Henry moved lower, suckling her as he fondled her bottom, until her mouth came open in bliss.

'I'd fuck you here and now if you weren't a virgin,' he growled as he pulled away.

'I wish you would,' she answered, watching as he began to fumble with his breeches and then leaning forward to help. Henry's cock sprang free, and he sighed as she took it in her hand and began to tug at it.

'Don't tempt me,' he said hoarsely. 'So where would you like it? Your mouth, or in that fine arse.'

'Henry!' she squeaked. 'Naturally it must go where you please.'

'Your arse, then, if I can hold myself.'

Caroline let go of his cock, scrambling eagerly into a kneeling position.

'Make me ready,' she said, 'and be gentle.'

Henry merely grunted, coming behind her to lift her skirts. Caroline shut her eyes in bliss as they came up, just as she had imagined it, with the cool air on her bare bottom and thighs, and a cock ready for her body behind her. Resting on one arm, she began to stroke her breasts as she felt Henry's lips touch her bottom. He began to kiss, first on the crests of her cheeks, then lower, where they tucked under, and towards the middle.

Caroline sighed, her mouth wide in ecstasy as his tongue came out, flicking against the sensitive flesh of her bottom, dabbing her cheeks, licking her crease, burrowing in, until at last he found her quim, with his face pressed firmly against her. His nose was on her anus, his tongue probing her sex, teasing her until she had begun to push back, wiggling her bottom in his face. He went to her clitoris, dabbing firmly at the little bud, making her gasp.

She could already feel a climax welling up inside her, extraordinarily fast, but also irresistible as he continued to lick. He began to nibble, very gently with his teeth and lips, sucking at her sex and rubbing his face in her bottom. In response she stuck her bottom up, as high as it would go, pressing her quim onto him as once more he found her clitoris.

The orgasm built, higher and higher, until her back was arched and her mouth wide in ecstasy. His lips took her clitoris, sucking it in. A jolt of unbearable pleasure went through her, again he did it, harder, then once more and she was coming, biting her arm to stop herself screaming and writhing her bottom into his face in a welter of ecstasy that went on until she could bear no more and was forced to pull away.

Henry laughed, moving back to leave Caroline splay-legged and panting on the ground. She was wet behind, and as he once more moved in she readied herself to be buggered. Once more he kissed her bottom, now moving quickly between her cheeks, down to her anus. He kissed the little hole tenderly, then spat and she felt the wetness of it on her hole. A finger touched her, popping inside and again her mouth came open as he began to explore her rectum.

'Be slow,' she managed. 'Please be slow.'

She closed her eyes, remembering how good it had felt before, but still afraid. His coat touched her thighs, tickling her. His cock nudged her quim, Henry rubbing it to smear her juice onto his flesh and brushing her agonisingly sensitive clitoris. She felt the head touch her vagina, then the shaft slide up along the wet crease of her buttocks. Henry's hand touched her and his cock went lower, probing for her anus, finding the hole and pressing. She gasped as she felt her ring start to open, squeezing it on his cock deliberately, letting herself open, waiting to be sodomised only for Henry to grunt as something warm and wet splashed against her anal skin. Suddenly he was rubbing his cock in her crease, finishing himself off and smearing the come over her anus and buttocks, groaning as he did it.

'Damn!' Henry swore as he finally pulled away. 'I couldn't hold back.'

Caroline said nothing, torn between disappointment and relief as the warm semen dribbled down over her quim. Her head was still hazy with pleasure, but as it faded the realisation of the risk she'd taken came to her.

'It . . . it's not inside me, your seed?' she asked.

'I, er . . . I don't think so,' Henry answered. 'Mind, there's no shortage, I'd not spent for three days. Do borrow a handkerchief.'

Caroline accepted the offer, rolling over to dab the come from her quim and between her buttocks. As she cleaned herself she felt her hole, with the tight skin of her hymen half-blocking the entrance. She was wet, very wet, although whether with semen or her own juices it was impossible to tell. When she had done her best she stood, letting her skirts and petticoats drop to cover herself. She was thinking, as she adjusted her bodice, of the consequences of pregnancy.

'I could wish you had been more careful,' she remarked. 'Is my gown quite clean?'

Henry didn't answer, but reached out to brush the back of her dress with his hand. His silence was more worrying than anything, and as they walked from the wood she found herself feeling increasingly guilty and regretful. At the edge of the wood they paused, looking before stepping out on to the grass of the avenue.

'I would ask a rather bold question, if I might?' she said as they reached the gate.

'Be as bold as you please,' Henry answered.

'As you know,' she said, 'your brother has been showing me some kind attention for some while now. Do you suppose, perhaps, that he intends to propose marriage?'

'Stephen?' Henry answered. 'Well, he's keen enough no doubt, but I wouldn't advise it. He's a dry fellow, and you have spirit. No, I'll not mince my words: Stephen's mean and dull. He needs a Methodist for a wife, not a bright little thing like you. In a year you'd be sour or he'd be a cuckold. There, that's as plain as I can be.'

'Thank you, then, I am grateful for your candour,' Caroline replied, returning to her thoughts of pregnancy.

Judith Cates walked briskly through Seven Dials. Every street, every alley, was familiar from her childhood. The scents of horse dung, smoke and filth brought back memories, of playing in the same streets in no more than a ragged dress, of begging scraps from the tradesmen and prostitutes, of the thrill of chasing cabs, knife in hand, to slash the fabric and grab for whatever might be beneath the seat. Now it seemed unreal, as if viewed in a picture, yet beneath her cloak she kept her hand gripped tightly on the hilt of a knife.

From the moment Henry's message had arrived she had been sure that Sir Joseph Snapes was responsible for Suki's kidnap. Not only did he bear them a grudge, but Suki was the only one who could control Lord Furlong, the chimpanzee. Charles had agreed,

110

suggesting they call the watch to Snapes's house in Bedford Square and demand to search it. Judith felt it more likely that Suki would have been taken directly to the estate in Suffolk, where there was little they could do about it, legally. They had gone to Bedford Square in any case, but found the house shuttered and apparently empty.

Passing the Dial itself, she turned into the mouth of an alley. Beyond was a yard, grimy with soot and cluttered with crates and vehicles. Two heavy drays stood nearby, with a group of men beyond, seated or sprawled on the ground, one lifting a jar of gin to his mouth. For a moment Judith stayed in the shadow of a wall, then stepped forwards towards them. One looked up, pointing to her and speaking to the others, who turned, lust and aggression clear on their faces. She pushed back the hood of her cloak and the expressions of two turned to surprise and recognition.

'Little Judy Cates! he exclaimed. 'And quite the fine lady!'

'Michael,' she answered, smiling at him and trying not to wince from the waft of gin, stale beer and unwashed bodies as she came up to them.

'Who's the mort?' another demanded.

'The mort,' Michael replied, 'is one what you could learn from, John Simms. Not that you could follow her trade. Born here, she was. Took to prigging of cabs, then went to prigging in one. Mother Agie's, as a dell. Run off with Agie's money and a killing cove. Now she's strumpet to a swell in St James. Is that not right, Judy?'

'Near enough,' she answered, seating herself on a doorstep.

Simms grunted, but the looks of those who didn't know her softened and the man holding the gin pushed it towards her. Judith took it, upending it

111

over her mouth and taking a swallow, with her eyes shut but knowing full well that every one of them was watching to see that she drank.

'Her speciality, at Agie's,' Michael went on, 'was the burning shame. One candle in the doodle sack, one where the sirreverence comes out and a dozen of the cane between the two. The culls used to pay a smelt a piece, just to watch.'

'Not quite so much,' Judith laughed. 'Now who's upright man to your crew?'

Michael jerked a thumb at one of the others, a squat, burly man who hadn't spoken. The man looked up, showing china-blue eyes in a rough-skinned face with a broken nose and a massive, square jaw. Judith fought for recognition, sure she had seen him before, and as his eyes steadied on her it came.

'Ben Jenkin.'

'That's right.'

'You fought Daniel Mendoza[8] by the Queen's Head.'

'I did.'

'Then you'll do me, if you'd care to earn.'

'We might. What's the game? Some cull you want cropping?'

'No more than a crew to stand by and see that what I say gets done.'

'I've no mind to play the whore's flashman.'

'Not that. I've a friend, a negro girl. She's been taken by a man, a gentleman, Suffolk way.'

'So call the traps.'

'I'd more in mind my own justice.'

'Born in the Dials, stay in the Dials, fancy speech and fine clothes or none. What's the gelt?'

'For four men, a crown a day each.'

'For four, a bull down and a bull a day. I hold the purse.'

112

Judith nodded. Jenkin grinned, holding out the gin to her once more. She took the jar and again upended it over her mouth, swallowing and wiping her lips as she passed it back to Jenkin. He drank and passed it on.

'Michael'll do,' Jenkin said, 'and John here, and Isaac.'

Judith nodded to John Simms, then to the other man indicated, tall and hook-nosed with a cluster of smallpox scars on one cheek. He swallowed his gin and passed the jar back to her.

'I'd rather give you a drink of cock ale, Judy,' Michael said as she swallowed her gin. 'That's the best way to seal a bargain with a whore, ain't it, Ben?'

'And I'd care to see this trick with the candles, if you're game?' John Simms added.

Judith gave a wry smile, saying nothing. Isaac laughed. John Simms sat back, grinning expectantly. Ben Jenkin nodded, looking at her. The others exchanged jealous glances. Judith hesitated, wondering if she could afford to refuse, or if she'd buy better loyalty by accepting. Jenkin was waiting for her to speak.

'Show 'em you're one of us, Judy,' Michael said softly.

Judith bit her lip, then nodded.

'All of us,' Jenkin said. 'I'll have no ill feeling. Inside with you.'

Again she nodded, glancing round at the seven men in the group. She stood, putting her hands on her hips with the handle of the jar held in two fingers. John Simms had pushed open the door he had been leaning against, revealing a dusty room, littered with harness, bits of leather, brass fittings and the tools of the trade. Judith stepped across and inside, looking around for somewhere comfortable. A rough stool stood by the bench, which she rejected, placing a saddle on the floor and sitting down astride in preference. With a gentle sigh she began to undo the laces of her bodice.

Jenkin had come in, John behind him and the others clustered in the open door. Reflecting that it had little difference if they watched or not, Judith tugged open the front of her dress, spilling her breasts out and adjusting the cloth to keep them pushed high and close. Jenkin grinned in appreciation; Michael nodded to his fellows and maked a rude gesture to indicate the size of her breasts. Judith licked her lips as Jenkin put his hand to his breeches-flap.

His cock came out, thick and pale. Judith opened her mouth, leaning forwards towards his crotch to take it in. The others crowded close, watching her suck. She mouthed at his penis, making saliva until the taste became less strong and beginning to suck, easing her lips up and down his shaft as it grew in her mouth. Michael's cock was also bare, and she took it in one hand, tugging to help him to erection. John took her other arm, guiding her hand to his crotch, which she squeezed, feeling the soft lump of his genitals below.

Jenkin took her by the hair, feeding his cock in and out of her mouth, faster than she had been sucking. She began to tug harder at Michael, wondering how many she could bring off in her hands and how many would need sucking. Jenkin was hard, and John was getting harder inside his breeches. The others also had their cocks out, watching her suck and stroking themselves in readiness. They were getting excited, and she began to wonder if she'd need to take more than one load of semen in her mouth.

Isaac knelt down beside her, reaching to fondle her breasts as he pulled at his erection. John paused to free his cock, now hard. Ben Jenkin's erection pushed deep into her throat as he pulled her in by the hair, making her gag. He pulled back, but did it again, grunting as her gullet spasmed on the head of his cock. Judith tried to push back but he held it in, deep in her throat so that she was gagging, then choking, unable to breathe until he suddenly jerked free, grabbed his own shaft and his semen erupted in her face. Judith was already gasping for air as the come splashed over her, landing in her mouth and over her chin. The second spurt caught her neck and breasts, spattering her skin with warm, sticky drops. Jenkin pressed it to her face, rubbing the head across her nose and smearing semen into one eye.

Some were laughing, others grinning lustfully as Jenkin pulled back, leaving Judith with her face and chest smeared with his come. One eye was shut with semen, her nose and chin were slimy, while it bubbled from her lips as she made a froth of it and let it dribble out for their amusement. John Simms called out in delight, pressing close. Judith took his cock in, then Michael's as he too pushed forwards, sucking each quickly, then a third as another man replaced Jenkin in front of her. She looked up, seeing the sharp, thin face of John Ingles, who she had known since childhood.

The others were crowding in, six hard cocks held out to her. She struggled to help, taking two in her hands and sucking the others in turn. They were getting desperate, jerking at themselves and demanding that whoever was in her mouth hurry. Michael came full into her mouth as she opened it to take him in; Isaac was unable to hold back as he ejaculated over her breasts and neck. Both were pushed back, John Simms shoving in to catch her hair and force his erection deep into her throat, holding it there and masturbating with his fingers ringed around the protruding base of his shaft. He came as Judith started to gag again, and she felt the come erupt in her throat, fighting down the urge to be sick on his erection and he finished himself off. Another man lost control in her hand, his come spraying out over her hair and forehead, the second spurt catching her cheek and closing her second eye. A cock was pushed into her mouth, then a second, the heads side by side only just in. She mouthed at both and one came, over her lips. The other pushed deep even as the first wiped his erection in her face, then the last was coming, down her throat and she was gulping on salty, slimy semen. The man pulled back, laughing in glee, and Judith recognised John Ingles.

Her mouth was full of it, her face was filthy, her hair hung with thick white streamers and blobs, her chest spattered white, with a single sticky droplet hanging from one hard nipple. She didn't care. Her head was swimming with the taste of cock and come, her quim swollen and urgent. Grabbing at her skirts, she wrenched them up, the men calling out in amusement as she exposed herself. Wiping the sperm from her eyes with the hem of her petticoats, she opened them, watching the men as she cocked her thighs wide. There was an awl on the bench beside her, the handle a long, smooth length of rounded wood. Judith took it, her eyes meeting those of the men as she put it to her quim, rubbing it on her sopping flesh before easing herself forwards and sliding it deep into her hole.

Jenkin was tugging at his cock, Michael too, all seven watching as she masturbated. She went lower, rolling her legs up with the awl deep in her hole. Reaching to her breast, she took one in each hand, smearing the men's semen over them. Revelling in the sticky fluid, she scraped off what was on her face, putting two fingers in her mouth to suck on them and two lower, rubbing the come into her sex.

The men were masturbating hard, trying to bring their cocks back to erection. Judith opened her mouth, letting them see the froth of white bubbles inside, then stuck out her tongue, inviting more. Putting both hands down, she began to fuck herself with the handle of the awl, in and out of her open hole. Her juice was running down between her bottom-cheeks, wetting her anus.

Pulling her legs higher still, she put a finger to the tiny hole, letting the men watch as she teased it open. Slipping two fingers in, then three, she spread it. Michael swore and John Ingles swallowed hard, his eyes bulging from his head. Judith pulled the awl from her vagina, holding her lips wide to invite entry. Jenkin stooped down, pressing his half-hard cock to her hole. It went in easily, half-filling the sloppy cavity. He began to push, working his cock inside her with eager thrusts. Judith spread her thighs joyfully as his cock started to stiffen properly inside her. Putting her fingers in her mouth, she sucked at the taste of her own body. Jenkin pressed down on her and the saddle slipped from beneath her, leaving her bottom on the hard boards of the floor. He was pushing hard, grunting into her, his face red, his hand gripping her hard under her arms. She was panting, groaning, then grunting aloud as each push knocked the breath from her body.

Jenkin stopped, suddenly, climbing off her to stand panting with a triumphant grin on his face. Judith rolled over, crawling to where a thick candle stood on the bench. She took it, reaching back, pressing it to her sex. It went in, filling her, well up. A second followed, longer and thicker, in her anus, which stretched to take it. On her knees, she began to masturbate, the men staring at the two candles protruding obscenely from behind her. She saw

Michael pick up a strap and fold it, advancing on her. It smacked down, between the candles, on the sensitive skin of her lower buttocks. She slowed her pace, frigging gently as he beat her, letting her pleasure rise.

Ingles appeared beside her, holding another candle, burning. He ducked down, lighting those in her quim and anus then pressing his limp cock to her mouth. Judith began to suck gratefully, lost in ecstasy, her body jumping to the smacks of the belt as she went low, bottom in the air. Ingles went with her, grinning at the others as she sucked on his cock and balls, taking as much into her mouth as she could. Her clitoris was hard under her finger, burning. Each time the belt hit she came closer, rubbing at herself in her ecstasy, then screaming as the first of the wax ran down into the crease of her bottom. More came, between the two bulging holes and on to her fingers as she stuck her bottom as high as it would go. Someone had the third candle, dripping hot wax on to her upraised buttocks and into her crease as Michael beat her. She was screaming around her mouthful of cock, trying to suck as she panted and gasped, writhing to make the wax splash on her skin, kicking her feet in her pain, squirming under the lash, her muscles clenching, then going into wild, helpless spasms as she came, collapsing to the floor as she lost the last of her control.

Judith went limp, exhausted, indifferent to the smarting pain of her buttocks and sex. The candles were pulled out and Michael mounted her, pushing his cock up her bottom from the rear. She took him in, unresisting, letting him struggle to orgasm in her rectum before at last climbing off.

Five

Henry Truscott rolled onto his back, allowing a feeling of sleepy contentment to steal slowly over his body. Eloise crawled close, sighing in pleasure as he cradled her head to his shoulder.

He had finally lost patience with her sulking. That morning a paste board had arrived, announcing the engagement of Caroline Cunningham to Lewis Stukely. Henry had found the news irritating, which he knew was an unreasonable reaction, and the knowledge had only made him more irritated.

Not wishing to ride or fish on a cool day with constant drizzle falling from a leaden sky, he had grown increasingly bored. Eloise had been equally restless and ill-tempered, until she had finally thrown a book at him in response to a badly judged comment about her hair. In answer he had grappled with her and dragged her across his knee, struggling and screaming in rage as both Mrs Orcombe and the nurse had looked on with bovine indifference.

Eloise had been spanked hard on the bare bottom, slap after slap falling until her angry protests had turned to gasps and finally moans. When she had at last stopped kicking and lay, limp and red-bottomed, over his lap, he had carried her up to her own bedroom. She had been made to kneel and taken from the rear, with her red buttocks well spread as Henry pushed into her and at length came inside her. Now, their anger faded and their lust satisfied, they lay together on the bed.

'Little Caroline Cunningham and Stukely, eh?' Henry remarked. 'Well, I dare say he'll do well enough by her. What I can't see is why wait a year before the marriage. Damn it, in his shoes I'd be wanting it next week. Unless he's having her anyway, I suppose, up the arse in all likelihood.'

'Not everybody is such a beast as you, Harry,' Eloise answered, 'and must you always be so coarse? I expect they do not wish to seem in undue haste, and to avoid the winter for the sake of the weather.'

'Could be,' Henry admitted.

'In any case,' Eloise continued, 'as they are having an affair to celebrate the announcement, we shall need to travel to Exeter. The seamstress in the village is really quite inadequate, Mrs Orcombe worse still. We must hire someone, and I need a maid, Harry.'

'You have a maid,' Henry said absently.

'Mary simply will not do,' Eloise answered. 'Suki was beginning to understand my hair, and she was attentive. Mary thinks of nothing other than herself, and never ceases to talk. If that beastly man Joseph Snapes has Suki, I do wish Charles Finch would hurry.'

'He's doing his best, as you know. If Snapes has her, this crew Judith's assembled should have her out in no time.'

'And if Joseph Snapes is not responsible?'

'Then I confess I am at a loss. I find it hard to believe that if Parson Gould were a kidnapper he'd have the gall to hector me on the wretched Pearses. Do you know he came up again yesterday? He says Joanna Pearse is living with a bookbinder in

Okehampton and demands that I go and set her straight. I told him that if I'd swapped William Pearse for a bookbinder I'd be dancing the hornpipe. He wouldn't have it, but kept on about God and moral right and what not. In the end I promised to speak with her, just to quieten the fellow's trap. I suppose I had better ride over to Okehampton this afternoon, at least if the rain stops.'

Sir Joseph Snapes sipped at his glass of boal, pausing to admire the golden-brown gleams struck through the wine by the evening sunlight before he returned the glass to the table. His companion, Luke Hurdon, sat across from him, listening with attention as Snapes explained his theories.

'I maintain my hypothesis,' he stated, 'that the enschego is a degraded form of mankind. The gorilla also.'

'The Man-Ape of Borneo?'

'Another of the same. Indeed, the existence of three such types strongly supports the hypothesis. Yet if such degeneration were a matter of diet, or disease, you would expect the same form to be produced in each case, rather than distinct forms.'

'Different diets or diseases?' Hurdon suggested.

'Possibly,' Snapes answered. 'Possibly. Unlikely however, as the enschego and gorilla co-exist, which also rules out the possibility of the type of degeneration being related to the environment. Also, there is no evidence that forms change with time, save in the case of human intervention, as with horses or dogs. Yet the form has changed, and in specific ways, so what is our conclusion?'

Hurdon shrugged.

'Our conclusion,' Snapes stated, 'is that at some past time the enschego, gorilla and the Bornean creature, the Orang-Outan, were all at some past time in history deliberately bred from human stock.'

'Remarkable,' Hurdon answered. 'Extraordinary, even, yet I see no fault in your logic.'

'There is no fault,' Snapes answered, warming to his explanation. 'Note the differences in physiology we see all around us. Men have red hair, and yellow, and black. We may be short or tall, delicate or robust. Skin varies in shade, from the palest white to near black. With time, and care, such monstrosities could be created, be sure of it.'

'Who would do such a thing, and why?' Hurdon demanded.

'Who is easily answered,' Snapes went on. 'On every continent we find evidence of ancient, godless civilisations, often capable of feats of construction that rival or exceed our own. Look at the pyramids and temples of Egypt. This is who. As to why, I point you to a problem that has long plagued the upper echelons of society, that of securing loyal and reliable servants from among the lower orders, or slaves in the case of less enlightened societies.'

'Come, come, my dear fellow, there is a fault in your logic after all, which is the temperament of the beasts. Lord Furlong, as you know, is neither tractable nor submissive. Hardly an ideal servant.'

'Exactly!' Snapes exclaimed. 'The cases we now see are those which failed, for one reason or another, escaped, and which possessed the fortitude to survive. Weaker creations would have died.'

Hurdon nodded.

'This is not easy to prove,' Snapes continued, 'and what proof there is doubtless lies in Africa. While the subscription for the prints of those pictures drawn on the Benin expedition have been remarkably remunerative, the erotic in particular, the sum raised is far from sufficient to finance another expedition. In any case the first step must still be to show that man and the enschego may breed.'

'Which you have yet to do.'

'Yes, a difficult matter, and made worse by the ignorant fear of our lower orders. Nor is a single failure proof against the theory. To be certain I would need perhaps ten or a dozen subjects, and to maintain the experiment over a period of months.'

'Hardly practical.'

'Quite impractical, when a practised whore like Judith Cates runs screaming at a single glimpse of Lord Furlong. Yet there is a way.'

'There is?'

'There is. Naturally you are acquainted with the work of Dr Edward Jenner?'[9]

Joanna bent forwards, peering into the water of her ablution stand. It remained obstinately clear, without a trace of red. It had been the same for three days, while she was certain that she had counted the days correctly. Yet there was no blood, while she had been regular since the age of thirteen. The answer was clearly that she was pregnant, and the father could not be Thomas Carew. He had sodomised her repeatedly, not to mention making use of her mouth, her breasts, even her armpits, and as often making her adopt lewd poses or perform intimate acts while he watched. Throughout, he had never even introduced his cock into her vagina, much less come inside her. So, unless William had managed what he had failed to do since their marriage, the father could only be Henry Truscott.

She put her finger to her mouth, thinking of Carew's likely reaction. He had repeatedly stated his dislike of children and his determination not to get her pregnant. Thus he was likely either to throw her out or, yet more likely, to take her to a surgeon to have the pregnancy destroyed. Both prospects terrified her. For all his sexual demands, Carew treated her well, and she found herself happier than she had been with William. She had several pretty gowns, two petticoats, one of them lace-trimmed, rings, a necklace, five pairs of shoes and two of boots. The food was also better, the meat seldom tough or rank, while she had become used to sweeter, smoother ciders and even wine. Carew had a reputation, and customers came from as far afield as Plymouth, Exeter and Truro to use his services, even Bristol on one occasion. The thought of destitution was unbearable, let alone with a baby. The prospect of the surgeon was worse.

One lonely hope offered itself. More than once she had seen men change from child-haters to doting fathers, either at the birth of their first child or at the prospect of the event. Carew, she hoped, might be the same, or at least he might be if he believed he was the father of the baby. The difficulty was getting him to come inside her, and if she was to do it there was little time to waste with her pregnancy already two weeks advanced. She finished her wash, struggling to think how she could get what she needed. It was Carew who instigated sex, always, and it was he who made the choices once they had started, unless she was driven to the need to make herself come. On the few occasions she had tried to interest him he had failed to respond, as if he needed the control of what they did.

He was in the workshop, preparing skins to bind a volume of collected poems delivered that morning. Joanna came downstairs, smiling as he looked up from his work. He was seated on a stool, his flaccid buttocks squashed out to both sides and the rear.

'Good morning, Joanna, my dearest,' he greeted her. 'You slept well, I trust? Not too sore?'

'A little,' Joanna answered, feeling her well-buggered anus twinge at his words.

Carew gave his dirty chuckle in response. Joanna went to the counter, leaning across it to make her bottom swell out the seat of her skirts. He appeared not to notice. Once absorbed in work he was hard to distract, and she considered waiting until the evening, only to find the idea horribly frustrating. A sudden idea occurred to her and she went to the shelves, taking down a book with plates illustrating the fauna and flora of Ireland. Carew ignored her as she admired the plates. He was bent close to his work, applying gold leaf to the calf' hide. Returning the natural history book, she took another, set between plates, which she carefully removed before opening it.

Glancing at her husband, she gave a little gasp as the book came open at a picture of a fat, red-faced priest feeding his penis into the mouth of a novice nun. He took no notice and she turned the page, finding a picture of similar style, with a French soldier apparently sodomising a richly dressed noblewoman. Quickly she turned more pages, to a series of illustrations showing women washing in front of one another, urinating together into the same pot and helping each other to masturbate.

'These are shocking, Thomas!' she remarked when he still failed to respond.

Carew chuckled.

'Do not be alarmed, my dear, at the tastes of more refined society. After all, have we not ourselves enjoyed many of the practices shown?'

'Not this.'

'No?' he answered, putting down his tools and leaning across. 'No, indeed not, and yet women frequently share their bodies.'

'I could not,' Joanna declared.

Turning the page, she found a picture of two dark-skinned footmen and a woman, with one penis in each of her holes.

'How could they?' she said.

'Easily enough, and probably at her instigation,' he answered.

'Nonsense,' she said. 'They are raping her. How else could it be? It would be so shameful, to have another man in me, not my husband. I would hate it, as would any decent woman.'

Again he chuckled. Joanna turned the page.

'And again, but three men!' she exclaimed. 'The poor girl, how horrid!'

'She is enjoying it,' he said. 'You need only see the expression on her face.'

'Then she should be blushing for shame. How must it feel?'

'Three times as enjoyable as one, I should imagine. Not all women have your delightful modesty.'

'I could never do any such thing. I should hate it. I should die for shame!'

Carew didn't reply, but went back to work. Joanna waited, expecting him to rise and lock the door, then order her upstairs. Once naked, with his little cock hard in her hand or mouth, she was sure she could bring him to orgasm on his back. She could then mount him, taking his come-smeared cock up herself before he had recovered enough to stop her. Afterwards she could claim she had been unable to resist, and then trust to fate.

He said nothing, but went on working as she studied Stukely's book. It was thick, with plate after plate showing men and women together, women alone, in couples and groups, merely naked or performing sex acts. Some even showed a dark-skinned girl, apparently identical to Suki, with a grotesque black-haired creature, which she had glimpsed the first time she had seen the book and since put down to a mere fantasy of the artist. She had finished and returned the book to its plates when he finally stopped work.

Looking at the pictures had aroused her, with her horror at the idea of pleasing more than one man at a time more feigned than real. She knew her quim was wet, and as Carew rose she was expecting more than ever to be sent upstairs.

'Luncheon, I think is in order,' he said. 'That and a little something. Take this shilling, and walk out on Meldon Lane. Call at the last house on the left – you know it, I'm sure – for Jane Parrish. Give her the shilling and ask her to accompany you.'

'Jane Parrish? Jane Parrish is . . . well, she's a whore.'

'Exactly, my dearest. Now run along.'

He gave her the shilling and sent her out of the door with a pat on her bottom and a last, dirty chuckle. Joanna set off, her face red with blushes. It was obvious that Carew intended to make her perform with Jane Parrish, in front of him, and probably with him once he was sufficiently excited. It was not at all what she had intended, and the prospect made her burn with shame.

'I could not ask for a more beautiful girl to be my wife, nor a sweeter one,' Lewis Stukely declared, stroking a finger gently down the smooth surface of Caroline Cunningham's cheek.

'You are quite bold, Mr Stukely,' Caroline answered.

'I think you may call me Lewis, now we are to be married,' he said, 'at least in private. Now, where's that toad-eater of yours?'

'May has asked Mrs Aldgrave to choose some roses, to brighten the dining room for this evening. She is a cousin, and fallen on hard times. You are cruel to call her names.'

'She's a toad-eater, I say, living on your brother's charity.'

'Speaking of my brother, he would be quite angry to find us upstairs.'

'Doubtless.'

He stepped close to her, reaching out to tweak lose one of the bows which held the front of her bodice shut.

'No corset?' he asked as her breasts quivered in response.

'It is warm,' she said, 'and Lewis, really, someone might see.'

'Yes, myself. You are to be my wife. Surely I might inspect what is to be mine?'

'So you say,' she answered, 'yet Mrs Aldgrave would think it most improper.'

'To the devil with Mrs Aldgrave. Come, let's have those bubbies out.'

'Mr Stukely!'

Her gasp of feigned shock turned into giggles as he tugged the remaining laces of her bodice loose. She could feel her stomach fluttering as his hand found her breasts, squeezing them and pushing them up and out of the restraining silk to bounce, bare and round, into his hands. He leaned down, pressing them together to nuzzle her cleavage. Again she giggled, placing her hands on her back. He was kissing her breasts, between them, then the nipples, sucking each quickly into his mouth to leave them hard and wet. His arms went down under her bottom and she was lifted, carried quickly across the room and deposited on the bed. She lay back, breathing hard, expecting to be mounted. He knelt up on the bed, taking hold of her skirts and lifting them and dumping them across her belly, leaving her breasts bare. Caroline spread her thighs, blushing at the exposure of her sex. Stukely licked his lips, his eyes flicking across her body.

'Perfect,' he said, 'flawless.'

His hand reached out, but not to her quim. Instead he began to stroke her thighs, very gently, tracing his knuckles over her skin, near her knees, then higher, towards her sex. Caroline sighed in response, opening her legs yet further to let him explore every detail of her body. He responded with a curious purring sound from deep in his throat. She shut her eyes, lying back as his fingers explored her, touching her, tickling gently at her thighs, then under her bottom. The bed creaked and she felt his lips, kissing one knee, then the other, then starting to lick.

'Like cream,' Stukely purred, his tongue tracing a slow line up the inside of her thigh.

She giggled, then moaned softly as his tongue touched the shallow crease where her thigh met the tuck of her bottom. He was inches from her anus, and she was thinking of how Henry had licked the little hole, opening it with his tongue until she was wet and loose enough to accept his cock. He ignored it, starting back up the inside of one thigh with tiny, precise kisses, then stopping. She held still, feeling her chest rise and fall with her breathing, aware of how open she was in front of him and how easily he could have her.

'What a darling little cunt,' he murmured, 'and so clearly virgin. It cries out to be entered.'

'You might, if you wish,' Caroline sighed.

'On our wedding night, my pretty one, not before,' he answered, 'but there's a trick I'll teach you that will make you mine for life.'

'Are you . . . are you going to put it in my behind?' Caroline asked, struggling to sound shy rather than hopeful.

'What a thought!' Stukely declared. 'My, but you do have a lively imagination, and don't I have the luck in that you are mine? No, my pretty, not up your delightful behind, although I'll confess I'm tempted. This is what I mean.'

His face pressed between her thighs. The tip of his tongue touched her quim and he started to lick. Caroline relaxed, content to be licked, even if that was all he meant. It was good, and she was sure he'd done it before, just as she had, although she had no intention of admitting to it.

'That is lovely,' she sighed after a moment. 'So lovely. I had never imagined, Mr Stukely, Lewis . . . I had never thought. Oh, you are so wonderful, such a man.'

She lay back to enjoy being licked, hoping that she had flattered him sufficiently. He was teasing her, probing her hole with his tongue and lapping at her sex-lips, making her pleasure rise slowly. After a while she rolled up her legs, holding them behind her knees to push her bottom out and open her cheeks. It was an invitation which Henry, and Alice too, would have responded to by licking her bottom-hole. Stukely didn't, but began to stroke her thighs with his hands and presently cupped her bottom so that he could pull her more firmly towards his face.

His tongue found her clitoris and she felt herself starting to come. Her hands went to her breasts, squeezing the plump orbs together. She began to stroke her nipples, sighing as his licking became firmer. Her muscles started to tense, her back arching, and she was crying out, aloud, unable to hold herself back, bucking her sex against his face and struggling not to scream as her whole body locked in ecstasy. Only as she was coming down did she remember that it was supposed to be the first time she'd been licked to climax.

'Beautiful,' she murmured, 'so wonderful. Oh, you are so right, Lewis. I will be yours. How could I even think of another when you give me such rapture?'

He knelt up, grinning and obviously well pleased with himself. Caroline held out her arms, but he ignored the invitation, shuffling round on his knees. She realised that his cock was out and managed what she hoped was a convincing gasp. It was hard, and near enough to her face for her to smell the excited, masculine scent.

'You'll understand, as a lady, that a favour given should be returned,' he said.

Caroline nodded and moved forwards to gulp in his cock, immediately wondering if she was being too knowing. He said nothing, but moved around, Caroline following, until he was on his back and she was kneeling, her bottom stuck high in the air as she sucked on his erection.

'A pretty view. Stay like that, just like that,' he ordered. 'You are beautiful, Caroline, so pretty. Such lovely eyes, a perfect mouth. Oh, how often I've imagined that perfect mouth around my cock, and now it is.'

He lay back with a sigh, stroking her hair as she sucked.

'In a while something rather startling will happen,' he said. 'Do not be alarmed, and lick up whatever you may find, which is considered good manners. Yes, just like that, up and down. You have a natural talent, Caroline, my pretty. Now kiss the head. Yes, perfect.'

She went on sucking, obeying his orders. Slowly he became more heated, groaning and taking her by the

131

back of her head to push his cock deeper. She began to gag, at which he stopped, only to quickly become excited again. Struggling to take it, Caroline let him force his cock down into the top of her throat. She was gagging, her gullet tightening on his knob, panting through her nose, and suddenly her throat was full of semen and he was jerking her head up and down by the hair. She was helpless, choking on semen, gagging on his erection, her mouth filling with thick, salty fluid, which burst from her lips as she struggled on his cock.

Stukely groaned deeply, letting go of her head. Caroline pulled back, coughing and gasping for breath, semen and saliva dripping from her open mouth and on to his genitals. Making a face, she swallowed, sucking her cheeks in to make more saliva before leaning down to lick up the mess of semen and spittle she had spilled on his cock and balls.

'My, what a good girl you are,' Stukely said, pulling his head up. 'As man and wife we shall get on famously, have no doubt of it.'

Joanna shut her eyes as her knees were pulled open, allowing Jane Parrish to manipulate her body despite the excruciating shame in her head. She was bare below the waist, her quim showing to the girl, who had accepted the shilling and the suggestion that they have sex together with a happy giggle. Now she was on the bed, her back propped on the bolster, her knees up and wide, her dress high and undone at the front. Carew was watching, red-faced as he nursed his erection. He had ordered everything, the way Joanna should show herself and Jane should strip naked, how they should kiss and touch each other's bodies, what poses they should adopt, and now, that Jane should use her tongue to bring Joanna to a climax.

Jane went down between Joanna's legs and immediately started to lick. Joanna sighed, her stomach pulling in at the sensation, her shame growing stronger still as she realised how easily she was going to come. Jane was probing her vagina and licking up the full length of her sex with long, slow laps which pressed down on Joanna's clitoris.

'Let me see it,' Carew ordered. 'Keep your head clear, girl.'

Jane sat up again, making a wry face at Joanna to show what she thought of Carew. Joanna felt the corners of her mouth twitch briefly up into a smile. It was hard not to respond to Jane's playful enthusiasm, for all her embarrassment at what they were doing. They had already been made to kiss, and she had found herself responding despite everything, while having Jane suck her nipples had been much more exciting than when Carew did the same.

'Move around, head to tail,' Carew ordered, 'and Joanna, you are to keep your legs well apart. Jane, hold them open if you must.'

'Yes, Mr Carew,' Jane answered, clambering around.

For a moment Joanna was unsure of what was happening, only to have Jane calmly cock a leg across her head. The move left the girl's quim spread wide, inches above Joanna's face.

'You are to feel each other's bottoms as you do it,' Carew ordered.

Jane made herself comfortable, lying along Joanna's body. Tentatively, Joanna reached up, taking hold of the girl's round, meaty bottom-cheeks. She could see Jane's quim, every little fold of flesh, pink and moist, rich with the smell of girl. Hands slid under her bottom, cupping her cheeks as Jane took hold of them and began to knead the flesh, squeezing

133

gently. Joanna imitated the motions, making Jane's bottom part to show the rosy pink dimple of her anus.

'Beautiful!' Carew declared. 'A fine sight! Now, get busy, and do not stop until you have both spent.'

Swallowing, Joanna poked her tongue out, her eyes fixed on Jane's plump pink quim, wondering if she could really kiss another girl's sex. Jane's lips touched her own unashamedly, lapping up her juice. Giving in, Joanna shut her eyes and poked her tongue into Jane's hole, tasting salt and the same thick, rich girl taste she had from herself when sucking fingers or a cock that had been inside her. Jane was licking her, and the feeling was too nice, too strong, making her want to return the favour. She started, giving in to what her body was telling her to do. Jane wriggled her bottom in delighted response.

Joanna could see very little, only the swell of Jane's bottom and the canopy of the bed. Carew was out of sight, and quickly out of mind as her pleasure grew. There was still shame at what she was doing, but fading as she came closer to climax, until she knew she would not have stopped if Carew had ordered it. She was coming into Jane's face, her thighs squeezing firmly around the girl's head, rolled high to make herself as exposed as possible. It went on and on, so good that she could only hold herself still, her hands locked on Jane's bottom until at last it began to fade.

She went back to licking, only for Carew to call a halt. Jane climbed off her face, and Joanna found her husband red-faced and sweating, but still nursing his erection. His teeth gritted, he pointed beneath the bed, a gesture she knew only too well. Ducking down, she drew out the chamber pot, sharing a glance with Jane, who shrugged.

'Both,' Carew panted, 'together. Naked.'

Joanna unfastened her dress and let it drop, stepping out of it as Jane positioned herself over the chamber pot, legs braced apart, belly pushed out to leave her quim directly over it. Blushing, Joanna adopted the same rude position, squeezing her bladder in an effort to pee.

'Last to finish drinks the pot,' Carew grunted.

Jane gave Joanna a look expressing disgust, but immediately began to pee, a thick golden stream of fluid gushing from her quim. Some missed the pot, splashing on Joanna's legs, the surprise making her lose her own concentration. She had peed earlier, and it was hard, but the thought of having to drink what she made, and Jane's, had her straining the muscles of her belly in an effort to do as she had been told. It came, a trickle and then a gush, splashing into the big china pot to mingle with what Jane had already done. Joanna watched, looking down as their pee ran out, praying Jane was full. Her own stream was already dying, only for Jane to stop suddenly and step back, giggling. Joanna looked down in horror at the yellow fluid in the pot, then at Carew, whose eyes were staring from his head as he masturbated.

'Drink,' he ordered, his voice cracking. 'All of it. Drink your piddle up, and hers.'

With her stomach knotting and a hard lump in her throat, Joanna knelt down. Hardly knowing what she was doing, she lifted the big pot in both hands. Jane was watching, one hand over her mouth, giggling in delighted horror as Joanna tipped the pot towards her face. The pee touched her lips, acrid and rich with female taste, and she was drinking, swallowing down her own piddle as Jane squeaked in excitement.

Carew was tugging desperately at his cock, faster and faster as Joanna drank, gulping the thick yellow pee down, swallowing as best she could. Some spilled, dribbling down her breasts and belly to the floor. Jane had put her hand to her quim and was masturbating, eyes fixed on Joanna. Carew came, suddenly, semen erupting from his cock in a fountain and falling back to clot on the head. Joanna lowered the pot as he slumped back in his chair. She straddled him, pushing his hand away from his erection, which she grabbed and stuffed into her quim and she settled her body across his. He looked up, startled, trying to say something but unable to. She was bouncing on his cock, taking it deep even as his erection began to fade, and calling out, faking climax but revelling in the slimy feel of the semen around her vagina.

Face down on the bed, Suki let her hand run over the contours of her waist and bottom. The one felt less firm, the other bigger, she was sure of it. Every day since she had been taken she had been fed three heavy meals and frequent slices of bread and jam or cake. Her breasts felt heavier, her buttocks fatter and her hips broader, she was sure of it. The explanation she was sure of. In her homeland there had been rumours of a king with many wives, all of whom were huge. They were said to be fed until they could no longer walk, but only lie in their hut, great mounds of soft, fat flesh, monuments to the king's wealth.

She had seen nothing of the sort in England, where women seemed to prefer to exaggerate the width of their hips and bust in contrast to their waists but were seldom more than fleshy. Yet, as the Truscotts liked to see women's bottoms beaten and to race her as if she were a draught beast, so it was easy to imagine a man who wanted her fat. She could also guess why it had been her rather than another. Her captor might have heard of the king's women and reasoned that she would fatten easily, or he might have been obsessed with her dark skin, as many of the white men she had met had been.

The stairs creaked, a sound she now recognised immediately, and she rolled over as Davy's voice sounded outside the door. It opened and Davy came in, carrying a tray laden with food. Nathan followed, pushing a heavy machine, a contrivance of rods and levers on an iron base. Suki glanced at it in alarm and Nathan laughed.

'There's no harm in it, girl,' Davy said. 'It's to calculate your weight.'

'Get on,' Nathan ordered, pointing to the flat base.

Suki climbed off the bed, tugging at her chain. As she stepped onto the machine a lever rose with a clang. Nathan made adjustments, placing a cylinder of dull grey metal on one rod and sliding a thick brass ring along another. Davy had set the tray down on the bed and approached, glancing at the apparatus.

'Ten and nine,' he said, nodding. 'Right, you can get off now.'

She climbed down as he indicated that she should. Her tray held a mug of milk, a large cake and three slices of bread with jam and cream, which she began to eat. Neither man took any notice, and Nathan left his cudgel fixed to his belt. They had become easier with her, still treating her with indifference, but more as a human being than as an animal, which they had done at first.

As she ate they talked, discussing ships and the sea, as they often did. Suki said nothing, listening but not looking, sure that they would be more cautious if they realised how much she understood. She had gathered that both were sailors. Nathan had been to somewhere far distant, apparently more so than her own homeland, in search of hides from sea animals. Davy had been a fighting man, a fact which he

137

seemed to resent. Neither had said anything to hint at why she was being held captive, or fattened up, yet she felt sure that eventually one or the other would.

They continued to talk even when she had finished, leaving only at the sound of a door slamming below them. Suki waited as the key grated in the lock. Davy's quick footsteps sounded on the stairs, Nathan's lower, heavier tread in the corridor. A voice sounded, then another, followed by the slam of a door and all was silence. For a moment Suki stayed still, listening, then picked her chain up and stepped quietly down from the bed. Crossing the room to the limit of her chain, she began to investigate the weighing machine.

Henry dismounted, throwing the reins across a convenient post before fixing a nosebag into place. The horse began to munch contentedly as Henry looked around, quickly spotting the sign announcing one of the shops as that of Thomas Carew. The rich yellow glow of a lamp showed within, with the shadows of the houses opposite already making the street gloomy. Walking briskly across, Henry knocked on the door, which was opened by Joanna herself.

'Joanna, my dear,' he announced himself. 'I had hoped to find you at home.'

'Mr Truscott,' she answered, bobbing an uncertain curtsy.

'Is your husband in?' Henry asked. 'Well, you know, the fellow who owns the place, Thomas Carew?'

'Mr Carew is out,' she replied.

'There's no need to be so damn formal,' Henry said, 'and my, haven't you changed in the space of a fortnight? Quite the lady, with airs and graces to boot.'

'Mr Carew likes me to dress well, and to speak well, for the sake of the customers.'

'Treats you well, does he? Better than Pearse in any case, I'll warrant.'

'He is very kind.'

'Damn it, Joanna, the last time I saw you I was being hammered by that damn husband of yours, and the time before you were strapped across a branch with your well-hued arse in the air. Don't you remember?'

'Yes,' Joanna answered quickly.

'Then be easy. Fetch me a glass of ale, or whatever old Carew keeps for best.'

'There is sack in a decanter, of Malaga.'

'Well enough.'

Henry threw his hat on to the counter and shrugged off his coat, walking across to Carew's display of books. Joanna had disappeared through a door and returned quickly, holding a tall glass of pale yellow liquid. Henry took it and sipped, letting the hot, dry taste warm his mouth before swallowing.

'Not bad,' he pronounced. 'Now, first things first. Those fellows who took Suki. William says they held you off and made away in a gig drawn by a pair of greys.'

'Right enough,' Joanna answered. 'I did try to give aid. Has she not been found?'

'Best not to try aid with a pair of barkers in your face,' Henry said. 'As to fetching her back, we've had no sign of her. Looks like they took her up country.'

'Poor Suki.'

'They'll not crop her, I wouldn't think. My reckoning is that she was taken for the way I treat her. Doubtless the righteous bastards'll have her scrubbing floors in a church poor-house somewhere. You didn't recognise the fellows who took her or anything? You might have seen them around the village perhaps?'

'No, sir, no strangers recently, none at all.'

'Hmm. You live, well, used to live, in plain sight of the rectory, didn't you?'

'Yes, sir.'

'Gould, the parson, did he ever have visitors, men you didn't know?'

'Parson, sir? Not that I can think, not often.'

'Hmm. Well no matter. There's another matter, which is this business of your being sold to Carew. Well it's not in the scriptures, you know. It's not the law either.'

'It's right, sir. Tilly Chillcott, she . . .'

'Yes, I know about the Chillcotts, and others. That don't signify, you see . . . Oh the hell with it. Are you happy with this fellow Carew?'

'Well enough.'

'You dress well enough for sure, and eat well enough by the look of you. I'll be damned if I'll drag you back to Pearse, especially when he don't want you.'

'Is he well, William?'

'Well enough, picking stones from the fields on a farm Meldon way, so I hear. So what's this Carew fellow like?'

'He is old, and fat, and ugly.'

'Don't suppose you're ridden too often then? Nor too well.'

'Mr Carew is . . . he has his way . . . he is given to sodomy.'

'Boys? What'd he buy you for, then?'

'Not boys, me.'

'He is, eh? Well, I can see the virtue in a tight breech myself, so long as it's sweet. With an arse like yours, I can't say I blame him.'

140

Joanna was blushing and looking down. Henry glanced at the window, outside which dusk was gathering rapidly.

'Gone long is he, your man?' he asked.

'He has gone to visit a customer,' Joanna answered, 'to Tavistock.'

'Tavistock, eh? That's what, sixteen mile, nearer eighteen if he doesn't care to pay the toll. Left early, did he?'

'Shortly after three.'

Henry didn't answer, calculating the time it would take to drive to Tavistock and back, even assuming Carew stayed only a short time.

'He is likely to take supper,' Joanna said quietly.

'Ever the bobtail, eh?' Henry laughed. 'Damn, but you are looking plump. I'll swear there's an inch on those bubbies.'

'I'm sure I don't know what you mean, sir,' Joanna giggled.

Henry rose and caught her around the waist, kissing her neck as his hands went to her bottom and a breast.

'The window!' she squeaked.

His mouth closed on hers as they stumbled towards the door. Pushing through, Joanna went backwards, on to the stairs, Henry coming down on top of her as he fumbled for the laces of her gown. They came open and he pushed her breasts up over the top, nuzzling them and biting her nipples.

'Turn over,' he grunted. 'We'll have that glorious arse out, shall we?'

She obeyed, turning to kneel on the stairs with her bottom level with his crotch. Henry took hold of her skirts and yanked them high, exposing her bottom, plumper and rounder than ever, the big cheeks slightly apart to show the crease between. Her quim

141

showed too, a plump mound of hairy flesh pouting out between her thighs, the centre parted to show moist pink.

'Like it in your breech, does he?' Henry said. 'The man has taste. I've a mind to do the same.'

'No, please,' Joanna answered. 'I am ever so sore.'

Henry laughed, tugging at his belt. She had turned back, watching as he opened his breeches and let them fall. He came close as she opened her mouth in invitation and she took him in, sucking eagerly until he was fully erect and not stopping until he pulled back.

'Come,' he grunted, 'grease your tail for me. Another won't hurt.'

'If you must,' Joanna answered, her hand already going back to her bottom.

Henry watched, stroking his cock as she touched the tight bud of her anus, briefly, before dipping a finger into her quim. It came out wet with juice, which she dabbed on to her anus. Again she did it, and again, until the little ring was wet with thick white juice. Only then did she push a finger up her bottom, deep in, then a second, then a third.

'By God, but he's got you well trained,' Henry swore. 'Come now, that's open enough if he takes you regularly.'

'He is not so long, nor so thick around,' Joanna answered.

Her fingers came out, leaving her anus a gaping black hole, wet inside and closing slowly. He took his cock, kneeling to press it to the juicy hole so that he could see. The head went in, leaving Joanna's anus a tight ring of stretched pink flesh. She moaned as it filled, then again as he began to push it up. Holding his cock, he watched as it was forced slowly up her bottom. Joanna grunted and mewled her way through her buggery, until Henry's knuckles met her flesh and he stopped. She gave a little groan as he took her by the hips, pushing the last of his penis into her rectum.

'You're tight for one so well used,' he grunted. 'Now frig your cunt and come with me in you.'

'He makes me do the same,' Joanna said weakly, but reached back and began to rub at her quim.

With his cock buried deep up her body, Henry kept a gentle rhythm, admiring her big, spread buttocks as he sodomised her. She began to sigh, then mewl, and as she started to come he remembered how she had screamed before. It was too late; Joanna was calling out her ecstasy as her anal ring tightened on his cock, over and over. It was more than he could hold back from, and he began to jam his cock in and out of her, his front slapping on her buttocks, sending waves through the plump flesh. She was screaming and he was near coming, only for contractions to die even as he reached the brink of orgasm.

'Hell!' he swore, stopping and beginning to pull out.

'Have you spent?' Joanna panted.

'No,' Henry answered as his cock left her rectum.

'Then be quick!' she gasped. 'A neighbour might have heard! No, not . . .'

Henry had grabbed her hair, pulling her round and silencing her by stuffing his erection into her open mouth. Her eyes went wide, but he had her firmly by the head, fucking her mouth with short, hard pushes. She began to suck reluctantly, then properly, shutting her eyes as her mouth worked on the penis that had just been up her bottom. As he saw her horror change to eagerness Henry felt himself start to come, his cock growing suddenly sensitive, unbearably so, and then he had ejaculated in her mouth and her cheeks were blown out with semen dripping from around her lips.

143

She sucked eagerly, swallowing her mouthful, then more, draining him before carefully licking up what had spilled from his balls and thighs. He leaned back against the door, hastily adjusting himself as she did the same.

'Fine,' he gasped. 'Better, I trust, than old Carew?'

Joanna nodded, still making sucking motions to clear her mouth of the taste. Henry laughed, opening the door as she quickly fastened the laces of her bodice. His drink was on the counter and he took a swallow, then passed it to her. She accepted the glass, sucked her cheeks in and swallowed.

'I shall tell the black fly,' Henry said, 'that you are content here, and that you will not leave. There is little he can do, so rest easy.'

'Thanking you,' Joanna answered, 'but ... but there is another matter.'

'Yes?' Henry enquired.

'I ... I am with child.'

'By William Pearse?

'No, by ...'

'All the better then. Even Gould must see the sense in you being with the father of your brat. Can you be sure of it?'

'My William is barren, certain sure. Thomas Carew cares nothing for my front. There has been only one other.'

Six

Seated on the terrace of his Suffolk house, looking out over the sea and at the waves breaking gently on the shingle of the beach, Sir Joseph Snapes steepled his fingers in thought. Everything had gone to plan, more successfully than he had dared hope, and his experiment was scheduled for the afternoon.

'Fourteen girls?' Luke Hurdon stated from the chair beside Snapes. 'Remarkable. I must congratulate you on your powers of persuasion.'

'A simple enough matter,' Snapes replied, 'and one for which I can take only limited credit. The true genius belongs to a certain Elizabeth Hickling, locally known as Mother Bessie.'

'Indeed?'

'Yes. She is a redoubtable woman, with a reputation locally as what is known as a "white witch".[10] Sheerest superstition, of course, but the local women have great faith in her. She acts as midwife, and is able to make poultices and draughts for minor illnesses. These cure themselves in the fullness of time, and she gains the credit.'

'I see, so where you would have been unable to persuade your subjects to co-operation, she has no difficulty.'

'Exactly so. Their ignorance is typical. Rather than enjoy the benefits of modern science, they entrust their health to country remedies of no proven efficacy. Frankly, I wonder if our own poor are any better than the natives of the Benin coast. They have knowledge of God, true, but little enough besides.'

'Sadly true, and yet in education there is the danger of what has overtaken France.'

'Nonsense, my dear fellow. Are the French peasantry any more educated than our own? No, not a bit of it, merely more downtrodden.'

'No longer, I fear, although Lake has achieved a notable victory at Lincelles,[11] I understand.'

'So I hear.'

'This woman, then, you persuaded her of the benefits of Dr Jenner's theory?'

'Hardly that. I paid her twelve shillings to explain to as many local girls as possible that an unpleasant disease has been brought into the country by French prisoners. Its effect is to render female victims barren, while males show no ill effects. The cure is an application of a certain preparation, of which I possess the formula. The woman Hickling is no fool and realises that matters are not as they seem. I imagine she thinks my intentions erotic in nature. Certainly she suspects nothing of the truth.'

'A clever device, as it also explains why the preparation need be applied in so intimate a place. There is naturally no such disease?'

'Naturally not, and so none of the girls will catch it. They are all young, married women, mainly the wives of bargees in the oyster trade, and doubtless unsure of their husbands' fidelity on trips up to London.'

'It is a most cleverly constructed plan, no doubt, Sir Joseph. Yet I confess that I am uncertain of the morals involved. What if one or more girls should conceive and produce hybrids?'

'That is my most earnest hope! As to the moral implications, in the cause of the advancement of science, such a trivial deception counts no cost at all.'

'And the hybrids?'

'The girls will be mortified and wish to be rid of the creatures. I will oblige, and in due course present them to the Royal Society, to the comprehensive astonishment of the world of science.'

'You would seem to have considered every detail.'

'I certainly hope so, my dear Hurdon, I certainly hope so.'

'What then is my part in the matter?'

'I wish you to apply the preparations. It is not a task I can entrust to Mother Hickling, while I am under no illusions as to my own lack of pulchritude. Women are curious creatures, and lack rationality. Despite the fact that they are not being asked to indulge in sexual congress, but merely to allow the insertion of the preparation into their vaginas, they will still prove more co-operative to a man of good physique. I shall also introduce you as a doctor, naturally.'

'I see.'

'It is a simple enough matter. Insert the syringe fully into the vagina of each and depress the plunger slowly until the full dose has been delivered. The seed is diluted with saline of exact concentration, under which conditions the individual spermatazoans are active and so the seminal matter presumably viable. I am confident of achieving several pregnancies.'

'With such elaborate preparation it is hard to imagine you failing,' Hurdon replied.

'In science, exactitude is everything.'

The barge creaked, the deck tilting as the boom swung across to take it on to a new tack. Judith watched the long, low line of Orford Ness start to recede once more as they moved out from the shore. The wind was light and easterly, making it impossible to sail north except in long, slow tacks, which meant that her hopes of reaching the estate of Sir Joseph Snapes at dawn had had to be abandoned. As it was, they seemed unlikely to reach their destination before mid-afternoon.

The bargees had taken the delay in the same calm, phlegmatic manner they had accepted her instructions, and the money Charles had paid for their services. The attitude of the four she had hired in Seven Dials was still more irritating. Ben Jenkin regarded the whole affair as little more than a pleasure trip, and easy money for not a great deal of work. The others took much the same attitude. All four had spent most of the night drinking and gambling, despite her demands that they be fresh for the day.

They had also made sure they got their fill of her services, which Ben Jenkin had insisted on as part of the bargain, a deal which had quickly come to include the two bargees. She had sucked Jenkin's cock while the others watched, egging him on and making lewd suggestions. He had obliged, making her pull the top of her dress down so that he could rub himself between her breasts, then strip completely. Judith had given in to the inevitable, accepting his cock from the rear as she bent across the cabin table. The others had wanted the same, and one by one she had sucked their cocks and taken them into her body from behind. She had only balked at letting them come in her quim, so that four men had splashed their semen across her upturned bottom before Isaac had decided it would be more amusing to sodomise her. He had rubbed his cock between her buttocks, in the slimy

148

mess left by his companions, then forced her bottom, the muscle giving with embarrassing ease. He had come in her rectum, as had the older of the two bargees, who had only managed to get his cock erect by watching the entire performance. It had proved too much for her, and she had come in front of them, rubbing herself with her other hand reached back to finger her semen-sodden anus.

She had tried to sleep, only to wake every time the barge changed tack. When the younger of the bargees had come to her at dawn, it had been with the information that the wind was wrong and that their was no hope of arriving at dawn. Now, tacking slowly up the coast in bright sunlight, the men were beginning to grow restless.

Sir Joseph Snapes folded his arms across his chest, smiling benignly and greeting each young woman with a paternal nod as she was shepherded into the room. They were in the hall of his house, in which a double row of chairs had been set up. Luke Hurdon stood beside him, the servants, Sale the butler, Hastable the cook and black John, against one wall, all in full livery uniform of dark blue and gold. Mother Bessie was at the door, marshalling the girls with an expression of stern forbearance on her heavy face.

Snapes considered the group as the last of the girls took her seat. There were now fifteen, one of the girls having persuaded her younger sister of the virtues of the treatment. Eight were the wives of bargees, whose husbands made regular trips to London to deliver oysters, cod and other seafood. Three more were married to drovers, men who took cattle to London on frequent occasions. A further two were fishermen's wives, one the daughter of a local brewer, the last the unmarried sister.

149

Some were plain, others pretty; most were brown- or tawny-haired; one, the tallest, was pale blonde. All looked reasonably healthy and well fed. Most seemed nervous, a few distinctly so, although as many appeared entirely complacent or even animated, presumably excited by a break in the routine of their lives. He waited until all fifteen were seated before stepping forwards, raising his hands for silence as he did so.

'Ladies,' he began, bowing slightly. 'As you know, I am Sir Joseph Snapes. I bid you good afternoon, and congratulate you all on having the forethought and good sense to attend this afternoon. With me is my colleague, Doctor Hurdon, a physician of excellent repute and an expert in these matters, whose task it is to apply the preparation.'

Snapes inclined his head, watching the expressions on the girls' faces as they cast glances at Luke Hurdon, some demure, some less so, a couple uncertain. Two whispered together, stifling giggles behind their hands. He waited until their attention had returned to him before continuing.

'As Mrs Hickling has explained to you, the preparation must be applied internally to show effect. Naturally I understand that you will be concerned for your modesty, yet you must appreciate that Doctor Hurdon and myself are men of science and so there can be no question of impropriety. Moreover, the good Mrs Hickling will be on hand at all times. Rest assured that the entire process will be conducted with the utmost decorum, discretion also.

'For the preparation to take full effect it is unfortunately necessary to remain in an inverted position, that is to say, upside down. It is also important to remain still for some small period of time. In order to effect this, and with so many of you, I have arranged for the experiment, er ... that is to say, the application of the preparation to take place in the barn, where there is sufficient space. It is there that I have set up my apparatus. Pray do not be alarmed by what you see, my dears. No harm will come to you, and a great deal of good, rest assured. So, if you would be good enough to follow Mrs Hickling?'

He indicated the door, where Mother Bessie was waiting. She gestured to the girls, calling on them to hurry. They followed her, across the lawn to the rear of Snapes's property, where a large barn stood between the lane and the mere, set up to store goods for transport to London on barges.

Snapes, Hurdon and Hastable followed the girls, who Mother Bessie was trying to make form a line on the lawn. Within the barn the floor was clear, a long, high space beneath beams of old ship's timber, black with age. To one side a table had been set up, with a clean tablecloth spread over it on which stood a microscope.

'Experimentation indicates that the spermatozoans persist in motion for the longest period when kept cool,' Snapes remarked to Hurdon. 'I had imagined the temperature of the body would be ideal, but this proved not to be the case. In view of this discovery the syringes are stored in the ice house.'

Hurdon nodded, looking over to where a pile of ropes and sacking lay on the floor. Snapes sat at the table, adjusting the microscope as Sale appeared in the doorway.

'The girls are ready, sir,' he announced. 'All fifteen appear willing.'

'Splendid,' Snapes answered.

'There is a barge on the mere, sir.'

'Not for me, I trust. It's probably going up to the cottages.'

Sale moved aside, allowing John to enter the barn. He held a long wooden case, which he placed in front of Snapes. Opening it, he revealed a line of thick glass syringes, metal-bound and each stopped with a tiny cork. Taking one, Snapes squeezed a drop of fluid on to the microscope slide. He pushed the slide beneath the lens and leaned close, adjusting the mirror, the eyepiece and focus until the picture swam into view. It was clear, the egg-shaped heads and long tails of the chimpanzee sperm swimming in the fluid, very much alive. As he sat back from the microscope he was struggling to prevent the cool formality of his expression from breaking into a broad grin.

'Very well, then, we are ready,' he announced. 'Sale, if you would be good enough to usher the first of the girls in?'

Sale bowed and walked to the door. A moment later a girl appeared, one of those who had shown more confidence. She was brown-haired, with a snub nose crossed by a bridge of freckles, taller than most, but tiny next to the bulk of Sale.

'You are?' Snapes asked.

'Mary Hodge,' she answered.

'Mary, you say, splendid, splendid. Now, as I said, you must not be alarmed. All is for the best. My man John, here, and Hastable, my cook, who you may well know from market, will assist you.'

Mary turned, to find the two men behind her, each holding a piece of sacking and a rope. Both ducked down, wrapping the sacking around her calves and quickly tying the ropes into place. Then, before she had a chance to protest, they had caught her legs and upended her, resulting in a squeal of surprise as her skirts fell away to expose her legs, bottom and belly.

'Gently, gently, she is not a sack of potatoes,' Snapes chided, then chuckled at his own wit.

The ropes were flung over a beam, well apart, and tied off, leaving Mary dangling upside down, her inverted skirt obscuring everything but her hair and her hands, both of which barely touched the ground. From belly to knees she was bare, her plump, well-furred quim on clear display between open thighs. She struggled to support herself, at the sight of which Snapes found himself unable to restrain his mirth.

'I do apologise, my dear,' Snapes stated. 'You must understand that it is entirely for your own benefit, and that if it obliges you to adopt a somewhat ridiculous posture, then that is but a small price to pay for the benefits. Sale, perhaps if you could usher the next of our subjects in?'

Sale nodded and ushered in the tall blonde girl, whose face briefly registered surprise at the sight of Mary hanging upside down from the beam, before she too was grabbed, upended and suspended by her ankles. One by one they were given the same treatment, until all fifteen hung upside down, with fifteen plump young quims spread bare and ready for Luke Hurdon's attention. Some continued to struggle, others to complain or simply squeal. Most hung limp and mute, accepting their fate. Snapes stood, contemplating the line of girls with his hand on his podgy chin before addressing Hurdon.

'Splendid, splendid, to work then. Here are the syringes, here the goose fat with which we shall ease their passages – a job, I think, best suited to myself.'

Crouched low in the barge, Judith had watched the last of the girls disappear out of sight behind the barn.

'So the cull's in there, you reckon?' Ben Jenkin asked.

153

'Seems so,' Judith answered. 'The fat man's the butler, Sale. The woman I've not seen before.'

'Neither'll be trouble,' Jenkin assured her.

Judith nodded. Her stomach felt weak with excitement and her fingers were trembling.

'Now, or in the darkmans?' Jenkin asked.

She hesitated, watching the house. The girls she had seen had been calm enough, but one or two alarmed squeaks had carried across the mere. Common sense told her to have the barge sail past and up the mere, returning under cover of darkness. Emotion told her to try and help the girls. They might have seemed willing, but she had been willing until the moment Snapes presented her with the chimpanzee. If her own experience was anything to go by their fate would probably be painful, humiliating and terrifying.

'Now,' she said in decision.

Jenkin nodded and Judith signalled to the older bargee, pointing to the little dock beside Snapes's barn.

'Bring her about!' he called.

The boom snapped across, the barge wallowing around until the bow faced the shore at the right point. The sail filled, driving them forward. They slid in quickly towards the dock, the barge cutting through the ruffled water of the mere. Judith and the men kept low, leaving the bargees to their work. As the barge slowed and bumped against the dock Jenkin leaped ashore, the others following. Judith scrambled after them, hindered by her dress, reaching the front of the barn as the door slammed behind the retreating Sale. The big woman she had seen was on the lawn, backing away in alarm as shouts and then screams rang out from within the barn. Ignoring the woman, Judith threw open the door. Inside was chaos, Jenkin grappling with one man, others beyond, and a row of girls hung by their legs, screaming and struggling frantically.

Snapes was there, backing hurriedly with his face set in terror, a thick syringe held in one hand. Another syringe protruded from the quim of one of the girls, who was kicking and struggling in panic even more than the others. The man with Jenkin she recognised as Luke Hurdon, now squaring up, fists raised. Beyond the pair, Michael was struggling with black John, while both Isaac and Simms were fighting to bring down the massive Hastable.

Judith's eyes ran along the girls, looking for Suki. All were white. Snapes had seen her, his fear wrestling with anger. He was shouting, calling for Hurdon, who took no notice as Jenkin drove a double blow in. Jumping back from the fight, Judith ran for the house. She made the door, yelling for Suki as she hurled it open. Inside she stopped, glancing at the chairs and catching sight of the big woman hidden behind the door even as a hand gripped the shoulder of her dress.

'Got you, you little thief!' the woman spat.

'Let go of me!' Judith demanded, striking out at the woman's arm.

The woman held her grip, jerking Judith off balance. She went down, hard on to the floor. A foot pressed to her abdomen, the big woman's weight coming on to her. Grabbing the other leg beneath the woman's skirts, she swung her body around. Her mouth found the coarse texture of the woman's stocking, with soft flesh beneath. She bit, hard, bringing an angry scream and a kick in her midriff. Again she bit and the woman stepped off, kicking at her.

Judith rolled, struggling to rise, but caught her boots in her petticoats. The woman came at her, red-faced with anger. She pushed back, sliding on her bottom across the polished wood of the floor and fumbling in her pocket. Her finger closed on the blackjack she had borrowed from Michael, an irregular lump of lead sewn into leather. The woman stopped at the sight of it, backing as Judith struggled to her feet. Extending one hand, Judith began to swing the blackjack in the other, her eyes locked on the woman's face. For a moment their eyes met, Judith judging her blow, only for the woman to dash for the door.

Immediately Judith ran at the stairs, calling for Suki. The house was silent, with the curses, yells and screaming from outside making it hard to listen. Then came a new sound, an angry chattering. She froze, raw fear welling up in her throat, only to shake her head and force herself to go on. Running, she threw open door after door, calling for Suki. Nobody came, neither in the main corridor, nor in the servants' quarters beneath the beams of the attic. She finished downstairs, still with the curses and yells of the struggling men sounding outside. Suki was nowhere to be found, and at last only one room was left, that which held Lord Furlong.

Judith went to the door, her hand shaking as she took hold of the handle. From within came the chattering, snickering noises of the chimpanzee, angry and puzzled, then the rattle of bars. Her stomach felt weak, and she was filled with the urge to run, remembering their last meeting and his awful, inhuman strength. Fighting down her panic, she threw open the door.

Lord Furlong stood in his cage, hands clutching the bars. His eyes met hers and his lips drew slowly back, exposing long, yellowing teeth. She could only stare, her gaze held by his, until the shaggy black hair at his groin twitched and she saw his cock growing to erection. She screamed and ran, and as she ran, piddle gushed out of her quim from her terror, soaking the inside of her petticoats and leaving a trail on the floor. She went out, onto the lawn, stopping only at the sight of the men, still fighting.

Hurdon was down, his courage and strength no match for Ben Jenkin's experience and raw, crude power. Jenkin stood, face masked with red from a cut to his forehead, knuckles bloody, squaring up to black John. Sale sat against the barn wall, dazed and clutching his head. Isaac was down, while Michael and John Simms stood against Hastable, all three showing the marks of their encounter. Of Snapes there was no sign, nor the big woman Judith had fought. Judith stood, letting her breath come back, watching and fighting for calm, the piddle still trickling down her legs.

Black John turned to glance at her, his eyes going wide in angry recognition. Jenkin struck in, right, then left, and black John went down without a sound. The upright man turned, giving her a bloody grin and stepped towards where Hastable stood. Seeing that he was alone, the cook ran, Michael and Simms chasing. All three vanished around the side of the barn, then Jenkin.

'Leave him!' Judith called. 'Where's Snapes?'

Nobody answered. She walked to the barn, suddenly weary. Sale looked up at her but made no move to stop her, and she stepped over Hurdon's unconscious body to push open the door. The girls hung as before, most with their faces peering in terror from beneath the hems of their skirts, pleading for her help. She began to untie them, twisting the ropes off from the cleats around which each had been wound. One by one they dropped to the floor, to sit struggling with the ties on their ankles and babbling thanks and fearful questions. Knowing full well what her crew

157

were likely to do, Judith told them to run. None hesitated, until as the last scurried for the door Ben Jenkin appeared. The girl screamed and ducked under his arm, dashing for the lane to the sound of his laughter.

'Where's Snapes?' Judith repeated. 'What did you do with Hastable, the cook?'

'Big fat cull? Tied him in the barge,' Jenkin answered. 'Rum douser, that one, and the other swell. You never said about either. Got your friend?'

'No,' Judith answered. 'I need Snapes.'

Jenkin shrugged, looking around the barn. A heap of sacks had been thrown into one dim corner, to which he walked, jerking a handful aside to reveal the cowering form of Sir Joseph Snapes.

'Your cull,' Jenkin said. 'Want me to make him leak?'

'No,' Judith answered, advancing on Snapes. 'Where's Suki, you filthy bastard?'

'Suki? Suki?' Snapes stammered. 'The negro girl? How would I know? Squire Robson had her, last I heard.'

'Lying piece of filth!' Judith spat, kicking out at him. 'Where is she?'

'I swear it!' Snapes answered, pulling himself in among the sacks. 'I've not seen her, not since last year, not since . . .'

'Not since you tried to give me to that damned enschego!' Judith answered and kicked him again.

'A misunderstanding,' Snapes babbled. 'I assure you, only that, nothing more, only that. I thought . . . I thought you would take pleasure in it . . .'

'Bastard!' Judith swore and all the tension and fear of the attack suddenly burst out as she slammed the blackjack down on his head, once, twice, and raising it once more when Jenkin's hand locked on her arm. She stopped, letting the big man draw her back. Snapes slumped unconscious among the sacks.

'He'll not leak like that,' Jenkin remarked.

'No,' Judith admitted. 'Search the outhouses, the grounds too, properly, and the house again. There's the attic, and a cellar even.'

'Right,' Jenkin answered, 'and, that done, the crew'll want to speak on our dust. We'd no reckoning for any fight.'

Judith hardly heard him, turning from Snapes to walk quickly out of the barn. On the lawn Michael and John Simms were helping Isaac to his feet. Michael laughed as he saw Judith's sodden dress, the wet patch at the front making it very obvious what had happened.

'Find the mort,' Jenkin ordered them, 'and be sharp. There's likely to be traps here soon enough.'

Judith hesitated as the men ran for the house and the cluster of buildings beside it. They had been noisy, very noisy, and she had heard nothing that might have come from Suki. As Snapes's estate was so remote, it seemed unlikely she would be kept gagged all the time. Also, Snapes's denials had sounded real, the more so for his obvious terror; while, whatever he had been doing to the fifteen girls, it seemed odd for him not to have included Suki.

Feeling dispirited, she made for the barge. Suki, she reasoned, might be in some outlying building, or even a boat on the mere, but then there would not be enough time to find her. To be certain, the only chance seemed to be to strike a deal with Hastable. The two bargees were turning their vessel, using long poles to swing it end on end. Hastable sat on the decking, his great red face starting out around a piece of dirty cloth knotted for a gag. Judith jumped on board, nodding to the bargees, then to the cook. He glared back.

'Don't think I forget how you helped me escape before,' she said, sinking to the deck in front of him.

'Now, I'll do the same for you, if you just tell me where Suki is?'

Hastable's immediate response was a questioning look, without a trace of any emotion other than puzzlement.

'She's not here, is she?' Judith asked.

Hastable shook his head. Judith slammed her fist on the deck. Taking a knife from the younger of the bargees, she quickly cut the cook's bonds, leaving him to jump to the dock and make a hasty retreat through the reeds.

Later, sat still in the bows of the barge, Judith stared out across the dull grey sea at the dim line which marked the Suffolk coast. They had turned north, sailing until well out of sight of Snapes's mansion, then heading out to sea. She had been recognised, and the accents of the crew were all too plainly London, yet Jenkin had insisted on the ruse and she had been in no mood to argue.

The four men were in the cabin, drinking Madeira and port from Snapes's cellar while Jenkin divided what they had stolen. She knew that there would be a share for her, but felt little interest, with her mind focused on her failure and what might have become of Suki. The search had been thorough, and she had not been there, while Snapes, Hastable and later Sale and black John had all seemed to be telling the truth. Even Jenkin's trick of telling Sale that his master had confessed to Suki's kidnap but died before revealing where she was had failed.

Despite their cuts and bruises, the crew were well pleased with themselves. They had looted the house and cellar, taking what they dared until Ben Jenkin had forced them to leave. Lord Furlong had been left, his bared fangs and furious screams enough to make

160

them cautious. Their sole regret was the village girls. Jenkin's intention had been to lower the ropes until they could kneel on the ground, presenting him and the others with a line of fifteen helpless bottoms. Every quim would have been fucked, every mouth and anus used, a loss which they were none too pleased about. It had been made very plain to Judith that she would be the one to pay for depriving them of their fun. She had expected it anyway, whether they succeeded or not.

Michael appeared, his face red with drink, an open bottle swinging from his hand, a second clutched in his other fist. He was grinning at her as he approached, a dirty leer, but friendly as well. She returned a weak smile.

'Get this inside you,' he drawled, holding out one of the bottles.

Judith took it as he slumped down on the deck beside her. She put it to her mouth, upending it, a strong, raw port, far from ready and full of sediment, but immediately sending a warm flush through her body. Michael leaned close, putting an arm around her shoulder, his eyes fixed unsteadily on her chest.

'We're going to fuck you, you know that, don't you, Judy?' he slurred.

Judith nodded and took another swallow of wine.

'Fuck you up the cunt and fuck you in the arse,' he went on. 'He's a dirty bastard, our Isaac, he is. Likes his feak with lumps in, if you follow. Dirty bastard. Deserves his tail, any roads, the way that fat bastard of a cook laid him clean.'

Judith nodded again, her bottom-hole twingeing at the thought of Isaac's thick, dark cock.

'Ben says we should hue your arse too,' he said, 'good and hard, on account of letting all that tail go wasted. Rum that was, prime rum. Fifteen there was,

161

rum cunt, prime rum cunt, and it's all wasted, you silly, fucking whore . . . Sorry Judy, sorry. You know I care for you. I've wanted you since before you went to that fat bitch Agie. How I wanted to lift that little raggy dress up and fuck that little white arse, an' look at you now, wouldn't spit in the street. Give Michael a feel, Judy.'

He began to grope her breasts, fumbling drunkenly at them through her dress. Judy let him, drinking from her bottle and thinking of the day as he pawed her. One breast was pushed up and out, and he began to suck on her nipple as he groped the other. Judith began to stroke his head as he suckled on her, thinking of hard cocks and the thrill that came from a beaten bottom in an effort to ready herself for what was coming. It had always worked at Mother Agie's, when she was to be punished or given to some particularly perverted client. With half-an-hour of dirty thoughts and slow mastur-bation she knew she could take anything the crew wanted to do to her, more easily still if she was drunk.

When at last they emerged from the little cabin, she emptied the last of the port down her throat, dregs and all. The sun had begun to sink into the west, and the men had their coats pulled tight around them against the light breeze. Judith felt warm, and sleepy, indifferent to the gentle rolling of the barge. They came to stand over her, Ben Jenkin to the front, the others to his sides. Michael rose, unsteadily. Judith looked up, watching the way the big boxer seemed to sway against the sky. Lifting her knees, she pulled up her skirt, exposing her quim.

'I'm yours,' she said. 'Take your pleasure.'

'You are, and we will,' Jenkin answered. 'Arse high, first; you're for a thrashing. Tie her hands, lad.'

'You don't have to,' Judith said, but extended her wrists as the younger of the bargees held out a piece of cord.

He wrapped the cord around them, pulling them across one another. Judith held still as her wrists were lashed together, the cord wound around each several times and tied off, leaving her with no way of releasing herself. Strong hands took her, rolling her over and tugging her dress high up around her waist. Stinging slaps to her thighs made her rise to her knees, while Michael took her bound wrists and held them, forcing her face down on to the deck.

She looked back, watching as thick belts of stained leather were pulled from breeches, all four of them as they arranged themselves so that each would be able to make a good target of her buttocks. In front of her, Michael began to fumble with the flap of his breeches.

Jenkins brought his belt down. Judith squeaked and jumped at the shock, then again as Isaac followed suit. They began to beat her, their belts falling on her naked buttocks, smacking down to make her flesh jump and tingle. At first it was gentle, but it quickly got harder, until she was mewling with the pain and writhing her bottom under the blows. She was pushing her buttocks up as well, hardly aware of what she was doing, her head swimming with drink and the dirty feeling of being so rudely exposed and so well beaten. Michael held firm to her bound hands, keeping her in place as he freed his cock. Shuffling forward, he pressed his genitals to her face.

'Lick it, Judy, you little bitch biter,' he growled.

'Let's whip her 'til he fouls her face!' Simms suggested, to a chorus of happy agreement.

She tried to obey, poking her tongue out to lick his balls, each shock to her bottom jamming her face into his leathery genitals. Her bottom was warming, her quim juicing as her flesh bounced and quivered, smack after smack falling, harder and harder, until she was crying out with the stinging pain and lapping desperately at Michael's cock and scrotum. He inched forwards, parting his legs to press his crotch hard into her face. His hand closed hard in her hair and her head was forced down.

Judith found her tongue against the base of his balls, then his anus. For an instant she held back, only for his grip to tighten in her hair and the slaps on her buttocks to double in force.

'Lick his arse, Judy!' Isaac called. 'Get your tongue in the dirt!'

A belt caught her thighs and she squealed in shock; Michael immediately pressed her open mouth to his anus. With a last, hopeless sob, she kissed it, letting them all see, then began to lick between his buttocks and on the actual hole. The sight was greeted with a chorus of cheers and toasts to her. For a moment the beating stopped, and Judith was left to lick Michael's anus clean until they grew bored of watching and once more began to beat her.

His cock was hard in front of her face. She pulled up, trying to get her mouth to it, but was moved on to his balls. She sucked one into her mouth, then the other, rolling them over her tongue until at last he could stand no more and jerked her head up, stuffing his penis into her open mouth. The others cheered and began to count the blows as they beat her. She began to suck to the rhythm of her beating, suck for smack. Michael's cock jerked and her mouth filled with salty, slimy come. One last time a belt smacked down across her rump and it was over, leaving her panting on the deck with Michael's come dribbling from her lower lip.

Her bottom was burning, a fat, hot ball of girl-flesh behind her, ripe for entry in either sweat-slick, juicy hole. She looked back, expecting to find the men struggling to release their cocks for her. Instead there was the younger bargee, with the others stood back around him. In his hands was the paddle from the shore boat, a six foot length of thick wood with a broad, flat end. Before she could protest it slammed down across her bottom, sending her sprawling into Michael. The crew laughed to see it, calling on the young man to do it again and telling her to get up and take it. Judith stayed down, only for the oar to smack down on her buttocks again, and a third time, leaving her sprawled on the deck, mouth open and panting in her pain.

'Fuck her, lad, fuck her with the oar!' she heard Simms call. 'Right up her cunt!'

Eager hands gripped her body, lifting her and spreading her wide. Her knees were pulled forward, forcing her to stick out her bottom, kicking weakly in their grip as the oar handle pushed against her buttocks, over her anus.

'No!' she gasped. 'No, not up there, no!'

Someone laughed, but the oar went lower, to her quim. Her eyes went round as the tip pressed to her hole. It hurt, but she knew her vagina was going to take it, stretching wide, impossibly full until she was gasping and swearing into Michael's crotch. It was going in, but it hurt so much, and she was shaking her head with pain when she caught Jenkin's voice.

'Don't spoil her, lad, we want that hole.'

Laughter greeted the remark, but the oar was pulled free. As her vagina closed Judith sank down on the deck, relief washing over her. She was exhausted, her buttocks burning, her vagina still wide. With her eyes shut, she lay breathing softly, half aware of sounds behind her, the chink of glass and the pop of a cork.

'Put some up her cunt!' someone called. 'She needs cooling off.'

'Cunt and arse both!' Isaac crowed.

'Put plenty up her feak, it gets 'em drunk!' Simms laughed.

'Arse up, bitch,' Jenkin ordered.

Judith struggled to obey, lifting her bottom and cocking her knees wide to make herself available. She knew she was to have wine put up her, a fresh degradation to amuse them and add to the state she was in. Hands took her thighs, pulling them yet wider. Cold wine splashed into the mouth of her vagina and down over her quim, followed by the touch of cold, smooth glass at the mouth of her hole. It went in, and she heard the bubble of air rise in the bottle as her vagina filled with port. They began to fuck her with the bottle, in and out, port sloshing out of her hole with each push and running down into her dress.

Another bottle touched, to her anus, cold wine filling the dimple until the bottle-mouth plugged her hole. Her ring was greasy with sweat, and it popped open easily, the neck slipping up. Both bottles were in her, pumping, her rectum filling with wine, more spilling down her sex. Already it was going to her head, the alcohol soaking through her thin membranes, softening her pain to make her feel dirty and ready. Michael still had her head in his lap, held by the hair, and she began to nuzzle his cock. Someone laughed as she began to suck it.

'Bitch biter and no mistake,' Jenkin said.

'Cork her arsehole, Ben!' Isaac called. 'Let's see her blow!'

Both bottles withdrew, and Judith struggled to hold in the wine, squeezing her ring shut. Something touched, a long port cork, sliding up her bottom as she let her anus relax. Again she held it, her anus plugged, the pressure in her rectum making her

166

breathing quicken, rising, until suddenly she could hold it no more. She let go. The cork exploded from her anus, the wine gushing after it in a high arch, to splash on the deck to the sound of jeers and clapping from the bed. Judith let it happen, eyes closed in dizzy, ecstatic relief as she let the full contents of her gut spray out behind her, over the deck and into her dress.

As the last of it dribbled down over her quim she opened her eyes and looked back. Her vision was blurred, but she could see the men, some with their breeches down, others with cock hanging from the flaps, erect or nearly so. Ben Jenkin got down behind her, taking his cock and rubbing it in the wet flesh of her quim. Judith sighed, and then it was in her, pushed firmly up her hole until his coarse pubic hair touched in her bottom crease and against her anus. He began to push, fucking her with quick, firm motions.

She let it happen, hardly aware of what was going on as they took turns with her. All the while she sucked on Michael's cock, making it stiffen slowly, only letting it loose when the pumping in her rear became too strong. Jenkins came in her, Simms over her bottom. Isaac buggered her, rammed to the hilt in her anus, again and again until she was dizzy with pleasure and panting into Michael's crotch. He came in her bottom, to be replaced by the young bargee, who took her in her vagina, only to change his mind and finish off in her aching, semen-slick anus.

All the while, since the pain of her beating had changed to a warm, rude glow, she had been wanting to come herself. With come oozing from both her holes and her head full of dirty thoughts, it was too much. Pulling off Michael's cock, she looked up at him.

'Untie me!' she begged. 'Please! You've had yours, you must let me, you must!'

'Five rum coves not enough for you?' Simms asked.

'Filthy bitch!' Isaac added.

'Just let me, please!' Judith begged.

'Untie her. She's earned it,' Jenkin ordered.

Judith found herself babbling thanks as her wrists were unstrapped. Free, she rolled on to her back, presenting them with her spread sex. She pulled her legs high to add her bottom and anus to the show, then reached up, tugging at her bodice until her breasts were both free. The men watched, gloating lust in their faces, amusement too, at what they'd done to her and her wanton reaction.

Lying in the sodden ruins of her dress, Judith began to masturbate. They stood over her, drinking and watching, their cocks hanging from their open breech-flaps. Her pleasure was rising, her orgasm approaching, only for the older bargee to appear, pushing between the other men, his hard cock already in his hand. They made way for him, and he sank down on her, his thick cock probing for her hole. It poked her clitoris, bringing her to the very edge, only to find her hole and slide up. He began to fuck her, grunting, his beard prickling her face and neck. It got faster and faster, his cock jamming deep inside her, until she was gasping and breathless, her legs tight around him, held on the plateau of ecstasy she had reached with her fingers.

At the last second he pulled out, his semen jetting over her pubic hair. She was reaching down even as he got off, her fingers slipping in the mess he had done over her. She pushed it down with her palm, over her quim, feeling the flesh with her fingers, hot and sore, then slimy as her semen-slick hand reached it. Two fingers went up her vagina, the little to her anus, tickling the sodden, gaping ring. It was wide and loose, slimy, pulsing and oozing mess into her petticoats, a delicious feeling as once more she began to rub at herself. Her thumb was on her clitoris, flicking at the tiny bud, bringing her quickly towards orgasm.

She could see them, all six, watching her frig, the cocks which had been put in her hanging out, limp and spent. Isaac was grinning, his ugly face leering down into hers as he took hold of his penis, twitching it out to point at her face.

'Let's piss on her while she frigs it!' he crowed and the urine sprayed from his cock.

Judith opened her mouth; it was impossible to stop herself. Immediately his stream was directed full into it, filling the cavity and bubbling out at the sides, splashing over her face as all six of them burst into uproarious laughter. Michael let go, full across her breasts, then Simms, aiming it into her face and hair so that she was forced to close her eyes. She felt the lad's stream splash on her middle and heard his high laugh. The old man's caught her belly, and last came Ben Jenkin's full between her legs, over her quim and between her buttocks, up her vagina and into her gaping anus, filling both to squirt out again as her muscles locked in orgasm and she was coming. Mouth agape, pee and semen and wine and saliva bubbling from every orifice, she snatched over and over at her quim, slapping herself, smacking at her clitoris, harder and harder, the men's urine spraying out around her hands, trying to put her fingers in every aching hole at once as it all came together in a blinding rush of absolute, perfect ecstasy, only to be ruined as her mind filled with the mad chattering of the chimpanzee.

Seven

Caroline Cunningham smiled at Lewis Stukely, then glanced back along the path. Mrs Aldgrave was a good hundred yards behind them, picking her way carefully among the ferns and rocks which closed in the narrow path to either side. Further back still was Stukely's man, Staddon, carrying the hamper which held all that they would need for the proposed moorland picnic.

Beyond Stukely, the gorge up which they were walking, Tavy Cleave, opened out to a view of fields, woods and distant hills. Beside her the river ran swift and shallow, sparkling in the bright sunlight, in stretches broken by tumbled boulders, in others still and smooth over deep pools. The sides of the gorge climbed steeply to left and right, brilliant green and still glittering from the night's rain, rising to peaks of jagged granite set against blue sky.

'Quite beautiful,' Caroline remarked.

'Indeed,' Stukely answered, 'a beauty to which you yourself add an exquisite touch, bringing it within a finger's breadth of perfection.'

'Only within a finger's breadth?' Caroline asked.

'Indeed,' he answered, 'not quite perfection. For true perfection you would need to be naked.'

Caroline giggled, thinking of the rare occasions they had managed to be alone together long enough

170

to indulge themselves and the way he never seemed to tire of applying his tongue to her body. Each time he had made her come, and then taken his own pleasure in her mouth. Twice more, when time had been short, he had simply held her, her dress lifted, his hand on her quim, rubbing until she came. Quicker still, she had three times been put on her knees and made to suck his cock, swallowing the come. Yet now, with Mrs Aldgrave following determinedly behind, it seemed unlikely they would even have time for that, leaving just the thought of a quick fumble behind one or another of those rocks large enough to conceal them. Yet ahead, the river turned sharply, promising better concealment.

'I would gladly go naked for your edification,' she said. 'When we are married, I shall, here, exactly as you imagine me.'

'What of moormen, shepherds and such?' he answered. 'They might see.'

'I don't care for them a single bit,' she said. 'Why should such low people spoil our pleasure?'

'Why indeed? Could it be, my little one, that the thought of such coarse types seeing your naked beauty excites you?'

Caroline found herself blushing and thinking of her fantasies of being caught by her brother's game-keepers or a gang of miners. She turned so that her bonnet hid her face and Stukely gave a knowing laugh.

'Why wait?' he said. 'You could go naked now.'

'Not at all!' she answered. 'What of Mrs Aldgrave? We might chance a kiss, perhaps, little else.'

'Too quick for my liking,' Stukely answered, 'and not enough. Don't fret, my little one. Do you see these rocks ahead, at the turn?'

'I do.'

'Mrs Aldgrave, I imagine, will have some difficulty in negotiating them. She will have to wait for Staddon to assist her and, as you see, he is some way behind.'

'A kiss then, of the nicest sort.'

'More, my little one. Beyond the turn is Devil's Pool, where we plan to picnic. Beyond that, the ground becomes difficult, certainly too difficult for a lady of Mrs Aldgrave's years.'

'You are a wicked man, Mr Stukely. I do believe you have arranged this all most carefully, simply in order to take advantage of me.'

Stukely laughed, offering his hand as they reached a row of stepping stones placed to help cross a patch of mud. Beyond was the turn, and he helped her over the rocks, climbing to the top and pretending not to be able to hear when Mrs Aldgrave called out to them to wait.

Beyond the turn was an area of flat rock, beyond that marshy ground, which Caroline crossed with her skirts held high and the feeling of mischief building quickly inside her. There was no more path, only narrow tracks made by sheep and moor ponies, which merged and split, then joined again as the gorge narrowed beyond the marsh. They reached a tumble of rock, massive grey granite boulders, fallen from the tor above them, which proved to screen a wide, still pool with a small waterfall at the far end.

'How lovely!' Caroline exclaimed. 'This is quite the most perfect place!'

'Perfect indeed,' Stukely agreed. 'Now, across the pool we can be seen; here, we cannot. So, my little one, off with your clothes.'

Caroline was shivering as she began to disrobe. Stukely watched, seated on a boulder and gently stroking his crotch. His attention made her shake even more, her fingers trembling as she loosened her dress. It fell down as she bent to undo her shoes, to leave her in a tangle of cloth with her breasts bare. She was forced to bend, leaving them hanging heavy from her chest, a view she was sure looked ridiculous. Giggling and blushing, she pulled at the folds of cloth, at last releasing herself to step from her dress.

She looked up, finding Stukely still watching, his hand on his crotch, stroking at a conspicuous lump. He smiled, his fingers going to his belt buckle. Caroline glanced up around the skyline as she started on the drawstrings of her petticoats. Nobody was visible, only sheep, and the long, ragged horizon. It still felt dreadfully exposed, with her breasts bare, then yet more so as her petticoats fell down and she felt the air on the bare flesh of her lower body. She was naked but for stockings, which she untied and peeled down quickly. Stark naked, she found herself feeling utterly, deliciously vulnerable, naked and bare to whatever Stukely chose to do to her, and just possibly with other men watching. His cock was out, a stiff pink pole of flesh protruding from his open breeches. He was holding it, grinning, his other hand in the pocket of his coat.

'Beauty indeed,' he said, 'yet perhaps we may yet improve on God's work. Apply this to your skin.'

He pulled a small jar from his pocket, throwing it onto the soft grass by Caroline's feet. She bent to pick it up, opening it to find a thick grease within.

'Seal oil,' Stukely said, 'it will make your skin glisten most beautifully. Come, I shall watch as you apply it.'

Caroline giggled, digging her fingers into the thick, oily substance to pull out a wad. She put it to her belly, smoothing it over her flesh, watching Stukely as he watched her. It was cool and slippery, a very pleasant sensation, and better still as she smeared it over her breasts and her nipples grew to erection. Stukely was nursing his cock, slowly, clearly in no hurry. For Caroline, her feelings of embarrassment and vulnerability dwindled as she oiled herself, the delicious naughtiness of being bare and pure arousal replacing them.

Increasingly she began to show off, no longer aware of her surroundings save that she was nude in the open air. With the jar on the ground, she made a display of her breasts, cupping both plump, greasy globes and squeezing them with her nipples poking out between her fingers. Stukely was getting more and more excited, his face reddening and both balls and cock in his hands. Caroline turned, presenting him her bottom, which she began to massage, sliding her greasy hands over her big cheeks until both were glossy pink balls of girl-flesh. Her legs followed, bent with her bottom towards him so that he could see her quim and every detail between her cheeks.

Only her back remained, and as she straightened up Stukely stood, still holding his cock as he walked towards her. Caroline giggled, reaching down for the pot. Stukely reached her, grabbing her shoulders. She went down under the pressure, to her knees, squeaking in delighted surprise only to be abruptly shut up as his cock was pushed into her mouth. She began to suck, cradling his balls as she did it and gently teasing her own breasts. He was breathing deeply, looking down at her, watching her oily body as she sucked him.

Caroline stuck her bottom out, improving his view and hoping that he would at last give in and put his cock where she wanted it, up her virgin hole, or at the least in her bottom. Reaching for the pot, she scooped out as much seal oil as she could, smearing it between her buttocks. Stukely groaned at the sight as Caroline's finger found the tight little hole, slipping inside. She began to finger her bottom, thinking how a cock had felt in the same tight hole. Stukely was getting urgent, his hand on her head, trying to push his erection down her throat, as he always did near orgasm.

She pulled back, easing her mouth off his erection. It stood up, proud in front of her and then she was scrambling round, pushing her bottom up, her knees cocked open to make her big cheeks flare, glossy with oil, her anus smeared and loose for his cock. He grunted as he sank down, and then his cock was between her buttocks, rubbing in the oily crease.

'Put it in, Lewis!' Caroline urged. 'Up my bottom, Lewis, please, up my bottom, I beg you!'

He answered with a groan and she felt the round, firm head of cock press to her anus. She sighed as it went in, filled her, the grease squeezing out around her anus as her cavity filled. He began to bugger her, groaning, his hands moving in circles on the oily skin of her buttocks, calling her name and saying how beautiful she was, his balls slapping on her empty quim, her breasts swinging to the motion of her sodomy.

Caroline put her hand back to masturbate, lost in the delightful sensation of having his cock in her greasy back passage. Her quim was slimy with oil, the hole wet and ready, her clitoris a hard, aching nub.

'Your skin, flawless,' Stukely gasped. 'Your bottom, my darling, so fat, so smooth, such flawless beauty, such skin, and to think you've let me, in you, in your little hole, between those fat, fat, smooth, soft cheeks . . .'

He finished with a cry, jamming himself home to knock the breath from Caroline's body. She was rubbing hard, close to orgasm, then coming, thinking of the pose she was in, of the rude things he'd said, of the beauty of her bottom, and of how utterly, shamelessly dirty it was to let men put their cocks up it. Her anus clamped tight on his erection, squeezing out the last of his come into her gut. She was gasping out her pleasure into the grass, biting at it, trying to hold herself, but failing, screaming and screaming, over and over, her whole mind focused on the feel of her clitoris and the cock up her bottom.

Judith Cates allowed herself to be helped down from the horse, then waited as her luggage was unloaded from the travois. It had been a long journey, two days on the post road from London to Exeter and a good part of a third around the north of Dartmoor to Okehampton. There she had managed to find a farmer travelling in the right direction, and had spent an uncomfortable journey perched behind the saddle of his carthorse with her luggage strapped to the old-fashioned travois behind.

The sun was already sinking into the western sky as the man unloaded for her outside the Truscotts' house. Henry and Eloise proved to be on the terrace, drinking sack and admiring the newly filled lake. After a moment's surprise she was greeted enthusiastically and was soon seated with a glass in her hand and the strain of the journey fading slowly under the influence of company and wine.

'So what came of things?' Henry asked. 'Charles said you had hired a crew to search Suki out.'

'A crew yes, searching no. We raided Snapes's place in Suffolk.'

'Raided Snapes! By God, but aren't you the one? I can see London's no place for you then, not if you were recognised. Well, you're welcome here, though don't be surprised if the traps come calling. He'll guess, will Snapes.'

'Most like he will. We left him with a sore head and his house rifled. What am I to do?'

'You shall be my maid,' Eloise answered. 'I shall swear you have not left my side. Who will doubt my word?'

'With Judith's hair?' Henry scoffed. 'I've seen carrots less orange. They'll not be fooled.'

'Many people have red hair,' Eloise objected. 'Myself for one . . .'

'And if Snapes himself comes?' Henry interrupted. 'No, hold on, why should he look at a servant when he's expecting a high-groomed tart, begging your pardon, Judith. Damn but you're right, her hair, a tawdry dress, and if she stays in the kitchens I'll give a guinea she'll not be noticed. We can take a damn high hand with the fellow – better still, play the innocent, let them search the place as they please. What then of Suki?'

'Not a sign. He's not had her, I'm sure of it. We searched the house and grounds. We threatened Snapes and others. He's not a brave man, Snapes, yet he said nothing, admitted to nothing.'

'Damn! Well, it looks like Gould then.'

'As I said from the first,' Eloise put in.

'He's a damn cool head if it is him, that I'll grant,' Henry replied. 'Well, what do we do? We can't just torture the fellow until he leaks, can we?'

'Why should we not?' Eloise asked.

'It's just not done, damn it!' Henry retorted. 'This is England, and we're not quite so damned bloodthirsty!'

'What else, then? You have spoken with him. He gives no hint. You should have Judith's courage.'

'What? Raid him? Damn it, Eloise, I'm a gentleman and a landowner. There'd be hell to pay and, besides, she's not with him. Gurney reckons she was taken up country.'

'We can at the least test him. You must go to Plymouth, where I feel sure another negro is to be had. Bring them here and I shall remark to Gould of how you bought them, from an American perhaps. We shall see how he responds.'

'By setting ruffians on me in all likelihood! A wonderful plan, Eloise!'

'Well, you must act in whatever way seems fit.'

'I intend to,' Henry mumbled, turning away.

'There is a book,' Judith put in quickly. 'You must see it.'

She rummaged in her luggage, pulling out a nearly square book, large, but thin.

'It is?' Henry asked.

'I had it from Snapes,' Judith said, carefully opening the book. 'The man Isaac, one of my crew, found it. It was open on Snapes's table. He's a dirty one, so he took it, but when it came to the choice it fell to me. The prints are from Snapes's expedition, when he brought back Suki and the enschego. Look, here, natives, stark naked, or near so. Again the same, and here, surely that is Suki.'

'Or her spit,' Henry agreed. 'Damn pretty piece, though, ain't she? I say, that posture wasn't struck for scientific interest, and look, here's that damn enschego.'

'*Mon dieu*,' Eloise said softly.

'My God, indeed,' Henry replied. 'Damn peculiar fellow, Snapes.'

He went quiet as Judith turned the next page, remaining so until she closed the book and not speaking again until he had poured each of them a full glass of sack. Judith took a swallow of hers, thinking of Suki and Lord Furlong. Henry drained his glass, blew out his cheeks and then spoke again.

'You recall that fellow Stukely? Well, he's to be married to little Caroline Cunningham. There's an affair tomorrow, which'll be damned frosty with her brother there, and mine too in all likelihood.'

'Yet we must attend,' Eloise put in. 'One must maintain civil relations with those neighbours of quality, especially when they are so few. The Duke could well be present.'

'More likely Lord John,'[12] Henry put in, 'and discussing agricultural progress and reform with my damn brother, most like. It's an evening affair, so we shall visit the periwig makers in Okehampton in the morning. I'll drive you over myself, Judith.'

Joanna paused in the act of fastening her dress at the waist. Outside, the morning sun was sending bright beams of light through the chinks in the shutters. She felt different, her belly swollen. With better food and so much more leisure she had been putting on weight anyway, but most of that had gone to her bust and bottom. Yet her head was fuzzy, and there was an unfamiliar sick feeling in her throat. It had to be the first signs of her pregnancy, about which she had yet to tell Carew.

She bit her lip, wondering how she would broach the subject. Soon it would be obvious, and she had already tried to persuade him of the pleasures and benefits of having children. He had been cold, even hostile, and when she had mentioned their duty to God he had merely laughed.

He was already in the shop, talking to Lewis Stukely, who had come to discuss his book. Tying her dress off and slipping her feet into her shoes, she hastily arranged her hair and went downstairs, curt-sying to Stukely as she joined Carew behind the counter. Neither man acknowledged her.

'I would recommend gilting, sir,' Carew was saying. 'I have somewhere some of those designs created by Mr Roger Payne,[13] of whom you have doubtless heard, rich yet elegant, delicate and of surprising complexity . . .'

'No,' Stukely broke in, 'I think not. A simple border, yes, perhaps a monogram, but the leather itself is too precious to be obscured by overmuch gilt.'

'Quite, quite, I see you are a man of taste, sir. The edges, perhaps, might also be gilted?'

'Yes, indeed. The leather is an unusually dark, rich brown, in view of which, and of the contents of the work, I hope to achieve an exotic effect, decadent even.'

'Ideal for the work, if I may say so sir, ideal. May I suggest then a red gold, formed by the addition of minute traces of copper? It is an extraordinary colour, which should suit your needs admirably. Naturally it comes expensive.'

'Expense is not a consideration. I expect perfection, and it is a fool who seeks perfection at a low price.'

'My philosophy exactly, sir. May I compliment you on your wisdom?'

'Is it possible to see a design?'

'Certainly, sir, certainly. Joanna, the book, come come, quick now, we must not keep the gentleman waiting.'

Joanna hurried to draw the book of gilt patterns from its place in the workshop, returning to place it on the counter, once more curtsying to Stukely. Carew opened it and the two men began to consider designs, leaving Joanna to wait, wishing Stukely had not called until after they had breakfasted. Eventually Stukely left, after a hurried glance at his watch. Retiring to the kitchen, Joanna began to prepare breakfast.

'Mr Stukely is to wed,' Carew informed her as he seated himself at the table. 'His bride will be Miss Caroline Cunningham, sister to Mr Saunder Cunningham, a most estimable gentleman.'

'I have met Miss Caroline,' Joanna answered. 'She is ever such a pretty maid.'

'Do not speak of your betters with such familiarity,' Carew answered her.

Joanna went quiet, feeling suddenly queasy as the smell of eggs and hot fat rose from her frying pan. With a sudden rush of courage she began to speak.

'We've a blessing the same,' she said. 'I . . . I am with child.'

'Indeed?' Carew demanded. 'You are? Can you be sure?'

'Certain sure,' Joanna answered. 'We must have been blessed the day Jane Parrish called, the first occasion.'

Carew said nothing, his brow furrowing.

'Isn't it fine?' Joanna went on. 'A little man to follow you in the shop, or perhaps a maid to marry . . .'

'It is not fine,' Carew broke in, 'not fine at all. How many times have I made it clear that I do not want my house filled up with brats? You are a wilful and disobedient woman, Joanna, nothing more. I have been generous to you – most generous, kind also – and see how you repay me!'

'But, Thomas . . .'

'It is fortunate that I have a call to visit Plymouth, to discuss the binding of a set of works by the poet Milton. I shall find a suitable surgeon, who will do what is necessary, and thus spare my time, if not my money.'

Joanna said nothing. A lump was rising in her throat, the tears welling in her eyes, her whole body shivering with fear and anguish.

181

'Naturally you must reimburse me for the surgeon's fee,' Carew went on. 'I shall find you a place at the tannery, where you shall work each afternoon for perhaps . . .'

Joanna spun, hurling the pan at Carew, and ran, tears streaming down her face, from the house and out into the street.

'An extraordinary difference,' Henry declared to Judith as they left the wigmaker's shop in the main street of Okehampton. 'The fellow is right, it is remarkable how the colour of hair appears to change the lines of a face. Once we've got you shaved and in a servant's dress, I expect I'd walk past you in the street myself, and never the wiser.'

Judith replied by biting her lip.

'Come, my dear,' Henry went on, 'it is not such a terrible thing. Hair grows back, while in any case it can hardly be a greater travail than Brideswell, where you'd likely be shorn anyway.'

Judith gave an absent-minded nod, her gaze drifting out over the moor where Yes Tor rose above the town. Henry took her arm, steering her gently in the direction of the carriage, only to stop as the Reverend Gould appeared around a corner.

'Ah, Mr Gould,' Henry greeted the priest. 'No slaves in this market. I fear you have come upon a wasted errand.'

'I beg your pardon, Mr Truscott?' Gould answered stiffly before giving a restrained bow to Judith. 'Miss Cates, if I remember correctly.'

'No, no,' Henry said quickly, 'er . . . the Demoiselle, er . . . Marie de la Tour Romain, the sister of my dear wife, don't you know? Fresh from France, to spare her head.'[14]

'France?' Gould replied. '*Ma Demoiselle, vous êtes . . .*'

He launched into a spate of fluent French, at which Judith looked completely baffled. Realising that he had dug himself into a hole, Henry looked around, frantically seeking a reason to leave Gould quickly. Nothing was obvious, until he realised that a young woman walking briskly towards them was Joanna Pearse. A moment later he also realised that she was in a flood of tears.

'Good God!' he exclaimed. 'That is, I mean to say, look here, Mr Gould, Joanna Pearse, in some distress.'

Gould turned sharply. Joanna had seen them, and was going to turn away, but Gould stepped forwards, blocking her path, Henry following.

'Whatever is the matter, my dear?' Henry asked.

Joanna stopped, sobbing too hard to speak. Judith stepped close, putting an arm about the girl's shoulders. Henry waited, throwing a puzzled look to Gould and getting a frown in return.

'My husband, he's . . .' Joanna finally began, only to burst into tears again, heavier than before.

'Mr Carew is not your husband,' Gould stated. 'This, Mr Truscott, is the sorry end to a disgraceful and unchristian tale! Doubtless Carew, tiring of poor Joanna, and with neither morals nor the obligations they bring, has thrown her into the street!'

'Looks like enough,' Henry admitted.

'We have failed in our responsibility, both you and I,' Gould continued, 'yet in bringing us together in this street at this time, the Lord our God has provided us with one last opportunity to make good.'

'Quite, absolutely. Look, er . . . ah yes. You must speak to this Carew fellow, Mr Gould, in your capacity as a Minister of God. Speak most sternly, and impress his sin upon him. I, meanwhile, shall take poor Joanna back to my estate. Should it prove necessary we shall provide work for her as a maid.'

'A most Christian attitude, Mr Truscott. Well spoken. I shall speak to Carew this moment.'

'Why bother?' Henry remarked as Gould strode away out of earshot. 'Send a couple of bullies to thrash the fellow instead. More your style, I should have thought.'

In front of Judith was a tall, gilt-framed mirror, in which she could see the upper part of her body. A heavy cloth obscured everything below her neck, leaving her head the only part of her clearly visible. Her hair was loose, pulled out of its usual elaborate style to hang down behind her. Next to her, Henry was also visible in the mirror, honing a scissor blade on a razor strop.

She waited, feeling numb, for her hair to be cut off. Henry was nonchalant, infuriatingly so, as if what he was doing was no more than routine, a simple task of no great significance. To her it was very significant indeed.

With the scissors ready, he took her hair in one hand, bunching up as much as possible and pulling it out so that she could feel the tension against her scalp. She screwed up her eyes. The blades touched, she heard the crunch of cut hair, and felt the tension go as it was cropped away, utter humiliation welling up inside her. She opened her eyes, slowly. Henry was holding up the hank of hair, nearly three feet of soft red curls.

'I doubt we shall have a deal to pay for the periwig,' he remarked, 'not with this for an exchange.'

Judith said nothing, but looked at herself in the mirror. All that remained of her glorious locks was a spiky halo of carrot-coloured frizz, sticking up at every angle. Henry tied the hair into a thick knot and put it carefully to one side. He went to the pail that stood on a table beside them, rolling up his sleeves before taking a lump of soap and dipping it into the water. Judith sat still, watching miserably as Henry worked the soap into a lather. When he was ready she closed her eyes tight as his hands found her scalp, working the soap well in across the full area of her head.

It stopped, and again he went to the table. Whistling cheerfully to himself, he began to work the razor back and forth along the strop, Judith listening to the horrible sound with her eyes closed hard. It stopped. His hand touched her hair, taking a clump of it. The razor touched, scraping and she felt the first of her hair go.

Henry continued to whistle, working casually and methodically, shaving upwards from her forehead, bit by bit, until he stopped to wash the blade. Cautiously, Judith opened an eye. In the mirror she looked more ridiculous than ever, with the front of her head bald to give her an absurdly high forehead. She felt a sob rising in her throat but choked it down, once more closing her eyes as Henry withdrew the blade from the water. Again the razor was put to her skin.

Her sense of humiliation built as she was shaved, growing worse and worse until she was sure she would cry. Henry was pulling up her locks one by one, applying the blade and scraping away her hair, still whistling. Eventually she opened her eyes and watched herself, her mouth set in a sorry pout as the bald area grew slowly, moving back from her forehead, then to one side.

Slowly her hair was scraped away, Judith unable to stop herself watching as she was shorn. One side went, then the other, the back next, leaving her with just a ludicrous topknot of wet, spiky hair. Again

Henry leaned close, taking a firm hold on her head. The razor came down, scraping once, twice, before being washed, then twice more and it was gone, the last piece, which was the worst.

She was bald. Every trace of hair was gone, leaving her pate shiny and bare, still covered in soapsuds and stray strands. Taking a cloth, Henry washed her head, then stood back, nodding as he admired his work. Judith gave back a resigned smile, although she was close to tears.

'Look at me,' she said. 'Who will want me now?'

'Do not be so despondent,' he answered her. 'Many women wear periwigs, many indeed of the greatest.'

'It was my glory,' Judith answered, 'the thing which set me apart.'

'And it shall be again,' Henry assured her, 'in no time. For the moment . . .'

'For the moment I am hideous,' Judith broke in.

'Not at all,' he answered. 'You are still beautiful, Judith, bald or otherwise. I say that without side, no side at all.'

She sighed.

'In fact,' Henry went on, 'just being so close is bringing me a familiar stiffness.'

'Yes,' she said, 'no doubt. Your cock grows hard from the pleasure my shame brings you. Do not dissemble, Henry Truscott, I know you too well.'

'Nonsense,' Henry answered, 'it is the scent of you, the feel of your body as we press together that excites me – everything about you.'

'It is a woman's shame,' she insisted, 'as when you strip poor Eloise's bottom for spanking.'

'Perhaps,' he admitted, 'in part at least, but do you not think the scent and sight of Eloise arouses me also?'

'No doubt.'

'Then the same is true of you, bald or not . . .'

'What would you do, Henry, were I to offer to pleasure you at this moment?' she demanded.

'Well . . .'

'I will tell you what you would do, Henry. You would come on my bald head and laugh as you rubbed your seed into my skin.'

'No such thought ever occurred to me! Not for a minute! What an idea, an absurdity!'

'An absurdity, you say? There was a girl at Mother Agie's, Rebecca, a pretty little piece with dark hair to the small of her back. A man took a fancy to her. A guinea he paid, one whole guinea, to shave her head. He did it as we other girls watched. When she was stark bald he had me take him in hand and pull him over her pate, then laughed to see it as it ran down her hairless skin.'

'No accounting for tastes.'

'It was so shameful. She was crying, and he loved it all the more for that. When he was done she ran to her room and I followed, but was detained by another man, on the stair. When I got to Rebecca she was seated in front of her mirror, still crying, but with her dress high and her thighs apart, toying with her cunt.'

'As I say, no accounting for taste.'

'For the sake of God, will you just do it, Henry? I can see you are aroused, and feel it also.'

She reached out, touching the bulge in his breeches. Henry shrugged, quickly working loose the flap as she stroked, until his cock sprang out, already close to erection. Judith bent down and took it in her mouth, sucking firmly until it grew hard. Drawing back, she bowed her head, closing her eyes in shame as Henry began to jerk at her erection.

His breathing came quicker; he began to moan, then grunted and she felt warm semen splashed across her newly shaven head. He kept jerking, three times ejaculating on her, while the come ran down, thick and sticky over her bald skin as she tugged up her dress to masturbate.

Henry chose a glass from the tray being held out to him, sipped and swallowed. The claret flowed down his throat without noticeable effect and he took another swallow. Looking around the lawn of Lewis Stukely's house, he tried to decide which group of his fellow guests would be least tedious.

None appealed. Stukely himself was talking earnestly to Lord John Russell and Henry's brother Stephen. Occasional snatches of audible conversation revealed that the topic was improvements in agricultural practise on the Bedford Estate, a subject Henry preferred to avoid. Undoubtedly they would attempt to persuade him to implement the same changes on his own land, a process which had been known to end in riots.

Saunder Cunningham, Caroline's brother, had not spoken to him since the establishment of Wheal Purity on land bought from the Cunninghams – or tricked out of them, to Saunder's way of thinking. Attempting to join him and the two other Cornish landowners to whom he was speaking was hardly a cheering prospect.

Eloise was chattering excitely to Caroline and May Cunningham, with Mrs Aldgrave standing by in an attitude of sober introspection. Various men and women were also present, few of whom he knew well and none of whose company appealed to him. The Reverend Gould was also present, nodding politely as he listened to a fellow priest Henry did not recognise. Deciding that he preferred his own company, he took another sip of claret, pretending to admire the great sweep of Dartmoor beyond Stukely's house.

He had been drinking steadily since arriving. Stukely's taste in claret at least was impeccable, serving only the Latour of the excellent 1784 vintage. So far some three bottles of it had gone to soothe his boredom, although he had lost count of the number of glasses he had drunk.

Another bottle followed, this time taken from the table as he at last gave in and joined his brother and Russell. His attempts to steer the conversation away from agriculture and land management only succeeded in bringing it to politics, then to the war with France. Finally Henry excused himself in exasperation, turning to watch the sun set over distant Bodmin Moor.

At the edges of the lawn Stukely's servants were busy lighting oil lamps, which quickly cast the area into a jumble of long, flickering shadows as the light faded from the sky. Henry glanced around, admiring the swell of Caroline Cunningham's bosom and the curve of May's hip. Eloise was beside them, in profile to Henry, and he let his eyes wander over her face and chest, only to switch back to Caroline, who seemed to be in some discomfort.

Henry smiled, even as Caroline bobbed curtsies to May and Eloise. He watched as she made for the house, disappearing behind the system of formal hedges which led down to the lawn. A glance showed that nobody was paying attention to him, and he followed, waiting in the shade of a hedge until Caroline emerged from the house. She jumped as he stepped from the shadows, putting a hand to her mouth.

'Mr Truscott,' she said, 'you quite startled me.'

'I do apologise,' he replied. 'I was keen to see you alone.'

'And now you may,' she said as he leaned close to her face.

'I need to have you,' he whispered.

'Not now!' she hissed. 'Henry, this is neither the place nor the time. This affair is to celebrate my betrothal!'

'Damn that, when will we have another chance?'

'Often, I am sure. We shall be neighbours.'

'Be that as it may, I want you now!'

'But where, and how? Should we leave the party, someone is sure to see!'

'Quickly, then, in here, between the hedges. They'll think you still on the pot.'

'Henry!'

He pulled her close, drawing her into the narrow gap between two hedges. She resisted, briefly, then went with the pressure, giggling excitedly. He laid her down on the grass, where the light from the torches above the door reached them. Her face was flushed with excitement, red in the dim torchlight, her eyes wide and round, her lips slightly parted. With a last hurried glance through the shielding bush, he joined her.

Even as he took her in his arms her hand was fumbling with his breeches flap. It came open and she burrowed, pulling out his cock to tug at it with frantic energy. Henry was kissing her, his lust rising fast as his cock hardened in her hand. He began to paw her, feeling her breasts and bottom through her dress and trying to get at the soft, plump flesh beneath. His cock was aching by the time he got her skirts up, his fingers sinking into the warm flesh of her quim to rub at her clitoris.

'What's it to be?' he growled. 'Mouth or arse?'

'You cannot possibly, the one is certain to ruin my face, and as for the other!' Caroline stammered. 'Kiss me there, quickly!'

Henry grunted, shifting down until his face came to Caroline's quim. He took his cock in her own hand as she spread her thighs, then buried his face between them, licking at the moist, salty flesh. She moaned, aloud, and gasped as he slid a hand under her bottom and began to tickle her between her buttocks with his thumb. His cock felt fit to burst, and when his thumb touched her anus to find it slimy with her own juices it was too much. Climbing up between her thighs to mount her, he pushed in his aching cock, probing for her bottom-hole.

'What are you about?' she demanded.

'I aim to bugger you, my sweet,' he grunted.

'Henry, no! How will you get in?' she squealed as his cock pressed in between the soft meat of her buttocks. 'No, Henry, not that!'

Despite her words, her legs had come up, allowing his cock to slip deeper in, nudging the soft, wet flesh between her legs. He was close to orgasm, just from the feel of her in his arms and the touch of his erection on her flesh. He pushed, desperate to get in before it all became too much and he wasted his semen over her crotch. Pushing his penis in, he felt the hole, tight but wet. Caroline gasped as he pushed, then cried out in pain. Henry mumbled an apology, but pushed his cock in, feeling the constriction of her ring move along his shaft as he buried it inside her.

'Ow!' she squeaked. 'Henry! Henry, you've broken me! You've . . .'

She finished with a sob. His cock felt warm and wet, wetter even than it should have done. Dimly, Henry became aware that he was not in her anus but her vagina, and that what he could feel was her virgin blood. The tight constriction had not been her poorly lubricated ring but the mouth of her vagina, her pain not sudden buggery but the tearing of her hymen.

'Damn!' he swore. 'Sorry, girl . . .'

It was too good, the tightness of her hole and the knowledge that he had just taken her virginity sending him right to the edge of orgasm. He was pushing hard, Caroline squealing and grunting beneath him, his cock a burning, agonised rod before a wave of ecstasy hit him, blotting out everything else.

'Henry! Henry! You've done it in me!' Caroline sobbed. 'You've spoiled me, and I had tried so hard not to!'

Henry rolled off her, his eyes closed. His head was swimming with drink, satisfaction warring with guilt over what he'd done. It was impossible not to grin, even as he was telling himself that it was an accident and trying to think of excuses Caroline might use to Stukely. Next to him, Caroline moaned, and Henry opened his eyes to find that she was masturbating.

He watched in drunken satisfaction, smiling at her eagerness and arousal. She was patting her sex and stroking her breasts, sighing with pleasure, her eyes tight shut. Her legs were cocked wide, her quim spread to the torchlight. On impulse he swung his body round, until he could see between her legs. Caroline took no notice, lost in pleasure. Henry watched, fascinated as her quim started to pulse and her bottom-cheeks to clench, along with the muscles of her thighs. Fluid was dribbling from her hole, his semen and her own blood, red and black in the torchlight. As her vagina opened in climax he glimpsed her hymen, torn and ragged, before the hole squeezed tight and she cried out in ecstasy, calling his name and then calling him a bastard.

Henry moved back, grinning, then jumped up at a startled gasp from behind him. He turned, bringing up his fists at the sight of a figure in black silhouette against the red light of the torches. The figure vanished, leaving Henry to scramble up, just in time to recognise the horrified features of Mrs Aldgrave as the light briefly caught her face.

Eight

Henry Truscott kicked the bollard, cursing. The *Indies Wildling* was pulling from the dock, her men busy on deck, including the two black men Henry had attempted to hire. Having eventually succumbed to the combined arguments of Eloise and Judith, he had spent the day in Plymouth. As the women had pointed out, on this occasion he could prepare, making sure that he was armed and with Todd Gurney at all times, perhaps a couple of miners as well.

Unfortunately hiring a black man had proved harder than he had hoped. He had found only two, both sailors on the *Indies Wildling*, and despite his best efforts to bribe the boatswain, he had failed to secure the services of either. His failure was frustrating, and all the more so for the constant tension which came from expecting to be called out by Lewis Stukely at any moment. Mrs Aldgrave was sure to report the incident with Caroline to Saunder Cunningham, who would jump at any chance of damaging Henry. Therefore the story was certain to get back to Stukely, who would have no honourable choice but to demand that Henry meet him in a duel. The only consolation was that as the challenged party he would have choice of weapons, and that he knew

Stukely was neither skilled nor experienced with a sword.

Turning his back on the sea, he walked quickly to the block of tall houses and narrow streets that stood directly behind the waterfront. In one, Basket Ope, was a brothel he occasionally frequented, which seemed to be the ideal place in which to consider his next move.

The madam greeted him enthusiastically, calling for claret and a cigar while she marshalled the girls. Henry had intended to decline, except perhaps to have one or another of his favourites serve him while he thought. With a row of girls walking out in front of him his resolve quickly weakened, then snapped entirely as the last appeared from the back room.

She wore a white corset, embroidered in blue, also stockings tied at the knee with blue ribbons, nothing more. Her breasts were bare, her thighs also, both plump, the flesh bulging gently from the constriction of her garments. None of this was what attracted Henry, rather the fact that she was black.

In colour, her skin was a rich olive, far paler than Suki's, but undoubtedly dark, giving her the same exotic air, as did her full lips, huge dark eyes and glossy black hair. Thick black curls hid the chubby swell of her pubic mound, with a hint of pink flesh just visible.

As she passed she threw him a coquettish look, turning to wiggle her bottom, almost in his face. Her rear was as fine as the rest of her, firm, meaty cheeks well tucked under, quivering as she walked. He caught her scent, deeply feminine and again exotic, similar to Suki's.

'A new tail in the cab, Mary?' Henry asked the madam, nodding to the black woman.

'Sally, Mr Henry, sir,' Mary replied proudly. 'Not new, no. My own daughter, from entertaining a negro gentleman back in my working days. Ever so willing, and as clean as I've taught her myself.'

'A handsome daughter from a handsome mother,' Henry answered. 'Damn handsome. How d'you do, Sally?'

The girl giggled and curtsied, holding out the lace that fringed her corset. Henry felt his cock stiffen in his breeches.

'Then if you'll be kind enough to provide a room, Mary,' he said, 'I shall endeavour to do your charming daughter justice. Have some claret sent up, the best you have, with two goblets.'

'On the instant, Mr Henry,' Mary replied, beaming proudly before clapping her hands to drive the other girls back into the rear room.

Henry extended his arm to Sally, who took it, her eyes glittering with mischief as they exchanged glances. He led her to the stairs, and up, following Mary's wobbling bottom to the landing. Inside the room, Sally composed herself on the bed, face down, her chin in her hands, watching Henry as he began to undress.

'I dare say you'd care to earn some extra money?' Henry asked, tugging off a boot.

'Money's Mama's bag,' Sally answered. 'What's your favour? My behind, I think. I saw you stare.'

'Your delightful behind could well come into matters,' Henry admitted, 'especially if you don't mind a slap or two across it. '

'I don't care to be whipped, but Mama'll send for a rope's end at a penny a stroke. You may spank me like a brat if it would amuse you.'

'It might very well, but for the work, I was thinking more on the lines of a few days' hire, up on my estate.'

'Mama does day rates,' Sally said, shrugging. 'My, you are in a hurry.'

Henry had pushed his breeches down and off, turning to reveal his erect cock sticking up from between the edges of his shirt front. Sally reached out as he sat down, taking his cock and moving to sit beside him. He put an arm around her back as she began to masturbate him, watching the white flesh of his cock bob in her dark hand. Henry waited until she had relaxed into the rhythm of wanking him.

'Maybe not such a hurry,' he remarked casually.

With a single hard tug he threw her down across his knee. She went over, squealing with surprise, then shock as his hand smacked down on her bare black bottom. He laughed, catching one flailing arm and pulling it smartly into the small of her back, then setting to work to spank her.

'How's this for the way to treat a brat?' he asked as her bottom began to bounce beneath his palm.

Sally didn't answer. She was squeaking, yelping with the smacks but giggling too, her legs kicking and her bottom jiggling to her playful struggles. Cupping his hand, Henry laid in, delighting in the loud smacks of palm on buttocks almost as much as the soft, female texture of her bottom and her excited squeals. She was sticking her bottom up, her buttocks parting, showing the brown star-shape of her anus and the plump, pouted lips of her quim. The smell of her arousal was getting quickly stronger, while her breasts were bouncing and slapping on his thigh, all adding to the straining feeling of his erection, which was pressed against her corset as he beat her.

She was squealing crazily, and panting, but he kept it up, spanking merrily away to the rhythm of her kicking legs and dancing buttocks. Only when he was sure he would come just from the friction of his cock on her corset did he stop, pushing her to the ground and spreading his thighs. She needed no invitation, rising immediately to kneel at his feet and suck eagerly on his cock. He could see her bottom, the dark skin flushed a rich, deep red, her back dipped to keep the chubby cheeks flared and the scent of her sex strong in the air.

Henry could wait no longer. Gripping her beneath the arms, he pulled her up, on top of him on the bed. She climbed on without hesitation, lowering her wet quim on to his erection. It went in easily, sliding up her open passage, and Henry laughed to see how quickly the spanking had made her juice. She began to bounce on her cock, all the while rubbing her crotch against him, wriggling and squirming with her eyes shut tight and one plump breast cupped in each hand. Knowing she was going to come, Henry let her do it, admiring her jiggling breasts and her pretty face, set in ecstasy as she brought herself off.

Only when she began to slump forwards in blissful satisfaction did he act. Rolling her off, he turned her, bottom up. She lifted it, obliging but slow, almost sleepy. Henry got his knees between hers, pushing them apart as she lifted her bottom, the skin still flushed dark from the spanking. Her quim was gaping, wet with juice, with more smeared down between her buttocks.

Henry put his cock to her and slid it up, taking hold of her by the hips as he began to fuck her. She responded with a soft moaning sound, burying her face in the bed. He kept pushing, his eyes locked on the swell of her bottom, dark skin smacked red beneath a fringe of white lace. His head was full of her scent, rich and musky, his hands locked in the soft flesh of her hips, his cock buried deep in her tight, slippery hole.

He was going to come, unable to hold back. Whipping his cock from her quim, he pushed it to her anus, spreading the moist, sticky hole wide as she gave a startled squeak. For a moment his cock was in her bottom-hole, the pale flesh of his knob ringed by the brown of her sphincter. Then he had come, pulling back, filling her anus with semen. He was jerking frantically at his cock as the little pink hole filled with spurt after spurt of thick white fluid, until it began to close, his come trickling out down onto her quim.

Sally got up, quickly douching herself at a stand in one corner. He sank down on the bed, happy and satisfied, lying still until a discreet knock on the door announced the arrival of the claret.

Judith stared back at her reflection. Henry had been right. In the black wig she could hardly recognise herself. It altered the lines of her face, the colour also, making her seem paler and thinner. The plain blue maid's dress added an extra touch, and if the girl staring back from the mirror seemed plain and rather timid, then it was unlikely that even Snapes would spot her for the flame-haired and vivacious woman he thought of as Judith Cates.

'The ruse is certain to succeed,' Eloise remarked from behind her. 'Why, I would hardly know you myself.'

'Nor I,' Judith admitted.

'Naturally,' Eloise continued, 'you must learn to behave as a maid.'

'Naturally,' Judith agreed, 'but it is no great matter, surely. Should Snapes or some agent of his appear, then I will address you as ma'am and do as you say.'

'Yet what if he should arrive while you are seated with us on the terrace?'

'Clearly I must remain ready.'

'Very true. You might, indeed, derive benefit from a little practice.'

'If you wish to beat me, Eloise, you need only ask. Unfortunately my behind is still a little sore from the attentions of my crew. They belted me, and used an oar, which is truly far too heavy an implement with which to beat a woman.'

'So I should imagine. Up with your dress then, maid. Let me see what they have done to you.'

Judith lifted her skirts at the back, looking over her shoulder as she put her bottom on show to Eloise. It was visible in the mirror too, sideways on, the skin still colourful with bruising.

'In due time,' Eloise remarked, 'I will beat you. For now, the day is hot, and there will be little to do until Henry returns with his negro. Have you ever enjoyed a negro, Judith? A man, I mean, not Suki.'

'Twice,' Judith admitted, dropping her dress.

'Is it true that their pegos are of superlative size?'

'I could not say, on so little acquaintance. Both seemed large at first, frighteningly so in the one case, yet they grew little with arousal.'

'A shame.'

'In other cases it may be different. Men vary remarkably in this matter. Do you hope to experiment?'

'You may be certain that Henry will wish to put me to his negro. It is best to take pleasure in the experience. Tell me about yours, both of them.'

Judith laughed.

'One of the bullies at Mother Agie's was a Lascar,' she began, 'but that was after my time. In any case they are no different from other men. Nor, in truth, are negroes.'

'Oh,' Eloise spoke, sounding disappointed.

'Save for the smell of their skin,' Judith went on. 'Which is like Suki's, yet masculine.'

'Their skin is difference enough,' Eloise said. 'It would be sensual, arousing.'

'The first,' Judith said, 'was servant to a gentleman from the Americas. Like many men, his pleasure was in watching, and in particular in watching girls with his negro servant. With my red hair and pale skin I was his choice.'

'He merely watched?'

'That, and had me take him in my mouth when the servant was done. I suspect his true pleasure lay in my humiliation.'

'That is often the way with men.'

'This is true, yet in this case it did not succeed. To him, doubtless, the status and colour of the man with me was important. To me it made no difference. Oh, I begged and pleaded not to be made to do it. I even cried. Mother Agie bought me six pennyworth of ribands for my performance.'

Eloise laughed.

'The second,' Judith said, 'was humiliating, though not for reason of the colour of his skin. It was a punishment, with lots drawn for who might have me. The winner was a negro, a tall man, very straight, with a proud face. He was off a ship, I think. He won the lot and was given two quart pots of watered ale by Mother Agie. I was made to strip, and kneel at the centre of the floor, with all around, watching. First the man beat me, a dozen cuts of a switch, which he enjoyed hugely. A pot was then brought out, over which I hung my head, with my hair hung down inside. The negro piddled on my head, a full two quarts worth, which I was made to drink, before them all. When he was done he took me upstairs, for the free use of me until morning.'

As Judith had spoken, Eloise had sat back on the stool she used while having her hair arranged. Her skirts had come up, then her petticoats, showing the plump mound of her sex. Judith understood, falling to her knees and putting her face straight to Eloise's quim. She kissed, her puckered lips pushing in among the ginger curls to find the soft flesh. Eloise sighed, and Judith began to use her tongue, licking very gently up and down the groove of Eloise's sex.

'Take off the wig,' Eloise said.

'You want me bald?' Judith asked, pulling back. 'You want me bald as I kiss you?'

'I have no wish to ruin the wig,' Eloise replied, rucking her skirts and petticoats further back and sliding forward until her quim was clear of the edge of the stool.

'In the pot?' Judith asked, swallowing.

'Please,' Eloise answered.

Judith was shivering as she turned, reaching in under the bed to pull out the big, china chamberpot. Eloise was plainly aroused, now stroking her quim as Judith removed the wig and put it aside. Kneeling, she went down, between Eloise's knees, her face over the bowl of the potty. Eloise sighed and Judith closed her eyes. Immediately she felt it, a warm drop, then the patter of liquid on her bare skin as Eloise began to urinate over Judith's bald head.

She could hear Eloise's breathing, fast and passionate. The pee was running down around her face, splashing on the dome of her head to trickle onto her neck and around her ears, dripping from her eyes, nose and lips. She poked out her tongue, tasting it, then opened her mouth to lick her lips. Her eyes were tight shut, but she could hear the piddle running from her face into the potty beneath, first tinkling, then splashing as the level rose.

As the stream of piddle died, Judith was left kneeling, her head soaked with urine, which dripped slowly from her face. Eloise's foot settled on Judith's neck, pushing her head down. Judith went, listening to the wet, fleshy sound she knew was Eloise playing with herself. Her face was pushed down, the pressure stopping for a second with her nose just immersed in the piddle, then reapplied, pushing her face firmly into the pee pot. Judith's nose filled with piddle, then her mouth as she opened it, sucking it up to the sound of Eloise's laughter.

Judith could hear Eloise masturbating, and as she drank the pee her hands went back to her own quim, scrabbling in among her skirts until she too could touch herself. Eloise was already coming as Judith started, moaning and pushing down to keep Judith's face well immersed in the piddle. As Judith's own pleasure rose her control started to go, blowing bubbles in the pee, then starting to choke on it as Eloise cried out in climax. Judith's head was kept down, her nose and mouth under the surface, gagging in the piddle as she tried to concentrate on her sex. It was impossible, until Eloise's foot at last came off her neck and she was free to lift her head. She came up, piddle running from her mouth and nose, coughing and spluttering as she rubbed at her clitoris. Eloise laughed at the sight and at that Judith came, dipping her face once more in the hot, acrid urine, drinking and swallowing, to let it run from her mouth once more as she climaxed.

Henry paused, pretending to study the inscription on a gravestone. Behind him, the congregation was filing out of the village church, in twos and threes, many pausing to speak briefly to the Reverend Gould. The service had been much as normal, but considerably more interesting for Henry as he had followed Gould's eyes, flicking, time and again to the rear of the church where Sally sat among the other house-hold servants.

Now, waiting for the church to clear, he was increasingly confident that it was Gould who was responsible for Suki's kidnap. With certainty came anger and resentment, and with them a rising bravado. Eventually the last of his fellow parishioners had left, save for Eloise and the heavily disguised Judith, who were talking together with the maids behind them. Henry walked back to Gould, smiling broadly.

'Ah, yes, Mr Gould,' he began. 'I was hoping for a word in private.'

'Certainly, Mr Truscott.'

'This matter of Joanna Pearse. I trust you left old Carew properly chastened?'

'I spoke to him, yes, briefly. He was in something of a rage.'

'Oh, yes?'

'Joanna, it seems, did not leave peaceably.'

'Ah, right. Full of spirit, that girl, when the mood takes her.'

'Yes, indeed, the main thrust of my conversation was to warn him that should he attempt to bring a prosecution, I would stand witness to his poor character.'

'As would I, naturally. Now, Joanna is settling in well with us, and I'm sure that you will agree that it would be both unwise and unchristian to oblige her to return to Pearse, who is a most uncouth fellow.'

'Quite so, Mr Truscott, quite so, so long as she is not living in sin.'

'Far from it. She is in the best of care, I assure you,' Henry said, nodding in the direction of the lich-gate, where Joanna was standing meekly behind Eloise, Sally beside her. 'Have you seen my wife's new maid? Pretty girl, ain't she?'

'Most fetching,' Gould replied cautiously.

'Fine maid too,' Henry went on. 'I had her from the skipper of a merchantman in on the Jamaica run with a cargo of coffee and rum. She's from Cuba originally, so he says. Cost a middling amount.'

'She is a slave?' Gould demanded. 'You purchased her, with money?'

'Ten guineas,' Henry answered. 'Damn good value when you think about it. After all, I need only feed and clothe her, which is no great expense, and then there are the additional benefits, if you follow my meaning.'

Gould answered with a wordless nod, his eyes wide with shock and possibly jealousy.

'Fancies, they call 'em,' Henry went on. 'Purpose-bred, so I'm told, for brothels in Havana and suchlike places. Maybe the truth.'

The priest was staring, pop-eyed, his head moving between Henry and Sally. Henry tried not to chuckle, thinking of Sally in her corset and stockings rather than the demure dress of blue wool she now wore, and wondering if Gould could have stared any harder.

'She is . . . she is not a Christian?' he finally asked.

'Oh, no,' Henry answered. 'Not a bit of it. Her head's full of some spirit business they have in the Indies. I've tried, of course, but there's no talking sense to her. Not really my strength, if the truth be told, proselytising and such.'

'I . . . er . . .' Gould stammered. 'That is to say, perhaps, er . . . possibly, she might benefit from a period of, er . . . tuition? She speaks English, I trust?'

'Better than many,' Henry answered. 'Tuition, eh? Well, I don't know . . .'

'If it is a question of propriety,' Gould broke in. 'Then I may assure you . . .'

'No, no,' Henry answered, 'more a matter of whether my wife can spare her. We have Joanna, naturally, but still ... Perhaps if you would excuse me a moment?'

Gould nodded and Henry stepped quickly away, trying to decide what to do as he crossed to Eloise and the other women.

'Fellow's damn interested,' he stated as he reached them. 'He swallowed the slave business, pips and all. Wants to give you Christian tuition, Sally, if you please.'

'I have some experience with "tuition" from parsons and such,' Sally said archly.

'I dare say,' Henry answered, 'but I doubt that's what Gould has in mind.'

'She must not go,' Judith put in.

'Naturally not,' Henry answered.

'To the contrary,' Eloise put in. 'The proposal is ideal. If Mr Gould imagines that we are so foolish as to allow him to take her so easily, then it is to our advantage. Send her, Henry. You yourself, and your man Gurney and others may wait until his men arrive.'

With only the skeleton Sunday crew minding Wheal Purity, Todd Gurney had taken the opportunity to relax, drinking beer on the tiny lawn in front of his cottage with his wife Natalie and Peggy Wray, the book-keeper. Of the three engines installed, only the one that kept the mine pumped free of water was working, its steady, slow thumping audible from the cottage, as always.

At the approach of Henry, riding towards him among the spoil heaps, he simply raised his beer pot in salute. Henry dismounted, exchanged greetings and drew himself a beer from the cask. Todd watched, sensing the tension in Henry despite his attempt at a casual manner. Rather than speak, he waited until Henry had taken a swallow of beer.

'I shall need you for a couple of days, Todd, maybe three or four,' Henry eventually said.

'Suki been found, has she?' Todd asked.

'No,' Henry admitted, 'yet we now feel sure it was parson Gould who took her. I shall explain.'

Gurney listened as Henry explained what had happened to Judith and how they hoped to trap Gould's men with Sally as the bait. He listened in silence, both women giving the occasional exclamation of surprise at the details of what Judith had done.

'We aim to catch them before they arrive,' Henry finished. 'They'll be wary, like as not, and armed, so we take them in the lanes, when they won't expect it.'

'Best after,' Todd Gurney answered. 'That way we can be sure we've the right men.'

'I don't care to risk Sally,' Henry answered. 'Besides, that's one reason why I've set the time so late. What other business would two strangers have, in a gig, at the dead of night?'

'True enough, sir. Which lane to choose, that's the question? East for Okehampton and the moor, south to Tavistock and such . . .'

'You are right,' Henry admitted. 'If they've sense they'll come around west and down the lane behind the church. Best way to the rectory without being seen. We wait there, but close enough to see should they chance to come the other way. We can put a man by the church, in among the yews.'

'Two mine men should serve in all, sir; best keep it close. There's a pair I've in mind, Saul Penhale and his brother Ewan, rough but safe.'

'Good, that's the sort we need. Fetch them presently. Nor need we trouble to be polite ourselves. We'll take the fellows down to the mine and hang 'em over the shaft by their heels. They'll leak quick enough with that.'

'Certain sure, sir.'

Henry laughed, enervated by the thought of revenge and a chance to restore his battered pride.

With the sun already a rich, brilliant orange as it moved towards the horizon, Henry walked down the steep lane towards the village. Sally was beside him, wearing the same blue woollen dress that Suki had been in on the day of her capture. She was nervous, despite Henry's reassurances, again and again glancing back up the lane as if expecting to find people following them.

'There's no danger, not a scrap,' Henry said, laughing. 'Leastways, not to you. The fellow wants to save your soul from the devil and your body from me, which I imagine he judges much the same.'

'He's a dirty one, I know from the look,' Sally insisted.

'Parson Gould? Fellow's all cold pudding and godly piety.'

'I've seen plenty look the same.'

'Well I dare say you know your trade. In any event, here's another shilling. Do as he says, whatever keeps him amused. Todd Gurney and I will be along presently, with two men besides.'

Sally gave an uncertain nod, taking the shilling and slipping it into her pocket. The church was visible ahead, beyond a stand of trees and the old yews of the graveyard. Todd Gurney, Henry knew, would already be in the lane which ran beside the church, along with the two miners, all ordered to stay hidden well out of sight until the sun had set.

Reaching the church, they made their way into the rectory garden. Henry knocked at the door. Gould answered, grinning and bobbing, obviously nervous as he ushered them inside.

'Well, here we are, Mr Gould,' Henry said. 'I trust that the hour is not too inconvenient and that you will have a fruitful evening.'

'No inconvenience at all, Mr Truscott,' Gould assured him, 'none whatever. Indeed, I have always found the time after evensong most restful, which I feel sure will be conducive to learning.'

'Quite,' Henry agreed. 'I will return when I hear the strike of eleven. The bells are clearly audible from my house.'

'Ideal. I shall expect you shortly after eleven.'

Gould gave a hasty bow, to which Henry responded, stepping back as the Rector ushered Sally further into the hallway. As the door closed, Henry's mouth spread into a savage grin. Gould had been nervous, undeniably so, far more than any man contemplating an evening of Christian tuition. Even if Sally's guess was right and Gould intended something more, then the reaction seemed excessive.

Walking briskly away, Henry turned towards the village, then along the side of the churchyard. The light was fading quickly, and as he reached a point from which the back of the rectory was visible he saw that a light was on in Gould's main room, showing at two windows, no others.

He settled down to wait, the air growing quickly cool as the light faded from the sky. After a while he heard the crunch of heavy boots and caught the glimmer of a dark lantern. Gurney appeared, the two miners behind him, both big, solid men who Henry recognised as two of those who moved ore and machinery on the surface. One was despatched to the churchyard, the other remaining with them.

They waited, grouped together in silence as the church clock struck first nine and then one quarter after another, until at last Henry began to grow impatient. It was pitch black, the thin lines of light coming through Gould's shutters the only illumination save the occasional star visible through gaps in ragged cloud. The only sound had been the distant barking of a dog.

'Damn this, I'm going to look,' Henry said quietly, his patience finally snapping.

'Well enough, sir. Go careful,' Gurney answered.

Scrambling over the low wall, Henry quickly made his way to the rear of the rectory. He caught the sound of a voice, then laughter, female. At a lit window, he pressed his face to the glass, peering within through a chink in the shutters.

The Reverend Gould knelt on the floor of his living room, naked. On his back, mounted as if astride a horse, was Sally, naked but for her stockings, a riding crop in one hand, with which she would occasionally flick at his buttocks. She was grinning, obviously enjoying herself. Henry watched, puzzled but unable to restrain his amusement. Gould's face was set in bliss, his cock half-stiff where it hung between her legs. He was crawling, Sally steering him by the hair and with the crop, while the cluster of pink marks on his buttocks and thighs showed that the game had been going on for some time.

However long it had been, Gould seemed in no mood to stop. Henry was unable to make out the Rector's words, only the tone, which was urgent and aroused. Occasionally he would stop, reaching back to tug at his cock, until Sally stopped him with a word and a smack of her crop. This didn't prevent him growing erect, and before long his cock was a hard pole, the red tip pointing at the floor and waving as he crawled.

Absorbed in the spectacle, trying not to laugh but himself aroused by the sight of Sally's naked black body, Henry at last remembered to pull back to check on his surroundings. Nothing was visible, only for his heart to jump as one shadow detached itself from the

209

other, then settle once more as Gurney emerged into the dim light, crouched low. Henry put his finger to his lips, pointing to another of the cracks in the shutters, before returning to his own station. Gurney moved in beside him.

Sally and the Rector were as before, she mounted on his back, whip in hand. His cock was now furiously hard, the tip glossy with blood, his balls pulled up into the scrotum. He was touching it, and talking, and as they reached the opposite side of the room he stopped, rising as Sally dismounted from his back. Gould was speaking, rapidly, Sally nodding, then placing her hands on her hips, the whip sticking out at an angle.

Gould nodded enthusiastically in response to her pose. His face was red, sweating, his eyes bulging from his head. Moving on his knees, he crossed to a chair, bending himself across it with his buttocks pushed out to the room. Sally walked over to him, spoke a sentence and whipped the crop down across Gould's buttocks. The whip left a welt, white at first, then rising to a vivid scarlet. Gould spoke, now loud enough for Henry to hear, demanding harder strokes.

Obliging, Sally brought the crop down hard across Gould's buttocks, only for him to demand yet more. Again she hit, and again, Gould still crying out for more, until she was striking with all her force, over and over, lashing the crop down onto his buttocks, now criss-crossed with red and purple welts. Finally she stopped at a word from him, still holding the crop as if wishing she could continue. She had begun to sweat, giving her skin a glossy sheen, while her chest was rising and falling in a manner that made Henry's cock stiffer still.

Gould rose to his knees, shuffling quickly across the room. He took a white pot marked with black lettering from a sideboard. Again he spoke, Sally nodding in reply and taking the pot, then turning her back on him, which left her full, dark bottom pushed out directly towards the window. Henry watched, fascinated, as she dipped a finger into the jar, pulling out a thick blob of grease. Reaching behind herself with one hand, she parted her buttocks, showing off the tight brown dimple of her anus. Her greasy finger went to the tiny hole, smearing the cream around it before jabbing at the opening. With her fingers pushing out her bottom-cheeks, Henry watched her grease her anus, pumping the digit in and out until she was satisfied.

'Strange fellow, to take a whipping then sodomise her,' Henry whispered.

Gurney merely grunted. Gould had left the room, but quickly returned, speaking as he held something out to Sally in the palm of his hand. It was a dirty white, sausage-shaped and lumpy. She took it, her face screwing up in disgust as she examined it.

'What the hell's that?' Henry whispered.

'Dough, look's like,' Gurney answered. 'Better question, what's it for?'

'A bull says it goes up her breech.'

'Not taken, sir, not for a moment.'

Sure enough, as they watched, Sally reached back once more, again holding open her bottom. Pressing the lump of dough to her anus, she forced it in, packing the thick, white paste up herself with her fingers until it had disappeared, save for a rough star-shape of dirty white where her ring had not fully closed.

As Sally had stuffed her bottom, Gould had lain down, full length on the floor. He spoke, taking his cock in hand as she stepped over to stand, legs apart, over his head. As he began to masturbate, Sally sank slowly down, her broad black bottom spreading above his head. He was staring at her, his gaze locked on her bottom, then obscured as she sat firmly on his face. She wiggled her bottom in his face, then moved, into a kneeling position, her bottom cocked back, her breasts swinging forward.

The crease of her buttocks was easily visible to Henry. He could see her anus, the tip of the lump of dough still visible, directly above Gould's mouth. His masturbation had become frenzied, a furious tugging at his cock. He kissed her anus, twice, speaking as he lay back. Immediately Sally's bottom tensed. Henry watched, mouth wide, as the girl's anus went loose. The little brown ring pouted, opening, the dough squeezing out, over Gould's mouth, then into it. He began to eat, jerking in desperation at his cock. It erupted, spraying come over Sally's breasts and belly as his mouth gaped wide around the lump of dough emerging from her anus. She sat back as the come hit her breasts, suddenly, immersing his face between her plump brown buttocks, wriggling it, then rubbing it on him, until at last his hand began to slap frantically on the floor.

Sally rose as Gould let go of his cock. His face was filthy, smeared with dough, the crease of her bottom in the same, dirty state. She was giggling, he silent and tight-lipped, as if he had not enjoyed the experience at all, despite his obvious ecstasy.

'They not be here tonight, his men,' Gurney said. 'He'd not want to get seen like that.'

'Likely not,' Henry agreed.

'What says we pay him a visit, sir?'

'We do,' Henry agreed, 'and quickly. Fetch the brothers.'

Gurney nodded and melted into the darkness. Henry waited, occasionally putting his eye to the shutters. Gould had risen, and was dressing when

Todd returned with the two miners. They ran quickly to the front door, where Henry knocked. There was a pause, with urgent voices just audible in the rectory, female and male. Finally Gould opened the door, now dressed.

'Ah, Mr Truscott, a little early, I see,' he greeted Henry, 'and with company?'

'My mine captain, Mr Gurney, along with a couple of Cornish lads who work the spoil heaps,' Henry answered. 'We've wanted to consult you on a spiritual matter.'

'A spiritual matter, Mr Truscott?'

'Yes,' Henry answered, 'that being the opinion of the Bishop of Exeter on those who take their pleasure in licking a negress's feak, not to say being ridden bare-back by the same.'

For a moment Gould's face registered outrage, then shock and finally fear as Henry and the others pushed past him into the house. Sally was stood against the sideboard, fully dressed if less than perfectly ordered. Henry crossed the room, helped himself from a decanter and sat down on the most comfortable chair.

'No sense in denying it, Rector,' he addressed Gould. 'Not that a negro girl's word would be taken against yours, but then there's mine, and Gurney's, all of whom'll take oath on what we saw.'

Gould nodded. He was pale-faced, standing between the three miners, not only dwarfed in height, but also bulk, with his thin form in sorry contrast to their massive frames and heavy muscles. Henry sipped the drink he had taken, an indifferent sack.

'What do you want?' Gould managed. 'I have little money . . .'

'I have no need for your money,' Henry answered, 'although, of course, I can't speak for my fellows here. No, what I want is the truth.'

213

'The truth?' Gould asked.

'The truth about Suki, my wife's maid,' Henry answered, with sudden, genuine anger. 'Where the hell is she, damn you?'

'The maid? The negro maid?' Gould stammered. 'I have no idea. I swear. Is she not at your house?'

'You know damn well she's not,' Henry answered. 'Damn you, Gould, what gives you the right to take her? I suppose you think she's better off as a drudge in some poor-house because I whip her tail now and again? Eh?'

On his denial, Saul and Ewan had picked Gould up, lifting him one to an arm so that his feet hung suspended a foot off the ground. His face was now white, his lip trembling as Henry got up and strode across the room.

'Where is she, damn you, Gould?' he demanded. 'Some church poor-house in Exeter, isn't she, or Bristol?'

Gould shook his head, his eyes fixed, apparently too terrified to speak.

'Where, then? Plymouth? Don't lie, you treacherous black fly, we found her bonnet, over to the moor.'

Again Gould managed to shake his head.

'Crediton, then?' Henry demanded. 'That's it, isn't it, in that hell-pit by the river? Nobody'd see her there, would they? Speak, damn you, Gould, admit it!'

Saul Penhale had drawn a knife, a crude, foot-long piece of iron, the blade edge glinting in the light of the oil lamps. Gould glanced down at it, mumbling prayers between his lips. Henry took the knife, holding it up in front of the Rector's face. Suddenly Gould was nodding frantically.

Nine

Suki placed a foot against the wall, tugging at the chain. Before, it had not so much as moved. Now, a shower of tiny dust particles rained down each time she put her weight against it. On the scale that morning she had recorded a weight of fourteen and twelve, figures she did not understand except in that it meant she was some half as heavy again as when they had first weighed her.

Her bottom and hips were now huge, her breasts so large it took both hands to hold each. Soft reams of fat girdled her middle, while her belly hung heavily over her pubic mound. Twice the men had changed her collar, the first time with Nathan standing ready with the cudgel as Davy worked, the second more casually. Suki had made no effort to escape.

Again she tried the chain, bracing herself against the wall. The chain creaked; a puff of mortar erupted from beneath the iron staple which held the bolt. She strained, gritting her teeth, only to stop suddenly at the sound of footsteps outside. Sitting down on the bed, she struggled to control her breathing, looking around when Davy addressed her.

'Lunch,' he announced. 'Have you been a good girl and creamed your skin?'

Suki nodded, pointing to the half-empty jar of Doctor Pilgham's Ablution Preparation on the floor.

'Good,' Davy said, 'now eat up, and then the Master says you're to have some reading matter. Drawings to look at, leastways, seeing as how you can't read your own name.'

He put the tray on the bed. On it was a great pot of stew, the surface rich with globules of molten butter and lumpy with meat and the round heads of a half-dozen dumplings. Beside it were four thick slices of bread, liberally buttered, a pair of grilled mackerel over which cream had been poured and a whole fruit cake. There was also a quart pot of thick, dark ale. Climbing on the bed, Suki licked her lips, trying to decide whether it would be better to start with the mackerel or the stew. Nathan had stayed back, in the doorway, and had not troubled to unfasten his cudgel from his belt.

Davy had brought a book, which he laid carefully on the bed. Suki paid no attention, concentrating on her food. When first captured, the meals had been hard to get down, simply because there was always so much. Now it was easy. She decided on the mackerel, both of which she ate before putting the bones aside and licking up the rich, oily cream from the plate. After a swallow of ale she started on the stew, picking out the delicious dumplings first, then the meat and vegetables, lastly draining the pot over her mouth and sopping up what remained with her bread. Finishing the ale, she started on the cake.

'Let's have your leg then, girl,' Davy remarked, drawing a tape measure from his pocket.

Still eating cake, Suki swung one leg over the side of the bed, perfectly familiar with the operation. Davy wound the tape around, first above her knee, then at the top of her thigh, so close that his knuckles brushed her fat quim. As usual, he took no notice, utterly indifferent to her nakedness. Suki ignored his touch, no longer fearful of rape, having long since realised that the men's sole sexual interest lay in each other.

'Thirty inches around, less a quarter, at top,' Davy stated. 'Twenty-six dead at the knee.'

'Twenty-six you say?' Nathan replied.

'Twenty-six it is,' Davy answered. 'She's just about ready, I'd say.'

'Seem so,' Nathan agreed. 'Master'll be glad, he's been getting precious impatient.'

Briefly Davy reached out to stretch the tape measure across the book, laughed and returned it to his pocket. Suki was cramming the last of the cake into her mouth as he lifted the tray, making for the door only to stop and turn back.

'That there book,' he said. 'You're to look, but if you makes so much as a thumb mark, Nathan here'll be taking a dog-whip to that fat arse. Got me?'

Suki nodded. Both men left, speaking briefly in the corridor before Davy returned downstairs. On the bed, Suki brushed the cake crumbs away and sat down, cross-legged.

She had understood every word they had said. So she was ready, fat enough, no doubt, for fucking. Every day she had grown more certain that it was what the man referred to as the Master intended. Like the coast king, he liked his women fat, very fat. Why having a thigh thirty inches around was right she had no idea, except that the English seemed obsessed with the dimensions of things, length and height and weight. When with Snapes, she had seen him weigh pieces of rock, then dip them in water and measure how much it rose. When done he would write numbers and symbols on a sheet of paper, often laughing aloud when finished.

With a dismissive shrug she leaned forwards, taking up the book. It was a thick sheaf of paper, pressed together at one margin by wooden slats with a pair of clips to hold them in place. She opened it in the middle, and immediately her mouth went wide. On the first sheet was a scene, a ship standing off a shore, a painfully familiar shore. Figures stood on the beach, tall, slender black figures, male and female, naked or nearly so, some holding knobkerries, others baskets of fruit. The ship was also familiar and, still more painful to look at, Snapes's vessel, in which she had spent two awful months.

Turning the page with trembling fingers, she found another scene, a village, much like her own, with the round huts of woven grass and the stockades beyond, people, cattle, cooking fires, pots, all arranged as if a feast was being prepared. A lump was building in her throat, and she was wondering why she had been given the book; from compassion, or cruelty, maybe to ask her questions about her homeland.

She turned another page, finding herself staring back at her, seated on the side of a longboat, smiling. The scene came back immediately, the ship's artist showing her pictures he had drawn and indicating that he wished to draw her. She had complied, in return for a handful of beautiful beads marked with swirling colours, something she had treasured but which she now knew the English held as of very little worth. She had posed, sitting happily in the sun, stark naked and entirely unaware of how much store the white men set by clothes.

Pleased with her willingness, the artist and Snapes had given her more beads, asking her to pose in increasingly sexual positions. She had responded with giggling enthusiasm; lying full length on the sand with her hip cocked up, standing with her hands behind her head and her breasts pushed out, crawling with her bare bottom towards them as she looked back over her shoulder.

218

The artist had ended up with a hard cock, which she had obligingly sucked and pulled off over her breasts as Snapes had watched. After that she had been given another handful of beads and sent off with a slap on her rump, thoroughly pleased with herself.

She turned the page, knowing exactly what to expect. Sure enough, there she was, depicted in exact detail, in poses which had been simple fun at the time but she now knew would be shocking to the prudish English and strongly arousing to the more debauched among them. The lump was growing in her throat as she looked at the pictures, unable to stop turning the pages and yet more and more fearful as she did so.

The day after she had posed for the artist she had been taken. They had tricked her into accepting a ride in the longboat and then simply tied her hand and foot, bundled her aboard and set sail. She had been terrified, lying helpless in the hold, in darkness, with no idea where she was going or what was to happen to her. It had not been long before she found out, and as she turned the next page she knew full well what she was going to see. Sure enough, there she was, and there too was the enschego, Lord Furlong. His mouth was drawn back in a demented grin, his shaggy hands holding her by the thighs as she knelt on the deck, his hips pushed tight to her buttocks as he fucked her.

She shut the book, unable to look, her mind burning with emotions. By the time they had reached England, Snapes had taught the beast to associate sex with a certain scent, and her. It had been the same in Suffolk, until at last she alone had been able to control the enschego, which had eventually proved Snapes's undoing. Then had come Judith, escape and revenge, ending with her secure with the Truscotts, for whom she felt deep and undying gratitude, despite their peculiar habits.

At the thought of Henry and Eloise her mind turned back to her captivity. Davy and Nathan had said she was ready, fat enough. Soon the Master would come and fuck her. She could fight, biting and scratching, but if she did they would tie her to the bed, or maybe hold her down, with the servants on her limbs while the Master mounted her struggling body. Afterwards they'd probably beat her to make sure that she was more compliant the next time.

The Master was going to fuck her, whatever she did, and so it was easier to do as she was told. It would save her bruises, maybe worse. For that matter, if she was to be fucked it made sense to be ready, and so save herself more pain. Biting back her pride, she opened the book again, wondering if there might not be other pictures, of handsome young men with women. As she did so she put a hand to one huge breast and began to stroke the nipple.

As she had hoped, the pictures from the African expedition were not the only ones. There were plenty of others, showing both men and women, usually naked or half-dressed, alone or together. Most were simple, girls masturbating with their dresses held up, men with their cocks out for women to fondle or suck, couples together, mounted on one another. Others were more complicated, such as one showing a group of men, all in the same colourful clothes, lined up to enjoy a pair of women in torn dresses. Others were strange, a man eating what seemed to be oysters from a woman's quim, two men urinating on a woman in a black and white costume as she lay on the ground, masturbating in the streams of pee.

Her spare hand had gone between her legs, to stroke the smooth skin of her thighs, deliberately avoiding her quim as she was determined not to come before the Master came for her. It was becoming harder, though, as her mind turned to thoughts of eager men and hard cocks, also to women in open, sexual positions, ready for fucking. By the time she reached her own pictures her fingers had gone lower, tickling the plump tucks of her bottom where they curved up to meet her thighs and quim. Her sex felt ready, and she knew that if the Master came she would be easy to enter.

He didn't appear, and she read on, become gradually more aroused until her nipples were straining out and her skin was slick with sweat. Finally, at the sight of a plump white girl being beaten as she masturbated, it became too much. Thinking of her own beatings, and the way Henry and Eloise encouraged her to touch herself as she knelt for punishment, she put her hand to the fat mound of her quim. Staring at the picture, she began to rub herself, her fingers deep in the fleshy cleft, thinking of how it felt to have her bottom hot and throbbing, and wondering whether Henry would enjoy her more or less now that she was so fat.

Abruptly she rolled on the bed, sticking her bottom up in prime spanking position. The pose left her huge breasts hanging down, squashed out on the bed, with her belly hanging too and her enormous buttocks high and parted. It felt good, and she wished she had a mirror, like the one in Eloise's room, with which she'd so often been shown the state of her freshly smacked buttocks.

Placing the book in front of her face, she began to turn the pages, her other arm back between her legs, fiddling with the plump, swollen flesh of her sex. It was the first time she had masturbated since being taken, and it felt wonderful. Her body was different too, making it better still, her massive, heavy breasts and overweight buttocks intensely sexual, something impossible to hide, now flaunted, and so female. All of it was wobbling as she rubbed at herself, mounds of flesh rippling and bouncing, the bed creaking in protest.

She reached the pictures of herself again, admiring her own body as she masturbated and thinking of how nice it had felt to show off in front of the artist. He had made her suck him and she had done it gratefully, giggling as she licked and nibbled at his stubby white penis. She had sucked his semen down, swallowing it, then kissing his balls the way she had been taught.

At the picture of herself crawling she was on the verge of orgasm, her initial intentions lost in a welter of pleasure. Her fingers were slapping in the plump, wet mush of her sex, making her flesh quiver, her breasts, buttocks and belly shaking as she masturbated. Even as she turned the page she knew what she was going to do, terrible shame filling her head as she saw the picture. There she was, Lord Furlong mounted on her plump, black bottom. Black hair and dark skin, her mouth gaping, her eyes shut, her bottom high with the grinning enschego on her, up her, mounted on the fat black buttocks that even now were quivering and shaking with her orgasm, spread, wide and huge . . .

Suki screamed, once, then bit hard on the bed, her eyes closed in burning, excruciating ecstasy as her orgasm tore through her body. Even as the bubble burst and the awful mind-numbing shame of what she'd done washed over her she was still rubbing, her body responding to her pleasure in rebellion against the demands of her mind.

Henry paused at the top of the slope, seating himself on a block of granite. Todd Gurney settled on another stone, both men silent for a moment as they looked down. They were at the top of Burley Down, among the blocks of a half-built folly intended to mark the limit of Henry's estate and provide a view back across the valley. Below them, the lake was just visible through the trees, light shimmering on its surface in the faint breeze. Beyond, the house was clearly visible, a sight which, as always, brought a smile to Henry's face.

'What do you think to an avenue down through the woods?' Henry asked. 'Eloise feels it would give a classical line to the estate, better still if we threw a bridge across the lake.'

'Waste of good woodland, seem so,' Gurney answered.

'You may be right,' Henry admitted. 'Classical regularity is all very well, but the elms we've planted will still be no more than half-grown when young John's an old man. Who's to say how the fashion will have changed?'

'It'll change, certain sure.'

Henry didn't answer, pondering the scenery until the niggling thought of Lewis Stukely once more pushed into his mind. He had been expecting a challenge, but none had come, and he was beginning to wonder if Mrs Aldgrave hadn't decided that silence was the wiser course. Despite that, he had taken to carrying his swordstick, not wishing to risk the chance of Stukely taking a less honourable course for his revenge.

There was Suki as well, whose whereabouts might be known, but who still needed to be brought free. Not wanting a protracted legal wrangle, he had determined to get her first and argue later. That morning Saul Penhale had been sent to the mine to collect a half-dozen more men, which Henry felt was sure to be enough to intimidate the poor-house men. The brother, Ewan, had been set to guard the rectory.

He could see the sense in Gould's choice. On his word a girl could be taken in at any poor-house, with few questions asked, a negress more easily still. In Exeter or other cities Suki might easily have been seen, and a black face was rare enough for rumours to spread quickly. Crediton was smaller, but the poor-house was by the river Yeo, a good mile clear of the town. Yet if it made Suki easier to hide, it also made her easier to rescue.

'Strange fellow, that parson,' Gurney said suddenly. 'When the brothers lifted him I thought he'd bewray himself. With what he fancied from Sally and all.'

'I've met fellows like that before,' said Henry. 'A taste of the whip across the arse gets them going. No different from women, in truth. It was common enough sport at Mother Agie's, so Judith tells me.'

'Unnatural, I call it,' Gurney said. 'I mean, if a wife's a strapping big woman and her man's some thurdle-gutted little fellow, then he's like to take a whipping now and again, certain sure. Maybe it'll get him going, like it does the women. I wouldn't know. Gould, now, he's two stone on little Sally, maybe three, so it ought to be him doing the whipping, by rights.'

'That's not the way of it,' Henry replied. 'Judith explained how she herself came to it, and I suppose it's much the same. When she was at Mother Agie's, she was put out for all sorts: young and old, fat and thin, sodomites, whipping coves. One fellow she spoke of used to come in off the street for her to clean his boots with her tongue, and never mind if he'd stepped in something a horse had done. She wasn't too well behaved either, by all accounts, and used to be punished no end, whipped on a frame, and that trick with the candles in her cunt and breech. She made it her pleasure, else she'd have gone mad. Now she needs it, and the more shameful the better. Hell, you've seen her fiddle with herself while her cunt's half-full of wax.

'Gould's the same, in his way. Being a good Christian doesn't rob a man of his needs. He feels guilty, I imagine, and it makes him feel better to be made low. Like Judith, in due time it must have come to answer his needs. The lower the better, I would suppose, and that'll be his kick with slaves. I mean to say, when that's your pleasure, what'd be better than having a slave girl sat on your face so's you can lick her arse clean?'

Henry chuckled at his own wit.

'That'll be all he wanted with Suki,' he went on. 'Doubtless he'd have suggested tuition if she hadn't been pinched. Still, he never did mention her being pinched . . .'

'Maybe you're right, sir. Maybe you're wrong,' Gurney interrupted. 'Look here.'

Henry looked up. Nobody was visible, only the broken ground of the track and the trees, their leaves rustling in the faint breeze.

'What?' he demanded. 'Damn it, man, what?'

Gurney nodded towards the trees, rising.

'Two men, maybe more, among the trees.'

'Gould's men?' Henry demanded, struggling to free his swordstick.

Gurney merely shrugged, pulling his bayonet free of his belt. As he did so two men stepped into the clear from behind trees. Both were masked, one big and broadshouldered, a cudgel swinging from his hand, the other smaller, and wiry, holding a knife.

The slim blade of the swordstick slid free as Henry rose to a crouch. The men came on slowly, cautious but showing no fear. Henry extended his sword, drawing his handkerchief from his pocket. The smaller man was facing him, arm extended, motionless, only to suddenly flip the knife back and hurl it.

Henry jumped, cursing as the knife cut through his coat at the shoulder and clattered away among the stones of the folly. The man had drawn another knife, holding the handle loosely as if ready to throw. Henry darted forward, flicking the swordstick at the smaller blade. Immediately the bigger man dashed in, swinging his cudgel. Henry danced back, his foot catching a stone, the big man coming in, crashing into him, screaming, Henry struggling to push him off, a dead weight, and as he finally succeeded he saw the bayonet handle sticking out from the man's side.

The other was backing away, knife still held out, Gurney facing him with his bare fists. Henry rose, struggling to control the shaking of his arm as he lifted the swordstick. The man glanced at him, back to Gurney, cursed and hurled the knife, which Henry dodged, and the man was running into the wood. Henry made to follow, only for Gurney to put out a hand, halting him.

'He's gone, sir. No sense risking a knife in the guts to follow.'

Henry nodded, sliding the swordstick back into its sheath. Gurney, apparently indifferent to what he had just done, reached down to pull his bayonet free, cleaning it on the dead man's coat.

'Let's see who he is then,' Henry demanded.

Gurney put out a boot, rolling the dead man over onto his back. Reaching down, he pulled off the mask, revealing coarse features made horrible by staring eyes and an open mouth with blood trickling from one side.

'That's one of Stukely's men!' Henry exclaimed. 'What's his name? Staddon, that's it, Staddon.'

'Nathan Staddon,' Gurney agreed. 'Sailor, he was. Plymouth man.'

'Bastard!' Henry swore, kicking the corpse as sudden sick fear welled up in his stomach.

'Stukely's man, as you say, sir,' Gurney went on. 'Stukely don't care to face you, seem so.'

'So it seems,' Henry agreed. 'Hell! What am I to do? I don't care to spend every waking hour watching my back!'

'Here's one won't be troubling you again, any-roads,' Gurney stated. 'How do we deal with the lich?'

'Can you lift these blocks?'

'That I can.'

'Then wall him into the base of the folly. I don't suppose Stukely's likely to come calling for him.'

Suki lay still, listening and trembling with fearful anticipation. For some while there had been voices audible in the house, too faint to make out words. The Master was coming, she was sure of it.

Since her orgasm she had kept herself on edge, wet and ready, also willing, despite her stung pride. Again and again she had moved on the bed, wondering which position would prove the most alluring. Some, kneeling or with her thighs spread, seemed too obvious for the English style. Others, lying face down or standing, too demure. At last she settled on her side, showing her ample curves to good effect and hiding nothing without being blatant.

The stairs creaked, as always. She heard Davy's voice, his tone respectful. Another answered and the door came open, revealing a man of middle height and build, expensively dressed, with a neatly made wig and a coat of heavy, bottle-green cloth. She recognised him immediately, but said nothing, watching him from beneath half-closed eyelids. He closed the door behind himself and came to the bed, immediately picking up the book to examine it.

'Undamaged, I see; clean also. Good, I am glad my men have taught you some sense. It is only my spare copy, naturally, but still valuable. I trust you have admired the plates?'

Suki nodded, moving a little to make room for him on the bed. He sat down, reaching out to touch her thigh and trace a slow line over the smooth, dark skin.

'Beautiful,' he said, 'flawless. From the moment I saw it I had to have it.'

Suki shivered, trying to stay calm as she waited for his fingers to go higher, towards her sex. He said nothing, just smiling as he stroked her skin, tickling until she was struggling to keep her face straight. She wanted to giggle, but didn't dare. There was something in his manner which told her it would not be welcome, despite his smiling compliments on her body, or at least the texture of her skin.

'Beautiful,' he repeated. 'Now, so that you do not feel wasted, I am going to explain what is to be done with you. I don't really expect you to agree, or even understand, but then why would you? After all, what would a savage know of aesthetics?'

He laughed, a cruel, vicious sound, which changed her apprehension to raw fear.

'I am a collector,' he went on, 'but no ordinary collector. Not for me the accumulation of bird's eggs or their stuffed parents. Not for me oriental artefacts or the heads of wild beasts. No, I collect, but I am also a perfectionist. What I seek, is the most perfect example of any given class. Were you to visit my study you would observe but a single egg, that of the dodo, a giant, flightless bird, apparently a pigeon of

228

sorts. The creature was confined to the island of Mauritius, in the Indian Ocean, and has been extinct since the late seventeenth century, a fact which greatly enhances the value of its egg. Even the stand on which it sits is carved from wood cut on Mauritius; again perfection.'

Suki listened, not understanding much of what he said but aware that he was saying it as much or more for the pleasure of hearing his own voice than to inform her.

'In this present case,' he continued, 'I have what I consider, without false modesty, to be the finest and most extensive collection of erotic prints ever assembled in a single volume. My father assembled a not insubstantial collection of such work, on which I expanded. The result is this book, painstakingly reworked and made to imperial quarto.'

He gave the book a tap, smiling in smug satisfaction. Suki met his eyes, which were bright but cold, looking at her without warmth, as if she was no more than an object. He stood, suddenly, and put the tips of his fingers and thumbs together, smiling at her.

'Having compiled my collection,' he went on, 'I naturally asked myself how I should present such a unique work. What binding I should select. I considered the skin of a new-born calf, or some rare beast from Africa or the Indies. Nothing suited; nothing had that rare quality which sets perfection apart. No, I could not decide.'

He spun on his heel, his smile broader than ever, showing a childish delight in the sound of his own voice and what he was saying.

'I had been amused,' he continued, 'and also fascinated, to discover that my new neighbour, Henry Truscott, had in his employ a negro girl, the very one depicted in certain prints purchased on subscription

229

from Sir Joseph Snapes. You have seen them, no doubt? At first I thought it only a chance resemblance, one negro looking much like the next. However, I subsequently had a remarkable tale from my old friend Luke Hurdon, revealing that it was indeed you.

'So there I was, perplexed by my binding difficulty and amused each time I visited the Truscotts and saw you, thinking of you in congress with that ludicrous beast!'

He laughed and shook his head, his smile broader than ever, then went on.

'It was not until that day at Meldon Pool that the two things dovetailed. Suddenly it was obvious. There you were, in all your naked, savage beauty, your thighs spread wide to the sun, your skin glistening with your own wet. It was perfection indeed, dark and beautiful, as smooth as silk, unblemished. I knew then I had to have it, the perfect binding for my collection, girl's skin.'

Suki stared, her mouth dropping open in mounting horror as his meaning sank in. For a moment it seemed impossible, that she must have misunderstood. He turned, smiling down at her and the realisation came that it was just a horrid joke, until again she met his eyes.

'So you see,' he said, 'you are not quite as worthless as you may have supposed. Carefully flayed and properly tanned, the skin of one of your thighs would make the perfect binding for my collection.

'Taking you was simple; two horses hired from different stables, a little misdirection concerning slaves and it was done. As to the Truscotts, I had little concern. Eloise would not know one maid from another, so long as they serve well. As to Henry, he is a drunken rake. What does he care for some Carib girl? So long as there is an adequate supply of willing cunt he is happy, and one is as good as the next. I did not imagine they would expend much effort in searching for you, nor that they would have the wit to find you. So it has proved.

'No, your only problem was that you were unreasonably slight. Hence your diet, which I am glad to say you have taken to well, greedy to the last. You will now provide ample skin – enough, indeed, to provide the leather for several other works. So now, as I have no taste for blood, I must leave you. My man Davy will be here shortly. I am fortunate in him; a more callous individual it would be hard to find. He is also an expert, from years of skinning seals in the southern seas, so rest assured that your precious hide will not be wasted. I bid you good day.'

Henry watched, grinning, as Eloise struggled to accommodate three of the miners at once. Her disappointment at his failure to provide a black male had been evident, while having decided to leave for Crediton at dead of night, there had been several hours to fill. He had also felt agitated after the killing of Stukely's man, and in no mood for introspection. Drink and sex had seemed the best options with which to fill the time. He had also decided that it would be both sensible and amusing to buy the silence of the miners with pleasure as well as money.

It had taken a little trouble to persuade Eloise, but in response to her protests he had put her across his knee, spanking her bare bottom in full view of the delighted miners. When her furious protests had finally died down and she had stopped trying to scratch and bite, he had let her down, red-bottomed and sobbing, also more than happy to do as she was told. Her only demand, when he had ordered her to pick three of the men and suck their cocks hard, had been for the other girls to join in too. Judith had readily agreed, Sally also. Even Joanna had shown little reluctance, another mark of the gratitude she had shown since being told she would be allowed to keep her baby.

Eloise now lay on the floor, among a pile of cushions, stripped naked. One man was beneath her, his cock well immersed in her rectum, jerking himself against the soft flesh of her bottom as he buggered her. Another squatted between her rolled-up legs, his erection sunk deep into her quim, his muscular buttocks clenching and unclenching to the rhythm of his pushes. The third was in her mouth, kneeling as she sucked on his cock with desperate eagerness.

Henry could not even remember which name went with which miner. All were much alike, picked for their size by Gurney, large, rough men who worked the surface and no underground. Their skin was rough and ingrained with dirt and stone dust. All three bore several scars and, Henry judged, were probably the ugliest of the group, yet Eloise had chosen them herself.

She had undressed in front of them, feigning coyness, only to get down on her knee once she was naked and suck each erect. Only then had she allowed the other girls to join in. Judith had gone first, taking Todd Gurney and Saul Penhale by their cocks and leading them to a couch. She was now bent over, on her knees, her skirts high, sucking on Todd's cock as Saul fucked her from the rear.

That had left three miners for Sally, who now sat naked between two with a cock in each hand as the third fed his cock in and out of her mouth. Joanna had come to Henry, and now sat on his lap, her skirts rucked high and her bodice open as he casually fondled her breasts and bottom while he watched his wife used. In return she was tugging at his cock, which stuck up from his breeches, erect and ready.

Henry had broached a cask of cider even before he had decided to spank Eloise into willingness. The rich, apple scent now hung in the air, along with the smells of sweat, cock and aroused females. Most were drunk, or at least tipsy. He himself had grown tired of cider after a couple of quart pots, and had gone to the cellar for a bottle of claret. A full glass now stood on a table beside him, so that he could take a sip each time he broke off from fondling Joanna.

Enjoying the sight of the miners using the girls, he was determined not to come too soon. The others were clearly less restrained. Todd had begun to masturbate into Judith's mouth, holding her by the head while her body jerked to Saul's increasingly urgent pushes. Henry thought one or the other would come first, only to hear Sally give a gasp of surprise as the man she was sucking came in her face. Henry turned, laughing to see her with a long streamer of white come lying across the dark skin of one cheek, with more hanging from her nose and chin. Her mouth and eyes were wide in shock and possibly disgust, but even before she could speak she had been pulled down, her mouth stuffed with the penis of one of the men she had been masturbating.

Saul Penhale groaned at that moment, trying to pull back but coming in the mouth of Judith's vagina. He sank back, and Henry saw the thick white fluid spattered in the deep red hair of her quim. Joanna began to tug harder at the sight, but he put his hand on top of hers, slowing her rhythm to long gentle strokes. The man in Sally's hand came, white semen erupting up to coat his cock as she finished him off with a flurry of sudden tugs. As she did so, more semen burst out around her mouth. She set to licking up both men's come, Henry watching until the thrusts of the man in his wife's quim became urgent, then desperate.

The miner came, full in Eloise's sex, even as her cheeks bulged with the semen of the man in her mouth. She pulled back, the mess dribbling from her lower lip, only for her to catch it and quickly lick it up before it could fall on the carpet. She was still being buggered, the man in her bottom rolling her onto her side. Her eyes closed, Henry watching in delight as the flesh of her breasts and bottom jumped and quivered to the man's powerful thrusts. He was red-faced, grunting, his great coarse hands locked in the soft flesh of Eloise's hips. The buggering got faster, harder, Eloise's soft groans turning to gasps, then a sudden, pained shriek as the man's face went slack and Henry realised he had come up her bottom.

He chuckled, watching his wife's face as the big man's cock was pulled slowly out of her bottom-hole. As it popped free she blew out her cheeks, rising into a crawling position briefly before slumping onto the cushions.

The miners began to make themselves comfortable, returning their cocks to their breeches and thanking Henry in gruff, somewhat embarrassed voices. Henry returned their remarks with bluff, hearty thanks, assuring them that the pleasure was his. Even the man who had come in her quim he reassured, pointing out that she was pregnant already, at which Eloise coloured more than when she'd been turned across his knee.

More cider was poured, while Henry fetched a second bottle of claret, decanting it into a jug. Joanna continued to attend to his cock, stroking and kissing at it with rising excitement, until the last of her bashfulness was gone and she began to suck in earnest. At that Henry pulled her gently up, sitting back to glance round at the four women, his face set in a mischievous grin.

'My turn, I think,' he announced, 'and what I've in mind is a row of bare bottoms, as we've so fine a collection. Across the table, the four of you. Come, come, ladies, bottoms up and be quick about it.'

Judith bent across the table, the others following, one by one, until there was a row of four female bottoms, plump and round, quims poking out from between chubby thighs. Henry stood back to admire the view. Judith was marked with bruises, Eloise pink from spanking, Joanna and Sally unmarked. Of the eight holes showing, four were running come – three vaginas and one bottom-hole, Eloise's. Henry chuckled, wondering where it would be best to put his cock and feeling spoiled for choice. In the end it made little difference, or he could have all four if he was able, although with their quims sopping with the miners' come, it was their bottom-holes which tempted. With a flush of drunken greed, he decided to make the attempt.

'Right,' he declared. 'A wager, I think, is what's needed. Who'll stake a hog I can't sodomise the four without spending?'

'Taken,' Judith said, looking back as she wiggled her bottom.

'I know your tricks, Judy Cates,' he answered, 'but I know how to get around them. I'll have you last.'

'I'll take the wager,' Gurney called, 'should you agree to spend but once, that in the last, and to finish in the hour.'

'Done,' Henry answered after a glance to the clock, which showed over a quarter to the hour.

'You will lose,' Eloise remarked without troubling to turn.

235

Henry slapped her bottom, drawing a squeak from her and leaving a fresh red handprint on the already pink skin. Glancing once more to the clock, he gave a mocking bow to the room and made for the kitchen, pausing only to check that neither Mrs Orcombe nor the nursemaid were about.

Taking a cup full of lard, he returned to the drawing room, where the girls were still waiting with their bottoms presented, Joanna still, Eloise with her chin propped in her hand, Judith and Sally chattering.

'On your toes, girls,' he ordered, 'and backs in. Let us see those admirable behinds spread wide.'

They obeyed as he came behind them, Eloise, Judith and Sally immediately, Joanna after a smart swat to her fleshy bottom and a gentle push in the small of her back to make her pose. Four bottom-holes came on full show, three neatly puckered, Eloise's soft and wet with semen. Henry smacked his lips, stroking his cock as he admired the view. All four were looking back. He nodded and smiled, letting them watch as he dipped a finger into the lard. It came out glistening with the thick, pale fat, which he held up to the light. Stepping forwards, he went to the first in the line, Joanna, prising her meaty buttocks a little wider before smearing the lard onto her anus. She gave a sob as the cold grease touched her anus, then another as his finger invaded her bottom. He pushed deep in, feeling the hot, slimy tube of her rectum and imagining how his cock was going to feel in the same deliciously tight hole.

His finger came out and Joanna farted, drawing a fresh sob from her and deep laugh from among the watching miners. Turning, Henry bowed, then returned to his task. Once more dipping his finger into the lard, he moved to Sally, whose heavy, dark

236

buttocks were fully parted, her anus an inviting star-shape of dun-coloured flesh. He put the lard to it, first with little circular motions, feeling her ring, then up the hole, deep in her rectum as he had with Joanna. Unlike Joanna, she took the invasion of her bottom with a soft moan, sticking it out to encourage him to go deeper. Henry laughed and slapped her, making the meaty brown cheeks wobble.

Pulling his finger from Sally's bottom, he went to Judith, giving her the same treatment, her ring greased, then penetrated, finishing with a slap to her pert white bottom. Eloise came last, her already slimy ring opening easily as he smeared the remains of the lard around it and then up the hole. The work complete, he stood back, stroking his cock. He had stayed rock hard, just from the feel of his finger invading the tightly puckered rings.

Each anus now glistened with lard, ready for entry. Henry smacked his lips, took a swallow of claret and got behind Eloise, his erection resting between her buttocks.

'My darling wife first, naturally,' he declared. 'After all, merely because she is being sodomised in public is no reason to neglect precedence.'

He laughed at his own wit, taking his cock and pushing it to his wife's anal opening. The ring stretched, taking the head, then more, pushing up the little hole with the lard forming a collar around his shaft as it went in. Eloise moaned, her hands clutching at the table top as her rectum filled with cock.

Henry could feel her flesh, hot and soft and moist, enveloping his erection. The temptation was to push, to ram his cock home up her bottom, over and over until he came in her guts. He gritted his teeth, trying to hold back, keeping his erection in but pushing only gently, also watching her red buttocks wobble as he buggered her. With each push he went a little deeper, until the full length of his cock was embedded up her bottom.

'One done,' he declared, through clenched teeth.

'Begging pardon, ma'am,' Todd Gurney remarked as he came beside Henry, pulling Eloise's buttocks apart to show the junction of cock and anus. 'Sure enough, he's well in.'

Pulling back, Henry watched his cock slide from his wife's anus. Her ring pulled out as it came, and she gave a little gasp of pain as the head came free, leaving her anus a gaping tunnel into the body, with the puffy red flesh visible inside. Taking hold of his cock, Henry gave Eloise a last hard slap across her bottom. Stepping past Judith, he put his cock to Sally's hole. She lifted her bottom, pushing back obligingly on to his cock. The head popped inside; Henry admired the contrast between her flesh and his, dark anal ring and pale cock. She took it well, with professional skill, squeezing and relaxing her anus to draw him in and incidentally bringing him to the edge of orgasm.

Judith was watching, her chin in one hand, smiling as Sally was buggered. Henry grinned back, pushing his cock the last inch up the black girl's bottom, until his front met her buttocks. Again Gurney leaned in, spreading Sally's bottom to check that as much of Henry's cock was inside as would go.

'Two,' Henry grunted.

'Frig your cunt while he's up you, Sally,' Judith suggested. 'They can seldom hold their seed at that.'

'You'll not catch me that way, not until it's up your own sweet arse,' Henry said.

Sally had reached back at Judith's words, and Henry felt her ring squeeze as she found her quim.

Trying to think of anything but the glorious dark bottom in which his cock was stuck, he pulled back, eyes closed. It came, slowly, Sally tightening her ring over and over, the last contraction closing on the neck of his cock. Henry swore, jerking it out even as he felt the first spasm in his groin. Her anus closed slowly behind him, the sight of the glistening, open hole making him fight not to plunge his cock back up it.

He stood back, drawing in deep breaths. His erection was agonisingly sensitive, the head scarlet and shiny with the pressure of his blood. Bubbles of fluid were already oozing from the tip, and as he glanced at the fat, proud hemispheres of Joanna's bottom he knew he would be unable to bugger her without coming.

She was looking shyly down, one eye peeping out from beneath a fringe of golden-brown hair, her pretty face flushed with arousal. Henry swore, turning his face away, towards the clock. It showed nine minutes to the hour. Blowing out his cheeks, he stationed himself behind Joanna's big, ripe bottom. Her hole showed, greasy with lard, winking at him in her shame and embarrassment at what was to be done to her.

Henry shut his eyes, counting slowly to ten, then twenty before opening them and pushing his cock in between Joanna's chubby buttocks. He felt the warm, slimy lard on his cock head, then the pressure of her anal flesh, resisting him.

'Loosen yourself, make it easy!' he grunted. 'Damn it, girl, it's not your first!'

Joanna gave a deep sob, then cried out in shock as a good half of Henry's cock jammed up her rectum in one push. She had relaxed, unexpectedly, her ring surrendering to the pressure. He too cried out,

239

tensing his muscles to stop himself coming up her on the instant. It worked, and he stopped, head thrown back, eyes shut, struggling to keep the picture of Joanna's penetrated bottom out of his head.

At last he felt safe, opening his eyes. Taking hold of her bottom, he spread the big cheeks with his thumbs. His cock was more than half up her, what remained a stout pink trunk joining his body to hers. He pushed, Joanna gasping as it slid in. Bit by bit it went up, painfully sensitive.

Todd Gurney watched as Joanna was buggered, nodding until at last the full length of Henry's shaft was buried in the girl's bottom. Only then did he pat Henry on the back and step clear. Henry sighed. It was in, Joanna's fat bottom squashed out against his front, his balls up against her quim. The problem was getting it out without coming. A glance at the clock showed six minutes remaining. He watched it, counting as the pendulum swung back and forth, until the minute hand clicked forwards.

Something of the agonising hardness had left his cock, and he began to pull out. Judith was watching him, giggling at his distress from behind her hand as he pulled from Joanna's bottom. Sally was still masturbating, lazily, one hand under Judith's chest, toying with a breast.

Henry returned a triumphant leer, only to realise that his erection was failing, the urge to ease his bladder rapidly replacing the urge to come. He tugged at his cock, the shaft slick and greasy with lard and the girls' juices, agonisingly sensitive, yet softening from the pain in his bladder. Thankful that he had left Judith's frequently buggered ring until last, he moved behind her, sure that he would be able to manage once his cock was wrapped in hot, wet girl-flesh.

240

Judith pushed her bottom out obligingly, surrendering her ring without fuss and giggling at his urgency. The head went in, filling the slimy little cavity as he pressed with his thumb. Judith looked back, laughing, and suddenly her ring was clamping on the neck of his cock, tight. Henry tried to drive himself up her, but his cock was only half-erect, while the tension in his bladder was growing to pain.

Cursing himself for drinking so much cider, and for not relieving himself before buggering the girls, he struggled to force his cock up Judith's bottom. She was laughing, and teasing him by winking her ring on his shaft, never relaxing long enough for him to get it up.

'Push then!' she laughed. 'So big and strong, and he can't even burst a girl's breech!'

Henry stopped, breathing deeply. Judith laughed, louder than before. Henry's bladder twinged, making him grit his teeth. One last time he tried to push, clutching Judith by the hips, before simply letting go.

Judith's laughter turned to a horrified shriek as the hot urine spurted up her bottom. Henry sighed in pleasure, holding her by the hips as he let the contents of his bladder drain into her rectum. Her shriek broke, she went silent, then began a pig-like squealing as her gut began to bulge with the pressure. Henry let it flow, ignoring her pained noises, curses and the frantic hammering of her fists on the table. He could feel it around his cock, hot and wet. Her anus was plugged, but not perfectly, letting the pee dribble out between her quim and spray onto Henry's balls. He could feel it, a delicious sensation, and as the pain and tension in his bladder began to ease his cock once more started to respond. Grinning, he looked down, admiring Judith's pert, raised bottom and those to either side, one pale, one brown, one spanked.

'Bastard! Bastard! Bastard!' Judith swore, then groaned as once more Henry began to bugger her.

His cock was stiffening quickly, and Judith's resistance had snapped. It went up, bit by bit, deeper and deeper into the warm puddle of urine inside her. His front met her buttocks and they began to bounce and jiggle to his pushes, while the fluid in her gut created an odd sloshing sensation as her body rocked back and forth. She was still cursing, her fists clenched tight, her breath coming in little, ragged pants.

With a last glance at the clock, Henry jammed the final inch of his now solid cock up Judith's bottom. She responded with a pained grunt, then gasps as he began to work in and out, the pee spurting from around his cock with each push. It felt glorious, better still with the thought of what he'd done to her. His pleasure was rising, his orgasm building once again, and then she had moved, reaching back with one hand, rubbing at her empty quim as she was buggered.

Henry laughed aloud, gritting his teeth as he struggled to make it in time, pushing, harder and harder. Judith was grunting with each push, also panting with ecstasy as she rubbed at herself. Henry felt her ring contract, then loosen and hot pee was spurting out around his balls, again, spraying wildly out as she went into orgasm, screaming and swearing in her ecstasy as he too came, with a long moan as his come erupted into the wet, pee-filled interior of her gut.

He stopped, his legs burning with pain, his knees shaking. Judith was still panting, her wig askew, the skin of her bottom and lower back prickly with sweat. Henry pulled back, slowly, suddenly conscious of the carpet.

'Hold it in,' he instructed. 'There's a good girl, clamp it tight as I pull out.'

'Bastard!' Judith said once more, but obligingly squeezed her ring as his cock came free.

She jumped up the moment it was out, running for the terrace, only to trip on the sill. Crashing down on to all fours with a yelp of surprise, followed immediately by a horrified gasp, she let go, in clear view of all of them. A long, yellow arch of piddle sprayed from her bottom, pattering and splashing on the stones. She made one final attempt to hold it in, her anus tightening and her buttocks clenched, then surrendered, once more letting the fountain erupt in a high arch as she sank face-down on the stone. She stayed like that, still clutching her dress, mouth agape, eyes shut, as the pee squirted out, forming a big yellow puddle behind her, which grew, then burst, trickling away down the steps.

As he watched Judith expel her enema, Henry was laughing so hard he was unable to stand. Clutching his sides in pain, he had sunk to his knees, while the miners and Gurney were also laughing at Judith, Eloise also, with Sally tittering behind one hand and only Joanna showing sympathy.

The gush from Judith's bottom gave way to a series of irregular spurts and finally a thin trickle of fluid running down over her quim. She rose, still holding her skirts clear of her dirty bottom, turned and gave Henry a filthy look, which broke suddenly to a broad smile with the blood rising to her cheeks.

Henry climbed unsteadily to his feet, reached for his glass and swallowed the contents. Todd Gurney was already holding out a shilling piece, which Henry took, acknowledging his victory with a broad grin.

'My game, I think,' he managed, 'and now perhaps a rest. Joanna, my dear, perhaps you would fetch a mop and bucket.'

Joanna, still bent over the table as if in a trance, quickly jumped up and ran from the room. Henry went for more wine, and Judith presently returned, still with her bodice undone but with her soiled petticoat bundled in her hands. Together with Joanna, she cleaned up, ignoring the ribald comments and compliments from the miners. Having sent the miners out on to the terrace with the cider barrel, they sprawled naked or near-naked in the drawing room. They sipped claret and talked, distinction forgotten save for Henry and Eloise occupying chairs while the others sprawled on the floor.

'To tomorrow,' Henry called, raising his glass. 'Mist on the Yeo at dawn, and the devil with any who set themselves against us.'

The others echoed him, raising their glasses and draining the contents. Henry refilled his, then Eloise's, before passing the jug to Judith.

'You show a deal of concern for a maid,' Sally remarked. 'Most would barely trouble.'

'I'll not pretend to be more gallant than the next man,' Henry answered, 'but damn it, it's a matter of pride. I'll not have some damn ruffian steal my wife's maid out from under my nose!'

'I reckon she was more than just a maid,' Sally giggled. 'There's been afternoons at Mama's with less going on.'

'True,' Henry admitted. 'I'll not deny it. Fine piece, Suki, and besides, she knows how to deal with Eloise's hair, top and bottom. Here, we've a picture of the girl, true to life.'

He went for the book Judith had taken from Snapes's house, opening it on his knee as the others crowded around to look. First choosing the picture of Suki sprawled on the sand, he turned the pages, revealing her in increasingly lewd poses.

'Mr Stukely had this same book,' Joanna remarked as they reached the one of Suki bending to flaunt her bottom. 'Larger, though. Hundreds of pictures it had. Ever so dirty.'

'Mr Lewis Stukely?' Eloise demanded.

'Mr Lewis Stukely, to Lydford,' Joanna said.

'Stukely collects,' Henry put in. 'Fancies himself something of a perfectionist. Only the best example of any one thing, he claims, as if such a thing existed. I mean to say, whoever heard of the best stuffed bird? He has something called a hoactzin in his study, from the southern Americas. Peculiar-looking creature, I'll grant him that. Even the stand's from some odd wood taken along the Amazon. Bloody fool. Serves good claret though.'

'Regular customer he was,' Joanna went on. 'Wanted it just so, he did, in special leather. Similar to Morocco, he said, and rich brown, but he wouldn't have none of Mr Carew's fine hides. The best we had, genuine Barbary goat tanned with sumac. Wasn't good enough for him. Fancy colour gold he wanted too. I never heard the like.'

'Typical,' Henry remarked.

'My father was from that way,' Sally put in. 'The colony to Senegambia.'

'Then he'd have seen these,' Henry remarked, turning to the picture showing Suki and the chimpanzee.

Henry chuckled as Sally gasped in shock.

'That's what your hide'll be, Joanna,' he laughed. 'Enschego skin. Typical of Stukely that'd be. The beast's in the book so he binds it with the hide!'

He sat back, grinning to himself, feeling thoroughly enervated and ripe for further mischief. His cock lay flaccid in his lap, the already the sight of the women's naked bodies was beginning to restore his interest. Reaching for the jug of claret, he filled his glass, drained it, repeated the process and filled it once more. As he drained the third glass he saw one of the

245

miners on the terrace rise, obviously speaking to somebody outside his range of vision.

'Damn!' he swore. 'We've company. Not genteel, I hope.'

There was a general scrabbling for clothes, Henry and Gurney tugging on their breeches, Judith and Joanna struggling with their bodices. Sally ran for it, stark naked, Eloise after her, fleeing the room with her dress clutched to her chest and her red bottom wobbling behind. Before Henry could finish buttoning his breeches flap, the visitors came into view, three men in coats of rough cloth, two in brown, one green. Saul Penhale was speaking to them, his brawny arms folded across his naked chest.

'Like to be the fellows who took Suki,' Henry grated. 'Well, this time there'll be a different story.'

'Right enough, sir,' Gurney answered.

Struggling into his shirt, Henry felt his anger rise, also the need to make a brave scene. Barefoot, in shirt and breeches only, he caught up the claret jug and his glass, striding out onto the terrace with Gurney behind him.

'This be he,' Saul Penhale said, nodding towards Henry. 'These men aim to speak to you, Mr Truscott, sir.'

'Do they, by George?' Henry answered. 'And who in hell might you three be?'

'We've a commission from Sir Joseph Snapes to seek out one Judith Cates, sir,' the man in the green coat replied, his voice firm but his eyes glancing to the seven heavy-set men behind Henry.

'Judith Cates?' Henry asked, trying to adjust his thoughts. 'Judith Cates? Well, she's not here. What the hell makes you think she might be?'

'We were told she'd likely be here,' the man went on, peering beyond Henry into the room. 'Who're they?'

'My wife's maids, damn your impudence!' Henry answered him.

Judith and Joanna stayed in the room, standing together in their blue maid's dresses. The man in green glanced at them, then at Henry once more.

'Neither of whom are Judith Cates, as you doubtless can see if you've had the wit to secure a description,' Henry said.

'We're to search for her, sir,' the man answered, hesitantly.

Henry laughed, about to tell the men to pass him if they could, when sudden inspiration struck. He poured himself a glass of claret, sipped at it and looked thoughtfully away across the valley.

'Judith Cates is not here, as you may plainly see,' he said. 'Indeed, despite the rudeness of your intrusion, I invite you to make a full search of the house and grounds. The search will prove fruitless, yet if you wish, I shall supply you with the information you require.'

'Yes?' the man asked, suspiciously.

'Indeed,' Henry replied. 'As you doubtless know, Judith is, or rather was, the er . . . lady of a good friend of mine, Mr Charles Finch . . .'

'We know all that,' the man interrupted. 'She's not there.'

'Indeed not,' Henry continued, 'and this is why I shall inform you of her whereabouts. Rather than remain faithful to Mr Finch, whose intentions were always honourable despite her status, she has taken up with another gentleman, although gentleman is hardly the word for one of so few morals.'

'Who would that be, sir, and where?'

'He is Mr Lewis Stukely, of Lydford. His house is off the Tavistock road, set back under the moor.'

'Where would that be then?'

Henry pointed across the distance, towards the moor, where the set of hills which marked the Lyd valley could clearly be seen.

'Over there,' he said, 'where you see the woodland cutting up into a valley. No? Well, as I bear her no good will after deserting my friend, I shall guide you, at least as far as the gates. Now, I warn you to be cautious. He's a devil of a fellow, this Stukely. Bad blood, you know – you must have heard of traitor Thomas Stukely, back in Queen Bess's time? No? No matter. Anyhow, he'll not surrender her lightly.'

'We're ready enough for that, sir,' the man answered, tapping the pocket of his coat.

'Then,' Henry finished, 'if you will permit me to dress, I shall join you at the gates presently.'

The man in green bowed, the others following as he left the terrace. Henry waited, sipping claret, until they were out of sight, then turned to Gurney.

'Care to join me, Todd? This should make fine sport!'

Suki pulled, bracing one foot against the wall, exerting everything she could on the chain. It groaned, plaster dust exploding in little puffs. She strained once more, pulling with the strength of her fear, ignoring the pain in her body. Again little bursts of plaster dust appeared, nothing more, and at last she sank down, exhausted. Before, she had always abandoned her efforts when the chain wouldn't give. Now she waited only to recover her breath, then stood again.

Wrapping herself in the blanket from her bed, she took the chain, turning on the spot to wrap it around her waist. Once more she braced herself, one foot on the wall, straining until the metal groaned and she felt the chain would cut her in half. Nothing moved, then

248

one stone, a crack appearing in the mortar. With sudden hope she pulled again, bracing her second foot against the wall, her full fifteen stone coming against the chain. There was a grating noise, the tiny gap widened, and suddenly she was falling backwards, crashing into the bed as mortar showered down on her.

Immediately there was a noise in the corridor, a voice calling, the sound of footsteps. The dust and debris was impossible to hide. Suki ducked down, waiting, her breath coming fast. The door began to open, Davy's face appeared and she hurled the two-pound brass weight from the scale. He swore, jerking the door closed an instant before the weight struck. Suki leapt up as he hurled the door back, dropping a box and snatching at the knife in his belt, to be sent reeling back as another weight caught him on the side of his head.

On the floor the box had burst, spilling knives and hooks, tweezers and strange, bladed implements across the floor. Seeing them, Suki threw herself at him in desperate terror, screaming and swinging the chain. Davy caught it and her body slammed into his. They went down on to the bed, grappling. He was trying to press her down, swearing and cursing at her, ordering her to be still, to surrender. She heard none of it, deaf with terror, struggling frantically, hurling herself from side to side as he tried to pin her down.

She was spitting, biting and kicking, but he was too strong, the muscles in his arms knotting as she was forced back. He had a knee on one of her thighs, forcing her leg down. His teeth were bared, right in front of her face, grinning as he realised he had her beaten. She lunged up, driving her forehead into his face, snapping his head back as she hurled herself to the side. They rolled, Suki clawing and biting at anything she could reach.

Once more he began to press her down. She had a leg over the side of the bed, one hip at the edge. Hurling herself sideways, she toppled him down, landing on top of him. There was a dull crack and his face creased in pain. He struck out, catching her in the face and she fell back, sitting heavily on the floor. Davy rolled away, clutching his chest. Suki rose, staggering with exhaustion. Davy had the chain, wrapped tight around one arm, wrenching even as she realised.

She cried out in pain as the iron collar dug into her neck. He wrenched again, jerking her across the room towards where his knife lay. Catching at the iron links, she hurled herself backwards. She went down, hard, Davy following, only to once more jerk the links. Suddenly he had dropped the chain. Dashing across the room, he grabbed at the largest of the skinning knives, his hand closing on the hilt, twisting around and up to stab out.

The blade caught in the heavy bed cover as she threw it. Hurling herself after it, Suki grappled with him, her fifteen stone bearing him down. He went, but stabbed up with the knife, slashing the cover inches from her face. She jerked back; he slipped, falling. She was on top of him, screaming in her own language, screeching in fear and fury, jumping up and down on his body beneath the cover, unaware of anything but her pain and fear.

He had stopped moving long before she gained enough control to realise. When she did, it was to find the Master looking down at her, a pistol in one hand, a raised cudgel in the other. The cudgel came down. There was a burst of pain, then blackness.

Lewis Stukely stood over the two bodies, one unconscious, one dead. He cursed, glaring in annoyance at

Davy's corpse. Davy had been meant to strangle the girl with the chain, and instead he had managed to get himself killed, and by falling on his own skinning knife. Suki was now unconscious, and so easy to dispatch, yet he was not at all certain of his ability to do the job. If it proved beyond him, then she would have to be kept alive until he could find a reliable replacement for Davy; no easy task.

Cursing again, he bent to lift Suki, only to find her too heavy to pick up. Instead he dragged her to the centre of the floor and rolled her on to her face. Using the chain, he bound her arms behind her back, making a double loop around her wrists, which he fixed together with Davy's bootlaces. The dead man's belt went to bind her ankles, again tied off with bootlaces. She looked helpless enough, and a quick inspection of her thighs showed no cuts or bruises.

Davy's skinning tools were spread out across the floor. Stukely began to pick them up, studying each before putting it down on the bed. The function of the knives was at least obvious, and the different sizes were presumably for different animals or types of skin. The various forceps, grips and hooks appeared designed to hold and stretch the hide, while he could only guess at the use of the peculiar truncated scissors and yet stranger instruments.

Again he glanced at Suki. Her huge, bare black bottom was uppermost, the fat cheeks smooth and glossy, the skin less fine than that of her thighs, but by no great margin. She was out cold, immobile, her breathing shallow. He put his hand to his chin, wondering if he would be able to test his skill without her coming around and spoiling it by struggling. He put his foot on one buttock, kicking.

Her bottom wobbled, quivering like an enormous brown jelly. Otherwise she remained still. He nodded to himself and turned to the bed, selecting a short-bladed scalpel, a pair of clasping forceps and a long, flat-bladed knife.

Henry pulled at the reins, turning his horse in between the high granite gateposts which marked the entrance to Stukely's property. He was reeling with drink, making it hard to stay in the saddle.

'This is it, my fine fellows!' he called, indicating the drive with a sweeping gesture of the claret bottle he held in one hand. 'The residence of Lewis Stukely, seducer, fornicator and collector. He is supposed to challenge me to a duel, so I'll join you if I may.'

The man in the green coat gave him a puzzled look, but followed as Henry started up the path. The two other strangers followed, Gurney bringing up the rear.

'The fellow's white-livered,' Henry mumbled, making his point with a stab of the claret bottle towards the house as it became visible. 'Damn it, I gave his betrothed a crimson cunt, and he's not got the spunk in him to call me out. White-livered, as I say. Mark you, she's a biter, is little Caroline, regular bobtail.'

'You spoke of him as a devil, sir, earlier,' one of the men said.

'Devil to be sure,' Henry answered, 'when he's barkers in both hands and some greenhorn against him. Full of bounce, he is, full of bounce, the bastard.'

'Best be cautious, sir,' Gurney remarked from behind him.

'Nonsense,' Henry answered. 'What can the fellow do? Not challenge me, with you four here? Damn it, I'll tell him how Caroline was on the grass, to his face, then see how he does!'

Henry turned, gesticulating with his bottle, vaguely aware that it was going to be hard to explain the absence of Judith, but not really caring. He put the bottle to his lips, draining it, and was about to throw it away when the air was torn by a piercing scream. Another followed, and a third, the men swearing and spurring their horses forward. Henry recovered his balance, starting after them. More screams rang out, high-pitched and shrill with terror, calling for help, in English, then in another language.

'Suki, by God!' Henry swore.

Gurney was off his horse, running for the door, Snapes's men behind him. They slammed into it, together, but it held. Slipping from his horse, Henry reeled to the ground. A window was nearby, and he hurled his claret bottle, shattering a diamond pane. His hand went through, grabbing the handle and wrenching it open.

Cursing violently, he scrambled through, across the seat within. Another scream rang out, then a broken babbling in Suki's language and a curse in English, male. Henry ran for the stairs, stumbling and clutching at the banister. A door was open across the landing; Stukely was standing in it, a long knife held in one hand, then abruptly ducked back. Henry hurled himself forward, slamming open the door to see Stukely, kneeling, the knife held to Suki's throat where she lay chained on the floor, staring in stark terror.

'A step and I kill her!' Stukely yelled.

Henry lurched forward, too drunk to care, driving his riding boot full into Stukely's face. Stukely's head snapped back, the knife flying from his hands. Off balance, trying not to step on Suki's head, Henry staggered to the side, landing on the edge of his foot and crashing into the window. His head caught the shutters, leaving him with his vision blurred and lights bursting in his head. Struggling to regain his senses, thinking of the skinning knife being plunged into his back, he turned.

There were people on the floor, more in the doorway, Todd Gurney and Snapes's men. Somebody cursed, another exclaimed in horror, and as Henry's vision cleared he saw Suki, rolled across Stukely's prone body, her face to his neck, her teeth sunk into his throat.

Notes

1 Ice houses were both a fashionable and functional feature of
   most eighteenth-century estates. Generally they were lined
   with brick, built wholly or partially underground and with a
   north-facing door, often in a wood or a copse planted for the
   purpose. Winters were considerably colder at the time, with
   even the Thames frequently freezing. Thick blocks of ice
   could therefore be collected easily in a way that would
   nowadays be impossible in most winters. Serving in much the
   same way as a modern fridge-freezer, a good ice house could
   retain icy temperatures from one winter until the next.
2 The eighteenth and nineteenth centuries saw a major change
   in agricultural practice. Primarily this involved the enclosure
   of common land, which was then redistributed among the
   inhabitants of each parish on the basis of individual owner-
   ship. An Act of Parliament was required for every individual
   enclosure and, despite self-interest among the gentry, this
   could be a slow and expensive process. Inevitably the wealthy
   and literate benefited at the expense of the poor, causing riots,
   great hardship and considerable rural depopulation. However, this, along with the introduction of new agricultural
   practices, allowed total production to be greatly increased.
   Without enclosure it would have been impossible to feed the
   populations of the cities and there would have been no
   Industrial Revolution.
3 By the late eighteenth century, the abolitionist Granville
   Sharp had managed to establish the precedent that 'as
   soon as any slave sets foot upon English soil, he becomes
   free'. This followed the cases of Jonathan Strong, Thomas
   Lewis and James Somersett, all black slaves brought to

England. However, the African slave trade was in its heyday and the picture was by no means clear. William Wilberforce presented his first bill to abolish the slave trade in 1791, but it was defeated. The slave trade was formally abolished within the British Empire in 1806, although slavery itself was not made illegal until 1833. Despite this the trade continued until the latter half of the nineteenth century. In 1793 any slave taken from an owner in Britain or from a ship in port would have had the support of the courts.

4 The late eighteenth century saw a severe shortage of coins, especially silver. A George III crown piece would have been a rarity to a country girl, and also have represented a week or more of work. Not only that, but the system of rents and tithes meant that anyone of the labouring class had great difficulty earning more than they owed. To offset the shortage of coins, tokens were frequently issued in their place, a much abused system. Mills, mines and so forth would pay their workers in tokens which could only be redeemed at the company shop, usually giving very poor value indeed and often trapping employees in debt to the company.

5 English law at this stage allowed any individual subject to prosecute a case against any other, with no official prosecution service. While fairer and less despotic than most systems of the time, it gave a considerable advantage to those with the right connections or money. Literate people could also 'plead clergy', if only once in theory, commuting a capital sentence to branding on the thumb.

6 Wife sales are one of those pieces of our history which the revisionists like to excuse, deny or simply ignore. There is no doubt they happened, although as the practice was largely confined to the rural poor it is not well documented. Even Thomas Hardy's famous account in *The Mayor of Caster-bridge* is said to have been derived from a newspaper report rather than first-hand experience. Most real sales seem to have been ritualised, with tradition demanding that the wife be sold at a regional market and that the halter be kept around her neck until she was brought to the buyer's house. Less formal sales occurred in pubs and by the wayside, mainly later examples.

In Devon, several cases are reported by the Rev Sabine Baring-Gould. The best documented is that of Henry Frise, of Lew Trenchard, Baring-Gould's own village. Frise bought his wife Anne at Okehampton market for half-a-crown in or

256

around 1800. Both Squire and Parson attempted to dissuade Frise, but he insisted that as the purchase had been made at the market and he had led Anne back from Okehampton on a halter, she was his wife. Anne had no objection to this and, indeed, in most cases the woman seems to have been willing or even the instigator of the sale. Another case reported by Baring-Gould is of a woman being purchased for a two-gallon jar of Plymouth Gin, but he declines to name her as she was still alive at the time, in 1908.

7 Thomas Stukely (1525?–1578) a notorious turncoat of the later sixteenth century. Reputedly a bastard son of Henry VIII, he served several European powers, often in conflict with England, but primarily the Spanish. Early in his extraordinary career he was also a privateer for Elizabeth I, and later claimed the title of Duke of Ireland, which he hoped to invade with Philip II of Spain. He was gifted with extraordinary powers of persuasion, talking several monarchs and Pope Gregory XIII into supporting him despite his reputation. He was also deceitful, vain and treacherous, placing a blot on the family name for generations. Actively involved in several battles, including Lepanto, he died fighting the Moroccans at Ksar el Kebir (Alcazar), after once again turning his coat from the service of the Pope to that of King Sebastian of Portugal.

8 Daniel Mendoza (1764–1836) the sixteenth English heavy-weight boxing champion. Active between 1784 and 1820, he took the title after beating Richard Humpheries in 1791, holding it until being beaten by John Jackson in 1795. His style was for fast movement and rapid punches, employing skill and speed rather than brute force.

9 Dr Edward Jenner (1749–1823) is credited with the invention of vaccination. It was known among the peasantry that those who had suffered from cowpox were subsequently immune to smallpox, knowledge which Jenner made formal. He carried out the first successful inoculation in 1796, experimenting on a boy of eight, although by then he had held his theory for some time in the face of considerable scepticism.

10 White witches were a common feature of English rural society at this time, by when witches had ceased to be actively persecuted. The last English witchcraft trial was that of Jane Wenham in 1712, and she was found innocent. The Witch-craft Act of 1735 repealed previous acts and made claiming supernatural powers punishable only as fraud (this was only

repealed in 1951, and the last prosecution was 1944). Such witches would have had more in common with modern homeopaths and therapists than occultists or even pagans.

11 Lincelles, a British victory against superior French revolutionary forces on 18 August 1793. Britain had been involved in the war since February of that year but it had yet to make much impact on day-to-day life.

12 Much of the land in this part of Devon was granted to the Russell family by Henry VIII after the dissolution of Tavistock Abbey in 1539. The Russells were Earls and later Dukes of Bedford. In 1793, Francis Russell, a noted agriculturist, was the 5th Duke and also Marquess of Tavistock. Lord John Russell, MP for Tavistock, became the 6th Duke in 1802 on his brother's death.

13 Roger Payne (1739–1797) was the most influential eighteenth-century English bookbinder. Highly skilled and inventive, his work was widely imitated and is still prized.

14 The French Revolution was in full swing in the late summer of 1793. Louis XVI had been executed in January, feudalism was fully abolished, the Committee of Public Safety had been set up and the terror was about to begin.

NEXUS BACKLIST

This information is correct at time of printing. For up-to-date information, please visit our website at www.nexus-books.co.uk

All books are priced at £5.99 unless another price is given.

Nexus books with a contemporary setting

Nexus books with Ancient and Fantasy settings

MAIDEN	Aishling Morgan ISBN 0 352 33466 5	☐
NYMPHS OF DIONYSUS £4.99	Susan Tinoff ISBN 0 352 33150 X	☐
THE SLAVE OF LIDIR	Aran Ashe ISBN 0 352 33504 1	☐
TIGER, TIGER	Aishling Morgan ISBN 0 352 33455 X	☐
THE WARRIOR QUEEN	Kendal Grahame ISBN 0 352 33294 8	☐

Edwardian, Victorian and older erotica

BEATRICE	Anonymous ISBN 0 352 31326 9	☐
CONFESSION OF AN ENGLISH SLAVE	Yolanda Celbridge ISBN 0 352 33433 9	☐
DEVON CREAM	Aishling Morgan ISBN 0 352 33488 6	☐
THE GOVERNESS AT ST AGATHA'S	Yolanda Celbridge ISBN 0 352 32986 6	☐
PURITY	Aishling Morgan ISBN 0 352 33510 6	☐
THE TRAINING OF AN ENGLISH GENTLEMAN	Yolanda Celbridge ISBN 0 352 33348 0	☐

Samplers and collections

NEW EROTICA 4	Various ISBN 0 352 33290 5	☐
NEW EROTICA 5	Various ISBN 0 352 33540 8	☐
EROTICON 1	Various ISBN 0 352 33593 9	☐
EROTICON 2	Various ISBN 0 352 33594 7	☐
EROTICON 3	Various ISBN 0 352 33597 1	☐
EROTICON 4	Various ISBN 0 352 33602 1	☐

Nexus Classics
A new imprint dedicated to putting the finest works of erotic fiction
back in print.

- - - - - - ✂ -

Please send me the books I have ticked above.

Name ....

Address ....

....

....

.... Post code ....

Send to: **Cash Sales, Nexus Books, Thames Wharf Studios, Rainville Road, London W6 9HA**

US customers: for prices and details of how to order books for delivery by mail, call 1-800-805-1083.

Please enclose a cheque or postal order, made payable to **Nexus Books Ltd**, to the value of the books you have ordered plus postage and packing costs as follows:

UK and BFPO – £1.00 for the first book, 50p for each subsequent book.

Overseas (including Republic of Ireland) – £2.00 for the first book, £1.00 for each subsequent book.

If you would prefer to pay by VISA, ACCESS/MASTER-CARD, AMEX, DINERS CLUB or SWITCH, please write your card number and expiry date here:

....

Please allow up to 28 days for delivery.

Signature ....

- - - - - - ✂ -

Laura made her escape before Jake could say anything else. And, as she went up the stairs again, she realised she was trembling. For heaven's sake, she thought impatiently, what was wrong with her? It wasn't the first time she had had a conversation with a strange man, and certainly he had given her no reason to feel this consuming sense of vulnerability in his presence. It wasn't as if he'd made a pass at her or anything. He'd been a perfect gentleman, and she was behaving like a silly spinster. Even if Julie had not been on the scene, there were probably dozens of women like her, waiting to take her place. She was just a middle-aged housewife, with a pathetic lust for something she had never had.

GUILTY

BY

ANNE MATHER

MILLS & BOON LIMITED
ETON HOUSE   18-24 PARADISE ROAD
RICHMOND   SURREY   TW9 1SR

*First published in Great Britain 1992
by Mills & Boon Limited*

© Anne Mather 1992

*Australian copyright 1992
Philippine copyright 1992
This edition 1992*

ISBN 0 263 77503 8

*Set in Times Roman 9½ on 9¾ pt.
01-9204-70469 C*

Made and printed in Great Britain

CHAPTER ONE

THE phone was ringing as Laura opened the door, and her heart sank. She had been anticipating kicking off her shoes, helping herself to a well-deserved drink, and running a nice deep bath in which to enjoy it. But all these pleasant prospects had to be put on hold while she answered the call. And as she could think of no reason why anyone should be calling her at this time of the evening, she was necessarily reticent.

After all, it was only twenty minutes since she had left the school, after a particularly arduous session with the parents of her fourteen-year-old students, and she had hoped to indulge herself for what was left of the evening. Mrs Forrest, who came in two days a week to keep the house in order, had, as she often did, left something simmering in the oven, and, although it was probably overcooked by now, the smell emanating from the kitchen was still very appetising. But someone, another parent perhaps, or a colleague—though that was less likely—or even her superior in the English department, had decreed otherwise, and she mentally squared her shoulders before going into the living-room and picking up the phone.

'Yes,' she said evenly, her low attractive voice no less sympathetic in spite of her feelings. 'Laura Fox speaking.'

'Mum?' Her daughter's voice instantly dispelled any trace of resignation in her attitude. 'Where've you been? I've been trying to reach you for hours!'

'Julie!' Laura's initial sense of relief at hearing her daughter's voice was quickly followed by concern. After all—she glanced at the slim gold watch on her wrist—it was almost ten o'clock. 'Is something wrong? Where are you? I thought you said you were going to New York this week.'

'I was.' But her daughter didn't sound concerned, and Laura sank down on to the arm of the sofa and tucked one foot behind the other. Experience had taught her that her

5

daughter's telephone calls—though infrequent—tended to
be long, and Laura prepared herself for protracted explanations. 'I told Harry I couldn't go.'

'I see.'

Laura didn't. Not really. But it seemed a suitable reply.
If Julie wanted to tell her why she should have chosen to
turn down a proposedly lucrative opportunity to work in
the United States she would do so. Laura knew her daughter
well enough to know that asking too many questions could
illicit an aggressive response. Ever since she was sixteen,
and old enough to make her own decisions, Julie had resisted any efforts on her mother's part to try and offer her
advice. Her favourite retort, if Laura had attempted to
counsel her, was that Laura was in no position to criticise
her plans, when she had made such a mess of her own life.
And, although the barb was hardly justified, Laura was too
sensitive about her own mistakes to carry the argument.

Now, however, her daughter was speaking again, and
Laura forced herself to concentrate on what she was saying.
Now was not the time to indulge in rueful recollection, and
there was no denying that Julie had made a success of her
career.

'So,' her daughter exclaimed impatiently, 'aren't you
going to ask me why I've been trying to get in touch with
you? Don't you want to know why I turned down Harry's
offer?'

Laura stifled a sigh. 'Well—of course,' she said, looking
longingly towards the sherry decanter residing on the
bureau, just too far away to reach. 'But I assumed you
were about to tell me.' A twinge of anxiety gripped her.
'What's happened? You're not ill, are you?'

'No.' Julie sounded scornful. 'I've never felt better. Is
that the only reason you can think of why I should want
to stay in London?'

Laura lifted her shoulders wearily. Her neck was aching
from looking up at people, and her spine felt numb. It had
been a long day, and she wasn't really in the mood to play
twenty questions.

'Have you left the agency?' she asked carefully, conscious that Julie could throw a tantrum at the least provo-

cation, and unwilling to arouse her daughter's anger. 'Have you found a better job?'

'You could say that.' Evidently she had made the right response, and Julie's tone was considerably warmer. 'But I haven't left the agency. Not yet, anyway.'

'Oh.' Laura endeavoured to absorb the subtler connotations of this statement. 'So—it must be a man.'

There had been a lot of men during Julie's five-year sojourn in the capital, but this was the first time Laura had known her daughter give up a modelling contract for one of them.

'You got it.' Julie was apparently too eager to deliver her news to waste any more time playing games. 'It is a man. *The* man! I'm going to marry him, Mum. At least, I am if I have anything to do with it.'

Laura's lips parted. 'You're getting married!' She had never expected this. Julie had always maintained that marriage was not for her. Not after her mother's unhappy experience.

'Well, not yet,' Julie conceded swiftly. 'He hasn't asked me. But he will. I'll make sure of that. Only—well—he wants to meet you. And I wondered if we could come up for the weekend.'

'He wants to meet me?' Laura was surprised, and Julie didn't sound as if the proposition met with her approval either.

'Yes,' she said shortly. 'Silly, isn't it? But—well—I might as well tell you. He's not English. He's Italian. An Italian count, would you believe? Although he doesn't use the title these days. In any case, he's not an impoverished member of the Italian aristocracy. His family owns factories and things in Northern Italy, and he's very wealthy. What else?' Julie uttered an excited little laugh. 'I wouldn't be considering marrying him otherwise. No matter how sexy he is!'

Laura was stunned. 'But—Julie...' She licked her lips, as she endeavoured to find the right words to voice her feelings. 'I mean—why does he want to meet me? And— coming here. This is just a tiny cottage, Julie. Why, I only have *two* bedrooms!'

'So?' Julie sounded belligerent now. 'We'll only need one.'

'No.' Laura knew she was in danger of being accused of being prudish, but she couldn't help it. 'That is—if—if you come here, you and I will share my room.'

'Oh, all right.' Julie made a sound of impatience. 'I don't suppose Jake would want to sleep with me there anyway. After all, it's his idea that he introduce himself to you. That's apparently how they do things in his part of the world. Only I explained I didn't have a father.'

Julie's scornful words scraped a nerve, but Laura suppressed the urge to defend herself. It was an old argument, and Julie knew as well as her mother that she had had a father, just like anyone else. The fact that her parents had never been married was what she was referring to, a situation she had always blamed her mother for. She had maintained that Laura should have known that the man she had allowed to get her pregnant already had a wife, and no amount of justification on her mother's part could persuade her otherwise. Even though she knew Laura had been only sixteen at the time, while Keith Macfarlane had been considerably older, she had always stuck to the belief that Laura should have been more suspicious of a man who worked in Newcastle and spent most of his weekends in Edinburgh.

But Laura hadn't been like her daughter at that age. The only child of elderly parents, she had been both immature and naïve. A man like Keith Macfarlane, whom she had met at a party at a friend's house, had seemed both worldly-wise and sophisticated, and she had been flattered that someone so confident and assured should have found her so attractive. Besides, she had enjoyed a certain amount of kudos by having him pick her up from the sixth-form college, and for someone who hitherto had lived a fairly humdrum existence it had been exciting.

Of course, with hindsight, Laura could see how stupid she had been. She should have known that a man who liked women as much as Keith did was unlikely to have reached his thirtieth birthday without getting involved with someone else. But she had been young and reckless—and she had paid the price.

Looking back, she suspected Keith had never intended to get so heavily involved. Like her, he'd evidently enjoyed having a partner who was not in his own age-group, and at sixteen, Laura supposed, she had been quite attractive. She had always been tall, and in her teens she had carried more weight than she did now. In consequence, she had looked older, and probably more experienced, too, she acknowledged ruefully. So much so that Keith had expected her to know how to take care of herself, and it had come as quite a shock to him to discover she was still a virgin.

That was when their relationship had foundered. Keith had seen the dangers, and drawn back from them. Three weeks later he'd told her he had been transferred to Manchester, and she'd never heard from him again.

Tom Dalton, the father of Laura's best friend, at whose house she had first met Keith, eventually admitted the truth. He had worked with Keith, and he knew why he spent his weekends in Edinburgh. Laura wished he had seen fit to tell her sooner, but by then it was too late. Laura was pregnant, and for a while it seemed as if her whole life was ruined.

Naturally, she had dreaded telling her parents. Mr and Mrs Fox had never approved of her generation, and she was quite prepared for them to demand she get rid of the baby. But in that instance she was wrong. Instead of making it even harder for her, her father had suggested a simple solution. She should have the baby, and then go back to school. There was no point in wasting her education, and if she was going to have a child to support then she ought to ensure that she had a career to do it. And that was what she had done, leaving the baby with her mother during the day, while she'd studied for her A levels, and subsequently gained a place at the university.

It had not been an easy life, Laura recalled without rancour. Julie had not been an 'easy' baby, and when her parents had died in a car accident during her first year of teaching it had been hard. Coping with the pupils at an inner-city comprehensive during the day, and still finding the energy to cope with a fractious five-year-old at night. But Laura had managed, somehow, although at times she was so tired that she'd wondered how she was going to go on.

Of course, much later, when Julie discovered the circumstances of her own birth, other complications had arisen. As a young girl, Julie had always resented the fact that she only had one parent, and as she grew older that resentment manifested itself in rows and tantrums that often escalated out of all proportion.

But Julie had one consolation. Her features, which as a child had been fairly ordinary, blossomed in her teens into real beauty. Not for Julie the horrors of puppy-fat and acne. Her skin was smooth and unblemished, her height unmarred by extra inches. Her hair, which she had inherited from her mother, was several shades darker than Laura's, a rich, burnished copper that flowed freely about her shoulders. She became the most popular girl in her class, and, although Laura worried that she might make the same mistakes she had made, Julie was much shrewder than she had ever been.

Laura hated to admit it, but when Julie left school before she was eighteen, and took herself off to London to work, she was almost relieved. The effort of sharing an apartment with someone who was totally self-absorbed and totally selfish had been quite a strain, and for months after Julie had gone Laura revelled in her new-found freedom.

And then, not wholly unexpectedly, Julie became famous. The secretarial job she had taken had been in a photographic agency, and not unnaturally someone had noticed how photogenic Julie was. Within months, her face began appearing on the covers of catalogues and magazines, and all the bitterness of the past was buried beneath the mask of her new sophistication.

Of course, Laura had been delighted for her. The guilt she had always felt at being the unwitting cause of Julie's illegitimacy was in some part relieved by her daughter's success, and it meant she could stop worrying about her finances, and buy herself the cottage in Northumberland she had always wanted. These days she lived in a small village about fifteen miles from the city, and only commuted to Newcastle to work.

Now, pushing the memories away, and ignoring her daughter's bitterness, Laura addressed herself to the present situation. 'Do I take it you plan to come up here tomorrow evening?' she asked, mentally assessing the contents of the freezer and finding them wanting. If Julie and this man, whoever he was, were coming to stay, she would have to do some shopping tomorrow lunchtime.

'If that won't put you out,' Julie agreed offhandedly, and Laura hoped she hadn't offended her by reminding her of the differences in their current lifestyles. Julie now owned a luxurious apartment in Knightsbridge, and her visits to Burnfoot were few and far between.

'Well, of course you won't be putting me out,' Laura assured her quickly, not wanting to get the weekend off to an uncertain start. 'Um—so who is this man? What's his name? Other than Jake, that is?'

'I've told you!' exclaimed Julie irritably. 'He's an Italian businessman. His family name is Lombardi. Jake's the eldest son.'

'I see.' So—Jake Lombardi, then, thought Laura nervously. Would that be short for Giovanni? Would Julie be living in Italy, after they were married?

'Anyway, you'll be able to meet him for yourself tomorrow,' declared Julie at last. 'We'll probably drive up in his Lamborghini. Personally I'd prefer to fly, but Jake says he wants to see something of the countryside. He's interested in history—old buildings; that sort of thing.'

'Is he?'

Laura was surprised. What little she had learned about her daughter's previous boyfriends had not led her to believe that Julie would be attracted to a man who cared about anything other than material possessions. But perhaps she was maturing after all, Laura thought hopefully. Was it too much to wish that Julie had learned there was more to life than the accumulation of wealth?

'So—we'll see you some time after five,' Julie finished swiftly. 'I can't stop now, Mum. We're on our way to a party. 'Bye!'

'G'bye.'

Laura made the automatic response, and she was still holding the phone when the line went dead. Shaking her head, she replaced the receiver, and then sat looking at the instrument for a few blank moments, before getting up to pour herself the long-awaited glass of sherry.

Then, after taking a few experimental sips of the wine, she pulled herself together and walked through to the tiny kitchen at the back of the cottage. As she had expected, the casserole Mrs Forrest had left for her was a trifle over-cooked. But, although the vegetables were soggy, the chicken was still edible, and, putting it down on the pine table, she went to get herself a plate. But all her actions were instinctive, and she had the sense of doing things at arm's length. The prospect of Julie's actually getting married, of settling down at last, had left her feeling somewhat off guard, and she knew it would take some getting used to.

Nevertheless, she was not displeased at the news. On the contrary, she hoped her daughter would find real happiness. And maybe Julie would learn to forgive her mother's mistakes, now that she loved someone herself. Or at least try to understand the ideals of an impressionable girl.

Friday was always a busy day for Laura. She had no free periods, and she usually spent her lunch-hour doing some of the paperwork that being assistant head of the English department demanded. It meant she could spend Saturday relaxing, before tackling the preparation she did on Sundays.

Consequently, when she went out to the car park to get into her small Ford, Mark Leith, her opposite number in the maths department, raised surprised eyebrows at this evident break with routine.

'Got a date?' he enquired, slamming the boot of his car, and tucking the box he had taken from it under his arm. 'Don't tell me you're two-timing me!'

Laura pulled a face at him. She and Mark had an on-off relationship that never progressed beyond the occasional date for dinner or the theatre. It was Laura's decision that their friendship should never become anything more than that, and Mark, who was in his early forties, and still lived with his mother, seemed to accept the situation. Laura guessed he preferred bachelorhood really, but now and then he attempted to assert his authority.

'I'm going shopping,' she replied now, opening the door of the car, and folding herself behind the wheel. 'Julie's coming for the weekend, and bringing a friend.'

'I see.' Mark walked across the tarmac to stand beside her window, and, suppressing a quite unwarranted sense of impatience, Laura wound it down. 'A girlfriend?'

'What?'

Laura wasn't really paying attention, and Mark's mouth turned down at the corners. 'The friend,' he reminded her pointedly. 'Is it a girlfriend?'

'Oh...' Laura put the key into the ignition, and looked up at him resignedly. 'No. No, as a matter of fact, it's a boyfriend. Well, a man, I suppose. She rang me last night, after I got home.'

'Really?' Mark arched his sandy brows again, and Laura felt her irritation return. 'Bit sudden, isn't it?'

Laura sighed, gripping the wheel with both hands. It was nothing to do with him really, and she found she resented his assumption that he could make remarks of that sort. It was probably her own fault, she thought wearily. Although she hadn't encouraged Mark's advances, she supposed she had let him think he had some influence in her life.

Now she forced a polite smile, and shrugged her slim shoulders. 'Oh—you know what young people are like!' she exclaimed dismissively. 'They don't need weeks to plan a trip. They just do it.'

'It's a bit hard on you though, isn't it?' Mark persisted, his chin jutting indignantly. 'I mean—you might have had other plans.'

Laura nearly said, 'Who? Me?' but she didn't think Mark would appreciate the irony. His sense of humour tended towards the unsubtle, and any effort on Laura's part to parody her own position would only meet with reproval. In consequence, she only shook her head, and leaned forward to start the engine.

'I was going to suggest we might try and get tickets for that revue at the Playhouse,' Mark added, as if to justify his aggravation. 'I've heard it's jolly good, and it finishes on Saturday.'

Laura squashed her own resentment, and managed a warmer expression. 'Oh, well,' she said, 'we'll have to catch

it some other time. And now I really must go, or I won't
have time to get everything I want.'

Mark's mouth compressed. 'You could still——'

'No, I couldn't,' declared Laura firmly, and put the car
into gear. 'I'll see you later.'

He was still standing looking after the car as Laura turned
out of the car park, and lifted her hand in a reluctant
farewell. Really, she thought, concentrating on the traffic
on the West Road, there were times when Mark could be
such a pain. Surely he could understand that as Julie paid
so few visits to her mother Laura couldn't possibly desert
her to go to the theatre with him? Besides, it wasn't as if
Julie were making a convenience of her this time. She was
bringing her future husband to meet her, and, even if it
was more his suggestion than hers, it might presage a new
closeness in her relationship with her daughter.

But Mark and Julie had never seen eye to eye. From the
beginning, he had found her spoilt, and headstrong, and
on the rare occasions when they had all been together Julie
had gone out of her way to be objectionable to him. So far
as she was concerned, Mark was a stuffed shirt, and her
comments about his bachelor lifestyle wouldn't bear
repeating.

The supermarket was heaving with people doing their
weekend shopping, and Laura, who generally supplied her
needs from the small store in Burnfoot, gritted her teeth as
yet another mother with toddlers blocked her passage.
'Excuse me,' she said, trying to edge along the aisle, and
was rewarded with a smear of ice lolly all along the sleeve
of her anorak.

'Oh—sorry!' exclaimed a smiling matron, drawing her
child's hand away, and examining the lolly for damage.
'These aisles are so narrow, aren't they?'

Laura glanced at the sticky red confection adorning her
sleeve, and then gave a resigned shrug. There was no point
in getting angry. 'Yes, very narrow,' she agreed, and, unable
to prevent herself from smiling at the cheeky toddler, she
moved on.

It was after one by the time she had loaded her purchases
into her car, and striking half-past as she turned into the
school car park. One or two stragglers were still sauntering

across the playground, and they gave her a knowing look, before turning to whisper to their friends. Laura could almost hear the comments about her being late as well, and she tried not to look too flustered as she strode towards the school buildings.

The afternoon seemed endless. Now that the time for Julie's arrival was approaching, Laura could feel herself getting tense, and it didn't help when her class of fourth-years started acting up. Usually she had no trouble with her pupils, and she had gained a reputation for being tough, but fair. However, today she found it difficult to keep order, and it wasn't until she apprehended how hoarse she was getting that she realised she had had to shout to make herself heard.

But at last three-thirty arrived, and after dismissing the fourth-years Laura packed what exercise books she could into her briefcase, and tucked the rest under her arm. By her reckoning, she had at least two hours left to prepare herself for Julie's arrival, and the way she was feeling she was going to need every minute of it. She didn't know why she let Julie tie her up in knots like this, but she always did, and Laura intended to have a bath and wash her hair, so that she could have confidence in her appearance, if nothing else.

Burnfoot was situated in some of the most beautiful country in Northumberland. A small community of some one thousand souls, it was surrounded by the rolling fields and hills of the border country, with the crumbling remains of Hadrian's Wall providing a natural barrier to the north. It was farming country, with tumbling streams and shady forests, and long, straight roads, unfolding towards the old Roman forts of Chesters and Housesteads.

Laura had always loved it. Even though she had been born and brought up in Newcastle, this was the area where she felt most at home, and when the opportunity to buy the cottage had presented itself she had jumped at the chance. She knew Julie had thought she was mad; a single woman, on her own, going to live in some 'God-forsaken spot' as she'd put it; but Laura had never had cause to regret her decision. The cottage had been in a poor state of repair when she'd got it, it was true, and it had taken

years to get it as she wanted. But that was all behind her
now. It was still small, and the ceilings were still too low,
but she had had central heating installed, and on a cold
winter's evening she could light the fire in the living-room,
and toast her toes.

She was perfectly content, she thought, except on these
occasions when Julie invaded her life, and then she was
forced to see the cottage's shortcomings. Julie was adept
at pointing out its disadvantages, and never once had she
admired the garden Laura had worked so painstakingly to
tame, or complimented her mother on providing a home
that was both attractive, and full of character.

Laura had decided to prepare fish for dinner. It was a
Friday, and she couldn't be sure that as an Italian, and no
doubt a Roman Catholic, Julie's boyfriend would be prepared to eat meat. She had bought some plaice, and she
intended to cook it in a white wine sauce. She had decided
not to provide a starter, and instead she had bought a
strawberry shortcake to supplement the cheese and crackers
that she herself preferred. She knew Julie had a sweet tooth,
and, although she was generally on some diet or another,
she could be relied upon to be tempted by the dessert. It
also meant she could prepare everything in advance, and
leave the fish on a low heat while she took her bath.

Before she could attend to her own needs, however, there
was the bed in the spare room to make up, and fresh towels
to put out. She drew a pretty, chintzy cover on to the duvet,
and then surveyed the room critically, trying to see it through
a stranger's eyes. She couldn't imagine what a man, who
evidently came from a wealthy background, would think
of this tiny bedroom, with its accent on feminine tastes.
The carpet was cream, the walls were a delicate shade of
pink, and the curtains matched the cover on the duvet.
Laura herself had made the pleated skirt that swagged the
small dressing-table, and even she had to duck her head to
look out of the window.

Oh, well, she thought after opening the window and in-
haling the cool air of an April evening, at least the view
from the window was worth looking at, even if the spring
was dragging its heels in this part of the world.

The bathroom was modern anyway, she reflected some time later, soaking in a warm, scented tub. Until she had been able to afford the renovations to the plumbing system, she had had to make do with rather primitive conditions, which was probably one of the reasons why Julie had only visited the cottage once before the new bathroom was installed. But now, although again everything had had to be scaled down to fit its surroundings, the tub was satisfyingly deep, and there was even a shower above it. Of course, it wasn't a proper shower cubicle, such as Julie had in her bathroom in London. But Laura didn't mind. She was usually the only one who used it, and she realised with a pang that, apart from Julie, this would be the first time she had had anyone to stay at the cottage.

She wondered what her daughter had told…Jake…about her mother. How had she described her, for instance? As a middle-aged frump, she supposed. She knew Julie thought she didn't make the best of herself, and her daughter was always saying that Laura ought to pay more attention to her appearance. Julie said she was a woman of thirty-eight, going on fifty, and in her opinion Laura ought to shorten her skirts and take advantage of the fact that she had nice legs.

But Laura was so accustomed to living alone and pleasing herself that she seldom considered what might or might not be flattering when she bought clothes. She was happiest in jeans and sloppy shirts or sweaters, pottering about the garden at the cottage, or taking Mrs Forrest's Labrador for long walks through the countryside. She would have had a dog herself, except she didn't think it was fair, as she was out all day. But when she retired…

She smiled, soaping her arms, and enjoying the sensation of the creamy compound against her skin. It was silly to think of retirement yet. She was only thirty-eight. But the truth was, she saw no evidence for change in her life, and she had to think of the future. She might get married, of course, but apart from Mark she could think of no one who might want to marry her. In any case, it was not an option she considered seriously. Having remained single all these years, she was probably too set in her ways to adapt to anyone else's, she decided ruefully. Besides, she could think of nothing a man could offer her that she didn't already have.

Washing her hair, however, she had to acknowledge that it did need cutting. The trouble was, most days she just coiled it into its usual knot at her nape, and by the time she thought of it again she was back at the cottage. In any case, it was essentially straight, and it was probably easiest to handle in its present condition. She was not the type to go for fancy cuts or perms. At least she didn't have many grey hairs, she thought gratefully. Her hair was still that nondescript shade between honey-blonde and chestnut, and if it was also thick, and shining, she scarcely appreciated it.

She heard the car as she was drying her hair. She had been sitting on the stool, in front of the mirror in her bedroom, trying to make an objective assessment of her appearance, and when she heard the powerful engine in the lane outside she knew a moment's panic. Obviously, she had spent longer over her toilet than she had intended, and now she met her own reflected gaze with some trepidation. For heaven's sake, she wasn't even dressed, she thought frantically. And the door downstairs was locked.

There was nothing for it. She would have to go down in her dressing-gown, she decided, shedding the towel she had worn sarong-wise around her body and snatching up her towelling bathrobe. If she hurried, she might be able to unlock the door and escape upstairs again without anyone seeing her. Julie would not be pleased if she met the man her daughter was going to marry in such a state of disarray. Although her hair was dry and silky, it was simply not suitable for a woman of her age. She looked like an ageing hippy, she thought frustratedly. If only she had paid more attention to the time.

Not stopping to put on her slippers, she started down the narrow staircase, and then stopped, aghast, when the handle of the front door was tried and rattled impatiently. It was immediately below her, the cottage having only a minuscule hallway, from which the stairs mounted on the outer wall. A second door led into the living area, which Laura had enlarged by having the wall demolished between what had been the parlour and dining-room, and there was no way she could unlock the door now without being seen.

Taking a deep breath, she gave in to the inevitable. She couldn't ask them to wait while she put on some clothes. That would be foolish. Besides, if this man was going to become her son-in-law, the sooner he saw her as she really was, the better.

But, even as she was making this decision, the flap of the letterbox was lifted, and Julie called, 'Mum! Mum, are you there? Open the door, can't you? It's raining.'

'Oh! Is it?'

Without more ado, Laura hurried down the last few stairs, and hastily turned the key. The door was propelled inward almost before she had time to step out of the way, and Julie appeared in the open doorway, looking decidedly out of humour.

'What were you——? Oh, Mum!' Julie stared at her with accusing eyes. 'You're not even dressed!'

'I was taking a bath,' replied Laura levelly, trying to maintain her composure. 'Besides,' she lifted her shoulders defensively, 'you're early.'

'It is after six,' retorted Julie, pushing her way through to the living-room. 'God, what a drive! The traffic was appalling!'

Laura's lips parted, and she stared after her daughter with some confusion. What did she mean? Surely she hadn't driven herself up to Northumberland. Julie did have a Metro, she knew that, for getting about town, but the engine she had heard hadn't sounded anything like Julie's Metro. It had been low and unobtrusive, that was true, but there had been no doubting the latent power behind its restrained compulsion.

Shaking her head, she moved to the open doorway, and peered out into the rain. And, as she did so, a tall figure loomed out of the gloom, with suitcases in both hands, and Julie's Louis Vuitton vanity case tucked under one arm. He was easily six feet in height—tall for an Italian, thought Laura inconsequently—with broad shoulders encased in a soft black leather jerkin. He was also very dark; dark-skinned, dark-haired, and dark-eyed, with the kind of hard masculine features that were harsh, yet compelling. He wasn't handsome in the accepted sense of the word, but he was very attractive, and Laura knew at once why Julie had decided that he was the one.

CHAPTER TWO

THEN, realising that by hovering in the doorway she was forcing him to stand in the rain, Laura made a gesture of apology, and got out of his way. He stepped into the tiny hall with evident relief, immediately dwarfing it by his presence, and Laura backed up the stairs to give him some space.

'Hi,' he said easily, and his deep, husky tones brushed her nerves like black velvet. With apparent indifference to her hair, or her state of undress, he put down the suitcases, and allowed the vanity case to drop on top of them 'You must be Julie's mother,' he added, straightening. 'How do you do? I'm Jake Lombardi.'

He spoke English without a trace of an accent, and Laura thought how awful it was that she couldn't even greet him in his own language. 'Laura Fox,' she responded, coming down the stairs again to take the hand he held out to her. And as the damp heat of his palm closed about hers, she had the ridiculous feeling that nothing was ever going to be the same again. 'Um—welcome to Burnfoot.'

'Thanks.'

He smiled, his dark eyes crinkling at the corners, and shaded by thick lashes. For all he had shown no obvious reaction to her appearance, she had the feeling that no aspect of her attire had missed his notice, and in spite of herself, a wave of colour swept up from her neck to her face.

She wasn't used to dealing with younger men, she thought impatiently, chiding herself for her lack of composure. And particularly not a man who displayed his masculinity so blatantly. Against her will, her eyes had strayed down over the buttons of an olive-green silk shirt, to where the buckle of a black leather belt rode low across the flat muscles of his stomach. The belt secured close-fitting black denims that

clung to the strong muscles of his thighs like a second skin.
The fact that Laura also noticed how they moulded his sex
with equal cohesion was something she instantly rejected.
For God's sake, she thought, horrified that she should even
consider such a thing. What was the matter with her?

'Are you going to close that door and come in?'

Julie's peevish complaint from the living-room came as
a welcome intervention, but when Laura would have stepped
round Jake to attend to it, he moved aside, and allowed
his own weight to propel the door into its frame.

'It's closed,' he said, still looking at Laura, and, with
the panicky feeling that he had known exactly what she was
thinking a few moments ago, she turned towards the stairs.

'I won't be a minute,' she said, not looking to see if he
was watching her, and, without giving Julie time to lodge
a protest, she ran up the stairs to her room.

Her mirror confirmed her worst fears. Her face was
scarlet, and, even to her own eyes, she looked as guilty as
she felt. But guilty of what? she wondered. It wasn't as if
she had done anything wrong. Heavens, she was no *femme
fatale*, and she was a fool if she thought he had been
flattered by her attention. On the contrary, he had probably
found her unwary appraisal amusing, or pitiful, or both.
Right now he was probably regaling Julie with the news
that her mother had been lusting after his body. Oh, God,
it was embarrassing! What must he be thinking of her?

However, right now she couldn't afford to let that get to
her. She was probably exaggerating the whole incident
anyway, and the best way to put the matter behind her was
to go down and behave as if nothing had happened. Then,
if Jake Lombardi had been discussing her with Julie, it
would look as if he had been imagining things, and not her.

Earlier, she had laid out the dress she had intended to
wear on the bed, but now, looking at it with new eyes, she
saw it was far too formal for this evening. Made of fine
cream wool, it had a soft cowled collar, and long fitted
sleeves, and, bearing in mind Julie's remarks about not
making the best of herself, Laura had bought it at
Christmas, to silence her daughter's criticisms. In the event,
however, Julie had not come home at Christmas, and the

dress had hung in the wardrobe ever since, a constant reminder of her extravagance.

Now, she picked it up, and thrust it back on to its hanger.
The last thing she wanted was for Julie to think she was
dressing up to impress her fiancé, she thought grimly. Or
for him to think the same, she added, pulling out a pair of
green cords, and a purple Aran sweater, that had seen better
days. Whatever Julie thought, she was almost forty, and
she refused to behave like a woman twenty years younger.

Her hair gave her no trouble, and she coiled it into its
usual knot without difficulty. And, as the colour receded
from her face, she began to feel more optimistic. She had
allowed the fact that she had answered the door in her
bathrobe and nothing else to upset her equilibrium, and
now she had had time to gather herself she could see how
silly she had been. It had probably amused Jake Lombardi
that she had been caught out. And why not? He was no
doubt used to much more sophisticated surroundings, and
more sophisticated women, she acknowledged drily.

She leant towards the mirror to examine her face. Should
she put on some make-up? she wondered, running her
fingers over her smooth skin. She had intended to, but,
now that she had been seen without it, was there much
point? She didn't wear much anyway, and she was lucky
enough to have eyelashes that were several shades darker
than her tawny hair. Golden eyes, the colour of honey,
looked back at her warily, and she allowed a small smile
to touch the corners of her mouth. Compared to her
daughter, she was very small change indeed, she thought
ruefully. So why try and pretend otherwise?

The hardest part was going downstairs again. She entered the living-room cautiously, steeling herself to meet
knowing smiles and shared humour, but it didn't happen.
Although Julie was stretched out in front of the fire her
mother had lit when she'd come home, Jake wasn't in the
room, and Laura's expression mirrored her surprise.

'He's gone to lock up the car,' remarked Julie carelessly,
extending the empty glass she was holding towards her
mother. In a fine suede waistcoat over a bronze silk blouse,
and form-fitting black ski-pants, she was as sleek and in-

dolent as a cat—and her attitude said she knew it. 'Get me another Scotch, will you? I'm badly in need of sustenance.'

Laura caught her lower lip between her teeth, but she took the glass obediently enough, and poured a measure of malt whisky over the ice that still rested in the bottom. Then, handing it back to her daughter, she said carefully, 'Is this wise? Drinking spirits so early in the evening?'

'What else is there to do in this God-forsaken place?' countered Julie cynically, raising the glass to her lips, and swallowing at least half its contents at one go. She lowered the glass again, and regarded her mother through half-closed lids. 'So—what do you think of Jake? Pretty dishy, isn't he? And he tastes just as good as he looks.'

Laura couldn't help the *frisson* of distaste that crossed her face at her daughter's words, and Julie gave her an impatient look before hauling herself up in the chair. 'I hope you're not going to spend the whole weekend looking at me with that holier-than-thou expression!' she exclaimed, using the toe of one of her knee-length boots to remove the other. Then she held out the remaining boot to her mother. 'Jake is tasty. Even you must be able to see that. Even if your criterion for what might—or might not—be sexy is based on that wimp Mark Leith!'

'Mark is not a wimp,' began Laura indignantly, and then, realising she was defending herself, she broke off. 'I—gather you didn't enjoy the journey here. I believe Friday evenings are always busy.'

'Hmm.' Free of her boots, Julie moved her stockinged feet nearer the fire. 'You could say that.' She shrugged. 'I hate driving in the rain. It's so boring!'

'Even with Jake?' enquired Laura drily, unable to resist the parry, and Julie gave her a dour look from beneath curling black lashes.

'You still haven't told me what you think of him,' she retorted, returning to the offensive. And Laura wished she had kept her sarcasm to herself.

'I'm hardly in a position to voice an opinion,' she replied guardedly, escaping into the kitchen. To her relief, the fish was simmering nicely, and the strawberry shortcake had defrosted on the window ledge. At least checking the food and setting out the plates and cutlery distracted her from

the more troubling aspects of her thoughts, and it was only
when Julie came to prop herself against the door that Laura
fumbled with a glass, and almost dropped it.

'Would you like to know how we met?' Julie asked now,
making no effort to assist her mother with the preparations, and, deciding it was probably the lesser of two
evils, Laura nodded. 'It was in Rome actually,' Julie went
on. 'D'you remember? I told you I was going there about
six weeks ago, to shoot the *Yasmina* lay-out. Well, Jake's
father—Count Domenico, would you believe?—sits on the
boards of various governing bodies, and this ball had been
organised to benefit some children's charity or other. Harry
got an invitation, of course, so we all went. It promised to
be good fun, and it was.' Her lips twisted reminiscently.
'Oh—Jake wouldn't have been there if his mother hadn't
raked him in to charm all the women, so that they'd get
their husbands to contribute more generously than they
might have done. But he was; and we met; and the rest is
history, as they say.'

Laura managed a smile. 'I see.'

'Yes.' Julie studied the liquid residing in the bottom of
the glass she was cradling in her hands. 'Events like that
are not really his thing, you see.' She looked up again, and
her eyes glittered as they met her mother's wary glance. 'I
intend to change all that, naturally.'

'You do?'

Laura didn't know how else to answer her, but then the
sound of the front door closing made any further response
unnecessary. Julie turned back into the living-room to speak
to the man who had just come in, and Laura bent to lift
the casserole out of the oven.

She knew she would have to join them shortly, of course.
Although she generally ate at the pine table in the kitchen,
the room was scarcely big enough for two people, let alone
three, which meant she would have to pull out the gate-
legged table at one end of the living-room.

However, before she had summoned up the courage to
leave the comparative security of the kitchen, Jake himself
appeared in the doorway. He had shed his leather jerkin,
somewhere between entering the house and coming to
disrupt her fragile composure, and as he raised one hand

to support himself against the lintel Laura was not unaware of the sleek muscles beneath the fine silk of his shirt.

'I've left the car parked behind yours beside the house,' he said, and she noticed how the drops of rain sparkled on his hair. He wore his hair longer than the men she was used to, and where it was wet it was inclined to curl. Otherwise, it was mostly straight, and just brushed his collar at the back. 'Is that OK?' he added softly, and Laura realised rather flusteredly that she hadn't answered him.

'What . . .? Oh—oh, yes,' she said hastily, taking a table-cloth out of a drawer, and starting towards him. Then, realising he was blocking the doorway, she halted again, and waving the cloth at him, murmured, 'If you'll excuse me . . .'

Jake frowned, but he didn't move out of her way. 'Can't we eat in here?' he suggested, looking about him with some appreciation. 'This is cosy.' He nodded at the begonias on the window ledge. 'Did you cultivate those?'

'Cultivate? Oh . . .' Laura glanced behind her, and then nodded. 'Yes. Yes, I enjoy gardening. You wouldn't notice today, of course. I think the rain has even beaten down the daffodils.'

'The rain!' Jake grimaced. 'Oh, yes, it is certainly raining. It reminds me of home.'

'Home?' Laura frowned. 'But I thought——'

'You thought that the sun always shines in Italy?' he asked, grinning. 'Oh, no. Like the fog in London, it is somewhat overrated.'

Laura felt herself smiling in return, but then, realising she was wasting time, and the meal was almost ready, she caught her lower lip between her teeth.

'Um—do you really think we could eat in here?' she ventured, not at all sure how Julie would respond to such a suggestion, and then her daughter appeared behind Jake. Sliding possessive arms around him from behind, she reached up to rest her chin on his shoulder, before arching a curious brow at her mother.

'What's going on?'

'Your mother was going to serve the meal she had pre-pared in the other room,' Jake interposed swiftly. 'I thought we should eat in here. I always enjoyed eating in the kitchen, when I lived at home.'

'Yes, but how big was the kitchen you used to eat in?' countered Julie, turning her head deliberately, and allowing her tongue to brush the lobe of his ear. 'Not like this rabbit hutch, I'm sure. I bet there were acres and acres of marble tiles, and dressers simply groaning under the weight of copper pans.'

'I don't think it matters how big the room is,' Jake retorted, displaying a depth of coolness she had clearly not expected. He moved so that Julie had either to move with him, which would have been clumsy, or let him go. She chose the latter, and stood looking at him with sulky eyes. 'It's the room where the cooking is done. That's what's important. The smell of good food isn't enhanced by wasted space.'

'How gallant!'

Julie grimaced, but Laura had the feeling that Jake's reaction had surprised her daughter. Evidently, he was not going to prove as easy to manipulate as Julie had expected, and, although she was probably nursing her grievances, she had decided to reassess her options before making any reckless moves.

'Well—if you're sure,' Laura murmured now, half wishing Jake had not chosen to champion her. She had no desire to be the cause of any rift between them, and, in all honesty, she would have preferred to keep the kitchen as her sanctuary. But it was too late now, and, ignoring Julie's still mutinous expression, she shook out the tablecloth.

'D'you want a drink?' asked Julie, after a few moments, apparently deciding that sulking was getting her nowhere, and to Laura's relief Jake accepted the olive branch.

'Sounds good,' he said, and when Julie backed into the living-room he followed.

Breathing a somewhat relieved sigh, Laura quickly laid the table with the silver and glassware she had prepared earlier. Then, after rescuing the plates from the warming drawer, she set the casserole dish containing the fish on a cork mat in the middle of the table. The attractive terracotta-coloured casserole looked good amid the cream plates, with their narrow gold edging, and the crystal wine glasses that had been her gift to herself last Christmas.

She had bought some wine, and, although if Mark came for a meal she had him uncork the bottle, this evening she tackled the job herself. It wasn't as if she was helpless, she thought irritably, removing a tiny speck of cork from the rim. It was only that Julie tended to intimidate her. And that was her own fault, too.

In the event, the meal was a success. The fish tasted as delicious as Laura had hoped, and, whatever Jake and her daughter had said to one another in the living-room, the atmosphere between them was definitely lighter. Evidently, Julie had been appeased, and, although Jake still didn't respond to her frequent attempts to touch him, he didn't reject them either. Instead, he spoke equally to both women, encouraging Julie to talk about her recent trip to Scandinavia, and showing an apparently genuine interest in Laura's teaching.

Although Laura was sure he was only being polite, so far as she was concerned, she was not averse to talking about her job, and only when Julie gave a rather pronounced yawn did she realise she had been lecturing. But it was so rare that she spoke to anyone at any length outside the teaching profession, and Jake's intelligent observations had inspired her to share her opinions.

When they eventually left the table, Julie asked if she could have a bath. 'I feel grubby,' she said, deliberately stretching her arms above her head, so that the perfect lines of her slim figure could be seen to advantage. She wore her hair short these days, and with its smooth curve cupping her head like a burnished cap, and her small breasts thrusting freely against the bronze silk, she was both provocative and beautiful. She cast a mocking smile in Jake's direction. 'But you won't be able to come and wash my back, darling,' she added lightly. 'Mum doesn't approve of that sort of thing, do you, Mum?'

Laura didn't know how to answer her, but as it happened she didn't have to. 'I'll be too busy helping your mother with the washing-up, anyway,' Jake returned, causing Laura no small spasm of trepidation. 'Go ahead. Take your bath, *cara*. We don't mind—do we, Laura?'

Laura turned to stare at him then, telling herself it was his attempt to link them together that disturbed her, and not her reaction to her name on his lips. But Jake wasn't aware of her scrutiny. He was looking at Julie, and for once her daughter seemed nonplussed. Laura guessed she, too, was trying to gauge exactly what Jake was implying by his remarks, and her response revealed her uncertainty.

'I—well, of course, I'll help to clear up first——' she began but she got no further.

'It's not necessary for either of you to help me. Really,' Laura retorted, her face reddening as she spoke. 'Honestly. I can manage. Please. I'd rather.'

'I wouldn't dream of it,' declared Jake, apparently indifferent to her embarrassment. 'You've been at work all day, while we've only had a rather leisurely drive from London. In addition to which, you prepared this very appetising meal, which we've all enjoyed. I suggest you go and relax, while we deal with the clearing up.'

Laura looked at Julie now, and she could tell that her daughter didn't like·this turn of events at all. It was so unexpected, for one thing, and, for another, Julie wasn't used to being treated like a servant in her own home. It did not augur well for the remainder of the weekend, and Laura decided she wasn't prepared to play pig-in-the-middle any longer.

'No,' she said clearly, gathering up the coffee-cups and saucers, and bundling them on to the drainer. 'Really, Mr—er—I insist. You're my guests. I invited you here, and I wouldn't dream of allowing you to do my job.' She couldn't quite meet his gaze as she spoke, so she looked at Julie instead. 'Go along,' she continued. 'Have your bath. The water's nice and hot, and there's plenty of it.'

'Are you sure?'

Julie hesitated, looking doubtfully from Jake to her mother and back again, but Laura was adamant. 'Of course,' she said. 'Heavens, there are only a few plates to wash, when all's said and done. Hurry up. I'm sure your—er—friend would much prefer your company to mine.'

Julie frowned. It was obvious what she wanted to do, but Jake's attitude had confused her. Still, her own basic belief, that she was not being selfish by allowing her mother to have her own way, won out, and, giving them both a grateful smile, she departed. Seconds later, Laura heard the sound of her daughter's footsteps on the stairs, and, breathing a sigh of relief, she moved towards the sink.

'You're wrong, you know.'

She had almost forgotten Jake was still there, but now his quiet words caused her to glance round at him. 'I beg your pardon?'

'I said—you're wrong,' he responded. He had got up from the table when she had, and now he was leaning against the base unit behind her, his arms folded across his chest, his long legs crossed at the ankle.

'About Julie?' Laura turned her back on him again, and proceeded to fill the sink with soapy water. 'Possibly.'

'You spoil her,' he went on. 'She's perfectly capable of washing a few dishes.'

'Maybe.' Laura didn't like his assumption that he could discuss Julie with her, as if she were some racalcitrant child. 'But—I choose to do them myself.'

'No.' Jake came to stand beside her as he spoke, and now she was forced to meet his dark gaze. 'No, you don't *choose* to do them yourself. You take the line of least resistance. Which just happens to coincide with what Julie wants to do, no?'

Laura took a deep breath. 'I don't think it's any of your business, Mr—er—Lombardi——'

'Jake will do,' he put in briefly. 'And so long as Julie and I are together, I consider it is my business.'

Laura gasped. His arrogance was amazing, but at least it served to keep her own unwilling awareness of him at bay. 'You don't understand,' she declared, depositing the newly washed glasses on the drainer. 'Julie and I don't see one another very often——'

'And whose fault is that?'

'It's nobody's fault.' But Laura couldn't help wondering if he knew exactly how infrequently Julie made the journey north. Recently, Laura had had to travel to London if she wanted to see her daughter, and as she could only do so during school holidays, and they often coincided with Julie's working trips abroad, these occasions were getting fewer.

'So—you are quite happy with the situation, hmm?' he enquired, picking up a tea-towel, and beginning to dry a glass.

'Yes.'

Laura's response was taut, and she hoped that that would be an end of it. It was bad enough being obliged to entertain him while Julie went to take her bath. A conversation of this kind tended to increase their familiarity with one another, and she would have preferred to keep their relationship on much more formal terms.

She finished the dishes in silence, but she was very much aware of him moving about the small kitchen, and the distinctive scent of his skin drifted irresistibly to her nostrils. It was a combination of the soap he used, some subtle aftershave, and the warmth of his body, and Laura had the feeling it was not something she would easily forget. It was so essentially masculine, and she resented the knowledge that he could influence her without any volition on her part.

As she was putting the dishes away, he spoke again, and as before his words commanded her attention. 'I guess you're angry with me now, aren't you?' he said, stepping into her path, as she was about to put the plates into the cupboard. It caused her to stop abruptly, to prevent herself from cannoning into him, and she pressed the plates against her chest, like some primitive form of self-protection.

'I—don't know what you mean,' she protested, and although it was scarcely true she thought it sounded convincing enough.

'Don't you?' Jake looked down at her, and, despite the fact that she had always considered herself a tall woman, he was still at least half a foot taller. 'I think you know very well. You resented my remarks about your daughter. You don't consider I have any right to criticise the way she treats you.'

Laura took a deep breath. 'All right,' she said, deciding there was no point in lying to him. It wasn't as if she wanted them to be friends, after all. If Julie married him, the greater the distance there was between them the better. 'I don't think anyone who doesn't have a child of their own can make any real assessment on how a parent ought, or ought not, to behave.'

'Ah.' Jake inclined his head, and Laura was intensely conscious of how she must appear to him. The Aran sweater was not flattering, and she was sure her face must be shining like a beacon. 'But I do have a daughter. Not as old as yours,' he conceded, after a moment. 'She's only eight years old. But a handful, none the less.'

Laura swallowed. 'You—have a daughter?'

He could apparently tell what she was thinking, for his lean lips parted. 'But no wife,' he assured her gently. 'Isabella—that was her name—she died when our daughter was only a few months old.'

'Oh.' Laura's tongue appeared to moisten her lips. 'I—I'm sorry. I didn't know.'

'How could you?' Jake responded. 'Until tonight, we had never even met.'

'No.'

But Laura was embarrassed nevertheless. Julie should have told her, she thought impatiently. If she knew. But, of course, she must. She had the feeling it was not something Jake would try to hide.

She half stepped forward, eager to get past him now, and put the plates away, so that she could escape to the living-room. The kitchen was too small, too confining, and that awful panicky feeling she had felt in the hall earlier was attacking her nerves again. He was too close; too familiar. He might not be aware of it, but she most definitely was.

But Jake moved as she did, probably with the same thought in mind, she guessed later, and unfortunately he chose the same direction as Laura, so that they collided.

The shock jarred her, but her first instincts were to protect the plates. She clutched them to her, instead of trying to save herself, and it was left to Jake to prevent her, and her burden, from ending up on the floor. Almost instinctively, his hands grasped the yielding flesh of her upper arms, and for a brief moment she was forced to lean against him.

Afterwards, she realised that the incident couldn't have lasted more than a few seconds. It was one of those accidents that in retrospect seemed totally avoidable. Only it hadn't happened that way. Almost as if she was moving in slow motion, Laura was compelled into Jake's arms, and for a short, but disruptive period she was close against his lean frame.

And, during those nerve-racking seconds, when the world seemed to falter around her, her body came alive to every nerve and emotion she possessed. Her skin felt raw; sensitised; as if someone had peeled away the top layer, and left her weak and open to attack. She had never experienced such a shattering explosion of feeling, and her mind reeled beneath its implications.

She jerked away from him, of course, more violently than she should have done, and one of the plates went flying. But it wasn't the sound of the china splintering on the tiles that first made her face burn, and then robbed it of all colour. It was the fact that the ball of Jake's hand brushed her breast as she rebounded, and in the sudden narrowing of his eyes she saw a reflection of her own awareness.

CHAPTER THREE

LAURA slept badly, and it wasn't just the unfamiliar experience of sharing her bed with her daughter. She was hot and restless, and although she longed for it to be morning, she was not looking forward to the day ahead.

Of course, it didn't help that Julie had appropriated at least two-thirds of the space, and every time Laura moved she was in fear of waking her. Indeed, there were times during the night when Laura half wished she had not been so adamant about the sleeping arrangements. If Julie had been sharing Jake's bed, she would not have been so conscious of him, occupying the room on the other side of the dividing wall.

As it was, her senses persistently taunted her with that awareness, and images of Jake's dark, muscled body, relaxed against the cream poplin sheets, were a constant aggravation. It was pathetic, she thought, disgusted by her thoughts. Apart from anything else, he was Julie's boyfriend, her property—if a man like Jake Lombardi could ever be regarded as any woman's possession. Somehow she sensed he was unlikely to let that happen. Nevertheless, whatever label she put on it, he was the man her daughter intended to marry, and any attraction she felt towards him was both loathsome and pitiful. For heaven's sake, she chided herself, he was probably ten years younger than she was, and, even if Julie hadn't been involved, he simply wasn't the type of man she attracted.

She was just a middle-aged school-teacher, who had wasted any chance of happiness she might have had by getting herself pregnant, when she should have been old enough to know better. And since then, she had never felt the need for a serious relationship. Over the years, there had been one or two men who had attempted to push a casual association into something more, but Laura had always repelled invaders. Only Mark had stayed the course, and that was primarily because he made no demands on her. She had actually begun to believe that, whatever sexual urges she had once possessed, they were now extinct, and it was disturbing, to say the least, to consider that she might have been wrong.

And what was she basing this conclusion on? she asked herself contemptuously. It wasn't as if anything momentous had happened to shatter her illusions. How stupid she was to read anything into Jake's almost knocking her over, and preventing it. It was what anyone would have done in the same circumstances, man or woman, and she was fooling herself if she thought his brief awareness of her had been sexual.

But he had grabbed her, she argued doggedly. He had propelled her into his arms. It didn't matter that on his part it had been a purely impersonal reaction. She could still feel the grip of his fingers, and the taut corded muscles of his legs . . .

God! She turned on to her back and gazed blindly up at the ceiling. How old was she? Thirty-eight? She was reacting like a sixteen-year-old. But then, she thought bitterly, her sexual development had been arrested around that age, so what else could she expect?

She was glad Julie had known nothing about it. By the time her daughter came down from her bath, clean, and sweetly smelling of rosebuds, her slender form wrapped in a revealing silk kimono, Laura had swept the floor, and

restored the kitchen—and herself—to comparative order.
That disruptive moment with Jake might never have been,
and she was able to excuse herself on the pretext of being
tired, without revealing any of the turmoil that was churning
inside her. She left them sharing the sofa in the living-room,
where Jake had been sitting since she had insisted on clearing
up the broken china herself.

She got up at six o'clock. She had been wide awake since
five, and only the knowledge that she would have no excuse
for being up any earlier had prevented her from going
downstairs as soon as it was light. But six o'clock seemed
reasonably acceptable, and as the others hadn't come to
bed until some time after midnight Laura doubted she would
disturb anyone.

Drawing the blind in the kitchen, she saw it was a much
brighter morning. The sun was sparkling like diamonds on
the wet grass, and the birds were setting up a noisy chatter
in the trees that formed a barrier between her garden and
the lane that led to Grainger's farm.

The cottage was the second of two that stood at the end
of the village, the other being occupied by an elderly widow
and her daughter. Laura knew that people thought she was
a widow, too, and she had never bothered to correct them.
In a place as small as Burnfoot, it was better not to be too
non-conformist, and, while being a one-parent family was
no novelty these days, people might look differently on
someone of Laura's generation.

After putting the kettle on to boil, she opened the back
door and stepped out into the garden. It was fresh, but not
chilly, and she pushed her hands into the pockets of her
dressing-gown and inhaled the clean air. The bulbs she had
planted the previous autumn were beginning to flower, and
the bell-shaped heads of purple hyacinths and crimson tulips
were thrusting their way between the clumps of wild daffodils. The garden was starting to regain the colour it had
lost over the winter months, and Laura guessed that sooner
or later she would have to clear the dead leaves, and dispose
of the weeds.

It was a prospect she generally looked forward to, but
this morning it was hard to summon any enthusiasm for
anything. She felt depressed, and out of tune with herself,

and, hearing one of Ted Grainger's heifers bellowing in the
top field, she thought the animal epitomised her own sense
of frustration. But frustration about what? she asked herself
crossly. What did she have to be frustrated about?

The kettle was beginning to boil. She could hear it. It
was a comforting sound, and, abandoning her introspection, she turned back towards the house. And that was
when she saw him, standing indolently in the open doorway,
watching her.

He was dressed—that was the first thing she noticed about
him. He was wearing the same black jeans he had been
wearing the night before, but he wasn't wearing a shirt this
morning; just a V-necked cream cashmere sweater, that revealed the brown skin of his throat, and a faint trace of
dark body hair in the inverted apex of the triangle. Unlike
herself, she was sure, he looked relaxed and rested, although
his eyes were faintly shadowed, as if he hadn't slept long
enough.

And why not? she thought irritably. She had still been
awake when Julie had come to bed, even if she had pretended otherwise, and by her reckoning he could not have
had more than five hours. Hardly enough for someone who
had driven almost three hundred miles the day before, in
heavy traffic, with goodness knew what hangover from the
night before that.

Laura was immediately conscious of her own state of undress, and of the fact that she hadn't even brushed her hair
since she'd come downstairs. It was still a tumbled mass
about her shoulders, with knotted strands of nut-brown silk
sticking out in all directions.

Laura's hand went automatically to her hair, and then,
as if realising it was too late to do anything about it now,
she clutched the neckline of her robe, and walked towards
him. Pasting a polite smile on her face, she strove to hide
the resentment she felt at his unwarranted intrusion, and,
reaching the step, she said lightly, 'Good morning. You're
an early riser.'

'So are you,' Jake countered, moving aside to let her into
the house. 'Couldn't you sleep?'

Laura went to take the tea caddy out of the cupboard,
and dropped three bags into the pot before answering him.

The steady infusion of the water sent up a revitalising aroma from the leaves, and Laura breathed deeply, as she considered how to reply.

'I—er—I'm always up fairly early,' she said at last, putting the lid on the teapot, and having no further reason to avoid his gaze. 'Um—would you like a cup of tea? Or would you rather have coffee? I can easily make a pot, if that's what you'd prefer.'

'Whatever you're having,' he said, closing the back door, and leaning back against it. 'I'm—what do you say?—easy.'

Laura's lips twitched. 'Milk, or lemon?'

'You choose,' he essayed flatly. 'Tea is tea, whatever way you drink it.'

'I doubt if the connoisseurs would agree with you,' declared Laura, setting out three cups and saucers. 'Tea used to be regarded as quite a ritual. It still is, in other parts of the world. China, for instance.'

'Really?'

He didn't sound as if it interested him greatly, and she guessed her line in small talk was not what he was used to. He evidently enjoyed the kind of sexual innuendo Julie employed to such effect. But Laura wasn't experienced in innuendo, sexual or otherwise, and, aware of how she had monopolised the conversation at dinner the previous evening, she knew she had to guard against being boring.

Then, remembering her hair, she started towards the door. That was something that couldn't wait any longer, and she paused, uncertainly, when he asked, 'Where are you going?'

'I—won't be a minute,' she answered, loath to admit exactly where she was headed. 'Um—help yourself; and Julie, too, if you want.'

'I'll wait,' he said, leaving the door, to pull out a chair from the table, and straddle it with his long legs. 'OK.'

Laura hesitated a little bemusedly, and then nodded. 'Of—of course.'

Brushing her hair entailed going upstairs again, and as she stood at the bathroom mirror, tugging the bristles through the tangled strands, she felt a helpless sense of inevitability. The last thing she had expected was that she would have to face another one-to-one encounter with Jake so soon. Her assessment of the day ahead had already gone badly awry, and she hoped the rest of the weekend was not going to prove as traumatic.

There were men's toiletries on the glass shelf above the handbasin, she saw, with an unwelcome twinge of trepidation. No doubt they were responsible for the spicy smell of cologne that lingered in the atmosphere, the unfamiliar scents of sandalwood and cedar. There was a razor, too. Not some sophisticated electrical gadget, as she would have expected, but a common-or-garden sword-edge, with throwaway blades. The man was a contradiction, she thought, frowning, hardly aware that she was running her fingers over a dark green bottle of aftershaving lotion. He was rich, and sophisticated; he wore handmade shirts, and Armani jackets, and he drove a Lamborghini. All aspects of the lifestyle to which he was accustomed. And yet, he had seemed genuinely pleased with the simple meal she had served the night before, and he had dried the dishes afterwards, as if it was a perfectly natural thing for him to do.

She realised suddenly that she was wasting time. It was at least five minutes since she had come upstairs, and, apart from anything else, the tea would be getting cold.

The hairpins she usually used to keep her hair in place were in the bedroom, and although she wouldn't have minded waking Julie, it was going to take too much time. Instead, she found the elastic headband in the pocket of her dressing-gown that she sometimes used when she was pottering about the garden, and, sliding it up over her forehead, she decided that would have to do.

Going downstairs again was harder, but she steeled herself to behave naturally. After all, so far as Jake was concerned, she was just Julie's mother: a little eccentric, perhaps, and obviously nervous with strangers.

He was still sitting where she had left him, but he got politely to his feet when she came into the room. However, Laura gestured for him to remain seated, and he sank back on to the chair, stretching the tight jeans across his thighs.

Laura knew her eyes shouldn't have been drawn to that particular area of his abdomen, but somehow she couldn't help it. He was disturbingly physical, and her stomach quivered alarmingly as she endeavoured to pour the tea.

'W—would you like to take Julie's up?' she ventured, the spout hovering over the third cup, but when she reluctantly glanced round at her visitor Jake shook his head.

'I doubt if she'd appreciate being woken at this hour, do you?' he remarked, his dark eyes intent and wary. 'When she's not working, she considers anything short of double figures the middle of the night. But you must know that yourself.'

Not as well as you, I'm sure, Laura was tempted to retort, but she restrained herself. After all, it was really nothing to do with her how they chose to live their lives, and just because she was finding the situation a strain was no reason to blame Jake.

However, he seemed to sense her ambivalence, for as she set a cup of the strong beverage in front of him he said quietly, 'What's wrong?' and the anxieties of the last fifteen minutes coalesced.

'I—beg your pardon?'

'You don't have to be so formal, you know,' he told her, making no attempt to touch his tea. 'I asked what was wrong. Do you resent my getting up so early? Would you rather I had stayed in bed?'

Yes. *Yes!* The simple answer sang in Laura's ears, but she couldn't say it. Not out loud. Besides, she wasn't even sure she meant it. It might be reassuring to pretend she would rather avoid talking to him, and quite another to consider the reality of doing so. The truth fell somewhere in between, and she was too conscientious to deny it.

'I—I—don't mind,' she said at last, not altogether truthfully. 'Um—would you like some sugar? I—know men usually do.'

'And how would you know that?' enquired Jake, still holding her gaze, and she knew a sudden spurt of indignation.

'Why shouldn't I? Just because I'm not married, doesn't mean I haven't had any experience where men are concerned,' she retorted, resenting his implication, and then could have bitten out her tongue at the recklessness of her words. She had no idea whether Julie had told him of the circumstances of her birth. And if she hadn't...

But Jake was speaking again. 'I know about that,' he countered mildly. 'You had Julie while you were still in high school. And I didn't imagine that was an immaculate conception.'

Laura flushed then, his cool, faintly mocking tone reminding her of how inexperienced she was when it came to his kind of verbal sparring. But she refused to let him think he had disconcerted her, and, squaring her shoulders, she added crisply, 'I am almost forty, you know. Why do young people always think sex wasn't invented until they came along?'

'Is that what they think?' Jake arched one dark brow, and, wishing she had never started this, Laura nodded.

'You tell me,' she responded tautly. 'It's your generation I'm talking about.'

'My generation?' Jake pressed his left hand against his chest, his expression mirroring his amusement. '*Dio*, how old you think I am?'

'It doesn't matter how old you are,' declared Laura, trying to steady the cup of tea in her hand. 'All I'm saying is, you shouldn't jump to what you think are obvious conclusions.'

'Did I do that?'

'Yes.' Laura drew a trembling breath. 'And I wish you'd stop answering everything I say with a question of your own. We—we hardly know one another, and I—I don't want to fall out with you.'

'Fall out with me?' Jake adopted a puzzled expression. 'What is that?'

'Argue with you—quarrel with you—oh, I'm sure you know exactly what it means,' declared Laura crossly. 'Anyway, I don't want to do it.'

'Do what?'

'Have an argument with you,' repeated Laura shortly. 'And there you go again. Making fun of me.'

'Was I doing that?' Jake grimaced. 'Oh, damn, that's another question.'

He was teasing her. Laura knew it. And, although she knew she ought to be able to take it all in good part, she couldn't. He disturbed her too much. She returned her attention to her tea, hoping he would do the same, but she didn't sit down with him. At least when she was standing, she felt she had some chance of parity, albeit in a physical sense only. And perhaps, after he had drunk his tea, he would go for a walk, she speculated. He surely didn't intend to hang about the house until Julie chose to put in an appearance.

'So,' he remarked, after a few silent moments, 'you live here alone, is that right?'

'Well, I don't have a live-in lover,' replied Laura tersely, and then, catching the humour in his eyes, she struggled to compose herself. 'I—yes, I live alone,' she conceded, putting her empty cup down on the drainer. 'But I don't mind, if that's what you're getting at. After dealing with noisy teenagers all day, it's quite a relief to come back here.'

'I can believe it.' Jake wasn't teasing now. He had folded his arms along the back of the chair, and was regarding her with a steady appraisal. 'And it's very peaceful around here, isn't it?'

'Mmm.' Laura endeavoured to relax. 'That's what I love about it. The peace and quiet. I'd hate to live in the city again.'

Jake frowned. 'You lived in London?'

'No. Newcastle.' Somehow, she didn't mind his questions now. 'I moved here just after—Julie went to London.'

'Ah.' Jake nodded.

'I work in the city, of course,' Laura added. 'It's only about fifteen miles away.'

'Newcastle.'

'Yes.'

Jake absorbed this. Then, quite obliquely, he said, 'You'd like Valle di Lupo. It's very peaceful there, too. If slightly less civilised.'

Laura hesitated. She was loath to appear too curious after the accusation she had made towards him, but she had to ask, 'What is—Valle di Lupo?'

Jake smiled, and she felt her breath catch in her throat as his lean features assumed a disturbing sensuality. 'My home,' he said simply. 'Or rather—my family's. It's in the wilds of Toscana—Tuscany. A few miles north of Firenze.'

'Florence,' ventured Laura softly, and Jake inclined his head.

'As you say—Florence,' he agreed. 'Have you been to Italy?'

'Oh, no.' Laura shook her head. 'I'm afraid not. Apart from a school skiing trip to Austria, I haven't travelled much at all. Not outside England, anyway.'

'A pity.' Jake pulled a wry face. 'I think you would like it.'

'Oh—I'm sure I would.' Laura hoped she didn't sound too eager. 'Um—is that—is that where your daughter lives?' She moistened her lips. 'At Valle di Lupo?'

'Sometimes.' Jake was thoughtful. 'When she's not at school. And when I'm not able to take care of her.'

Laura was interested in spite of herself. 'You—don't live at Valle di Lupo?'

Jake smiled again. 'Who's asking questions now?'

Laura's face flamed. 'I'm sorry——'

'Don't be. I don't mind.' Jake shrugged his shoulders. 'I've got nothing to hide!'

Laura pressed her lips together, and glanced awkwardly about her. 'I—er—I think I'd better go and get dressed,' she murmured, and then caught her breath again, when Jake propelled himself up from the chair, and swung it round, so that it fitted back under the table.

'I thought you wanted to know where I lived?' he protested. 'Or were you just being polite?'

Laura caught her lower lip between her teeth. 'I—just wondered, that's all,' she improvised, smoothing her damp palms down the skirt of her dressing-gown. 'It's really none of my business——'

'I have an apartment in Rome, and another on the coast near Viareggio,' he told her softly. 'But my real home is at Valle di Lupo. That is where I was born.'

'Oh.'

It all sounded very extravagant to Laura. Two apartments, *and* a family home. It was the kind of lifestyle she had only read about in glossy magazines, or seen portrayed in American soap operas. It was quite amazing to meet someone who actually lived like that. It seemed a long way from Burnfoot, and the modest appointments of this cottage.

'You don't approve?' he suggested now, and Laura was guiltily aware that she had been frowning.

'Oh—no,' she murmured. 'I mean—it all sounds very beautiful. Your home, that is. I'm sure Julie is longing to see it.'

'Are you?'

Jake rested his hands on the back of the chair, and Laura's eyes were drawn to their narrow elegance. It reminded her of how they had felt the night before, and how strongly they had supported her weight . . .

But he was waiting for her answer, and, lifting her shoulders, she said quickly, 'Of course.' A sudden thought occurred to her, and she felt the colour invade her cheeks once again. 'Unless—unless she's already——'

'No.'

Jake was adamant about that, and Laura's eyes widened. 'No?'

'Julie isn't interested in the provincial life,' Jake informed her carelessly. 'She doesn't care for fields, and trees, and rolling vineyards. Only in what they produce.'

Laura swallowed. 'That's a little harsh——'

'Is it?' Jake's eyes were enigmatic. 'How do you know I don't feel the same?'

She didn't, of course. And on the evidence she had so far, she had little reason to believe otherwise. And yet . . .

'I—really think I must go and get dressed,' she insisted, moving towards the door. 'Er—if you'd like another cup of tea, help yourself. I—won't be long.'

She made her escape before he could say anything else. And, as she went up the stairs again, she realised she was trembling. For heaven's sake, she thought impatiently, what was wrong with her? It wasn't the first time she had had a conversation with a strange man, and certainly he had given her no reason to feel this consuming sense of vulnerability in his presence. It wasn't as if he'd made a pass at her or anything. He'd been a perfect gentleman, and she was behaving like a silly spinster. For God's sake, she told herself, locking the bathroom door and taking a good look at herself in the mirror, she was too old and too jaded to be attractive to a man like him. Even if Julie had not been on the scene, there were probably dozens of women like her, waiting to

take her place. She was just a middle-aged housewife, with
a pathetic lust for something she had never had.

CHAPTER FOUR

SO MUCH for her efforts to move quietly earlier, Laura reflected half an hour later, having made as much noise as
possible as she'd got dressed. Even though she had slammed
drawers, rattled hangers, and dropped a make-up bottle on
to the dressing-table, Julie hadn't stirred. She was curled
languorously in the middle of the bed, and nothing her
mother could do would wake her.

Of course, she could always take her by the shoulders,
and shake her daughter awake, Laura considered grimly.
After all, Jake was Julie's guest, not hers, and she should
be the one to entertain him. But that particular alternative
was not appealing. The girl was probably tired, and it wasn't
fair to deny her the chance to catch up on her sleep.

The reasons why Julie might be tired were less easy to
contemplate. Even though she had denied them the chance
to sleep together at the cottage, Laura had no doubt that
Jake had slept at Julie's apartment in London. And
although her experience of sexual relationships was fairly
negligible, she had a more than adequate imagination.

The brush she had been using on her hair slipped out of
her sweaty fingers, and landed on the carpet, and she
glanced round, half apprehensively, at the bed. But Julie
slumbered on, undisturbed by her mother's vapid fantasies, and, clenching her teeth, Laura wound the silky mass
around her hand, and secured it on top of her head with
a half dozen hairpins.

She was a fool, she told herself irritably. This simply
wasn't the time to have a mid-life crisis, and the sooner she
pulled herself together, and started acting her age, the better.

She went downstairs a few minutes later, slim and work-
manlike, in an unfussy cotton shirt, and her oldest jeans.
As soon as breakfast was over, she was going to make a
start on the garden, and, if Jake Lombardi didn't like it,
it was just too bad. Maybe he would have more luck in

waking Julie than she had had. He was unlikely to want to
spend the rest of the morning on his own, but it really wasn't
her problem.

However, when she entered the kitchen, she found Jake
wasn't there. The teacups had been washed and dried and
left on the drainer, but there was no sign of her visitor. He
had either retired to his room—and she certainly hadn't
heard him come upstairs—or he had gone out. The latter
seemed the most likely, but she couldn't help remembering
that he had had no breakfast.

Still, it was only half-past seven, she discovered, looking
at her watch. She wondered what time he usually had
breakfast. Later than this, she was sure. But she wondered
where he had gone all the same.

Conversely, now that she was on her own, she found she
didn't know what to do. It was too early for gardening. If
Mrs Langthorne, next door, saw her in the garden at this
hour, she would wonder what was going on. After all, she
wasn't a professional gardener, just a rather enthusiastic
amateur. And enthusiastic amateurs didn't start digging up
weeds at half-past seven!

She sighed, feeling definitely peevish. This was Jake's
fault, she thought, needing someone to blame. If he hadn't
come down so early, she would probably still be in her
dressing-gown, having another cup of tea, and trying to do
the previous day's crossword in the newspaper. That was
what she usually did on Saturday mornings. But today, her
whole schedule had been thrown off-key.

She was making a desultory inspection of the fridge, when
the back door opened, and Jake came in. And with him
came the delicious scent of newly baked bread.

'Miss me?' he asked incorrigibly, depositing a carrier-
bag on the table, from which spilled plain and sweet rolls,
scones, and a crisp French stick. 'I wasn't sure what you'd
like, so I got a selection.'

Laura stared, first at the table, then at him. 'But—
where——?'

'The bakery,' declared Jake, pulling a chair out from the
table, and flinging himself into it.

Laura's brows drew together. 'The—village bakery?'

'Where else?'

'But—Mr Harris doesn't open until nine o'clock!'

'No?' Jake gave her a quizzical look. 'Well, I didn't steal,
them, if that's what you're implying.'

'Of course, I'm not implying that, but . . .'

Laura was lost for words, and, taking pity on her, Jake
leaned forward to rest his elbows on the table. 'He was just
getting his delivery,' he explained, with a disarming grin.
'And I—persuaded him to let me be his first customer. He
didn't mind. I mentioned your name, and he was happy to
oblige.'

Laura shook her head. 'But—I hardly know the man.'

'No. He said that, too.' Jake's eyes were warm with
humour. 'You should patronise the local shops. They
depend on your custom.'

'I do.' Laura was indignant. 'Well, the general stores
anyway. I usually get my bread there.'

'Pre-packed, no doubt,' remarked Jake drily, and she
bridled.

'It's good enough for me,' she retorted shortly, ignoring
the mouth-watering smell of the warm rolls. 'I don't find
food a particular fetish. I eat to live, that's all. Not the
other way about. As you probably noticed last night.'

Jake's features sobered. 'Now what is that supposed to
mean?'

'Nothing.' Laura refused to say anything else she might
regret later, but Jake was on his feet again, and his height
and the width of his shoulders dwarfed her slender frame.

'Come on,' he said, and, although his tone was pleasant,
his expression was less so. 'What about last night? What
am I supposed to have noticed? I said the meal was good,
didn't I? What else was I supposed to say?'

'Nothing,' said Laura again, half turning away from him,
and fiddling with the teapot on the drainer. 'I shouldn't
have said what I did. It—it was just a defensive reaction,
that's all.'

'And why do you feel the need to be defensive with me?'
demanded Jake, evidently unprepared to give up so easily,
and Laura sighed.

'I don't know——'

'Don't you?' Now it was her turn to look at him with
unwary eyes.

'I beg your——?'

'Don't,' he said harshly. 'Don't say that again! Ever since I got up this morning, you've been on edge with me. Everything I say, you take exception to——'

'That's not true!'

Laura was indignant, but Jake simply ignored her. 'You don't like me,' he went on. 'Well, OK, I can live with that, I guess. If I have to. But what I want to know is why. What did I do to make you turn against me?'

'I didn't. I don't—— Oh, this is silly.' Laura pressed her lips together for a moment, to steady herself, and then continued evenly, 'I—don't dislike you, Mr Lombardi——'

'Jake!'

'Jake, then.' She paused a moment, after saying his name, trying to restore some sense of normality. 'I don't know you well enough to make any kind of assessment——'

'Grazie!'

'—and Julie cares about you. That's what matters.'

'Scusi, but I am not talking about Julie,' retorted Jake, and when she would have turned her back on him completely, his hand came out and took hold of her wrist. 'Don't walk out on me again.'

She was glad he hadn't touched her arm. The lean fingers coiling about her wrist were unknowingly hard, and the flesh above her elbow still ached from the night before. Even so, she couldn't prevent the spasm of pain that crossed her face, when he pulled her round to face him, and his eyes narrowed consideringly between his thick lashes.

'What is it with you?' he demanded, and she noticed how his accent was suddenly glaringly pronounced. Was that what happened when he lost his cool? she wondered dizzily. When the heat of his emotions melted the ice of his control?

But more important than that was her own reactions to his nearness. This time, his hold on her was deliberate, not the involuntary result of circumstances, and the blood his fingers were constricting rushed madly to its source. Her heart was pounding. She could hear the sound echoing hollowly in her ears. And its palpitating beat throbbed through every vein in her body, its rioting tattoo causing her temperature to soar.

'I think,' she said carefully, 'you should let me go.'

'*Come?* Oh…' He looked down at his hand curled around the fragile bones of her wrist, and his mouth twisted. 'Am I hurting you?'

'That's not the point.'

'Then what is the point?' he asked provokingly. 'I am allowed to look, but not to touch, hmm? Is that what you are saying?'

Laura couldn't look at him. She was half afraid of what he might see in her eyes. 'I—this is ridiculous——'

'I agree.'

'Then why can't you——?'

She broke off, her eyes darting towards his face and away again, and Jake's brows arched enquiringly. 'Go on. Why can't I what? Perhaps now we can get down to—how do you say it?—basics?'

Laura sighed. 'You know exactly how to say it,' she told him huskily. 'Don't think you can fool me by pretending you don't understand the language.'

'And don't you think you can fool me by persistently avoiding answering my questions,' he countered softly. 'I thought we could be friends.'

Friends! Laura swallowed. Was that what all this was about? She shook her head. God, she had to get a hold on herself.

'Please,' she said unsteadily, 'if—if you'll just let go of my wrist, perhaps we can talk about this.'

'Why?'

'Why what?' Laura was confused, and it was all she could do to keep her eyes fixed on the hair-darkened V of his sweater.

'Why must I let go of you before we can talk?' he replied, his thumb moving almost reflexively against the fine network of veins on the inner side of her wrist, and Laura shuddered.

'I don't think you need me to tell you that,' she retorted, snatching her wrist out of his grasp, and putting the width of the table between them. 'I don't know what you think you're doing, Mr Lombardi——'

'Jake,' he corrected, and then, on a harder note, 'Perhaps I'm just trying to find out what makes you tick, *Ms* Fox!'

Laura expelled her breath in a rush. 'I think—I think you're trying to make a fool of me, Mr Lombardi,' she declared, rubbing her wrist with a nervous hand. 'Perhaps it amuses you to make fun of older women; to play games behind Julie's back. Well, I don't like it. I may seem very old-fashioned to you, but that's the way I am. Now—if you don't mind——'

'Or even if I do, hmm?' he suggested, in a dangerously bland tone. 'I'm not a boy, Laura. And you're not a grand-mother—yet. Even if you do insist on acting like one.'

She had no answer to that. She was hurt. She didn't want to be; she ought not to be; but she was. His harsh words had bared her soul, and it took all her composure to gather up the bread from the table, and spread the cloth.

By the time she had set out plates and cutlery, spooned coffee into the filter and set it to perc, she had herself in control enough to ask, albeit tensely, 'What can I get you for breakfast? Would you like orange juice, or a cereal? Bacon? Eggs?'

'Nothing, thank you.'

Straightening from the lounging position he had adopted, while he'd watched her preparations for the meal, he walked to the living-room door.

'Nothing?'

The anxiety in Laura's voice was evident, but he was not disposed to humour her. 'I'm going out,' he told her, saun-tering across the living-room and into the hall, where he had hung his leather jerkin. He appeared briefly in the living-room doorway again, as he shrugged the jacket over his shoulders. 'Tell Julie, if she manages to regain con-sciousness before I come back, I'll see her later.'

'But——'

Laura pressed her hands together helplessly, but Jake didn't show any sympathy. 'No buts, Laura,' he essayed smoothly. 'Later, right?' and a moment later the front door slammed behind him.

Julie eventually put in an appearance at half-past ten. She came trailing down the stairs, wearing only the satin night-shirt she had worn to sleep in, her bright hair finger-combed, but appealing. She came into the kitchen, where Laura was making a dogged effort to mix pastry, her bare toes curling on the tiled floor.

'Hi,' she said sleepily, sinking down into a chair at the table. 'Is there any coffee?'

'In the jug,' Laura pointed, her hands caked with flour and water. However, when her daughter made no attempt to help herself, she dipped her hands into the bowl of soapy water she had ready, and rinsed them clean. 'There you are,' she said, setting a cup of the dark beverage on the table, and pushing the cream jug within reach. 'It's been made about half an hour, but it shouldn't be too bad.'

'Thanks.' Julie reached for the cup and savoured its contents, before adding only the minutest touch of cream. 'Hmm, I needed this,' she added, swallowing a mouthful. 'Where's Jake?'

Laura turned back to her pastry-making. 'I—he's gone for a walk,' she said, over her shoulder, calculating that it was a fairly reasonable conclusion. He hadn't taken his car, and she didn't think he was likely to have walked to the crossroads, and picked up the local bus service.

'*God!*' Julie sounded disgusted. 'What time did he go out?'

'Oh—early,' replied Laura, flouring the board rather more liberally than was necessary. 'I—suppose he was bored. There's not much to do around here, as you know.'

'Hmm,' Julie assented. 'I suppose he was up early, too. When he's at home, I believe he likes to go riding before breakfast. Can you believe that? Leaving a perfectly good bed, to go hacking about the countryside, before it's barely light!'

Laura peeled the pastry off the rolling-pin, and wondered if she could make do with omelettes for lunch. The quiches she had intended to make were proving more of a liability than she had expected, and the cool hands she needed were continually letting her down.

'Do—er—do you want something to eat?' she asked now, hoping to divert the conversation into other channels, but Julie shook her head.

'Just another cup of coffee will do,' she said, giving her mother a wheedling look. 'Get it for me, will you Mum?

I don't think I have the strength right now to get up from this chair.'

Laura resignedly rinsed her hands again, and refilled Julie's cup, before rolling the unfortunate pastry into a ball, and depositing it in the waste-bin. So much for home cooking, she thought bitterly. Perhaps she could get some ready-made quiches from Mr Harris.

Julie watched her with some surprise, and then sniffed. 'Have you been making bread?' she asked, frowning. 'It smells delici——'

'No,' Laura broke in, before Julie could pay her any unwarranted compliments. 'Your—that is—Mr Lombardi got some fresh bread from the bakery. That's what you can smell.'

'Really?' Julie grimaced. 'Before breakfast?'

'I—yes.' Laura couldn't bring herself to say that Jake hadn't had breakfast. 'D'you want some?'

'No, thanks.' Julie was tempted. 'I guess he was afraid you were going to offer him sliced bread. Italians like their bread fresh every morning.'

'Yes.' Laura had heard enough of what one particular Italian liked for one day. 'Well, now, are you going to get dressed?'

'Did Jake say where he was going?' Julie persisted, ignoring her mother's enquiry. 'How long has he been gone?'

'Oh——' Laura made a display of looking at her watch, although she knew exactly how long he had been gone '—about—a couple of hours, I suppose.'

'A couple of hours!' Julie was aghast. 'D'you think he's got lost?'

'I shouldn't think so.' Laura expunged a little of her frustration by scraping the remainder of the pastry from the board. 'He doesn't strike me as the kind of man who wouldn't know exactly what he was doing.'

'No?' Julie gave her mother a quizzical look. 'That was said with some feeling. What's wrong? Has he been rubbing you up the wrong way?'

'Of course not.' Laura was cross with herself for allowing Julie to even suspect how she was feeling. 'I just meant—he seems—very capable.'

'Oh, he is.' Julie cupped her chin in her hands, and sighed rather smugly. 'Believe me, he is.'

Laura lifted the board to put it into the sink, but a combination of its slippery surface, and her own unsteady hands, caused it to fall heavily against the taps, and Julie's attention was diverted again.

'I thought you were baking.'

'I was.' Laura struggled to keep the resentment out of her voice. 'But I changed my mind.'

'Why?'

'Why?' Laura cast her daughter a half-impatient glance. 'Oh—no reason. I'm just not in the mood, after all.'

'Are you sure you and Jake haven't had a fight?' Julie was curious. 'It's not like you to waste perfectly good flour and water.'

Laura sighed. 'Don't be silly, Julie!' she exclaimed shortly. 'I barely know the man. What could he and I have had a fight about?'

'Me,' said Julie simply, and Laura's jaw sagged.

The realisation that her daughter's interpretation of the facts was perfectly reasonable stopped Laura in her tracks. It hadn't occurred to her that Julie might see herself as the only possible reason for her mother and her boyfriend to have words, and, although it wasn't right, it was vaguely reassuring. Of course, Julie would never think that Jake and her mother might have had a more personal exchange, Laura thought, with some relief. So far as Julie was concerned, such an idea was ludicrous.

'Well—no,' she said now. 'Really. If—if I seem on edge, it's probably just the time of the month. Anyway,' she added, realising it was probably less suspicious to talk about Jake, than to avoid doing so, 'you didn't tell me he has a family.'

'I did.' Julie frowned. 'I told you we met at that charity bash his mother had organised.'

'I don't mean his parents,' replied Laura evenly. 'I meant his daughter.'

'Oh—*Luci*!' Julie pulled a face. 'He's told you about her, has he?'

'Obviously.'

Julie shrugged. 'So?'

'So, if you marry—Jake, you'll have a ready-made daughter.'

'Stepdaughter,' amended Julie shortly, her expression losing some of its complacency. 'Don't worry. I don't intend to see a lot of her. She's a bore!'

Laura turned to look at her. 'But she is his daughter. You can't expect him to ignore his responsibilities.'

'You know nothing about it,' retorted Julie rudely. 'In any case, she's at school in Rome. She lives with Jake's parents in term-time.'

'But I thought—that is…' Laura moistened her lips before continuing, 'I understood—his parents lived in Tuscany.'

Julie's eyes grew thoughtful. 'Did you?' She paused. 'We have been having a heart-to-heart, haven't we? Has he told you about Castellombardi, too?'

Laura frowned. 'I don't think so. *Castel*—that means castle, doesn't it?'

'Something like that.' Julie was offhand. 'It's also the name of the village where the house is situated. As for its being a castle—I don't think it's any more than a rather large country house. Old, of course. And probably draughty. Though Jake did say his grandfather had spent a lot of money restoring it.'

'I see.'

'Not that we'll live there,' went on Julie carelessly. 'Jake has homes all over the place. Rome; Viareggio; *Paris*!' She sighed. 'And, of course, the Lombardis have an apartment in London.'

'Really?' Laura put the baking board away and dried her hands. 'And—and when is all this going to take place?'

'Our getting married, you mean?' Julie lifted her shoulders in a considering gesture. 'I'm not sure. Has he said anything to you?'

'To me?' Laura was taken aback, but Julie nodded.

'Yes. To you,' she repeated. 'I assumed your little tête-à-tête was Jake's way of letting you know he was able to keep me in the manner to which I've become accustomed.' Her lips twitched. 'I wish!'

Laura shook her head. 'Well—no. I mean, we did talk about you, of course, but—but——'

'You didn't ask him what his intentions were,' finished Julie shortly. 'I should have known.'

'Now, come on.' Laura had had quite enough of being accused of things she wasn't responsible for this morning. 'You can't expect me to ask questions like that!'

'Why not?'

'Why not?' Laura gasped. 'Julie, you know him better than I do, for God's sake! If you don't know what he thinks, who does?'

Julie looked sulky. 'He wanted to come here. Not me.'

'I know that.' Laura did her best to ride the pain of her daughter's indifference. 'Nevertheless it's up to—to him to speak to me. Not the other way about.'

Julie hunched her shoulders. 'If you say so.'

'I do.' Laura took a steadying breath. 'And now, I suggest you go and get dressed, before—before Jake comes back. He may want you to go for a drive or something. You could go to Alnwick, or Bamborough. And I'm sure he'd like to see the Roman wall. Or—you could always go into Newcastle. It's busy on Saturdays, but it's better than hanging about here.'

Julie sniffed. 'Didn't he say what time he'd be back?'

'No.' Laura picked up her daughter's empty cup and carried it to the sink. 'But I'm sure he won't be much longer.' She paused to gather her composure, and then added, 'After all, there isn't much to see around here.'

'Hmm.'

Julie seemed to accept this, and to her mother's relief she pushed herself to her feet. Laura waited until she had gone upstairs, before sinking weakly into the chair her daughter had vacated. Lord, she thought wearily, running her hand over her head, and then allowing it to rest at her nape. This was going to be the longest weekend of her life.

CHAPTER FIVE

'DID you have a nice weekend?'

Mark caught Laura as she was going into the school on

Monday morning, and she was forced to turn and speak to
him.

'Um—very nice, actually,' she lied, unprepared to confide
her deeper fears in him. 'Did you?'

Mark frowned. 'It was all right, I suppose. I had the car
serviced on Saturday morning, and on Sunday I took
Mother over to a friend's in Carlisle. Nothing very exciting, I'm afraid.'

Laura forced a smile. 'Oh, well——'

'Did you?'

She looked confused. 'Did I what?'

'Do anything exciting?' prompted Mark impatiently.
'What was this boyfriend of Julie's like? I expect she let
you run around after her, as usual.'

'That's none of your business, Mark,' returned Laura
icily, glad of a reason to break off the conversation. She
thrust open the glass door. 'Excuse me.'

'Aw, Laura...'

Mark came after her, but she ignored him, and as they
caught up with one of the other teachers in the corridor
there was no further chance for him to try and redeem
himself. The staff-room, where all the teachers gathered,
was not the place to try and have a private conversation,
and Laura made certain they didn't leave together.

But, later on in the morning, when she had a free period,
Laura couldn't prevent thoughts of the weekend from im-
pinging on the English papers she was marking. She knew
it would be a while before she could put what had happened out of her mind. It was all very well dismissing Mark's
comments with a terse rejoinder. She couldn't dismiss the
things Jake had said with quite the same detachment.

Not that he had said much more to her, after he'd returned from his walk on Saturday morning. To her relief,
he had confined his attentions to Julie. And if her daughter
thought there was anything strange about his attitude
towards her mother, she was too wrapped up in her own
affairs to attribute it any consequence.

Besides, Laura thought ruefully, Julie was unlikely to entertain any worries about Jake's relationship with her
mother. It simply wouldn't occur to Julie that there could
be any personal contact between them. And there hadn't

been, really, Laura reminded herself severely. Just a silly misunderstanding that had alienated them both.

She refused to dwell too long on what Jake might have meant by the things he had said. As she had said to him, she wasn't used to his kind of word games. And not just word games, she appended doggedly. He had played with her emotions, and made her look a fool.

Or, at least, he had tried to, she thought defensively. She didn't think she had left him in any doubts as to her disdain for his promiscuity. The way he had behaved the rest of the weekend proved he hadn't liked her lack of response. He had been polite—just—but there had been no further attempts to disconcert her.

Of course, she hadn't seen a lot of them really. By the time Jake came back from his walk, Julie had been ready and waiting. And if she hadn't got her own way about going shopping in Newcastle, because Jake wanted to see the Roman remains, the result was the same as far as Laura was concerned. They were out for the rest of the day.

Dinner on Saturday evening had been rather fraught, Laura remembered now. She had gathered the outing hadn't been an unqualified success, and none of them had done justice to the roast beef and Yorkshire pudding she had so painstakingly prepared. But at least she had been left to do the dishes in peace, and afterwards she had excused herself on the pretext of having lessons to prepare. There had been no objections; indeed, she was aware that Julie had welcomed her departure, and, if Laura had found herself speculating over what might be going on in her living-room, she had resisted the temptation to find out. The less she and Jake Lombardi had to do with one another, the better, she had decided grimly. He was not at all the kind of prospective son-in-law she had anticipated.

They had left Burnfoot the following morning. Laura had waved them off in the low, powerful sports car, that had probably attracted quite a bit of interest in the village. It was not unusual to see the odd Mercedes or BMW gliding along the High Street, and old Colonel Renfrew had an ancient Rolls-Royce. But Lamborghinis were something else again, and she was quite sure she would have to face a few pointed questions, next time she went into the village stores.

Still, she was unlikely to see either of them again for quite
some time, she consoled herself, trying to concentrate on
her fourth-years' interpretation of the *The Merchant of
Venice*. Julie had made the usual promises that she would
see her soon, and so on, but Laura privately suspected that
once her daughter was married, she would see even less of
her than she did now.

She shook her head, trying not to let it bother her. After
all, it wasn't a new phenomenon. She should have learned
to live with it by now. She and Julie were simply not compatible, and there was no point in blaming herself for a
situation over which she had no control.

The next few days were uneventful. Mark made his peace
with her, catching her in the school car park one evening,
and apologising for what he had said. But, although Laura
accepted his apology, she didn't accept his invitation to
dinner the following weekend.

'Ask me next week,' she told him, pleasantly enough, so
he would know it wasn't his fault she was turning him down.
She didn't want to hurt his feelings. She just couldn't cope
with Mark's pedantic company at the moment.

Jess Turner, a friend from her college days, rang on
Friday evening. Jess was married, and lived in Durham these
days, but the two women still kept in touch.

'I wondered if you'd like to meet me for lunch tomorrow,' Jess suggested, after they had exchanged greetings.
'I'm going shopping in Newcastle, and I hoped you might
like to join me.'

'Well——' Laura had planned to start on the garden the
following day, but Jess was very persuasive.

'Do come,' she urged. 'It's ages since I've seen you.
And—well, I've got something to tell you.'

'Oh—all right.' Laura gave in, mentally resigning her
plans to weed out the winter's casualties for another week.
It wasn't as if she was really in the mood for gardening,
and Jess was such an undemanding companion.

They arranged to meet at Grey's Monument at half-past
twelve on Saturday, and Laura spent the rest of the evening
wondering what Jess had to tell her. Perhaps she and Clive
were moving again, she considered pensively. As Clive was
in the police force, it seemed the likeliest option.

When she went to bed, Laura hesitated a moment, and then went into the spare bedroom. She hadn't been into the bedroom since the morning of Jàke's departure, when she had stripped the sheets he had used from the bed. It hadn't been a conscious avoidance, she told herself now. Just a lack of necessity to go in there. Nevertheless, she recoiled from the faint aroma of the shaving lotion he had used, though its fragrance lingered in her nostrils, long after she had closed the door.

On Saturday morning, she spent some time deciding what she was going to wear. Jess would probably expect her to turn up in jeans and a sweater, but Laura felt like dressing up, for a change. It wasn't as if she had that many opportunities to do so, she thought defensively, and after last weekend she felt like changing her image.

It was still too chilly to wear just a suit, and combining her winter coat with a suit would be far too bulky. She could always wear the cream wool dress, with the cowl collar, which she had planned to wear last weekend, she reflected positively. In fact, it might be a good idea to take the opportunity to smarten up her wardrobe. Just because she had a twenty-one-year-old daughter was no reason to behave as if she had one foot in the grave.

She refused to consider the reasons behind her sudden change of heart. She owed it to herself to dress up sometimes, she told herself firmly. She was still a comparatively young woman. Julie was right. She ought to pay more attention to her appearance.

Nevertheless, when she viewed her reflection in the mirror of the wardrobe some time later, she did have reservations. She looked smarter, it was true, but what was Jess going to think when she saw her? It was so long since she had worn dark, filmy stockings, and three-inch heels, in the daytime. And the soft folds of the woollen dress emphasised a figure she had long since ceased to admire. Breasts were not fashionable any more—particularly rather generous ones that swelled above a narrow waist.

She turned sideways, sucking in her stomach, and then allowed it to relax again. What was she doing, for heaven's sake? she asked herself irritably. She was too old to start fretting about her shape. She had lived with it for thirty-eight years, and there wasn't much she could do about it now.

The doorbell rang as she was stroking mascara on to the tawny tips of her lashes. The unexpected sound caused her hand to slip, and she only just managed to prevent the stuff from smearing her cheek. Lowering the brush to the dressing-table, she glanced impatiently towards the window. Who could it be? she wondered, frowning. It was barely ten o'clock.

Shaking her head, she cast one final look at her appearance, before going downstairs. Whoever it was was going to get a surprise when they saw her. This was definitely not the usual way she dressed on Saturday mornings.

She paused at the foot of the stairs, ran smoothing fingers over her skirt, and opened the door. Then, she almost collapsed on the spot. A man was standing on the step outside, his broad shoulders successfully blocking her view of the road. He was tall, and lean—and distractingly familiar, and her jaw sagged helplessly, as her eyes met his.

'Hi,' he said, and she thought he sounded rather tense. 'May I come in?'

Laura caught her breath. 'I——' She looked beyond him. 'Is Julie with you?'

Jake shook his head, and her heart flipped. 'She's not—I mean nothing's happened——?'

'Julie's fine,' returned Jake evenly. 'As far as I know, that is. I came alone.'

'You did?' Laura swallowed. She had the distinct feeling she was imagining this. Jake couldn't be here. He was in London, or Italy, or some other place. But not here. Not in Burnfoot. Not at her door!

'So—may I come in?' he asked again, and although she wasn't sure it was exactly wise, she stepped aside.

He looked tired, she thought, reluctantly closing the door, and following him into the living-room. There was at least one night's growth of beard on his chin, and his eyes were red-rimmed and hollow. If she didn't know better, she would have said he looked like a man who had spent the night sleeping rough, and even the jacket of the dark suit he was wearing had creases across the back.

She paused just inside the doorway, linking her fingers together, and regarding him warily. She couldn't think of any reason he might be here, unless he and Julie had had a row. That was possible, of course, but why would he come to her? What could she possibly do to help him?

Jake halted in front of the hearth. As she was going out, Laura hadn't lit the fire; but the heating system was working, and the room was pleasantly warm, even so. However, it wasn't particularly tidy. The exercise books Laura had been working on the night before, were tipped in a haphazard pile beside her chair, and various items of clothing, awaiting ironing, were draped over the back of one of the dining chairs.

Oh, well, she thought impatiently, she hadn't been expecting a visitor, particularly not a visitor who was used to much grander surroundings than these. And if he didn't like it, no one was asking him to stay. *To stay* . . .

'You look nice.'

His words took her by surprise, and Laura gazed at him blankly for a few moments, before gathering her scattered wits. 'Thank you. But——'

'Are you going out?'

Laura moistened her lips. 'I—yes. Yes, I am, as it happens.' She took a steadying breath. 'Look—what's going on, Mr Lombardi? Why have you come here? I should warn you, if it's anything to do with Julie——'

'It isn't.'

'It isn't?' Laura released her fingers, to press her palms together, and realised they were sticky. 'I—but—it must be.'

'Why must it be?'

Laura's lips flattened against her teeth. 'Don't you ever answer a question?' she exclaimed. 'I want to know what's happened. Have—have you and Julie had a row?'

'No.' Jake pushed his hands into the pockets of his trousers, and as he did so his jacket fell open, revealing a bloody stain on the shirt beneath.

Laura gasped, and pressed her fingers to her lips, and Jake, realising what she had seen, pulled one hand out of his pocket to finger the ugly discolouration of the cloth. 'A small accident,' he said, his lips twisting cynically. 'I don't think I'll die of it, do you?'

Laura stared at him disbelievingly. 'You—cut yourself?'

'I didn't say that exactly.' Jake glanced behind him at the armchair. 'D'you mind if I sit down? I appear to have lost my balance.'

He sank down into the chair, as Laura rushed across the room towards him. He had gone so pale suddenly that she was half afraid he was going to lose consciousness as well. He must have lost a lot of blood, she thought, halting nervously beside the chair. But why was he here? What was going on?

'That's better,' he said, sinking back against the cushions, and gazing up at her through the thick veil of his lashes. 'Sorry about that. I guess I'm not as tough as I thought I was.'

Laura hesitated a moment longer, and then came down on her haunches beside him. 'Do you—would you like me to—to look at it?' she ventured, and his lips twitched with a trace of humour.

'Look at what?' he countered lazily, and she tore her eyes from the revealing tautness of cloth across his crotch.

'You know what I mean,' she declared, getting swiftly to her feet again. 'You're evidently hurt. I might be able to help you.'

'OK.' Jake tugged his shirt out of the waistband of his trousers, and unfastened the first couple of buttons. 'Go ahead.'

Laura didn't want to touch him. Just being near him like this was nerve-racking enough, without having to look at his bare flesh. It reminded her too much of the way she had pictured him, lying in her spare bed upstairs. He was so disturbingly male, and she simply wasn't equipped to deal with it.

Nevertheless, as she drew his silk shirt aside to reveal the brown flesh of his midriff, her reticence was quickly overtaken by concern. He had a gash, some three inches in length, and perhaps a quarter as deep, just below the curve of his rib-cage. Someone had endeavoured—not very successfully—to close the wound with adhesive sutures, but it had opened again, and was now bleeding fitfully.

Laura knew a momentary sense of panic, and then, determinedly quelling the feeling of sickness that had risen inside her, she lifted her eyes to his pale face. 'Who did this?' she exclaimed, forcing herself to speak levelly. 'Was there a fight? Is that how it happened? If so——'

'It was my fault,' Jake interrupted her wearily. 'It was a fight, but it was perfectly controlled. Or it was supposed to be. I was fencing—you understand? I wasn't giving my opponent the attention I should. Believe me, the man who did this was more upset than me.'

Laura shook her head. 'But—don't you wear protective clothing for fencing? And aren't there foils?'

'Very good.' Jake made a weak attempt to applaud her. 'Yes, you're right, of course. One is expected to take precautions. But—I didn't feel like being careful, and this is the result.'

Laura caught her lower lip between her teeth. 'You could have been killed!'

'I think not.' Jake's lips twisted. 'Believe it or not, I am usually capable of holding my own, as they say.'

Laura shook her head. 'Have you seen a doctor?'

'I don't need a doctor,' retorted Jake flatly. 'I've just lost a little blood, is all. Doctors ask too many questions. And I was not in the mood to answer them.'

Laura bit her lip, hard, and then, realising she was wasting time, she turned and hurried into the kitchen. Armed with a bowl of warm water, some antiseptic, and bandages, she returned to the living-room, and knelt down beside his chair.

'I'm afraid this is going to hurt,' she said, deciding the reasons why—and how—he was here would have to wait for the moment. Somehow she had to stop the bleeding, and then maybe she could persuade him to seek professional help.

He winced as she drew the gaping sutures away, and at once the wound began to bleed more freely. Her hands were soon wet with his blood, and the knowledge was terrifying. She just hoped she knew what she was doing, and that she wasn't making it worse.

'You should go to a hospital,' she protested, pressing a damp cloth against the gash. At least it was clean, she thought unwillingly. If she could bind it tightly enough, he might get away with just a bad headache.

'You're doing fine,' he told her, but she could see the beads of perspiration on his forehead. Whatever he said, she knew he must be in a great deal of pain, and that awareness troubled her more than it should.

'You should have had more sense,' she added crossly, spreading some antiseptic ointment on a gauze dressing, and applying it to the cut. She guessed it must have stung like crazy, but all Jake did was suck in his breath. 'I suppose what you were doing was illegal. That's why you didn't want to call a doctor.'

'Something like that.'

Jake's response was barely audible, and, although she knew he needed to rest, Laura steeled her emotions, and said, 'I'm afraid you're going to have to sit up.'

'Sit up?' Jake looked a bit sick at the prospect, but he pushed his hands down on the arms of the chair, and propelled himself forward. 'OK.'

'You'll have to take off your jacket—and your shirt,' murmured Laura awkwardly, wishing she was not so aware of him as a man. He was her daughter's property, she kept telling herself. Apart from anything else, he was too young for her. But it didn't help, and her breathing was as shallow as his as she watched him struggling to take off his jacket.

Of course, she had to help. Even coping with the knot of his tie exhausted him, and she was forced to remove his jacket, and unfasten the remaining buttons of his shirt. His skin was clammy. The result of her inexpert ministrations, she guessed. No matter how successful he was at hiding his feelings, he couldn't hide the reactions of his body.

But it made it a little easier for her. However, although the room was warm, while he was sweating he could easily catch a chill, and she applied the length of bandage with a swift and—she hoped—impersonal efficiency. The fact that his skin was smooth, with ridges of corded muscle beneath the flesh, and an arrowing of fine dark hair that disappeared below the waistband of his trousers, were passing observations. Nevertheless, she couldn't fail to notice how white the bandage looked against his dark skin, or help her own response to his potent sexuality.

Leaving him to put his shirt on again, as best he could, Laura carried the dish, and the dressings she had used, back into the kitchen. She tipped the bloodstained water into the sink, and watched as it curled away, out of sight. It looked worse than it was, she reassured herself, but even so, he was lucky to have reached the cottage without passing out. But how had he reached the cottage? she wondered, gnawing at her lower lip. And why had he come here? Dear God, what was Julie going to say when she found out where he'd been?

She pushed herself away from the sink, and looked around. Tea, she thought practically, refusing to consider Julie's feelings at this moment. Hot, sweet tea! Wasn't that what they always gave you in hospital? Something to warm you, and give you energy, all at the same time.

She filled the kettle, and plugged it in, and then faltered again, unsure of how to continue. Was he fit to answer questions now? she pondered uneasily. Was he fit to leave, without seeing a doctor? And could she turn him out, if he wanted to stay?

But, of course, he didn't want to stay, she told herself impatiently, marching to the door of the living-room, and then halting, her fingers clenching and unclenching frustratedly. Her questions were going to have to wait. Jake was asleep.

Or was he? Anxiety brought her to the side of his chair again, and she bent to listen to his breathing. How would she know if he was unconscious? she fretted. It wasn't as if she had any experience in these matters.

But he *seemed* to be sleeping. And he had managed to put on his shirt again, although it was just dragged across his chest, and no attempt had been made to fasten the buttons. Even so, she thought he looked a little better. There was the faintest trace of colour in his cheeks, and, with his eyes closed, their hollowness seemed less pronounced. Instead, his lashes lay like sooty fans above his cheekbones, and she knew an unholy desire to reach out and touch their softness with the tips of her fingers . . .

It was enough to set her back several paces. Dear lord, she thought, aghast, what on earth was she thinking of? She was behaving as if she had never seen a man sleeping before. How amused he would be, if he opened his eyes and saw her.

Swallowing her impatience, she strode across the room, and climbed the stairs to her bedroom. There were blankets, stored in the cedarwood ottoman at the foot of her bed, and, pulling out the largest, she carried it downstairs again. Then, trying not to inhale the pungent scent of sweat that still lingered on his body, she eased the blanket up to his chin. At least, it wouldn't be her fault if he caught a chill, she thought resentfully. She could do without that on her conscience as well.

The kettle was boiling, and, giving him one last, uneasy look, Laura went into the kitchen to turn it off. There was no point in making any tea yet, she reflected ruefully. He could sleep for an hour or more, and she might have to provide him with lunch. *Lunch* . . .

She cast a horrified look at her watch. It was after eleven o'clock already, and although she was not meeting Jess until half-past twelve, she had planned to give herself plenty of time to find somewhere to park. It wasn't always easy on Saturdays, and the traffic into the city was always heavy.

She groaned. What was she going to do? There was no point in phoning Jess's home. Her husband was unlikely to be there, and besides, Jess had said she was planning to make a day of it. There was no way she could let her friend know what had happened—even if she wanted to.

Even if she wanted to? The ambiguity of that statement caused another crisis of conscience. Of course, she wanted to tell Jess what had happened. She couldn't leave her friend, waiting around, not knowing what was going on. Why shouldn't she tell her? What did she have to hide?

What indeed? Laura gazed blankly through the window, into the back garden of the cottage. What was she afraid of? That Jess might suspect Jake had come here, because of something she had done—or said? That she might suspect Laura was *attracted* to the man? A man who was obviously years younger than she was?

Of course. She had her pride, just like anyone else, and Jake's appearance had put her in an invidious position. What could she tell anyone? How could he have done it?

Gripping the edge of the formica-topped work unit, Laura struggled to find some perspective in this. Jake must have had some other reason for coming to this part of the country, she decided. Julie had said his family was in business, hadn't she? And everyone knew that the north-east of England was an enterprise zone. He had probably come to finalise some business deal, and, because she was in the area, he had decided to look her up.

But no. That didn't hold water. For one thing, he'd said he had been fencing, and he would hardly have been doing that prior to attending some business meeting. So did that mean he had driven all the way from London, with that gash in his side? My God, she thought sickly, how could he have done it? And where had he spent last night?

The questions just went on and on, and she simply didn't have the time to find the answers. Jake was here, and, for the moment, there was nothing she could do about it. But that didn't mean she had to alter her schedule. She had made plans, and he couldn't expect her to abandon them, just because he had chosen to practically collapse on her doorstep.

She sighed. But could she go and leave him as he was? What if he was unconscious, after all? What if she was wrong, and he slipped into a coma, or something equally ghastly, in her absence? Would she ever forgive herself if something awful happened to him? If only she had ex-plained the situation, before he'd passed out. He could sleep for hours, and there was nothing she could do.

CHAPTER SIX

'DID I hear a kettle boiling?'

The low, attractive sound of Jake's voice brought Laura round with a start. She had believed he was asleep, or worse, and seeing him, albeit swaying, in the doorway, caused a sudden surge of impatience.

'What are you doing?' she exclaimed, forgetting for the moment that seconds before she had been lamenting his unconscious state. 'You shouldn't be walking around. That wound needs time to heal.'

Jake glanced down at his stained shirt, and laid a brown hand over the area of the injury. 'It feels much better,' he assured her, lifting his eyes to hers again. 'I'm sorry for losing consciousness like that. I guess I'm more tired than I thought.'

Laura's hands clenched at her sides. 'Did you have any sleep last night?'

'Some.' Jake was non-committal.

'Where?'

He sighed. 'In a service area.'

Laura was horrified. 'In your car?'

'Does it matter? I made it, didn't I?'

'That depends.' Laura found it was too much to cope with, right at this minute. 'Well—I've got to go. I—I'm meeting someone.'

'Are you?' Jake's eyes were dark and enigmatic. 'Does that mean you'd like me to leave?'

Laura hesitated. 'Not—necessarily,' she replied, ignoring the small voice inside her, that said that was exactly what she ought to ask him to do. But how could she? she argued with herself. He wasn't fit to go anywhere!

'No?' he said softly. 'You want me to stay?'

'I didn't say I *wanted* you to stay,' Laura countered hotly. 'I—just don't think you're fit to leave. Not if you have to drive anyway.' She pressed her lips together. 'Where did you leave your car?'

Jake inclined his head, his mouth taking on a vaguely ironic slant. 'I parked near that stretch of grass, beside the church.'

'The green!' exclaimed Laura, with an inward groan. 'Why'd you park there?'

Jake's face paled alarmingly, and he gripped the frame of the door for support before replying. 'I—thought you might prefer it,' he replied unevenly. 'I didn't want to embarrass you.'

'Embarrass me?'

Laura could have laughed, but it would have been a bitter laugh at best. She could just imagine the stir his reappearance would have caused. After last weekend, she doubted there was anyone in the village who wouldn't have recognised Jake's car, if they saw it. And parking on the green . . .

But Jake was obviously in no state to stand here trading words with her, and, forcing herself to move forward, she took his arm. 'I think you'd better go and sit down again, before you fall down,' she told him, intensely aware of the heat of his flesh through his shirt-sleeve. 'Come on. Then I'll make you some hot tea. Are you hungry?'

Jake shook his head, but he leaned on her fairly heavily as they progressed across the living-room to where the blanket was tumbled on the armchair. Without letting go of him, Laura quickly whisked the blanket away, and then supported him, as he lowered himself into the chair. He was sweating again, she noticed, with a pang; a combination of the shock he had had, and the amount of blood he had lost, she surmised. It was draining his strength.

'*Mi dispiace,*' he said, and she noticed how, in moments of stress, he was apt to lapse into his own language. 'I'm sorry. I am a nuisance, *no?*'

Laura straightened, resisting the impulse to smooth the damp strands of dark hair back from his forehead. 'It's—all right,' she said, offhandedly, glancing towards the kitchen. 'Um—here's the blanket. I'll get the tea.'

'But your—appointment?' he queried, looking up at her through his lashes, and Laura's heart palpitated wildly.

'I've got time,' she said, leaving him, and hurrying back into the kitchen. She had—just, but only if she managed to get parked at the first attempt.

At least the kettle didn't take long to boil again, and she made the tea with hands that shook a little. It was a hangover from supporting his weight on her shoulder, she told herself firmly, but she was trembling inside, too, and she had no excuse for that.

She set a tray with the necessary cup and saucer, milk, and sugar basin, and then added a plate of biscuits, just for good measure. She supposed she should have opened a tin of soup or something, but he had said he wasn't hungry, and when she came back...

She arrested her thoughts right there. She was not going to think about what might happen when she got back. He might not be here, for heaven's sake. If he drank the sweet tea, and rested for a while, he might feel well enough to drive to a hotel, at least—and that would all be for the best,

she told herself severely. Least said, soonest mended: wasn't
that what they said? So long as their relationship remained
on this impersonal level, she had nothing to worry about.

Jake's eyes were closed again, when she went back into
the living-room, but they opened when she set the tray down
on an end-table she had set beside his chair.

'*Grazie,*' he said, levering himself up from the cushions,
to take the cup she handed him. 'I am most grateful.'

Laura folded her hands. 'The teapot's on the tray, and
I've put plenty of sugar in your cup,' she said, realising she
was sounding more and more like his mother. Well, why
not? she thought cynically. If Julie had her way, she'd be
his mother-in-law, at least. 'I—I should be back by about
half-past three,' she went on, mentally abandoning any
thoughts of prolonging the outing. 'But if—if you want to
go before then—which I don't advise,' she added reck-
lessly, 'just drop the latch, and close the door.'

Jake regarded her over the rim of his cup. 'I'll stay.'

'You will?' Laura swallowed convulsively.

'If you have no objections,' he averred, grimacing at the
sweetness of the tea, and Laura's breathing felt suspended.

'I—no,' she mumbled, turning away, before he could say
anything else to disturb her efforts to remain objective.
Nevertheless, her heart was pounding, and it took an
enormous effort to walk across the floor.

Her coat and handbag were upstairs, and by the time she
came down again, the warm folds of her plum-coloured
cashmere coat wrapped about her, Jake was resting back
against the cushions.

'Drive carefully,' he said, as she collected her car keys
from the sideboard, and, with a jerky nod, Laura let herself
out of the house.

She saw the Lamborghini, as she drove through the
village. As Jake had said, it was parked on the verge, beside
the wall of the churchyard. Several of the village children
were peering through its windows as she passed, and she
hoped they wouldn't do any damage to it. In any case, she
didn't have the time to move it now, even if she'd had the
guts to try.

She was late meeting Jess, but only about ten minutes,
and her friend accepted her explanation of not being able

to find anywhere to park. The city was busy, and Laura had been lucky to find a space in one of the multi-storey car parks. Luckily, someone had been leaving, as Laura had cruised along one of the upper floors, and, although she had had to contend with some irate glares from motorists, who'd considered they had a prior claim to the space, she'd bought her parking ticket, and stuck it bravely to the windscreen.

Jess was waiting beneath the monument that had been raised to Earl Grey, one of England's earliest prime ministers, and her eyes widened when she saw her friend. She was smaller than Laura, and, although she generally wore high heels to increase her height, today she had chosen boots, and woollen trousers. In consequence, the contrast between them was quite pronounced, and she frowned as Laura crossed the square towards her.

'Did I miss something?' she asked, after Laura had made her explanations, and, aware that Jess was referring to her appearance, Laura grimaced.

'No,' she protested, but she couldn't help the wave of hot colour that ran up her cheeks at the words. Even though the way she was dressed owed nothing to Jake Lombardi's arrival, the connotations were irresistible.

'Are you sure?' Jess regarded her with some suspicion. 'We are just going shopping, you know.'

'I know.' Laura sighed. 'I just felt like making the most of myself for once. Do I usually look such a fright?'

'Of course not.' Jess shook her dark head. 'It wouldn't have anything to do with Julie, would it?'

'Julie!' Laura managed to sound indignant, but it took an effort. 'Jess!'

'Well!' Jess was unrepentant. 'You haven't seen her, then?'

Laura took the other girl's arm. 'Can we move away from here?' she asked, without answering. 'Where are we having lunch?'

'I thought we might go to Fenwicks,' replied Jess, giving her friend a studied look. 'Then we can look round the clothes department first.'

'Fine.'

Laura nodded, and they crossed the square to the swing doors of the large department store Jess had mentioned. Walking through the store, it was difficult to talk at all, and it wasn't until Jess led the way into the maternity department that Laura realised what her friend had to tell her.

'You're pregnant!' she exclaimed, and, when Jess nodded, rather sheepishly, she gave her a hug. 'How wonderful!'

'Is it?' Jess looked a little less confident now. 'I'm not so sure.'

'What do you mean?' Laura frowned. 'Don't you want a family?'

'Well, you know I do—*did*,' amended Jess, sighing. 'But, Laura, Clive and I have been married for almost *fifteen* years. I'm almost forty. You don't think I'm too old, do you?'

'Too old?' Unbidden, thoughts of Jake sprang into Laura's mind, and she had a hard time putting them aside. 'Of course you're not too old. What does Clive think?'

'Oh, he's over the moon,' said Jess glumly, examining a navy and white maternity dress, with straight, classic lines. 'But after all these years! I never imagined I'd be having my first child at my age!'

'Lots of women have their first child in their late thirties,' declared Laura staunchly. 'Women who've put their career first, and a family second.'

'Yes, but that's not me, is it?' said Jess, sighing. 'I wanted a baby when I was younger. Now, I'm not so sure.'

'Aren't you?'

Laura looked at her disbelievingly, and Jess managed a rueful smile. 'Well, all right, yes. I want this baby. But not if anything's going to go wrong.'

Laura shook her head. 'Stop being such a pessimist. If you want to look at it that way, younger women have problems, too. If you look after yourself, and do what the doctor tells you, you'll be fine. It's not such a big deal, Jess. Honestly.'

'That's easy for you to say,' Jess argued. 'You were only a kid when you had Julie. I'm an old married woman.'

'Nonsense,' said Laura firmly. 'You'll take it in your stride. So—when is the baby due? You don't look any different.'

'At the end of September,' Jess replied, running an involuntary hand over the curve of her stomach. She smiled. 'There's not much to see yet, thank goodness.'

'No.' Laura smiled. 'I'm so pleased for you. I'm sure Clive will make a marvellous father.'

'Mmm.' Jess was thoughtful. 'Well, I hope so.'

'I'm sure he will.' Laura knew a momentary sense of envy for her friend. She had never known what it was like to share those simple human emotions.

But later, as they were sitting enjoying scampi and chips in the restaurant, Jess returned to her earlier tack. 'So,' she said, 'how are things with you? Have you seen Julie recently?'

'You don't give up, do you?' Laura regarded her friend with some resignation. 'All right, yes. Julie came up last weekend. But she didn't browbeat me into doing something about my appearance, so you can stop looking so smug.'

'So who did, then?' Jess countered, and, once again, Jake's dark features swam into Laura's consciousness. She didn't want to think about him. She particularly didn't want to admit that he had had anything to do with her desire to improve her image. But she couldn't help wondering if he was all right, and if he really did intend to stay.

'I . . .' Realising Jess was looking at her rather curiously now, Laura endeavoured to speak casually. 'Um—no one influenced me,' she said, not altogether truthfully. 'I just felt like smartening myself up, that's all. I look all right, don't I? You're making me feel conspicuous.'

'Don't be silly. You look great, and you know it,' declared Jess warmly. 'I just wondered if—by any chance— some man——'

'No!' Laura knew her response was too vehement, but she couldn't help it. 'Honestly, Jess, just because you think marriage is the best thing since sliced bread, don't imagine everyone has to have a man in their life, before they begin to care how they look!'

Jess flushed then, and Laura felt awful. 'I didn't mean——' Jess began, but Laura broke in before she could go any further.

'No, I know you didn't!' she exclaimed, expelling her breath on a rueful sigh. 'Oh, Jess, I'm sorry. I didn't mean to blow up at you like that. I don't know what's the matter with me today.'

Didn't she?

'It doesn't matter. I shouldn't have said anything,' protested Jess hurriedly. 'Honestly. I just wondered if Mark—— '

'Mark?' In spite of herself, Laura's voice rose an octave. 'Oh—well, I still see him from time to time, of course. Outside school, I mean. But he's like me. He's not interested in surrendering his freedom for some precarious sexual commitment.'

Jess studied her friend doubtfully. 'At the risk of getting my head bitten off again, I don't think that's how you really feel,' she declared, and, when Laura raised her eyebrows, she went on, 'You think you're so self-sufficient, Laura. You go to school, and support yourself. You've even bought your own home. But can you honestly say you never wish you'd got married?'

Laura bent her head. 'Yes.'

'Well, I don't believe it.' Jess finished her meal, and propped her elbows on the table. 'I think you've let one bad experience sour you for a real, loving relationship. Or perhaps you've just never met a man who could turn your world upside-down.'

'Oh, Jess!' Laura fell back on sarcasm, as a means to divert her friend. 'Is this really Mrs Turner, the terror of the maths department, talking? Look out, Barbara Cartland! You've got a rival!'

'You can mock,' declared Jess imperviously. 'But I mean it. You just never go anywhere where you might meet someone.'

'I go places,' said Laura, aware that Jess's words were not as ridiculous as she would like to think. 'I go to parties, occasionally, and the theatre—— '

'With Mark Leith,' put in Jess, as the waitress came to remove their plates. 'No one's going to make a pass at you, with him keeping a proprietorial hold on you.'

'Just because you don't like Mark——'

'I hardly know him,' retorted Jess. 'But I'm pretty sure he's not the man for you.'

'There you go again.' Laura wished she had never started this. 'Jess, have you ever considered that I might not be the marrying sort?'

Jess gave her an old-fashioned look. 'No.'

'Why not?'

'Will you take a look at yourself some time?' exclaimed Jess forcefully. 'You're tall, and slim——'

'Not so slim!'

'—and attractive. You've got good legs.'

'Jess, please.' Laura shook her head. 'Can we talk about something else, please? Like—what are we going to have for dessert?'

'Doesn't Julie say anything?' persisted Jess, and Laura felt as if she was lurching from one awkward topic to another.

'I—Julie's fine,' she said, hoping Jess would take the hint, but her friend looked at her over the menu, and her expression was not encouraging.

'I meant—doesn't Julie ever mention the prospect of your getting married?'

'Me?' Laura stared fixedly at the menu. 'No, of course not. Why should she? I'm her mother. I'm too old to—to——'

'To have a sex-life of your own?' suggested Jess drily. 'Yes, I can believe she thinks that.'

Laura sighed. 'Jess, please——'

'Oh, all right.' Jess capitulated. 'So—tell me about Julie. Is she all right? I gather she's not thinking of getting married any time soon either.'

Laura's head came up. 'Why do you say that?'

'You mean, she is?' Jess's eyes widened. 'Have you met him?'

'Jess!' In spite of all her efforts, Laura could feel the colour rising to her cheeks. 'You do jump to conclusions,

don't you? I haven't even said she has a boyfriend. I only—
wondered why——'

'Laura, you're not a very good liar.' Jess smiled. 'Now,
I can tell from your face that something's going on, so you
might as well tell me what it is. I don't keep any secrets
from you.'

'I'm not keeping secrets!' But she was, and she was guiltily
aware of it. 'As it happens—Julie did…bring a friend home
with her last weekend. He's an Italian. His name's—Jake
Lombardi.'

'I see.' Jess was intrigued, and looked it. 'Was he nice?
Did you like him?'

Laura felt hot. And it wasn't just the fact that the restaurant was heated. It was as if she were enveloped in the
steam from a Turkish bath, and it took the utmost effort
not to use the menu as a fan.

'He's—very nice,' she said, grateful for the reappearance
of the waitress, to ask if they wanted a dessert. 'Er—just
coffee for me, please. I—couldn't eat another thing.'

'I'll have the same,' said Jess, and, after the woman had
departed, she lay back in her chair. 'Is he sexy?'

'Who?'

Laura pretended not to understand, but Jess was not to
be diverted. 'This—Jake Lombardi, of course,' she
answered. 'What does he look like? How old is he?'

'Oh.…' Laura realised she was not going to get any peace
until she had told her, and, adopting what she hoped was
a careless tone, she said, 'Julie seems to like him, so I
suppose he must be. Sexy, I mean. He's—an Italian, as I
said. What do Italians look like? He's dark, of course. Quite
good-looking, I suppose. And young. No more than about
twenty-eight.'

'I see.' Jess looked at her friend with knowing eyes. 'So—
what's wrong?'

'Wrong?' Laura blinked. She wished she had known what
was going to happen this morning before she'd accepted
Jess's invitation to lunch, but it was too late now. 'Nothing's
wrong.'

'No?' Jess was not convinced. 'You don't usually get so
flustered when you talk about Julie's boyfriends.' She
paused, and then added softly, 'You know, if it weren't so

unlikely, I'd wonder if you weren't attracted to him yourself!'

It was after four o'clock when Laura started back to Burnfoot. She had intended to make some excuse, and leave directly after lunch. She hadn't been happy about leaving Jake as it was, and the fact that he had had no food since God knew when was preying on her mind incessantly. At least, that was what she told herself was preying on her mind. Anything else was not to be considered.

But she had had to abandon the idea of leaving early. After the conversation she and Jess had had, it would not have been politic to beat such a hasty retreat. Jess might have begun to wonder why she had felt the need to curtail their outing, and if she ever found out that Jake had come back to Burnfoot...

It had been hard enough as it was, making her friend believe that she had no personal interest in her daughter's boyfriend. She had pretended it had been Julie's idea to bring him to meet her, thus fuelling Jess's speculation that their relationship was serious. And she had made a lot of their affection for one another, and maintained that she had felt like a gooseberry the whole weekend.

Of course, she hadn't been entirely honest in that respect. At no time had she actually interrupted them in what might be called a compromising position. But the fact was, she could have. And after playing on the fact of Jake's youth, and how no man was likely to look at her when Julie was around, she thought she had convinced Jess she was barking up the wrong tree.

She hoped she hadn't been too vehement in her denials, she thought now, accelerating past a slow-moving vehicle. Jess was fairly shrewd, and they had known one another too long for Laura to find lying easy. No, not lying, she corrected, her hands tightening on the steering-wheel; just prevaricating, that was all. Jess had probably felt sorry for her, she decided grimly, slamming the car into a lower gear, with a distinct disregard for the mechanism. After what she had said about marriage, it was obvious the way her mind worked.

The car splashed through the ford into Burnfoot at about
five minutes to five. Laura would have been quicker—she
had driven fast, if rather badly—but she had been balked
since she'd left the main road, by the vicar's modest
Vauxhall. There weren't many opportunities to overtake on
the narrower country roads and, besides, the Reverend Mr
Johnson would probably have looked askance at one of his
staider parishioners, storming past him like a teenager who'd
just got her licence.

The vicar waved as he turned into the vicarage gates, thus
confirming Laura's suspicions that he had recognised her
behind him. But her response was barely perfunctory as she
passed the vicarage and drove along the village green. Her
attention was arrested by the fact that the Lamborghini had
gone. The verge beside the churchyard wall was deserted,
the drizzle which had started as she'd left the city sending
even the children home earlier than usual.

Her stomach sank. There was no other word to describe
the way she felt. Jake had gone, and the steaks she had
bought for their evening meal would end up in the freezer.
Of course, she was later than she had said she would be.
And it was obvious he couldn't stay at the cottage over-
night. She should have thought of that when she was wasting
so much time in the dress stores. She should have realised
what he would think when she didn't return.

There were tears in her eyes as she reached her gate, and
she was glad it was raining, so that she wasn't likely to
encounter her next-door neighbour in the garden. She was
in no mood to talk to anyone, and she turned into the
narrow driveway with a heavy heart.

And then, she gasped. The Lamborghini was parked
alongside the cottage, just as it had been the previous
weekend. Although she didn't have a garage, there was
plenty of room to stand a car beside the cottage, and her
hands tightened convulsively on the wheel of the Ford. He
was still here, she thought incredulously, aware that her
heart was hammering wildly. He hadn't gone away. He had
just moved his car.

She sat for several seconds, after switching off the engine,
trying to get a hold on her emotions. For heaven's sake,
she thought, screwing the heels of her hands against her

damp cheeks, it wasn't as if it meant anything. He had said he would stay until she got back, and he had. And she had to pull herself together, before he got the wrong idea as well.

Eventually, of course, she had to move, and, throwing open her door, she got out and leant into the back to collect her coat and her shopping. On the pretext of needing something to wear for work, she had invested in two new blouses, a skirt, a pair of wide-legged trousers, and a fine wool sweater. All necessary stuff, she had assured Jess, dismissing the silky trousers as pure indulgence. After all, she had argued, she seldom spent money on herself. And Jess had agreed.

There was also a bag of food from Marks and Spencer. Steak, fruit and vegetables, and a cheesecake. Quite a haul, she reflected, trying to concentrate on what she was doing, and not on Jake Lombardi. But she couldn't help wondering how he was.

She was fumbling for her key on the doorstep. Her arms were full, with her coat and the carriers, and she was wishing she had had the sense to find her key before loading herself down, when the door gave inwards.

Jake stood on the step above, looking down at her with dark unreadable eyes. He had changed his clothes, she saw at once, and the snug-fitting jeans, and dark blue shirt, hid any trace of his injury. He still looked a little pale, but rested, his face clean of the designer stubble he had sported when he'd arrived.

'Hi,' he said, reaching to take the bags from her, but when he did, her brain reasserted itself.

'I—I can manage!' she exclaimed, hugging the bags close. 'You—you might hurt yourself.'

'As if,' said Jake drily, wresting the carriers from her hands. 'It was only a jab, Laura. Not a major laceration!'

He turned then, and walked into the house, and after glancing about her, as if to reassure herself that no one else had witnessed their struggle, Laura stepped inside, and closed the door. Then, draping her coat over the banister, she followed him across the living-room, and into the kitchen.

Jake had deposited all the bags on the table, and he turned when she came into the room after him. 'I don't know where you want these——' he was beginning, when he saw her face. 'Hey!' he exclaimed, and, because the kitchen was so small, he reached her with only one step. His thumb smudged an errant tear from her cheek, and then brushed her lower lip, before her instinctive withdrawal caused his hand to drop. 'What's wrong? Did I breach some feminist principle, or something? Where I come from, women do not carry heavy bags. Not if a man is there to do it for them.'

'Don't be silly.' Laura bent her head, wishing she had a tissue. 'Nothing's wrong. It's raining, or hadn't you noticed?'

'I'd noticed,' he said tautly. 'But raindrops don't usually fall into your eyes, do they? What's the matter? Are you sorry I'm still here, is that it?'

'No.' Laura sniffed, and turned aside. 'I—you moved your car.'

As soon as she had said the words, she knew she had made a mistake. Jake frowned, and then, side-stepping her, he put himself into her path. 'So what? I got the impression you weren't very happy with it where it was.'

'I wasn't.' Laura's skin tingled with uneasiness. 'It—it was too conspicuous. Everyone was looking at it——'

But Jake had sucked in his breath. 'Wait a minute,' he said, and the hand that only seconds before had grazed her cheek, moved to grip the back of her neck, imprisoning her in front of him. 'You thought I'd gone, didn't you?' he said hoarsely. '*Dio*, Laura, as if I would.'

'You're wrong,' she cried, trying to get away from him, but, instead of letting her go, he jerked her towards him.

'No. You're wrong,' he said thickly, bending his head, and, before she could even comprehend what he planned to do, his mouth covered hers.

Even then, she knew, she could have tried to stop him. He had no right to touch her; to take her in his arms; to hold her so close she could feel every ridge of the bandage she had applied earlier. Her knees bumped against his, and one powerful thigh was thrust between her legs, as he moved to keep his balance. It made her overpoweringly aware of his sex, trapped against her hip, and the warm male scent of his body, that rose irresistibly to her nostrils.

But it was his mouth that caused the most havoc, that lean sensual mouth, that she now admitted had haunted her sleep for the past week. It ravished hers with all the skill of which he was able, and her timid objections were trampled in the dust.

Her mind swam beneath the dark hunger of his kiss. Every nerve in her body was alert to the sensuous needs he was arousing. Her lips parted beneath his, and no experience she had known had prepared her for Jake's urgent assault on her senses. When his tongue invaded her mouth, its hot wet tip raking every inch of quivering flesh, her legs turned to water. She had never, ever, felt so utterly helpless, in the grip of emotions she hadn't known existed, drawn into a maelstrom of wild seductive passion.

But when his hand slid from her waist to encircle one swollen breast, a need for self-preservation fought its way to the surface. Dear God, she thought, aware that her hands were clutching his shirt for support, whatever was she doing? Apart from anything else, this was the man her daughter had told her she intended to *marry*. How could she be standing here like this, and letting him maul her? It was insane.

'No,' she gasped, and, although the word was muffled and barely distinguishable, Jake heard her.

'No?' he repeated softly, his thumb describing a sensuous circle around her nipple, tautly—and shamefully—visible, beneath the cream wool of her dress. 'Why not? It's what you want. It's what we both want——'

'No!' Laura could hardly get her breath. 'You—you're disgusting,' she choked, thrusting his hand away from her, and taking a backward step. 'How can you do this? You know that Julie——'

Jake's mouth hardened, and, although he didn't move away from her, he didn't stop her when she widened the space between them. 'Julie's not here,' he said harshly, his accent thickening his tone.

Laura clenched her fists. 'Is that all you have to say?' she cried. 'Julie's not here! My God, is that supposed to mean something?'

Jake straightened, and when he moved Laura couldn't help watching him. He had an indolent, almost feline grace, and, when he wiped his palms down the seams of his trousers, it was all she could do not to follow them with her eyes. She wanted to. She knew what she would see if she did, what she *wanted* to see, she admitted, sickened by her own duplicity. The tight jeans were no barrier to the bulging proof of his arousal.

'What do you want me to say?' he asked now, and she hated the fact that he probably knew exactly how she was feeling. 'I am not interested in Julie at this moment. I am only interested in you.' He paused. 'And I think you are interested in me, only you have some prudish notion that you shouldn't be.'

'That's not true!'

The words were hot and vehement, and, although she sensed he didn't believe her, he knew better than to argue her down. 'If you say so,' he conceded, lifting his hand as if to massage his midriff, and then, as if thinking better of it, he let it fall. 'So—I suppose you would like me to go now.'

Laura bit her lower lip. His involuntary action had served to remind her of his injury, and although she could hardly accuse him of making use of it she was guiltily aware that she had forgotten it. Had she hurt him? she wondered. When she'd clutched at his shirt, had she grazed the tender skin? She hoped not. She didn't like to think that she might be responsible for it starting to bleed again.

'I—suppose you should,' she answered at last. But when his lips twisted rather cynically, she added, 'But that doesn't mean you have to.'

Jake took a deep breath. 'No?'

'No.' Laura squared her shoulders. 'In spite of what you think of me, I'm not a complete idiot. I don't think there was a shred of decency in what happened just now, but I'm prepared to forget it, if you are.'

'Really?'

'Yes, really.' Laura held up her head. 'It was just a—a mistake, an aberration. You'd been on your own all day, and you mistook my reactions, that's all. You felt sorry for me, and—and I was flattered. It's not every day a—a young man makes a pass at an older woman like me.'

'It wasn't a pass,' said Jake flatly, but Laura was already tackling the bags on the table, sorting the one that contained the food from the others.

'Are you hungry?' she asked brightly, determined to show him that she meant what she said. 'I thought we could have steak, and roasted parsnips——'

'You're not an older woman,' persisted Jake, sliding his hands into the hip pockets of his jeans, apparently equally determined to have his say. 'How old are you? Thirty-five? Thirty-six?'

'With a twenty-one-year-old daughter?' Laura gave him a withering smile. 'I shall be thirty-nine next birthday. But thank you for the compliment.'

Jake swore. At least, she thought he did. The word he used was incomprehensible to her, but its meaning was not. 'Why are you doing this?' he demanded. 'Why are you trying to pretend you didn't want me to touch you, just as much as I wanted to do it? You're not old. You're in the prime of your life. D'you think I'm likely to be deterred by the fact that there's a handful of years between us?'

'A handful!'

Laura was proud of the scornful way she threw his words back at him, but Jake only stared at her with raw contempt. 'Yes, a handful,' he said, his mouth curling derisively. 'I'm thirty-two, Laura. I shall be thirty-three next birthday. Not exactly a boy, wouldn't you agree?'

Laura jerked her head aside. 'You're still too young. Not—not just in years, but in—in experience. You young people, you think you invented sex. I was having Julie, when you were still a schoolboy.'

Jake's eyes glittered. 'As I understand it, you were just a schoolgirl yourself at the time,' he retorted, and Laura caught her breath.

'That doesn't alter the fact that you're my daughter's friend, not mine,' she countered, forcing herself to take the steak out of the carrier, and set it on the table. 'Now—do you think we could change the subject? If you'd like to go back into the living-room, I'll start preparing dinner.'

CHAPTER SEVEN

JAKE looked as if he would have liked to have argued, but to Laura's relief he didn't. With a grim inclination of his head, he walked out of the kitchen, and it wasn't until she was left alone that Laura realised she hadn't asked him how he was.

Oh, well, she thought unsteadily, it was obvious he was feeling much better, and although it was impossible to tell if the cut was hurting him he was apparently capable of driving his car. Not to mention everything else, a small voice taunted mockingly. He might have been in dire agony, but his emotional organs weren't impaired.

Her hands were trembling, and, feeling in need of a drink, she filled the kettle and plugged it in. She would have liked a glass of the sherry she kept for special occasions, but that was in the living-room. It was always out of reach, she reflected, remembering the night, a week ago, when Julie had rung to tell her she and Jake were coming for the weekend. It had been out of reach then, too, but she definitely needed it more at this moment.

Still, a cup of coffee would do instead, she decided. And at least it would have the added advantage of not containing any alcohol. The last thing she needed right now was the soporific effects of a fortified wine. She needed to keep her wits about her.

She wondered now why she had ever invited him to stay. There was no question about it: it was madness. She had allowed the desire to prove to him that she could dismiss what had happened without a qualm to override basic common sense. She had wanted to show him that, as she was Julie's mother, he was welcome to her hospitality; to clear the way for their continued association. It would do her no good to try and turn her daughter against him. If she tried to tell Julie what had happened, she would never believe her. She would simply have to hope Julie detected his true character, before it was too late. And turning him out—however attractive that might sound—was the right way to achieve the opposite.

It couldn't be that difficult, could it? she asked herself. If she just kept her head, and behaved naturally with him, he was bound to get the message. She would serve him dinner, ask him about his trip, bring Julie's name into the conversation as often as she dared, and then send him off to a hotel to spend the night.

Deciding she could hardly make herself a cup of coffee without offering him one, she schooled her features, and marched to the door of the living-room. 'Would you like a cup of——?' she began, in a confident tone, and then broke off abruptly, at the sight that met her eyes.

Jake already had a drink in his hand. And it wasn't her sherry either. A newly opened bottle of malt whisky resided on the table beside his chair, and Jake was in the process of lowering the glass from his lips.

'Where did you get that?'

All Laura's plans to keep their relationship cool and impersonal were banished by the accusing edge to her voice, and Jake arched a mocking brow. 'I bought it,' he said carelessly. 'At the village store. Why are you looking so outraged? Did I need your permission?'

'As a matter of fact, there's whisky in the cupboard,' declared Laura defensively, mentally imagining the gossip his shopping in the local stores must have generated. She could hear the stiffness in her voice, and endeavoured to redress her sense of balance. 'I—I was surprised, that's all. I was going to offer you some coffee.'

'I'll pass,' said Jake smoothly, pouring another measure of whisky into his glass. 'But you can join me, if you like,' he added, looking up. 'You look as if you need something to give you a bit of—life.'

Laura didn't trust herself to speak. Suppressing the angry retort that sprang to her lips, she swung on her heel and left him. He would not make her lose her temper again, she told herself fiercely. He knew what he was doing. When she lost control, he had her at his mercy, and she was determined not to give him that satisfaction. Nevertheless, as she turned on the grill, and began seasoning the steak, she knew a helpless sense of frustration. Whether it was a de-

liberate ploy on his part or not, Jake was not going to be
able to drive. If she wanted him to spend the night at a
hotel, she would have to take him there herself.

In spite of her state of mind, the meal was not the disaster she had been afraid of. The food was surprisingly well-
cooked, and Jake ate everything she put in front of him.
Laura served the steak with asparagus, sweetcorn, and new
potatoes, and then set out the lemon cheesecake, alongside
crackers, cheese, and celery. She had made fresh coffee,
too, and she was relieved to see that Jake drank two cups.

She hadn't served any wine with the food, but Jake had
carried his whisky glass to the table. However, she noticed
he didn't drink while he was eating, and the whisky bottle
remained in the living-room.

It was a minor victory, vastly outweighed by their lack
of communication with one another. Conversation was
confined to comments about the food, and, even then,
Laura had had to take the lead. The anger she had felt
earlier had dissipated to a weary resignation. And still she
wasn't sure that the way she felt was Jake's fault. He
shouldn't have come here, that was true, but she was to
blame for how things had developed.

Laura had done most of the washing-up before the meal,
so that afterwards there were only the plates to deal with.
But, although Jake helped her to clear the table, he didn't
offer to dry the dishes, as he had done the week before.
And, when Laura had spent as long as she dared in the
kitchen and went into the living-room, he was seated in his
chair again, with the whisky glass in his hand.

'Um—shall I light the fire?' she asked, striving for normality. Although she hadn't lighted it that morning, she
had raked the grate, and laid it ready. It would be a simple
matter to set a match to the paper, and the room seemed
bare without its comforting glow.

Or perhaps it was just her mood, she thought gloomily,
and the fact that it was getting dark already. She had anticipated this evening with a certain amount of excitement,
and now it had all gone wrong. She realised she had
probably been deluding herself by imagining she and Jake
could have a normal relationship. In effect, she was only
compounding her guilt by letting him remain.

'Light it, if you want,' Jake replied now, and, although she would have preferred to seek the security of her armchair, Laura picked up the matches, and complied.

It was quickly done, the flames licking swiftly up over the dry kindling. It reduced the time she had to crouch before him, and after replacing the matches on the mantel she went and sat down.

Silence could be deafening, she discovered. It stretched between them like a yawning void, and although there were things she had to say, she found it very hard to begin.

But, at last, with the crackling wood providing at least some support, she asked, 'How does the—er—injury feel this evening? I assume it's much better.'

Jake rested his head back against the striped fabric of the cushions. Reclining in her chair like that, with his long legs stretched across the hearth, and his body relaxed and dormant, he looked very much at his ease. But his eyes were far from quiescent, and when he looked at her she flinched beneath the contempt in his gaze.

'Do you really care?' he countered, and the hand hanging loosely over the chair arm moved in a dismissing gesture.

'Of course I care,' said Laura, keeping her voice neutral with an effort. 'I did do my best to attend to it. At least you don't appear to be bleeding any more.'

Jake's mouth compressed. 'No,' he said. 'Not visibly anyway.' And then, more evenly, 'No, I'm sorry. You were most—helpful; most kind. I do appreciate it, even if I haven't acknowledged it.'

Laura swallowed. 'Well—that's good,' she murmured, not prepared to debate what he might mean by the latter half of his statement. 'I still think you should see your own doctor, when you get back to London. Cuts can become infected, and there are injections you can have to avoid problems of that kind.'

'I know.' Jake inclined his head. 'Thank you for your advice.'

Laura sighed. She was fairly sure he wouldn't take it, but there was nothing more she could do. She wondered if she ought to offer to change the dressing, but she recoiled from that idea. She couldn't do it. She couldn't touch him again, knowing, as she did, how his skin felt beneath her trembling hands. She might tell herself he disgusted her; that what he had done earlier this evening had demeaned and humiliated her, and that any woman in her right mind would have thrown him out there and then. But to actually consider removing the bandage from his midriff, to imagine cleaning his wound and re-applying the gauze dressing, made a mockery of her indignation. It wasn't revulsion that kept her from doing her Christian duty. It was the certain knowledge that she couldn't trust herself.

There was silence again, for a while, and then, compelled to dispel her treacherous thoughts, Laura said, 'Will you be going back to London tomorrow?'

It was an innocent question, she told herself, when Jake looked at her again, with those dark, mocking eyes. Hooded eyes, in a face that, she admitted, unwillingly, had a rough male beauty. He had no right to look at her like that, she thought resentfully. He was the interloper here. Not her.

'Perhaps,' he answered, at last. 'It depends.'

'On the reason you came north, I suppose,' said Laura sociably, hoping she was now going to find out the real reason why he was here. If she could just keep their conversation on this level, she might stop feeling so on edge.

'As you say,' Jake conceded, pouring himself more whisky. He lifted his glass. 'Are you sure you won't join me?'

Laura shook her head. In fact, she would have welcomed the warming influence the alcohol would have given her, but she had to keep her head clear for driving. The nearest decent hotel was about eight miles away. And on narrow roads, she would need all her skill

'I—Julie said your family was in manufacturing, is that right?' she asked politely. 'I suppose you have contacts all over England.'

'If you're implying I came north to conclude some business deal, you couldn't be more wrong,' Jake declared, shifting so that one booted foot came to rest across his knee. 'I'm sorry to disappoint you, but I have no business contacts in this area.'

Laura took a breath. 'You don't?'

It was all she could think of to say, and Jake shook his head. 'No,' he agreed, resting the hand holding his glass across his raised ankle. 'My family's interests are primarily in motor manufacturing, and wine. But, as far as I am aware, neither the Italian car industry, nor its subsidiaries, have made any great inroads in northern England. As for wine...' He shrugged. 'We are not involved in distribution.'

Laura swallowed. 'I see.'

'Do you? I wonder?' Jake's mouth flattened. 'Why don't you ask what I'm doing here? That is what you want to know, isn't it?'

Laura avoided his dark gaze, and looked at the flames leaping up the chimney. 'Your affairs are nothing to do with me,' she retorted, wondering if she had been wise to light the fire after all. The room seemed so hot suddenly, and she ran a nervous hand around the cowled neckline of her dress.

'You're wrong, you know,' Jake said softly, and it took the utmost effort for Laura to remain where she was. Her instincts were telling her to get out of there now, while she still had the chance to avoid a confrontation. Whatever he had to say, she didn't want to hear it.

'You said you'd been fencing,' she said, hurriedly, pressing her palms down on to her knees. 'How—how interesting! Are you a—a professional?'

'Hardly.' Jake's voice was harsh. 'For your information, I do my fencing in London. At a private club.' He paused, and she saw his fingers clench around his glass. 'And usually, I am quite proficient—though not, I might add, of a professional standard. However, on Friday evening, I was—how can I say it politely?—cheesed on?'

'Off,' put in Laura automatically, and then flushed. 'Cheesed off,' she added in a low voice, wishing she hadn't said anything, when he gave her a savage look.

'Very well,' he amended, 'I was—cheesed off, as you say.' But she was left in no doubt that he would have preferred to use a stronger term. 'It had not been a good week for me, no? I needed—a diversion.'

'So you tried to get yourself killed! You must have been mad!'

'If that is your interpretation of my actions, then so be it,' he declared bleakly, and Laura's intentions to remain impersonal shattered.

'Well, what else can I think?' she demanded, steeling herself to meet his disparaging stare. 'Sensible people don't play with weapons, when they've only got half their mind on the job. If you wanted a diversion, why didn't you go and see your daughter? I'm sure she'd have been delighted to see you.'

'More than you, no?' he suggested drily, and Laura's throat constricted.

'I don't come into this——' she began, but now Jake's temper got the better of him.

'No,' he said, putting his glass on the table, lowering his foot to the floor, and leaning towards her, his arms along his thighs. 'Not even you are that stupid!'

His jaw compressed, and although Laura wanted to protest, his expression kept her silent.

'You know exactly why I came here,' he went on grimly, 'and it has nothing to do with your daughter, or mine, or any of the other irrelevancies you keep throwing in my face. All right. Perhaps it was a little crazy to tempt fate as I did. When I went to the club, I wanted to do something dangerous. Perhaps I hoped I'd be hurt, I don't know. I was not—how would you say it?—in my mind?'

'In your *right* mind,' corrected Laura, barely aware of what she was saying, but her interruption only angered him even more.

'*Dio,*' he swore, 'will you stop acting like a school-mistress? I came here because I needed to see you again. Ever since last weekend, I have thought of little else. Does that answer your question? Or would you like me to draw you a picture?'

Laura took a steadying breath. 'I—don't—believe—you——'

'Why not?'

She shook her head, her eyes a little wild. 'It doesn't make sense.'

Jake's lips twisted. 'Unfortunately, it does.'

'But, Julie——'

'Forget about Julie. This has nothing to do with Julie. This is about—*us*!'

'*Us?*' Laura got up from her chair then, unable to sit still any longer, and caught her breath when he did the same.

'I—there is no *us*, Mr Lombardi. I'm afraid if you thought
there was, you've had a wasted journey.'

'I don't think so.'

Jake made no move to touch her, but she was intensely
aware of him, and of the fact that he was standing directly
in her path. Oh, she could get past him, if she set her mind
to it, she was sure. Apart from anything else, he was
probably still suffering the after-effects of losing so much
blood, and a jab to his ribs would probably be most
effective.

But, the truth was, she knew she would never hurt him,
not deliberately at least. And while she would have preferred for them not to have had this conversation, it was
probably just as well to clear the air.

'Look,' she said, endeavouring to keep her voice cool
and even, 'I don't deny that you're an attractive man. Any
woman would think so, and—and I'm happy for Julie, truly.
Really, she thinks you're wonderful, as I'm sure you know,
and——'

'Will you stop this?'

Jake moved, and, although she would have backed away,
the chair was right behind her. His hands descended on her
shoulders, his hard fingers moulding the narrow bones he
could feel beneath the fine wool. At the same time, his
thumbs brushed the underside of her chin, forcing her to
lift her face to his.

'Listen to me,' he said, and although Laura jerked her
head aside she couldn't dislodge his fingers. 'Why don't
you stop throwing me at your daughter, and accept what
I'm trying to tell you? For God's sake, if we must speak
about Julie, let's at least be honest. We both knew what
she sees in me, and it isn't just the colour of my eyes.'

'I know.' Laura held up her head. 'She thinks you're—
good-looking—and intelligent—and sexy——'

'And rich,' said Jake flatly, bending his head to touch
her earlobe with his tongue. 'Let's not forget rich!'

Laura shuddered, her whole world turning upside-down.
'Is that important?' she choked, as he bit the tiny gold circlet
she wore through her ear, and Jake shrugged.

'It is to Julie,' he said, his accent thickening as his mouth brushed the nerve that fluttered in her throat. 'I wasn't sure before. But after last weekend——'

'You decided I was the easier option, is that it?' Laura demanded raggedly. 'Why not try the mother? She's too old to offer much resistance. Besides, she's probably so desperate to have a man——'

Jake's hands around her throat silenced her. 'Will you shut up?' he muttered angrily. 'It wasn't like that! It *isn't* like that!'

Laura swallowed. 'But, you can't deny it crossed your mind——'

'It did not cross my mind.' Jake stared down at her savagely. 'Hear what I have to say, will you? I told you this had been a bad week for me, but not why.'

'I don't want to know why!' exclaimed Laura, aware that the longer he held her, the harder it was to keep her head. She was trembling, her whole body quivering with emotions she couldn't even identify, and, hateful as it might be, she was succumbing to those feelings.

'I'm sorry about that,' Jake said now, but he didn't sound sorry. When he braced himself to resist the hands she lifted to push him away, there was no compassion in his gaze. Instead, his hands slid from her neck, down to the small of her back, curving over her hips, and propelling her against him.

Laura almost panicked. Her nose was pressed against the dark silk of his shirt, and, whether she wanted to or not, she couldn't escape the raw male scent of him. He must have taken a shower, she thought unsteadily, because his skin smelt so fresh and clean, overlaid with just the faintest trace of antiseptic, a reminder of the dressing she had applied that morning.

But even that prosaic awareness didn't detract from the overall awareness she had of him, of his warmth, and his nearness, and the lean muscled strength of his body.

'What happened is, I spent the whole week trying to get you out of my mind,' he told her huskily, his breath fanning her heated forehead. 'I didn't want this to happen. So far, my life has gone the way I want it. Oh, when Isabella died, I was distraught, for a while, but although we were—how would you say?—compatible with one another, there was no great passion in our relationship. Our greatest achievement was in having Luci, and I do not deny that I love my daughter very deeply. But this——' he brushed her cheek with his finger '—this is something else. Something I have never experienced before. And, whatever you think of me, I do not usually want what I cannot have.'

'Well—well, you can't have me!' Laura's voice wobbled, but the words had to be said. 'Even—even if you weren't involved with—with my daughter—it just—wouldn't work.'

'Why not?' His lips brushed her ear, and she was unsteadily aware that if this continued, he would prove her a liar.

'Because—because it wouldn't,' she replied, not very convincingly. And then, on a sob, 'Oh, please—let me go! What do I have to do to prove to you that I'm not—not interested?'

His response was unexpected. Without another word, his hands fell to his sides, and he stepped back from her. He didn't say anything, however, and, although Laura told herself that this was what she had wanted, she felt unaccountably bereft.

'I—thank you,' she said, striving for sarcasm, without much success, and put a nervous hand to her hair. Several silky strands had come loose from the coil at her nape, and she busied herself, tucking them into place again, as she struggled to regain her composure. 'I—think you'd better go now.'

Jake studied her without comment, his dark gaze lingering on the parted contours of her mouth. She pressed her lips together then, to hide their revealing tremor, but his eyes drifted down to the equally revealing tautness of her breasts. She wanted to cross her arms, and hide their blatant betrayal from him, but she rigorously restrained herself. To do so would reveal she was aware of his appraisal, and he should not have the satisfaction of knowing how much he disturbed her.

'Go?' he said, at last, his gaze returning to her flushed face, and she nodded. 'Go—where?'

'To—to a hotel, of course,' she got out jerkily. 'You—
you surely didn't expect to stay here? Not—not in the
circumstances.'

Jake tucked his thumbs into the back of the low belt that
encircled his hips. The action strained the buttons of his
shirt across his chest, and Laura couldn't help staring at
the brown flesh, visible between the fastenings. She defended herself with the thought that, unlike Jake, she was
not consciously looking at *his* body. He was simply drawing
her attention to it, like the sexual *animal* he was.

'What circumstances are we talking about?' he asked now,
and Laura had to think for a minute before she could remember what she had said.

'The—er—circumstances of you and I—spending the
night together,' she declared at once. And then, realising
how ambiguous her words had sounded, she hurried on, 'I
mean—spending the night here—*alone*—together. I—people
in Burnfoot are rather—conservative.'

'You'll be telling me next that you have your reputation
to think of,' remarked Jake drily, and Laura's face burned.

'Hardly that,' she retorted, twisting her hands together.
'But someone might tell Julie that you spent the night in
the village.'

'So?'

Jake sounded indifferent, and Laura sighed. 'I just think
it would be—easier all round, if you stayed at a hotel,' she
said firmly. 'There's one on the Corbridge road. I think
it's called the Swan.'

'And how am I to get there?' enquired Jake, lifting his
shoulders. 'I hesitate to say it, but I don't think I should
drive.'

'I'll take you,' declared Laura swiftly.

'In my car?'

'In your car—oh!' Laura had forgotten about his car.
Even if she took him to a hotel, his car was going to stand
outside the cottage all night. 'I—well, no. In mine.'

'So, whatever happens, people are going to think I spent
the night here.'

Laura pressed her lips together. 'Perhaps.'

'But you still want me to go?'

Her tongue circled her lips. 'I—think you should,' she agreed doggedly.

'I guess you don't trust me, then.'

'It's not that.' Laura was dismayed at her own inability to control the conversation. 'I just think——'

'Or perhaps you don't trust yourself,' he murmured provokingly, and Laura knew that she was beaten.

'That would be foolish, wouldn't it?' she said, refusing to give him the satisfaction of admitting that possibility. She assumed what she hoped was a resigned expression, and steeled herself to meet his gaze. 'All right,' she said, as if it were of extreme indifference to her, 'as you say, if your car is going to stand outside my house all night, it does seem rather pointless to turn you out.'

CHAPTER EIGHT

LAURA lay awake, in the familiar surrounds of her own bedroom, and wondered how she had got herself into such a mess.

It was all her fault. She admitted that freely. If she hadn't been so desperate to uphold appearances, Jake would have left before dinner. He had expected to go. And after what had happened, she should have insisted upon it. But instead, she had carried on this stupid charade, of pretending his lovemaking had meant nothing to her—practically inviting him to stay here, and do it again.

Only it hadn't been like that, she defended herself swiftly. At the time, all that had seemed important was restoring a sense of normality. She still hadn't been prepared to believe that what had happened was anything more than a momentary infraction; a deviation from the rules, that he regretted as much as she did.

Of course, he had come here, uninvited and unannounced, bleeding from a wound he had received while dicing with his life, and perhaps she ought to have been more wary. But things like that didn't happen to her, and the whole situation seemed totally unreal. But Jake was still

here, that much was certain, and, although she hadn't
locked her door, she was undoubtedly uneasy.

Yet, since he had received her permission to stay, Jake
had done nothing more to disturb her. Not consciously
anyway, she conceded wearily. His just being there was disruptive enough. However, he had behaved with the utmost
propriety, and the uneasy alliance had lasted until bedtime.

What Julie would think about it all, Laura didn't dare
to speculate. *If* she ever found out, she appended heavily.
And these things had a habit of getting found out, she knew.
It would probably be better if she tried to tell her. Whatever
she had thought earlier, it was different now that Jake was
spending the night.

But what could she say? 'Oh, by the way, Julie, Jake
slept at the cottage on Saturday night. Yes, I was surprised,
too, but he'd had an accident, you see, and he wanted me
to deal with it.'

No! Laura shifted restlessly. No, there was no way she
could drop something like that into the conversation. She
could tell her daughter the truth, of course. She could describe what had happened, and allow Julie to draw her own
conclusions. But would she believe her? And if Jake chose
to lie, whose story was Julie likely to accept?

The answer was obvious—Jake's. *'God,'* Laura groaned.
Julie might even think she had instigated the whole affair.
With Julie's distorted image of her mother's life, she might
imagine Laura was jealous of her. That she had deliberately
come on to Jake, to humiliate her daughter.

Laura rolled on to her stomach, and punched her pillow,
wishing it were Jake's head. It was all *his* fault, she decided, performing a complete about-face. If he hadn't come
here, none of this would have happened. She would be
happily going on with her life, and the destructive emotions
he had aroused would never have been brought to life. He
was probably asleep now—sound asleep in the spare bed
she had made up earlier in the evening. Were all Italians
like him? Didn't he have a conscience? What perverted
streak of his character had inspired him to humiliate her?

And yet, when he wasn't tying her up in knots, he could
be so nice, she conceded, and then scorned herself for her
own gullibility. He was only nice when he was getting his

own way, she told herself grimly. Just because they had spent the rest of the evening in comparative harmony was no reason to pretend he wasn't totally unscrupulous. He was hurting Julie. He had probably caused a rift between herself and Julie that would take years to heal. How could she let him stay here, when he cared about no one but himself?

She turned on to her back again, and stared up at the ceiling. Moonlight, through the cracks in the curtains, cast a shadowy patchwork above her head. Somewhere, the eerie sound of an owl, going about its nightly business, broke the silence, and the ivy outside her window rustled against the stone.

She had never been aware of the stillness before. Usually, when she went to bed, she was so tired that she never had a problem sleeping. Besides, she invariably read for a while, until her eyelids started drooping. But tonight, she had been eager to put out her light, and pretend to be asleep, just in case Jake went to the bathroom, and thought she was waiting for *him*. It had been a silly idea, particularly after she had spent the latter half of the evening marking exercise books, while Jake read a book he had borrowed from her shelves. Nothing less romantic could she have imagined. Except that it had crossed her mind how companionable it had been.

She turned over again, and picked up the clock from the table beside the bed. It was half-past one, she saw impatiently. For goodness' sake, was she ever going to get to sleep? She was going to look absolutely haggard in the morning.

Unwillingly, her mind drifted to the man in the next room again. She couldn't help wondering what would have happened, if she had let him make love to her. They would not now be sleeping in separate beds, she acknowledged. And sleep might be the last thing on her mind.

A wave of heat swept over her body at the thought. Her breasts, already sensitised by her constant tossing and turning, tightened in anticipation. The knowledge aggravated her, but there was nothing she could do about it. She couldn't help their reaction, any more than she could prevent the sudden moistness between her thighs. She might have thought she was past all that, but Jake was a very attractive man. And she was human, after all.

She sighed. It was so unlikely that, after all these years, she should find herself in such a dilemma. After the unhappy associations of her youth, she had begun to believe she was immune to any unwanted feelings. She had had friends, both at college, and since she'd started teaching—male, as well as female—good friends; but none of them had got close to her emotionally. Her experiences with Keith had left her unimpressed, and wary, and, although she was quite prepared to believe that other women might find happiness in marriage, she had felt no desire to try it.

Of course, she knew that her practical experience of sex was necessarily limited. If what she read in books was true, Keith had not been a very generous lover, but at the time she had been too immature to care. She had liked the way he'd kissed her; she had liked the way it had made her feel. And if the culmination of the feelings he had aroused inside her had been something of an anticlimax, she had had more immediate things to worry about.

Not least the fact that Keith had gone, and she had missed a period, she reflected, remembering how frightened she had been then. She had had no one to confide her troubles to. The idea of telling her parents had seemed an unacceptable alternative.

She knew better now, naturally. Without them, life would have been very bleak indeed. That was what was so sad about her relationship with Julie. She had wanted to be there for her, as her parents had been, when she'd needed them.

But now...

Laura combed restless hands through the tangled mass of her hair. What would her daughter think, if she could see her now? she wondered unhappily. Julie would find it hard to believe that her mother was lying awake, fretting over the man *she* intended to marry. She would never understand the circumstances that had led her to this, and, if Laura was to tell her, there would be the most almighty row. Justified, no doubt, Laura acknowledged tiredly. And Julie would know all the right words to put it in perspective.

Words like *pathetic*, or *repulsive*; *vulgar*, or *detestable*! Oh, Julie had cornered the market on ways to make her mother feel like a monster, and, with this kind of ammunition, she could destroy her self-esteem completely. The trouble was, when it came to confronting her daughter, Laura was halfway defeated before she began. She had never been allowed to forget that youthful indiscretion, and admitting she was attracted to a man who, in spite of everything else, was years younger than she was, would only reinforce Julie's opinion that she was a fool.

Well, there's no fool like an old fool, thought Laura wearily, resorting to platitudes. Her best hope was to put everything that had happened out of her mind. She couldn't be sure, of course, but she didn't think Jake would be telling his prospective fiancée that he had taken a fleeting fancy to her mother. However open their relationship might be, she didn't think a casual fling of this kind allowed confession.

Laura eventually fell asleep as it was getting light. Exhaustion had at last taken its toll, and she sank into a dreamless slumber, just as the Graingers' dairy herd was being guided into the sheds for the first milking of the day. With her hand cupped beneath her cheek, and the tumbled sheets wrapped about her, she finally found oblivion. She didn't hear the bellows of protest from the milk-laden cows, or rouse to the birds' morning chorus. She was dead to the world for a good four hours, and when she did open her eyes her room was flooded with sunlight.

She blinked unwillingly, a sense of something ominous hanging over her, causing a heavy weight of depression that gripped her as soon as she opened her eyes. It wasn't until she turned her head, and looked at the clock, that comprehension dawned. It was nearly half-past nine!

She stilled the momentary panic, that made her think, just for a second, that it was a working day. It wasn't. It was Sunday. And she had overslept. Or rather, she had slept late, she amended grudgingly, remembering the night she had spent. God, she felt as if she had been hauled through the mincer! Every nerve in her body felt raw and abused, and a slight ache in her head promised a migraine later.

Groaning, she rolled over on to her back, and confronted the problem that still plagued her. She assumed Jake was still there. She couldn't imagine he would have made it easy for her, and left. Was he still in bed? she wondered apprehensively. It was still early by his standards, no doubt. Just because he had got up early last weekend was no reason to suppose he would repeat the exercise. She knew Julie didn't like getting up early, and if they usually slept together...

But thoughts like that were not conducive to initiating a good start to the day. It was galling, but she couldn't anticipate such a scenario without feeling slightly sick. The picture of Jake, sharing a bed with her daughter, caused an actual feeling of revulsion inside her. She didn't want to think about it in those terms, but she couldn't help it.

Something else she couldn't help was her own memory of the sensuous warmth of his mouth on hers. She could still feel his tongue, pressing its way between her teeth, and the throbbing heat of his arousal, hard against her stomach. Damn, but she couldn't help wondering how it would have been, if she had let him make love to her. Probably no different from when Keith had taken her innocence, she decided irritably. Men were impatient animals. They sought their own satisfaction first.

Her hand had stuck to her cheek as she'd slept, and although she had removed it now, she could feel the marks where it had been. Oh, great, she thought resignedly, pushing herself up on her elbows. As if she didn't have enough lines already.

And then, she saw the tray of tea. It was residing on the bedside cabinet, nearest the door. Her teapot, a milk jug and sugar basin, and a cup and saucer. Someone must have placed it there, but how long ago?

She clenched her lips. *Someone!* she chided herself impatiently. There only was one person it could have been, and that was Jake. Dear God, he had come into the room as she'd slept. What must he have thought of her? Her hair every which way, and the bedclothes a clear indication of her disturbed night!

She put out a reluctant hand, and touched the side of the teapot. It was warm, but not hot. The tea must have been there for at least an hour, she surmised. Which meant Jake could be up and gone, without her prior knowledge.

She hesitated only a moment, before sliding out of bed. She had to know if he was still here. Padding barefoot across to the bedroom window, she squinted down into the garden. The Fiesta was still where she had left it, and she could just see the tail of the other car.

The breath left her lungs on a gulp. She told herself she was disappointed he was still here, but it wasn't true. The fact was, if he had gone without telling her goodbye, she would have been shattered. So what price now her averred intention to get him out of her life?

Parting the curtains a few inches, she turned back to her dressing-table, and surveyed her appearance in the mirror. In spite of the troubled night she had spent, she didn't look as bad as she had expected. Her hair was untidy, of course, but for the first time in ages she didn't immediately reach for the brush. With her hair loose, and in the cotton night-shirt, that skimmed her hips, and exposed her slender legs, she looked amazingly young, and vulnerable. She didn't look like a woman who had a twenty-one-year-old daughter. She looked like someone who had definite possibilities.

She lifted the weight of her hair, and swept it loosely towards her face. She had seen women who wore their hair this way, but she had never considered that she might be one of them. Because her hair was straight, she tended, always, to keep it tightly confined. But now she contemplated how it would look, if it were shorter, and cut to frame her face...

She was so intent on discovering what the possibilities might be that when the knock came at her bedroom door, she called 'Come in,' without thinking. Perhaps she had thought she was at school. It was only when Jake stepped into the room that she realised what she had done.

'What—what do you think you're doing?' she exclaimed, dry-mouthed, but her outburst was barely reasonable, and she knew it.

'You invited me to come in,' remarked Jake mildly, pushing his hands into the pockets of his jeans, and she was sure his studied evaluation missed no part of her anatomy. 'Did you sleep well?'

Laura turned away from her dressing-table, allowing her hands to slide down from her hair, as if it was a perfectly natural thing for her to do. She kept telling herself that in Jake's world it was no particular novelty to see a woman in her nightgown, and as her cotton shirt could hardly be considered provocative she mustn't overreact.

'I slept—very well,' she lied, not prepared to discuss her restless night with him. 'Um—thanks for the tea. I didn't—hear you bring it in.'

'No. No, I know.' Jake's acknowledgement was accompanied by a vaguely rueful smile. 'No, you were sound asleep. It seemed a shame to wake you.'

'How kind!'

The thread of sarcasm in Laura's voice was not wholly intentional, but Jake's response showed he had noticed. 'It was,' he said, his eyes darkening sensuously. 'I might have decided to join you.'

'I don't think so.' Laura met his challenging gaze with an effort. She was trying not to sound as uptight as she felt, but it wasn't easy. 'I'm not your type.'

'You don't know anything about my type,' retorted Jake lazily, subjecting her to another thorough appraisal. 'How do you know I don't like tawny-haired women, with long legs and golden eyes, and the kind of body a man wants to bury himself in?'

'An overweight matron, right?' Laura quipped, hoping to dispel the sudden shift in the conversation, but Jake only shook his head.

'Go on,' he said. 'Put yourself down. It seems to be an occupational hazard with you.' He paused, and then went on, 'Did you know you kick the sheets off when you're sleeping? And that thing you're wearing barely covers you. You were cold, when I pulled the quilt over you.'

'You pulled——' Laura broke off abruptly, aware that she had been in danger of showing how easily he could disconcert her, and she was not going to give him that satisfaction. 'Well—thank you.'

'My pleasure.' Jake rocked on his heels. 'I guess that's why the bed's in such a state. If I didn't know better, I'd wonder if you'd had company——'

'I always sleep alone,' Laura broke in tersely. 'And I don't think it's any concern of yours what my bed looks like. Now——' she took a breath '—I think you'd better go.'

'OK.' To her relief, he turned towards the door, but he paused on the threshold, and gave her a dangerously attractive smile. 'But, just for the record, I don't think you'd have kicked me out, if I had got in beside you. In that easy time, between sleeping and waking, you'd have had no chance to think of an excuse. I'd have seen to that.'

Laura had had just about as much as she could take. 'Will you get out?' she demanded, her hands opening and closing convulsively, and with a gesture of resignation Jake closed the door behind him.

When she went downstairs some fifteen minutes later, the aromatic scent of fresh coffee and toast was filling the air. Evidently, he wasn't unused to taking care of his own needs, and, although she told herself she should resent his casual assumption of her role, there was something decidedly appealing about having her breakfast prepared for her. She wasn't used to it. Not since she'd used to live with her parents had anyone taken the trouble to wait on her, and she couldn't deny it was—nice.

For her part, she was still struggling with the need to put what had happened in perspective. Jake had spent the night at the cottage, that was true, but apart from those few minutes, when she'd got back from town the previous afternoon, she had done nothing to be ashamed of. The trouble was, the longer they were together, the harder it got to withstand his easy charm, and she was not immune to his attraction. On the contrary, it would be all too easy to believe the things he told her, and only her strength of will stood between her and certain disaster.

When she carried the tray into the kitchen however, the idea that Jake might exert any unwelcome influence over her seemed totally misplaced. With a tea-towel draped over his shoulder, he was in the process of ladling a pan of scrambled eggs on to a serving dish. A plate piled high with golden-brown toast was keeping warm on the hob, and her coffee-pot was simmering on its stand.

'I don't know if you like scrambled eggs,' he said, when she set the tray down on the drainer. 'But I thought you might like something substantial, as you barely touched your dinner last night.'

She didn't think he'd noticed, but she should have known Jake didn't miss a thing. And when she turned to put the serving dish on the table, and she met his lazy eyes, she felt the potent heat of their awareness.

'Sit down,' he said, when she stood there like an idiot, gazing at him, and, although she felt she ought to put up some opposition, she did so. 'Help yourself,' he added, setting the plate of toast in front of her. 'Go on. It won't poison you, I promise.'

Laura dragged her eyes away from his, and stared at the food. It did look inviting, certainly, and she was hungry. Ridiculously so, in the circumstances. Her whole system seemed to have been thrown off balance, but starving herself was not going to achieve anything. She needed her strength if she was going to come out of this with some semblance of dignity, and with a faint upward lift of her lips, she spooned some of the creamy eggs on to her plate.

'Good?' he asked, bringing the coffee to the table, and seating himself across from her, and she nodded.

'Very,' she said, her voice sticking in her throat, and Jake grinned as he helped himself to a generous portion.

It was difficult to remain detached with someone when you were eating the food they had prepared, and when Jake began asking her how long she had lived in the village, and what the people did hereabouts, Laura felt obliged to tell him. She found it helped to talk about impersonal things, and only now and then did the incongruity of the situation cause a corresponding ripple of unease to disrupt her uncertain stomach. But the food definitely helped, and by the time she had eaten her eggs and two triangles of toast, and drunk two cups of coffee, she was feeling decidedly less threatened.

But, when the meal was over, and Jake was lying back in his chair, regarding her through lazily narrowed eyes, Laura knew she had to address the subject that she had been avoiding for the last half-hour. Putting her coffee-cup aside, she moistened her lips, and then said evenly, 'Will you be telling Julie where you spent the weekend?'

Jake's expression didn't alter. 'Do you know, you have an incredibly sexy mouth?' he remarked softly, and Laura closed her eyes against his blatant sexuality.

'I think it would be—unwise,' she continued at last, resting her elbows on the table, and tucking her hands around the back of her neck. 'Don't you?'

'I suppose that depends on when we're going to see one another again,' Jake responded now, running a hand into the opened neckline of his shirt, and Laura wondered if everything he did was designed to disconcert her. He must know how her eyes followed his every movement, and it took the utmost effort to look down at the square of table in front of her.

'We—won't be seeing one another again,' she declared steadily, and then gulped back a startled cry, when he abruptly thrust back his chair, and got to his feet.

'What are you saying?' he demanded, coming round the table to stand over her, and Laura steeled herself to tilt back her head and look up at him.

'I said——'

'I comprehend the words you used,' he told her bleakly, his accent appearing again as he strove to keep his patience. 'What I am asking is—why are you saying this?'

'Why am I——?' Laura broke off, and, jerking her gaze from his dark exasperated face, she crumbled the corner of the last piece of toast left on the plate. 'What do you want me to say?' she demanded at last. 'I've told you how I feel about your coming here. Oh—tell Julie, if you must, but don't be surprised if she refuses to see you again——'

'And do you think I care?'

His violent response tore into every nerve in her body, and, when she lifted her horrified face to his, his mouth curled contemptuously.

'Have I shocked you?' he asked bitterly. His lips twisted. 'What kind of a man do you think I am?'

'I don't—I didn't——'

'Oh, yes, you did,' he told her thickly, and before she had time to realise his intentions he bent his head towards her. With one hand supporting himself on the back of her chair, and the other imprisoning hers to the table, he covered her mouth with his.

It wasn't a gentle kiss. There was none of the tenderness he had shown the day before; just an unleashed passion, that savaged her emotions, and laid bare the unguarded hunger of her soul. She had no more hope of resisting him than she had of resisting a whirlwind, and when his tongue thrust possessively into her mouth her head tipped back helplessly on her shoulders. Her legs felt incapable of supporting her, and when he let go of her hands, they made no move to stop his assault. Indeed, when his knuckles brushed the tender peaks of her breasts, she sagged towards him, and when he suddenly let go of her she felt a bruising sense of bereavement.

She watched him leave the room with lacklustre eyes, hardly capable of understanding what he was doing, until he appeared in the doorway again wearing his leather jacket.

'So,' he said, as she struggled to her feet to face him, 'if you will move your car, I will trouble you no longer.'

Laura blinked. 'You're leaving?'

She was unaware of the depth of feeling in her voice, and Jake's mouth took on a mocking slant. 'That is what you want, isn't it?' he queried huskily, and his sardonic words brought a belated sense of self-preservation.

'What—I—of course,' she got out unevenly, as the full awareness of what he had done swept over her in sickening detail. Her fists balled with frustration. 'I'll get the keys.'

'If that's what you really want.'

Jake's hand brushed her cheek in passing, but she flinched away from him. 'It's what I really want,' she averred, and she had the doubtful satisfaction of having the last word.

CHAPTER NINE

'MATTHEW SUTCLIFFE! What kind of shoes are you wearing?'

'These, miss?' The boy Laura had addressed lifted his foot and examined it with apparent thoroughness, much to the amusement of the rest of the class. 'They're trainers, miss.'

'I know what *kind* of shoes they are, Sutcliffe,' retorted Laura, regarding the chunky-soled sports shoes, with their thick protruding tongues and untied laces, with some disgust.

'Then what——?'

'You know you're supposed to wear proper shoes for school,' Laura interrupted him crisply. 'What's happened to those black leather ones you were wearing the first few weeks of term?'

The fifteen-year-old adopted a cheeky grin. 'I've lost them, miss.'

Laura sighed. 'You can't have lost them,' she began, and then, realising she was setting herself up for an argument, she amended it to, 'When did you lose them?'

'Last week,' said Sutcliffe at once.

Although she knew she was wasting her time, Laura persisted, 'Where?'

'On my way home from school, miss.'

'On your way home from school?' Laura gave him a sceptical look. 'Why don't I believe you?'

'I don't know, miss.'

Sutcliffe gazed at her with a look of wide-eyed innocence, but Laura was not deceived. 'I suppose you'll be telling me next that someone took them away from you,' she remarked tersely, and the youth grinned.

'How did you know?'

'Don't be insolent, Sutcliffe.'

'I'm not being insolent, miss.' Incited by the admiration in the faces of the pupils around him, he added cockily, 'Just because you're in a bad mood——'

Laura gasped, and a ripple of anticipation ran round the room. 'What did you say?' she exclaimed.

Sutcliffe shrugged, not a whit daunted by her furious expression. 'I said, just because you're in a bad mood, miss, you don't have to take it out on us.'

'Out here, Sutcliffe!'

Laura pointed to a spot directly in front of her, and the stocky teenager pushed himself resignedly up from his seat, and sauntered forward. 'Yes, miss?'

He was unrepentant, that much was obvious, but Laura was half sorry she had to send him to the headmaster to be disciplined. This class of fourth-years was one of her favourites, and she was loath to alienate any of them by over-reacting.

The trouble was, he was right. Oh, not about the shoes. She had no doubts on that score. Half the pupils in the school were wearing prohibited footwear, and picking on Matthew Sutcliffe would do no good at all. She was fairly certain the black shoes he had previously worn, as part of the school uniform, were residing in a cupboard back home. But, like the other boys, who had persuaded their parents to buy them a pair of the current craze in canvas boots, he wanted to show off in front of his friends.

No, it was the fact that she wasn't in the best of humours that now stirred her conscience. For the past two weeks, she had been living on her nerves, and, although she had done her best to carry on as normal, the frayed edges were beginning to show.

It infuriated her that this should be so. It wasn't as if anything had happened on which she could hang the blame for her impaired sensibilities. Since Jake had driven away that Sunday morning—exactly two weeks and three days ago—she hadn't heard from either him or Julie, which seemed to point to the fact that he had kept their sordid little affair to himself.

Not that it had been an affair in the usual sense of the word, she reminded herself impatiently. He had kissed her, that was all. Even if she added everything together, she couldn't get past the fact that their romance added up to very little. He had wanted her, and she had refused. That was all there was to it.

Of course, it wasn't. In her more honest moments, she had to admit that, given time, she would have succumbed to him. He had known that, as well as she did. But that was because he knew exactly how to play upon her senses, she thought defensively. She had been a tempting challenge; an older woman, with the added twist of being his girlfriend's mother!

She told herself it was perverse; that, no matter how she phrased it, he had been attracted by their relationship. Or perhaps by the fact that she was so inexperienced, she pondered. A timid, middle-aged woman, who had never really known a man...

Now, making one last attempt to rectify the present situation, she said quietly, 'If you apologise for that last remark, and give me a serious answer as to why you're wearing those unsuitable shoes, I'll overlook your behaviour this time.' She paused. 'Well? What do you say?'

But she should have known she'd be wasting her time. For the boy to back down now would be to humiliate himself in front of his cronies. At the moment, he was regarded as something of a hero, and his shoulders hunched against any retreat.

'Very well.'

Laura squared her own shoulders, as she prepared to deliver her verdict. But before she could say a word, the classroom door opened, and Janet Mason, one of the school secretaries, put her head through the gap.

'Oh, Mrs Fox,' she said, her eyes indicating that she had some news to impart. 'Could I have a word?'

Laura sighed. It had been Mr Carpenter the headmaster's idea that she should be addressed as *Mrs* Fox, but there were times when she wished she could just be herself. Still, being regarded as a married woman—or a divorcee— did have its advantages. At least, she was not continually being taunted by her unmarried status.

Now, bidding Matthew Sutcliffe to remain where he was, she stepped out into the corridor. 'Yes, Janet?' she said, trying to keep a watchful eye on the class. 'What can I do for you?'

'You're wanted on the phone,' said Janet at once, and Laura could tell from her expression that whoever was

calling had aroused some curiosity in the office. For one
wild moment, she wondered if it could be Jake, and her
knees went weak. But Janet's, 'It's your daughter,' quickly
squashed that thought, even if the news that Julie was calling
her at school was something of a body-blow. What could
she want? she asked herself. What could possibly be important enough to warrant interrupting her mother during
lessons? The answer seemed rather obvious, and Laura's
nerves clenched. Jake must have finally got round to telling
her daughter about his fall from grace.

She couldn't reveal her dismay to Janet however. The
other woman was quite curious enough as it was, and Laura
wished Julie was not so impulsive. But it wouldn't occur
to her that speaking to her mother at school might prove
rather awkward. Or if it did, it was not something she would
care about.

But for now, she had other matters to attend to. After
assuring Janet that she would be right there, she went back
into her classroom to deal with Matthew Sutcliffe.

'Saved by the bell,' she told him, well aware that her
conversation with Janet would not have gone undetected.
'Sit down, please. I'll deal with you later. The rest of you,
open your books at the first scene of act four. I want you
to read Portia's speech about the quality of mercy while
I'm away. I shan't be long, and I shall expect you to be
able to tell me what Portia's definition of mercy is, when
I get back.'

There was the rustle as books were opened, but Laura
had no doubt that once they were alone, there would be
little actual reading going on. For all they were one of her
better groups, there was still a sufficiently unruly element
among them to curtail any attempt by the rest of the class
to work quietly. In consequence, she put her head round
the door of the adjoining room, to ask one of her colleagues to keep an eye on the group while she was away.
She wanted to trust them, but she had no intention of
coming back and finding half the class had disappeared.

The phone she had to use was in the staff-room.
Thankfully, at this time of the afternoon, there were only
one or two members of staff in there, but, all the same, it
wasn't very private. Nevertheless, Laura picked up the re-

ceiver with an air of confidence. There was no point in looking anxious. It was too late for that now.

'Hello?' she said, when the call had been connected. 'Julie? Is that you?'

'How many daughters have you got?' asked Julie drily. 'Yes, of course, it's me, Mum. Have I caused a problem?'

Laura moistened her lips, and exchanged a rueful smile with Mike James, who taught woodworking. 'Well, I was teaching,' she murmured, her mind racing furiously. Julie didn't sound as if she was angry, but was that any assurance?

'I guessed you would be,' Julie responded now. 'But I've got to fly to Belgium later this afternoon, and I wanted to speak to you as soon as possible.'

Laura was confused. 'You did?' She took her life into her hands. 'Why?'

'I've got an invitation for you,' said Julie flatly, and now Laura was sure this call had nothing to do with *that* weekend. 'It's from Jake's mother. She'd like you to spend a weekend at Castellombardi. Jake and I will be going in a couple of weeks and it was his suggestion that you should come with us.'

Laura spent the evening trying to prepare a worksheet on war poetry for her first-year pupils. But the words of Wilfred Owen and Rupert Brooke only danced before her eyes, and when the flickering lights of an approaching migraine forced her to put her books away she did so willingly.

But what could she expect? she asked herself despairingly. She hadn't been able to concentrate on anything since Julie's call, and her brain just kept running in circles, trying to find some way to extricate itself from the proposed invitation.

Of course, when she had attempted to make her excuses to Julie, her daughter had proved quite implacable in her determination that Laura should not let her down. 'Jake's parents want to meet you,' she'd said, in answer to her mother's wavering uncertainty. 'Don't ask me why. They do, and that's all there is to it. Besides, I should have thought you'd welcome the chance to get away for a few

days. It will be half-term, won't it? I told Jake I thought
it was.'

So they were still seeing one another, Laura had acknowledged unsteadily, wondering why that news didn't give
her the reassurance it should. Were they still sleeping
together? Of course they were. She had practically guar-
anteed it by her attitude.

'Well——' she'd begun, but Julie wasn't taking no for
an answer.

'Don't start making up reasons why you shouldn't come!'
she'd exclaimed impatiently. 'It's not as if I'm asking much.
Just a few days of your time, that's all.'

After that, there wasn't a lot Laura could say, and, as if
she knew she had won the day, Julie went on to tell her the
exciting news, that her agent had been approached by a
film producer, with a view to Julie's being offered a screen
test.

'Isn't it fantastic?' she'd exclaimed, and Laura could tell
by her tone that this was more important to her daughter
than a weekend spent in the Tuscan countryside. 'You know
how much I've always loved acting and, according to Harry,
anyone can act on film. It's just a question of learning your
lines, that's all.'

Laura thought she had managed to sound reasonably enthusiastic, although she couldn't honestly remember her
daughter showing any particular interest in drama classes
at school. Still, if that was what Julie wanted, who was she
to try and stop her? Julie had rung off with the promise
that she would ring again in a few days, to make the final
arrangements. In the meantime, Laura should check that
her passport was in order, and be ready to leave in a little
over two weeks.

'And buy yourself some decent clothes,' Julie had added,
as an afterthought. 'The Lombardis are bound to live in
some style, and I don't want you letting me down.'

At the moment, however, Laura was convinced she would
never be ready. The idea of flying to Italy with Jake and
Julie, of spending a weekend in their company, parrying
Jake's parents' questions, and pretending she approved of
their relationship, sounded like the worst kind of nightmare.
How could she *meet* Jake again, let alone behave as if

nothing had happened? Dear God, could this possibly be *his* idea? A way of punishing her for repulsing him? A way of trying to make her jealous?

But she wasn't jealous, she groaned, leaving the table, where she had been working, and flinging herself on to the sofa. The unaccustomed exertion caused her aching head to throb, and she thrust restless hands into her hair, dislodging the pins, and bringing its weight down around her shoulders. She couldn't be jealous, she told herself again. Jake meant nothing to her. She was just working herself up into a state unnecessarily, making herself miserable over a man who had no compunction about betraying her daughter.

Nevertheless, in the days that followed, Laura could think of no way to avoid the coming trip. Although she might have had perfectly valid reasons for not going, they were not reasons she could voice—not unless she wanted to alienate her daughter, once and for all. Of course, there was still the possibility that Julie might find out that Jake had spent two days at the cottage, without her knowledge. But, as time went by, that was becoming less likely. Julie spent so little time at Burnfoot, and it would be something of a coincidence if anyone made such a connection. After all, she had been with him the previous weekend, and it had probably been assumed that she was with him again. Why not? It was the most obvious conclusion, when all was said and done.

Which left Laura with the problem of preparing for a trip, for which she might have no enthusiasm, but which she couldn't ignore. As Julie had so unkindly pointed out, her present wardrobe would not stretch to the kind of occasions she might be expected to attend. She didn't even possess an evening dress, and, although she had no intention of buying some entirely extravagant creation, she knew a shopping trip to Newcastle was unavoidable.

However, the idea of going alone was not appealing, and a week later she rang Jess, and asked her if she fancied repeating their previous outing. 'Something's come up,' she said, hoping Jess wouldn't expect her to go into too much detail over the phone. 'I need a suit, and maybe a couple of dresses. I'll tell you why when I see you. What do you say?'

To her relief, Jess was enthusiastic. And she didn't ask her why she needed to supplement the shirts and trousers bought on their earlier trip, though Laura sensed she was dying to. But Jess was obviously prepared to wait until Saturday to hear all about it, and, after making the necessary arrangements, Laura rang off.

She was in the bath, when her phone rang on Friday evening.

Laura guessed it was Julie. She had seen Mark earlier in the day, and reluctantly agreed to have dinner with him that evening, so she was fairly sure it wasn't him. It could always be Mrs Forrest, of course. Her twice-weekly cleaner sometimes rang to change her arrangements, but very rarely. Besides, something told her it wasn't Mrs Forrest. Although she wasn't psychic, Laura sensed the call was long-distance.

She sat for a moment, calculating her chances of getting out of the bath, and getting downstairs to answer it, before it stopped ringing, and decided they were poor. She had been caught that way before, and she was loath to leave the warm, soapy water for an abortive spring to the phone. Even so, when it continued to ring, long after she had expected it to stop, her conscience pricked her. If it was Julie, she ought to answer it. It was no use avoiding the inevitable.

But, although she made a belated foray for the towel, the phone stopped ringing before she had chance to leave the bathroom. Instead, when she opened the door, just to make sure she wasn't mistaken, the house was silent, and with a guilty sense of aggravation she climbed back into the bath.

But her mood of relaxation was shattered, and she didn't spend any longer than she had to in the water. Instead, she concentrated on getting ready for her date with Mark, unwillingly aware that she was going to spend the whole evening worrying about that call.

She decided to wear the cream wool dress again. Mark hadn't seen it, and, although it aroused a disturbing memory of the evening she had spent with Jake, she refused to let that deter her. She couldn't afford to discard the dress, just because of its associations, and by wearing it to go out with Mark she would dispel that particular myth.

She was making a final examination of her appearance, when the phone rang again. Her immediate reaction was one of relief, but as she went down the stairs to answer it, that was followed by an irresistible sense of apprehension. She couldn't help it. Any thought of the coming trip to Italy sent shivers of trepidation down her spine, and she knew Julie would be ringing to confirm the arrangements.

'Hello,' she said, picking up the receiver, and she was relieved to find her voice didn't sound as anxious as she felt. 'Burnfoot, two, four, seven.'

'Laura?'

She almost put the phone straight down. That dark, disturbing voice was unmistakable, and a wave of indignation swept over her. How dared he ring her here? How dared he get in touch with her at all, after what he had done?

'Come on, Laura, I know you're there.' There was just the faintest trace of impatience in his voice now. 'At least, have the decency to speak to me.'

'Me—have decency!' Laura swallowed. 'My God, I don't know how you have the nerve!'

'We all have nerves,' Jake assured her tensely. 'And you may be interested to know that mine aren't exactly undisturbed at this moment.'

'Good!'

'This has been the longest month of my life.'

'It serves you right.'

'All right.' His voice hardened, and Laura, attuned to every nuance of his tone, felt her own nerves tingle. 'You've had your fun at my expense, but now I want you to be sensible.'

'I am being sensible,' she retorted, realising she must not allow him to get the upper hand. 'I can't imagine why you're ringing me, Mr Lombardi. What's the matter? Has Julie been giving you a hard time?'

The word he used then was incomprehensible to her, but its meaning was not. Even in his own language, the ugliness of its intent was evident, and Laura wondered why she didn't just put the phone down, and be done with it.

'You have a foul mouth, do you know that?' he grated, after a moment, and Laura gasped.

'*I* do?' she countered, indignantly. 'After what you——'

'Did you understand what I said?'

Laura hesitated. 'N—o——'

'Well, I understand you, only too well,' he told her harshly, 'and, believe me, you could use a little instruction in the art of *not* saying the wrong thing!'

'I don't think it matters what I say to you, Mr Lombardi,' Laura told him, albeit a little less forcefully, and he expelled his breath on a low groan.

'Laura,' he said, his use of her name sending a shuddering wave of heat to the surface of her skin. '*Dio*, Laura, have you no pity?'

Laura could feel herself weakening. It wasn't in her nature to hurt anyone, but she wouldn't—*she couldn't*—give in.

'How—how is Julie?' she asked, deliberately bringing her daughter's name between them once again, and Jake sighed.

'She was perfectly all right when I spoke to her yesterday evening,' he replied at last, and Laura's fingers tightened around the receiver she was holding.

Closing her eyes against the images his words had evoked, she said tautly, 'Was that before—or after—you went to bed?' and waited, with a sense of dread, for his answer.

'Before—in my case,' declared Jake obliquely, and then, before she could ask him what he meant, he added, 'I wouldn't know about Julie. I'm in Rome, and she's not.'

'Rome?' Laura quivered. 'How—how long have you been in Rome?'

Jake's laugh was ironic. 'Do you really want to know?' He paused. 'I thought you weren't interested in what I was doing.'

Laura caught her breath. 'I'm not. That is—I was just being polite, that's all——'

'I know what you were being, Laura, and it wasn't polite. But we'll let it go for now.' Jake paused. 'I assume you got my mother's invitation.'

'Yes.' She could hardly deny it. 'But, I don't know——'

'Good.' Jake broke into her attempt to question its validity. 'My parents are looking forward to meeting you. And Lucia, of course.'

'Lucia?' Laura frowned.

'My daughter. Lucia—*Luci*.'

Laura tensed. 'She'll be there?'

'Of course. She's with me now, as it happens.'

'In—Rome?'

'In Rome,' he agreed, and she guessed that was why Julie wasn't with him. It put a whole new perspective on the situation.

'So,' she said tersely. 'Was that the only reason you rang? To ensure that I had received your mother's invitation?'

'Hardly.' Jake was evidently controlling his impatience with difficulty. 'I wanted to talk to you. I wanted to explain the arrangements to you. I wanted to be sure there'd be no misunderstandings. Now—a car will pick you up at your cottage at six o'clock on Saturday morning, a week from tomorrow, and transport you to Newcastle airport——'

'That's not necessary——'

'I think it is,' said Jake inflexibly. He paused a moment, and then went on, 'You will then board the shuttle to London, arriving at Heathrow at approximately ten minutes past eight.'

'Ten-past eight!' Laura was disconcerted. 'That's rather early, isn't it?'

'Unfortunately, the next flight from Newcastle is not until nearly half-past eleven,' replied Jake evenly. 'In those circumstances, we would not arrive at Castellombardi until dinnertime.'

'I can get the train——'

Jake expelled his breath heavily. 'No.'

'Why not?'

'Because that is not the way I want it to be,' he retorted wearily. 'Laura—*cara*——'

'Don't call me *cara*!'

'—just allow me to have my way, hmm?'

Laura took a steadying breath. 'And if I don't, you'll tell Julie what happened, right?'

'Wrong.' Jake sucked in his own breath, with the same intention. 'Laura, please—can't we suspend this ani-

mosity? For—for all our sakes? I want you to enjoy these
few days in my home.'

Laura closed her eyes against the disturbing appeal in his
voice. Just for a moment, she allowed herself to imagine
what it would be like if she were going to Castellombardi,
to meet Jake's parents, as his fiancée. If she, and not her
daughter, were the reason for this trip. Oh, she would still
have qualms, of course. What prospective bride hadn't,
when meeting her fiancé's family for the first time? But it
would have all been worth it, to know that Jake loved her…

'Laura?'

The frustration in Jake's voice brought her out of her
reverie, but a little of the warmth her thoughts had engendered lingered on in her tone. 'All right,' she said, unaware
of how much softer her voice sounded. 'Wh—what do I
do when I get to London? What time is the flight to—
to——?'

'Pisa,' put in Jake swiftly, responding to her mood. 'And
it's as soon as we can make it. We'll be flying to my
father's——'

'We?' Laura halted him there, the anxiety reappearing
in her voice. 'But—you're already in Italy.'

'I shall be flying back to London next Friday,' Jake explained, with some resignation. 'We—that is, you, Julie,
and myself—will fly back together on Saturday morning.'

'I see.' Laura bit her lower lip.

'Do you? Do you, honestly?' Jake uttered a harsh sound.
'You surely don't object to my escorting you, do you?'

Laura hesitated a moment, and then realising how futile
it all was, she submitted. 'I—suppose not,' she murmured,
and as she did so the doorbell rang.

She guessed it was Mark and, glancing at her watch, she
discovered she had been on the phone for almost fifteen
minutes. It must be costing Jake a small fortune, she
thought worriedly, before the cynical realisation that he
could afford it swept all other considerations aside.

'I'll have to go,' she said now. 'There's someone at the
door.'

'Answer it. I can wait,' declared Jake impatiently, but
Laura knew Mark wouldn't appreciate being kept waiting.

Besides, it would mean having to tell him who it was—or lying.

'I can't,' she said, as the bell pealed again. 'It—it's my date.'

'Your *what*?'

There was no mistaking Jake's savagery now, and Laura had to wet her dry lips before saying, half defensively, 'My date. I—I'm going out for dinner.'

'With a man?' Jake was grim. 'You're going out with a man?'

'Yes.' Laura found she was breathing much faster than she should. 'So, you see——'

'Who is he?'

'I—just a colleague.'

'A colleague? You mean he's a schoolteacher also?'

'That's right.' The bell rang yet again, and, realising Mark had only to peer through the front windows to discover her hovering by the phone, she added, 'I must go. Really——'

'Wait!' Jake's voice constricted. 'Are you—sleeping with him?'

'That's none of your——'

'*Tell me!*'

'No!' Laura felt a choking sensation in her throat. 'No, I'm not,' she replied wretchedly, and, slamming down the receiver, she pressed both hands to her burning cheeks.

CHAPTER TEN

LAURA had read that the light in Tuscany was the secret of the region's magic. In the early morning—or at dusk—painters and architects had marvelled at its clarity of illumination, and, even though it was late afternoon, she could see exactly what they meant.

From the balcony of her room, she had an uninterrupted view of the valley and the surrounding hills, and the colours were quite fantastic. From the silvery radiance of the River Lupo that wound along the valley floor, to the rich dark forests of pine and cypress that coated the hills all around,

she was entranced by their brilliance. In addition to which,
the air was like wine—fresh, and clear, and redolent with
the fragrance of the flowers that grew in such profusion in
the gardens below.

'Valle di Lupo.'

Laura said the name softly to herself. It meant the Valley
of the Wolf. She had looked it up in the library at school.
She guessed there had once been plenty of wild animals,
wolves included, sheltering in the shadowy depths of these
forests. There was still a sense of primitive beauty about
the place, of ancient civilisations worshipping ancient gods.

And, for Laura, there was also a sense of stepping back
in time. Everything was strange, and it was not unnatural
that she should feel unsure of herself, but it was the sense
of feeling young again that troubled her most. Of course,
it shouldn't be something she should object to, but she did.
She was not supposed to be here to resurrect her own youth,
but as Julie's mother, meeting her daughter's proposed in-
laws for the first time.

But, it hadn't been like that, and it was all Jake's fault.
Or Giacomo's—as his mother chose to call him. She should
have known—and been warned—when Jake had met her
in London. When he'd walked into the baggage collection
area at Heathrow, and casually informed her that Julie was
not with him, she should have refused to go any further.

And she would have, she remembered, ruefully, if he had
not gone on to explain that Julie had merely been delayed
in California. Apparently, the screen test her daughter had
been so excited about had materialised, and she had flown
off to Los Angeles at a moment's notice, leaving Jake to
explain the situation to her mother. However, she hoped to
join them on Sunday, so there was absolutely no reason
why Laura should feel so apprehensive.

In the hustle and bustle of Terminal One, it had seemed
ridiculous to imagine that Jake might have planned the
whole thing. Dressed in a dark brown suede jacket and
matching jeans, a bronze collarless body shirt open at the
neck, to display the brown column of his throat, he looked
so cool and attractive—and *young*—that it was incon-
ceivable that he should have any serious interest in *her*. Tall,
and dark, and undoubtedly male, he attracted female eyes

wherever he went, and even in her newly bought trouser-
suit, with her hair trimmed and styled, so that the ends
tucked under her chin, Laura knew she couldn't compete.
It had amused him to show her how inexperienced—and
unsophisticated—she was, despite being older, but that was
all. This wasn't a game any longer. This was for real. And
like it or not, she had to carry off the next few days with
as much confidence as she could muster.

And the journey had been surprisingly smooth. When
she stopped worrying about Jake, and accepted his com-
panionship for what it was, she could almost enjoy herself,
and there was no doubt he had gone out of his way to make
it easy for her. After all, there had been so many new things
to see and absorb, not least the helicopter ride from
Heathrow to Gatwick airport, and boarding Jake's father's
private jet for the flight to Pisa.

She had been introduced to the pilot, who had turned
out to be an Englishman himself, and the pretty Italian
stewardess had made sure that their every need was catered
for. They had eaten lunch, as they'd crossed the Alps into
Switzerland, before flying over northern Italy, and down
the Gulf of Genoa, to their landing at Pisa.

There had only been one bad moment, and that was just
before they'd landed, when Jake had taken it upon himself
to point out any visible places of interest. This coastline,
he'd told her, was known as the Riviera di Levante, with
the fishing harbour of Portofino being one of the prettiest
spots.

Directing her gaze to the hazy outline of Viareggio, miles
below them, had entailed his leaning over her chair, and
she was disturbingly aware of his muscled chest, pressing
against her arm and shoulder. As he spoke, his breath
fanned her cheek, and, although he did nothing to warrant
the sudden quickening of her blood, she couldn't deny its
wild crescendo.

In an effort to distract him, she'd asked the question that
had been troubling her, ever since he'd rung eight days ago.
'Your—your stomach,' she said. 'That is—the cut: did it
heal all right?'

It was only after the words were uttered that she realised
how intimate they were. Reminding him of his injury could

only serve to increase their awareness of one another, and
he might easily think that was what she intended.

But to her relief, Jake chose not to use the question to
his own advantage. Instead, as if sensing her ambivalence,
he drew back into his own seat, and running a careless hand
over his midriff, he replied evenly, 'It is improving, thanks
to you.' And then, more obliquely, 'Much like our relationship, wouldn't you agree?'

They'd landed in Pisa shortly afterwards, and Laura had
been grateful. It meant she'd had little time to wonder what
Jake had meant. Instead, she'd still been exclaiming,
somewhat fulsomely, over the brilliance of the sun on the
old city's towers and churches that she had seen from the
air, when Jake's father's chauffeur had come up to them,
as they'd cleared Customs.

A stocky, middle-aged man, with friendly features, and
a thick moustache, and wearing the same purple and gold
uniform that the pilot and stewardess had worn, he'd greeted
Jake with evident warmth and affection. The two men had
spoken together in their own language, as they'd walked to
where the car was waiting, and Laura had been happy to
trail behind, marvelling at the warmth of the day. It was
much warmer here than in England, and she'd been glad
she had not succumbed to the temptation—at five o'clock
that morning—to wear a heavier outfit. As it was, the
brushed cotton trouser-suit had been just about right.

The drive from the airport to Castellombardi had been
uneventful—inasmuch as Laura had concentrated on the
scenery, and Jake had obligingly discussed soccer with their
chauffeur. It had enabled Laura to absorb a little more of
her surroundings, though the glimpses of handsome villas
she saw, sheltering behind citrus and olive trees, as they'd
left the city, had given her more than a twinge of trepidation. They'd given her some indication of what
Castellombardi might be like, and the prospect had been
quite unnerving.

Beyond the city's limits, the motorway signs had all
seemed to lead to Firenze—Florence—but although they'd
driven for a short distance along the *autostrada*, they'd soon
turned off on to narrower country roads. The flat coastal
plain had soon been left behind, and they'd climbed into

cypress-shaded hills, where every summit revealed a hidden
valley, or the gleaming walls of a medieval town. There
were farms, and vineyards, and countless churches, each
with its own tower, or *campanile*, as it was called. There
were ruins, too, evidence of the Etruscan civilisation that
had once flourished in this area. And occasionally a barren
stretch of ground, whose melancholy landscape epitomised
the dignity of death in ancient cultures.

And then, Jake had turned from his conversation with
the chauffeur, to tell her that they were now nearing his
home. This pine-scented valley, with the tumbling waters
of a narrow river at its foot, was Valle di Lupo, and the
crenellated towers she could see, nestling against their dark
green backcloth, belonged to Castellombardi.

Laura's nerves had tightened apprehensively, and not for
the first time, she had wished Julie was with them. She,
Laura, should not have been here, seeing Jake's home for
the first time, meeting his parents, and sharing their hospitality. That should have been Julie's prerogative. This
whole trip had been arranged for Julie's benefit, not hers.
If only she could stop feeling like a usurper. If only she
could stop thinking about Jake altogether.

But, arriving at Castellombardi, Laura had found herself
worrying more about meeting Jake's parents than coping
with Jake himself. And the sprawling manor-house had been
daunting enough, without the added complications of a
handful of servants, whose names she was sure she would
never remember.

A little of her consternation must have shown in her face,
however, for Jake had taken time out from instructing a
lusty youth where Laura's bags were to be taken, to say
reassuringly, 'Don't worry! They're going to love you.' And,
in her hysterical state, she wasn't sure whether he meant
his parents or the members of their staff.

The creeper-hung portico, with its narrow mullioned
windows, gave access to a marble-floored entrance hall. The
age of the building was much in evidence here, with a restored frescoed ceiling arching above tapestry-hung walls.
There was a veritable arsenal of ancient weapons, forming
a grim collage above a huge stone fireplace. The number
of swords and daggers on display had made Laura look

automatically at Jake, and his lazy grin had stirred an unwanted awareness in the pit of her stomach.

'Now, you know why I enjoy sword-play,' he murmured,
for her ears only. 'Be warned, my ancestors were not known
for their tolerance.'

Laura might have replied—if she could have dismissed
the shiver of sentience that shivered down her spine at his
words, but she was forestalled by the appearance of another
woman. And not a servant, Laura surmised, noticing the
rings that adorned her slender fingers. Even without her
resemblance to her son, Laura would have guessed that this
was Jake's mother. Although the similarities between them
were more in colouring than appearance, she walked with
such grace and economy of movement—just like her son,
Laura had acknowledged unwillingly.

'Mama!'

Jake's greeting had confirmed what was already a certainty, and he went to greet her with an easy confidence.
For a moment, he was enfolded in his mother's arms, and
then, before Laura could begin to feel an outsider, he turned
and beckoned her forward, to make the introductions...

And that was when her misgivings had multiplied, Laura
acknowledged now, turning back into the classical beauty
of the bedroom behind her. For, in introducing her to his
mother, Jake hadn't mentioned Julie. Not once. He had
presented her simply as Laura Fox. Not *Julie's mother*,
Laura Fox, or even as Laura Fox, the mother of a friend
of his. Just Laura; nothing else; as if she, and not Julie,
were the reason for this visit.

The Contessa Sophia Lombardi had been especially
charming, Laura conceded, even though she must have
wondered why their guest was staring at her son with such
consternation. Tall, like Jake, with narrow patrician features, she had welcomed Laura into her home with real
cordiality, asking if she had had a good journey, and acknowledging Laura's compliments about her country. She
had made Laura feel like a wanted visitor, not the intruder
she believed herself to be.

Of course, Laura hadn't been able to say anything that
might create any awkwardness in his mother's presence, and
she had not had a chance to speak to Jake alone since his

mother's appearance. Instead, the Contessa had taken charge of her well-being, suggesting that Laura might like to see her room and rest for a while before the evening meal. Like her son, she spoke in English, and Laura had felt obliged to accept her suggestion. But that hadn't stopped her from giving Jake a quelling look, as she'd followed one of the maidservants up the stairs. It had said, she would speak to him later, and he'd been left in no doubt what she meant.

But that was over an hour ago now. Since then, Laura had taken a shower, and unpacked her case, and made a tentative exploration of her apartments. Her room—rooms, she corrected herself drily—were situated in the west wing of the building, overlooking the whole sweep of the valley. But it was the rooms themselves that had first drawn her admiration, with their skilful blend of ancient and modern.

Although, perhaps modern was not an appropriate adjective, she conceded now. Obviously, much of the renovation of the building had been done in the early part of this century, when time and materials had been no object. There was an abundance of gilt and decoration, and, despite their obvious age, the silk-encrusted walls and velvet carpets still wore the patina of an earlier age.

Nevertheless, the plumbing was reassuringly efficient, and the bathroom sported all the usual accoutrements. If the claw-footed bath and pedestal basin were rather large and ungainly, their function was not impaired. On the contrary, Laura was looking forward to taking a bath. She had the feeling that when the huge porcelain tub was full only her head would show above the rim.

Between the bathroom and the bedroom, there was a spacious dressing-room, with long walk-in wardrobes. Laura's handful of outfits looked rather lost in such an excess of space, but it was quite a novelty to have so much freedom.

Beyond the bedroom, whose generously proportioned four-poster also attracted Laura's admiration, a modest sitting-room provided reading and writing facilities. All the latest magazines—regrettably, Laura saw, in Italian—were spread on a low glass-topped table, while an exquisitely

carved bureau was set with writing paper and envelopes
and, Laura saw to her delight, a real quill pen.

She thought of sitting at the bureau and writing to Jess,
but the connotations of that exercise were more than enough
to deter her. She could just imagine her friend's reaction
if she wrote and told her she was spending the weekend
with Jake's family, without Julie. No matter that her
daughter was supposed to be arriving the following day.
Jess was bound to have suspicions. Heaven knew, she had
suspicions herself.

Which brought her back to the crux of her dilemma,
Laura sighed heavily. What was she going to do about Jake?
And Julie? The trouble was, she didn't know what Jake
had told his mother about his relationship with her daughter,
and she could hardly ask. And yet, what else could she do?
She had to know if Julie was expected here tomorrow, or
whether that had just been a lie.

But what if it had? she asked herself now, admitting the
incredible thought that it might be true. What if Julie wasn't
in California at all? What if she was, even now, trying to
reach her mother at Burnfoot?

But no. Julie herself had told her about this trip to Italy.
Julie had tendered the invitation, and just because Jake
had made the final arrangements was no reason to assume
her daughter wasn't involved.

She shook her head, and, walking across to the bed, she
flopped down on to the embossed coverlet. The mattress
gave beneath her weight, and, squeezing the edges on either
side of her, she realised it wasn't the spring interior she had
expected. If she was not mistaken, the mattress was stuffed
with feathers, and in spite of her worries she couldn't
prevent a rueful smile from tugging at the corners of her
lips. God, she thought, resting back on her elbows. Jess
would never believe this place!

A knock at the outer door brought her to her feet with
a start. As she tentatively walked to the door of the sitting-
room, her hands automatically dragged the folds of the terry
robe she had found hanging on the back of the bathroom
door, closer about her. But, she could do nothing about
her bare legs, protruding from its hem.

However, when she called a tentative, 'Come in,' the maid, who earlier had brought her a light meal of tea and pastries, appeared to collect the tray.

'Scusi, signora,' she said, picking up the tray. 'Mi dispiace di disturbarsi.'

The words were mostly unfamiliar, but their meaning was clear enough, and Laura raised a deprecating hand. 'Prego,' she said, quite pleased with her response. But when the maid launched into a voluble stream of her own language, she wished she had not been so clever.

'Non capisco, non capisco,' she exclaimed, trying to stem the tide, and she was almost relieved when she heard a low mocking laugh.

'Grazie, Maria,' Jake said lazily, straightening from his position by the door, and the young maid flushed becomingly, as she sidled past him, and out of the room.

With the maid's departure, however, Laura was immediately aware of her state of undress. Jake had evidently bathed and changed. There were drops of moisture gleaming on his hair, and his dark trousers and jacket, and the cream silk shirt and tie, were obviously what he was going to wear this evening. Laura, meanwhile, felt quite dishevelled, but rather than give him another reason to have fun at her expense, she put her hands into the robe's pockets, and faced him bravely. 'Did you want something?' she asked, in the dismissing tone of someone whose patience was wearing thin, and Jake glanced behind him at the open door before answering quietly, 'I rather thought you wanted to speak to me.'

'Oh...' Laura was disconcerted then, not least because he was right, and for a few moments she had forgotten the ambiguity of her position. 'Um—well, yes. Yes, I did want to speak to you. But—not like this.'

She glanced pointedly down at the bathrobe, and Jake's mouth took on a decidedly sensual slant. 'Ah,' he murmured, a wealth of understanding in the sound, and, as his insolent gaze roved down her body, Laura could almost feel the heat of its passing.

'Please!' she exclaimed, unable to withstand this kind of sexual gamesmanship, and Jake's eyes came obediently back to hers.

'Anything,' he said, his tone scraping her nerves with its husky vibration. 'Shall I close the door?'

'No!'

Laura made the denial rather louder than she had intended, and Jake arched a mocking brow. 'You want the rest of the household to hear this?' he queried politely, and she turned away, running both hands under the hair at the back of her neck.

'No. I—oh, close the door. Behind you,' she mumbled wearily. 'I'll talk to you later.'

The door closed, and she expelled her breath on a heavy sigh. But when she turned around again, she found Jake was still there.

'You——' she began, her voice taut with frustration, but Jake was not prepared to argue with her.

'Yes, me,' he said, crossing the space between them, and cupping her hot face in his hands. 'You despise me, I know.' His eyes darkened. 'But you want me just the same.'

'I don't——' she started, but his mouth silenced her. With hungry expertise, his kiss trapped her instinctive protest, his tongue sliding between her lips to make a statement of its own.

Laura's world tilted. Much as she wanted to deny what he was saying, what he was *doing*, her body betrayed her. The moist fusion of their mouths made any protest superfluous anyway. No one could respond as she was responding and still pretend she was a victim of circumstance. If she was a victim—and of that she had few doubts—it was a victim of her own needs, her own inadequacies. What Jake was doing was simply confirming all those guilty fantasies she had entertained about him.

But no fantasy had prepared her for the treacherous delight of feeling Jake's hands on her bare flesh. She was so weak, so accessible, and the terry-cloth robe parted easily beneath his purposeful hands. Not that she was aware of it—not immediately, anyway. Her own hands were too busy clinging to his lapels, in an effort to withstand the shakiness of her knees, to notice at once what he was doing. It was only when one mohair-clad leg brushed her thighs that she perceived the reason why the tips of her breasts felt so aroused. The sides of the robe had parted, and her quivering body was open to his touch.

Sanity craved that she draw back from him now, while she still could, but her mind was swimming in a haze of emotion. She wanted to be sensible. She tried to remember where she was, and what she was doing, but her feelings got in the way. And Jake didn't make it easy for her. When he released her mouth, it was only to seek the sensitive skin below her ear, and his teeth fastening on that skin, drenched her limbs with moisture.

'I knew you were beautiful,' he breathed, tipping the robe from her shoulders, his tongue finding the pulse that fluttered in her throat. His hands slid to her waist, and then moved upward until they were brushing the undersides of her breasts. '*Bella* Laura, do you have any idea how much I want you?'

'Jake——'

Laura was finding it an effort even to breathe normally, but her panting use of his name seemed to please him, and whatever protest she had intended to make was stifled by the groan he emitted. His hands closed over her breasts as his mouth sought hers again, and she was weakly aware that so long as he was touching her like this she had no will to resist him.

Her lips opened wide to the wet invasion of his tongue, and almost without her own volition her own tongue moved tentatively to touch his. A sensuous warmth was sweeping over her, and although she had never experienced such intense lovemaking before she seemed to know instinctively what to do.

Jake was biting her lips now, little nibbling kisses that caused her chest to rise and fall with the intensity of her emotions. And, in so doing, her hard nipples thrust into his palms, sensitising them to an almost unbearable extent.

Dizziness overwhelmed her, and, as if sensing her weakness, Jake swung her up into his arms, and carried her to the bed. He deposited her in the middle of the coverlet, and although the coolness at her back was briefly sobering Jake didn't allow her to escape him.

Careless of his clothes, he came down on the bed beside her, and his hands and lips drove all sane thoughts from her head. When his mouth found the creamy rise of her breasts, and trailed a searing path of wet kisses to the throbbing nipple, she reached for him. With wondering hands, she cradled his dark head against her, tangling her fingers in his hair, and raking her nails against his scalp.

There was an ache between her thighs now, an actual physical ache, that she knew only he could ease. But the means of that easement was too mind-bending to contemplate, even if at this moment he had her at his mercy.

His tongue thrust into her mouth again, its greedy possession an indication of his own diminishing control. When her eyes fluttered open she surprised a look of raw hunger on his face, and his eyes narrowed passionately as his hands slid over her naked body.

His touch was urgent, abrasive, shaping the gentle curve of her hip, before slipping down to her knees and up again, this time between the quivering flesh of her inner thighs. He caressed the skin from her knees to the apex of her legs with slow deliberation, always brushing the triangle of curls with the back of his hand, but never really touching. It was as if he was intentionally withholding something she desired with increasing urgency, and it was all Laura could do not to grab his hand, and press it between her legs.

Her trembling cravings shamed her. Jake knew exactly what he was doing, she was sure of that. And while a small corner of her mind clung to that knowledge, and taunted her with it, it was easily overwhelmed by the needs and desires he was so effortlessly promoting. She knew he wanted her aroused and clinging to him. It was the only way he could destroy her inhibitions. But that didn't stop her from bucking against his hands.

By the time he chose to cup the throbbing core of her womanhood, Laura was almost mindless with relief. Her legs were shaking so much that she couldn't have kept them together, even if she'd wanted to, and only when Jake bent to press his face against the tight curls did she utter a choked sob of protest.

'What's wrong?' he asked huskily, lifting his head and looking at her, and she thought how unfair it was that she was so naked and vulnerable, while he was still fully dressed.

'You—you can't,' she got out unsteadily, levering herself up on her elbow, but his smile was purely possessive.

'Why not?' he demanded. 'It's what you want. It's what we both want.'

'No——'

'Yes.' He moved so that he could take her resistant hand and press it against the rigid shaft of his own arousal, tautly visible against the fine cloth of his trousers. 'Only there isn't time to please both of us. Not right now. Only you.'

'Jake——'

'I'm here.'

He moved again, slanting his mouth across hers, and bearing her back against the covers. And as he did so, his fingers slid into the silky female flesh that was wet from wanting him. With infinite skill, his tongue mimicked the movement of his hand, and Laura was swamped with longing. This was what she wanted, she conceded dizzily, as feelings she had not even known existed rioted inside her. She did want Jake to touch her, to kiss her, and make love to her. And she wanted *him* inside her, not just an imitation.

But rational thought became impossible, as Jake's expert caresses began to arouse an unfamiliar hunger. It was no longer enough just to submit passively to what he was doing to her. She started to push against his fingers, and unfamiliar needs caused her to twist and turn beneath his hands. Even Jake's breathing quickened, she noticed unsteadily, his laboured heartbeat jerking in tune with her own.

She opened her eyes again, almost disbelievingly, as her body began to strive towards some goal she was barely aware of. Certainly, her experiences with Keith Macfarlane had not led her to believe she was capable of any depth of feeling, and the fear that she might never escape this craving brought panic-stricken intensity to her expression.

But Jake knew what she was feeling. Even though his face was taut now, his forehead and temples beaded with sweat, he understood her fear. When Laura raised a trembling hand to smooth the moist hair back from his forehead, he turned his head, and pressed his mouth to her wrist, and the heat of his lips sent a searing flame along her veins.

'Easy, *cara*,' he muttered thickly, lowering his head to her breast, and taking the burning nipple into his mouth. And, as he suckled on the rosy flesh, Laura's control deserted her.

'God—oh, God,' she groaned, hardly aware that she was digging her nails into his shoulders. A blinding wave of pleasure had overwhelmed her, and with it an urgent need to share her joy. Unaware that she was doing so, she wound her arms around his neck, and pulled him down on top of her, covering his face with kisses, until the tremors slowly receded.

But Jake did not share her abandonment. With grim determination, he extracted himself from her clinging fingers, and rolled on to his back beside her. And for a few moments, there was silence in the room, broken only by the individual sounds of their breathing.

It was the coolness of the evening air, drifting in through the open balcony doors, and chilling her bare flesh, that brought Laura fully to her senses. When Jake had first moved away from her, she had lain there, too stunned, both mentally and physically, over what had happened, to do anything. But, as her blood cooled—and likewise her flesh—she gradually felt the full impact of her own wanton behaviour.

Dear lord, she fretted wretchedly, what had she done? After all she had said; after the way she had castigated Jake for taking advantage of her, she had actually allowed him to—to——

To what? To reduce her to a trembling mass of nerves and sensations, she allowed disgustedly. He had used his not inconsiderable skills to show her exactly how vulnerable she was, so far as he was concerned. He had brought her to a peak of physical pleasure she had never known before, without even availing himself of her body. Let's face it, without even taking off his clothes, she acknowledged bitterly. Damn, how he must be laughing at her now!

She turned her head, her face twisted with contempt at her own weakness. There was no way she was going to get out of this, without humiliating herself still further, but she had to try. For her own sake. For *Julie's* sake! Oh, God! *Julie!*

Jake was still lying beside her. She had half expected to find he had moved, while she was recovering her senses, but he hadn't. He was still lying on his back, one hand raised behind his head, the other resting on the coverlet between them.

However he had sensed the nervous movement of her head, and he turned his head on the pillows to look at her. 'Better?' he enquired, a little thickly, and, although Laura was sure there must be some sarcasm in his question, his expression was free of derision.

It took her completely by surprise, however, and the words she had been prepared to say in defence of herself, stuck in her throat. 'I—this should never have happened,' she said instead, realising how feeble that sounded. Particularly after she had just betrayed everything she had thought she believed in, she added miserably. 'Um—you'd better go.'

Jake sighed then, and rolled on to his side to face her. 'Is that all you have to say?' he exclaimed, his tone harshening. 'Laura, this was not a mistake! This was for real. And believe me, my magnanimity does not extend to soothing your pretty sensibilities!'

Laura caught her breath. 'I beg your pardon?'

'I said——'

'I know what you said,' she responded, in a trembling voice. She sat up, and presented her back to him, 'I—I want to know what—what you meant by—by my pretty—sensibilities!'

'Dio!' Jake's oath was heartfelt, but when he would have grasped her arm she scrambled off the bed, and snatched up the discarded bathrobe. She felt a little better with its soft folds between her and Jake's scathing eyes, though she shifted a little nervously when he came up off the bed to face her.

'What do you think I meant?' he demanded grimly, and when she moved her head in a little indifferent gesture he raked back his hair with a frustrated hand. 'You don't suppose I enjoyed what just happened, do you?'

Laura's face flamed. She couldn't help it. It was an involuntary response to his lack of discrimination. 'I—don't—

think—we need to—to conduct a post-mortem——' she
began, but his anger overruled her prim denial.

'Do you not? Do you not?' he grated, and she noticed
how his accent had appeared again. '*Mama mia*, she doesn't
want to talk about it! She doesn't even realise how hard it
was for me to touch her!'

Laura swallowed convulsively. 'Well—if—if that was the
case,' she stammered, 'why did you?'

'*Dio*!' He pressed the ball of one hand against his
forehead. 'You don't even understand what I am talking
about, do you?' He glared at her. 'Laura, do you honestly
believe I *didn't* want to touch you? That is not what I meant.
Not what I meant at all.' He groaned. 'I have told you
already, I want you, Laura. I want to be a part of you. Do
you know what I am talking about now? I want to lie with
you. I want to slide between your thighs, and slake my thirst
in your most beautiful body, but I am careful. I know I
must not rush you. I know you are not ready yet to admit
your feelings, so I—I pleasure you. Not myself. Only you.
And you have no idea, no idea, believe me, how I am feeling
at this moment!'

Laura quivered, drawing her lower lip between her teeth,
as her eyes flickered down his body. They lingered on the
unmistakable evidence of his frustration, and then, when
he swore, rather colourfully, her gaze returned nervously
to his.

'Yes,' he said harshly, dragging his hands down his thighs,
as if to ease the constriction of the tight trousers. 'So now
you know. I want you, Laura. And I suggest you do not
look at me like that, unless you are prepared to take the
consequences.' He drew a laboured breath. 'Now, I suggest
you get dressed. My parents expect you to join them for
drinks in the library in——' he consulted the plain gold
watch on his wrist '—a little over fifteen minutes.'

Laura caught her breath. 'I can't join them now——'

'Why not?'

Jake was buttoning his jacket as he spoke, smoothing a
hand that was not quite steady over his hair, checking that
his tie was straight. Laura watched him, almost possessively, aware, as she did so, that she was actually beginning
to believe the things he said. He did want her. That was

undeniable. But what he wanted of her—that was something else again.

'Jake——'

'Get dressed, Laura,' he said flatly, walking towards the door. 'It's impolite to be late, when you're the guest of honour!'

CHAPTER ELEVEN

'PAPA!'

Lucia nudged her pony nearer her father's bay stallion, and whispered something Laura could barely hear. She knew it was about her. Her name—Lucia called her Signora Fox—figured fairly significantly in the little girl's oratory, but as she spoke in her own language Laura couldn't understand what she was saying.

Which was all par for the course, thought Laura bitterly, holding on to her mount's reins with a grimness that bordered on desperation. She didn't understand any of this, and Lucia's shy reserve was the least of her worries.

So, instead of fretting over what Jake's daughter might be saying about her, Laura stared determinedly at the view. If she could forget that she was on the back of a horse, and that the horse was standing on a ledge, some one hundred feet above the valley floor, it should be possible to appreciate the beauty of her surroundings. Jake had said the only way to see this country was on horseback, and, although Laura had never ridden before, he had insisted he would take care of her.

The trouble was, she didn't want him taking care of her. It was bad enough, knowing she was here under false pretences. She didn't want his mother and father to get the wrong impression. They had been kind to her, and she appreciated that, but she had to keep things in perspective.

Yet it had proved harder than she had ever imagined. Dinner, the night before, for instance. When she had eventually gathered herself together, and gone downstairs, she had found her plan to explain the situation to Jake's parents had had to be shelved. Contrary to her belief, she had not been the only guest for dinner. Jake's younger brother and his wife; two actors, who were performing in the area; an artist of some note; a priest; and various other business colleagues of Jake's father, and their wives, were gathered in the library, when Laura finally found the courage to join them. She had realised there was no chance then of any private conversation, and her head was soon swimming with so many introductions.

Not least her introduction to Jake's father, she remembered ruefully. Count Domenico Lombardi—Nico, to his friends—was simply an older version of his elder son. He was handsome, and courteous, and in other circumstances, Laura was sure, she would have been charmed by him. But he was too much like Jake for her to feel completely relaxed in his presence, and the ambiguity of their relationship made her feel like a fraud.

Jake's brother, Lorenzo, was much less threatening. Smaller than the other members of his family, he had a shy, self-deprecating manner, a little like Lucia's, that endeared itself to Laura. His wife, too, was relaxed and friendly, and, like most of the Italians Laura had met, she spoke extremely good English.

Laura was grateful she had taken some trouble over her appearance, however. Even if her hands had shaken as she'd been applying her make-up, the results were quite satisfying. The sequinned jacket she had shocked Jess by buying the previous week, worn with a simple black silk vest and trousers was definitely well-chosen. She hadn't needed Jake's studied approval to know she looked good. For once in her life, she had confidence in her appearance, even if her reasons for making the effort hadn't been what she'd expected.

Nevertheless, the evening had proved to be quite a strain. Oh, everyone had been very kind, and she had been made to feel that she was a welcome visitor. But, perhaps because of that, Laura remained on edge, aware, more than anyone, of the falseness of her position.

Her meeting with Lucia had struck a happier note. Unlike any English child of her age, she had been allowed to stay up for dinner, and the little girl was naturally curious about anyone who might focus her father's attention away from

herself. It was understandable, Laura supposed, bearing in
mind that the child's mother was dead, but she wished she
could tell her she was not who the child evidently thought
her. Even though Jake had introduced them, and had said
nothing to arouse her interest, Laura was sure Lucia sensed
there was something between them. But not for long, Laura
had wanted to cry. Just for this weekend...

Lucia had been taken off to bed, by her nursemaid, before
ten o'clock, but the evening had not ended until around
midnight. Laura had wished that she, and not the protesting Lucia, could have escaped so much earlier, but she
was obliged to be polite, and stay until the bitter end.

Not that it had been really bitter, she acknowledged now,
as the chestnut gelding shifted beneath her. Trying not to
show how nervous she really was, Laura pressed her knees
against the leathers, and hung on. The meal, which had
been served in the vaulted dining-room, had been mouth-
wateringly delicious, and had Laura not been so tense, she
would have enjoyed the food immensely. Smoked ham,
served with a delicate grapefruit mousse, pasta, stuffed with
meat and cheese, and a sugary fruit dessert to finish, would
normally have aroused her appetite. But in the event, she
had eaten very little, relying on the wine to keep her throat
from drying up completely.

Bed, when she'd reached it, had offered few reassurances. Looking at the satin bedspread, smooth now, and
neatly folded back, she had been irresistibly reminded of
what had happened on the bed before dinner. It had been
impossible to look at that soft mattress without thinking
of how her own body had betrayed her. And yet, much as
she hated to admit it, she had known a strange exhilaration
at the memory. She might tell herself she was mortified,
but her skin had tingled just the same.

Of course, she had been half afraid Jake would come
back, once his parents had retired. Long after the house
had settled down for the night, Laura had lain awake, determined to remain on her guard. She couldn't help remembering what he had said before he'd left her, and she'd
been fairly sure he would try to finish what he had started.

But Jake hadn't come back. Although she had wedged
a chair beneath the handle of the sitting-room door, no one

had tried to dislodge it. She had eventually fallen asleep, too exhausted to care any longer. Only her dreams had disturbed her, and they were no one's fault but her own.

But now, sitting here, on this cypress-studded hillside, with the sun cresting the hills, and casting dark pools of shadow between the trees, she was aware of the instinctive response her thoughts had engendered. Her mind might be determined to resist Jake, to put him out of her life, but her emotions were not so controllable. Even now, a hot sweet swirl of weakness was invading her lower limbs, and the memory of how he had made her feel was not one she was likely to forget.

The chestnut snorted softly, and tossed his head, and Laura's attention was drawn back to the precariousness of her seat. Below her, the ground fell away steeply to the river, and the knowledge that only the gelding's good nature stood between her and serious injury brought a wave of perspiration to her forehead.

'Luci thinks you're holding the reins too tightly,' Jake murmured beside her, and his knee bumped hers, causing the chestnut to shift in protest.

'Don't—don't do that!' gasped Laura, paying little attention to what he had said, and Jake reached across to anchor her reins with an expert hand.

'Hey,' he said, and she could tell by his expression, he knew exactly what she was thinking. 'Don't be scared,' he added. 'Caesar won't hurt you.'

'That's easy for you to say,' retorted Laura, her throat constricted, as much by his gloved hand resting on her knee, as by her fear. 'It just seems a long way down into the valley, that's all. And—and——'

'And you don't like it?'

'I didn't say that.' In all honesty, Laura had enjoyed parts of the outing, and she knew she would store up the memory of the beauty of this valley for when she was back in Burnfoot.

'Good.'

Jake looked into her eyes, and although he said nothing else, she knew he was remembering how she had looked the last time they were alone together. There were little sparks of awareness in the night-dark depths of his eyes, and Laura suddenly understood the meaning of drowning in someone's eyes. She wanted to drown in Jake's eyes, and the knowledge was terrifying.

'*Papa! Papa! Cosa stai facendo?*'

Luci was tugging his sleeve, wanting to know what they were doing, and, tearing his gaze away from Laura, Jake turned to his daughter. '*Niente, cara*, nothing,' he assured her soothingly, gesturing for her to lead the way down the winding track. 'We were just admiring the view, that is all,' he continued in English, but slowly, so that Luci could understand what he was saying. '*Avante, cara*. We are coming.'

Luci looked doubtful, but she urged her pony forward, and Jake used his hold on the chestnut's reins to draw him away from the ledge. Then, patting the beast's flanks, he urged him past his own mount, returning the reins to Laura, as she came up beside him.

'OK?' he asked, looking at her mouth, and Laura's lips parted nervously.

'I suppose so,' she said, a little tensely, and, keeping her eyes on Caesar's neck, she let him take her down the rocky incline.

There were terraces of vines on the lower slopes, and the sharp scent of citrus trees in blossom. It was a smell that Laura knew, from now on, she would always associate with this area, and her sweating palms cooled as the ground levelled out.

Luci came back to ride with her father as their mounts trod through lush meadows, bordering the river. It meant that Laura had little chance to talk privately with Jake, but, realising that once they got back to the house, it might be even harder to get him alone, she said tautly, 'What time is Julie coming?'

Her question had evidently disconcerted him, for he glanced swiftly at his daughter, as if gauging her reaction, before giving Laura a wooden look. 'Julie,' he said at last. 'I do not know.'

Laura noticed the 'do not', rather than the more casual 'don't', and was immediately suspicious. 'She *is* coming, isn't she?'

Jake sighed, and lifted his broad shoulders in a dismissing gesture. 'Julie does not like my country—only its
cities,' he responded, guiding his horse nearer the water.
Then, swinging down from the bay's back, he looked at
Laura's hands, clutching the thin strips of leather that controlled her mount. 'You're still holding the reins too tightly,'
he said. 'Can't you feel the way Caesar is trying to get the
bit between his teeth?'

'Damn Caesar!' Laura's gaze skimmed Luci's startled
face, before coming to rest on that of the man standing
beside her. 'That's not an answer, Jake, and you know it!'

'Perhaps it is the only answer you are going to get,' he
retorted coolly. 'Shall I help you down?'

'No!' As Luci prepared to swing out of her saddle, Laura
shook her head. 'I—I want to go back.'

'Back?' Jake's features hardened. 'To the *castello*?'

'No. To England,' declared Laura unsteadily. 'I should
never have come.'

Jake's mouth compressed. 'Not again, Laura. Now—will
you get down, or must I haul you out of that saddle?'

Laura shook her head again, jerking the reins, so that
Caesar's head came up, and his ears went back in protest.
The gelding shifted backwards, as if trying to escape the
bite of metal against the soft inner side of his mouth, but
Laura was unaware of the animal's unease. She was too
intent on showing Jake that, although he might have some
precarious control over her body, he had none over her
mind.

'I'm going back,' she said again glancing over her
shoulder. The walls of the *castello* were just visible above
the trees, and although she realised she was still some distance from the house she was determined he should not
think he could dictate what she could or could not do. She
had ridden out here, hadn't she? Why shouldn't she ride
back?

But she had spoken without giving any thought to the
animal beneath her. It never occurred to her that the gelding
might have a mind of his own. She had been nervous on
the ridge, it was true, but she had learned to trust him.
And, because he had brought her safely down into the valley
again, she had assumed she was in control.

However, her behaviour had unsettled Caesar. The animal had sensed her anger, and her frustration, without realising it was not directed towards himself. Her tight hold on the bridle, her anxious knees digging into his sides, excited him. He was not usually a nervous beast, but Laura's persistent use of the restraint disturbed him, and he whinnied loudly as she tugged his head around.

What happened next seemed to occur as if in slow motion. Jake had evidently sensed that the gelding was becoming agitated, and he lunged for the reins himself, as Caesar backed off. But although he managed to grab the bridle, the horse was too excitable to control. He reared wildly on his hind legs, almost throwing Jake off his feet, and Laura slid off his back, with only a muffled gasp of protest.

Jake let go of the animal then, and Caesar, finding himself free at last, galloped away. But Laura didn't notice. She was too busy fretting over the fool she had made of herself again, and hoping she didn't look as stupid as she felt.

But she barely had time to register the fact that the sleeve of one of her new blouses was covered in mud, before Jake flung himself on to his knees beside her. Uncaring that his daughter was still sitting on her pony, staring at them with wide, anxious eyes, he ran his hands intimately over Laura's body, checking her legs and arms, and skimming the slim curve of her waist.

'*Come si sente?*' he demanded hoarsely, and then, realising she was gazing at him uncomprehendingly, he translated, 'How do you feel? Are you all right?' He cupped her rueful face between his fingers. 'If Caesar has hurt you, I'll get rid of him!'

Laura's tongue appeared to circle her lips, which wasn't the most sensible thing to do in the circumstances. She could tell from the sudden darkening of his eyes that Jake was remembering how her tongue had felt in his mouth, and she guessed that if Luci had not been there he would have repeated the experience.

'I—I'm fine,' she assured him, a little unsteadily none the less, though he was not to know his nearness was as much to blame as Caesar's rearing. But it was difficult to think of anyone but him, when he was looking at her with

passionately concerned eyes, shattering her defences, with
the unmistakable tremor in his hands. 'Honestly,' she added,
realising she was in very real danger of showing him her
response, 'I just got a shock, that's all.'

'A shock!'

Jake's lips twisted, but before she could say anything else,
Luci appeared at his elbow. 'The *signora*—she has hurt her
head, Papa?' she asked, her English remarkably good for
someone of her age, and with reluctance Jake released
Laura, and got to his feet.

'Signora Fox is a little shaken, *bambina*,' he replied, offering Laura his hand to get up, and, although she would
have preferred to get up independently, she accepted his
assistance. She wasn't entirely sure her legs would hold her,
and she was more than a little relieved to find she was able
to stand without support.

'*Dov'e Caesar?*' Luci soon lapsed back into her own
language, and Jake dragged his gaze away from Laura's
pale face to reply that the horse was probably back at the
stables by now.

'He'll be all right, won't he?' Laura ventured, running
a trembling hand over her hair, and Jake's eyes darkened.

'Of course he will,' he declared succinctly. 'So long as
you are.'

'Oh—oh, I am.' Laura nodded vigorously, and then
winced at the sudden throbbing in her head. 'Well—almost,'
she conceded, giving Luci a rueful smile. 'I'm sorry if I've
spoiled your outing.'

Luci shrugged, not quite knowing how to deal with this
situation. It was obviously not what she had expected, and
her expression mirrored her indecision.

However, her father's terse rejoinder brought her head
up. 'You haven't spoiled anything!' he declared, giving his
daughter an impatient look. 'Luci, get on your pony. We're
going back.'

There was nothing Laura could say. She knew she couldn't
walk back to the *castello*, and she hoped Luci wouldn't
blame her too much for ruining their outing.

Still, it wasn't until Jake captured the reins of his horse,
and brought him back to where Laura was standing, that
she realised what he was intending to do. Until then, she

had assumed that he and Luci would ride back to the house, and probably return with some sort of vehicle to fetch her. Now, a shiver of panic swept over her at the thought of getting on to the stallion's back.

'You—you don't expect me to—ride him, do you?' she gasped, and Jake's expression softened.

'You and me both,' he reassured her gently.

Laura swallowed. 'Couldn't—couldn't I just—ride Luci's pony?' she murmured, and Jake expelled his breath on a heavy sigh.

'No,' he said, looping the horse's reins over his shoulder, and cupping his hands. 'Come on. Put your foot in here, and I'll help you. That way you won't get tangled up in the stirrup, and I can get up behind you.'

It wasn't a very elegant accomplishment, but when Jake swung into the saddle behind her Laura forgot her qualms in the sheer pleasure of feeling his muscled thighs enclosing hers. And when his arms came about her waist to take the reins, she felt the reassuring strength of his body all around her. It was pointless to deny it. No one else made her so aware of being a woman.

And, even though she had initially been alarmed at the idea of riding on the huge bay stallion, Laura was almost sorry when they trotted into the stable-yard some twenty minutes later. For the past fifteen minutes, she had abandoned any attempt to resist the desire to enjoy the experience, and it wasn't until Jake had dismounted and was reaching up to help her down, that she saw his strained expression. It was only then that she comprehended how her yielding body must have affected him, and the reasons why he had become progressively less relaxed during the ride were blatantly obvious.

'I can manage,' she said, a little breathily, but Jake ignored her. He waited until she had swung her legs across the pommel, and then lifted her out of the saddle. He lowered her to the ground slowly, allowing her to slide down the whole length of his body, and Laura couldn't help but be as aroused as he was by the time she found herself on her feet.

'*Ti voglio,*' he said, brushing her parted lips with his, and then walked away as Luci emerged from the stables.

Jake's parents were most concerned to hear that Laura had had a fall, and, although she tried to assure them it had been nothing, Sophia insisted that she rest for the remainder of the day.

'It is the shock that we do not always realise we have sustained,' she said, as they sat at lunch, in a delightful conservatory, overlooking the gardens at the back of the house. 'Is that not so, Nico? Laura must take care of herself.'

'I think Giacomo can be left to ensure that Laura does not overdo things, Sophia,' Count Lombardi replied smoothly, and Laura felt a renewed sense of duplicity for the ambiguity of her position.

'Your—your son—has been very kind,' she began, ignoring the intensity of Jake's eyes upon her. 'But—but really—I think my daughter——'

'Ah, yes,' Jake's mother broke into her stammered attempt at confession, with polite dismissal. 'We know your daughter, Laura. You must be very proud of her. She is a most successful model, is she not?'

'I—well, yes.'

Laura was taken aback, but, although she looked at Jake for inspiration, his expression was now unreadable.

'Yes, we met her in Rome,' went on Sophia Lombardi affably. She looked at her son. 'Giacomo introduced us.'

Laura swallowed. She suddenly realised how little she knew about her daughter's association with this family. How little she knew about these people at all. For all she knew, they might condone their son's behaviour. And if even half what the gutter Press wrote was to be believed, sexual relationships, of one kind or another, were common enough among people of his background.

The maid came to clear their plates, and Laura decided not to say any more. If the Lombardis knew that she was Julie's mother, then maybe her daughter was expected to arrive that afternoon. She hadn't forgotten Jake's avoidance of an answer earlier, even if subsequent events had tended to overshadow its importance. She could only wait and see. She had discovered she didn't have the stomach to pursue it.

She escaped to her room after lunch, grateful that she had an excuse for doing so. But every sound she heard, every footfall outside her door, had her heart beating wildly, and she eventually gave up trying to rest, and went out on to the balcony instead.

It was very peaceful out there. The only sounds were those of the birds and insects, with the occasional drone of an aircraft to remind her this was the twentieth century. Everything else had an agelessness about it, not least the *castello* itself, and she found it incredible to believe she was actually here, a guest in such surroundings. It seemed a long way from Burnfoot, she reflected wistfully, and not just in miles.

She sighed. Or course, she would be going home to-morrow. Whatever happened—Julie notwithstanding—she had no intention of prolonging her stay. Which reminded her of the argument she had had with Jake earlier. She couldn't help wondering if she would have had the courage to leave today, if she hadn't fallen off the horse, and made such an idiot of herself. It was encouraging to believe she would, but now she was not so sure that she would have gone through with it. After all, if she had managed to ride back to the *castello*, she would still have had to find a way to get to Pisa. And what excuse could she have given Jake's parents? It wasn't their fault that she found their son so disturbing.

Her lips tightened. It was easy to be brave in the heat of the moment. But accomplishing her boast was something else again. Apart from anything else, she didn't even have a return ticket to London. A major drawback to your hosts' having their own private plane, she thought ruefully.

It was seven o'clock before Laura left the balcony to prepare for dinner. The afternoon had given way to evening, and the sun was leaving caverns of darkness in its wake. The valley was settling down for the night, and tiny pin-pricks of light were appearing between the trees. Smoke drifted from the few farmhouses that nestled in the valley, and a solitary bell was tolling from the church in the village.

But apart from this evidence of human habitation, there had been no sign of any activity at the *castello*. Although Laura had spent the afternoon waiting for the sound of a car to prove that Julie had arrived, she was disappointed. Her daughter was not coming, she acknowledged flatly. Had she ever believed she was?

But she stopped thinking at that point. She knew that if she ever conceded she had had serious doubts about Jake's intentions before she'd left London there would be no living with herself. And if she ever allowed herself the luxury of admitting that she had come here, knowing that her daughter was unlikely to return from Los Angeles, and fly straight on to Italy, she was lost. For her own sanity, she had to go on believing. Anything else was madness . . .

CHAPTER TWELVE

LAURA packed her case before she went to bed. It was a small gesture, but she felt better after she had done it. It proved, to herself at least, that she meant what she said, and that was important to her.

Not that anyone was likely to offer any objections, she admitted painfully. She had thanked the Lombardis for their hospitality before coming upstairs, and if they had had any doubts about the arrangements they had been too polite to say so. Besides, she argued, climbing between real silk sheets, that she noticed had been changed after only one night's usage, she had only come for the weekend, and it was Monday tomorrow.

As for Jake, she preferred not to think about him. In spite of the fact that he had been waiting for her when she'd gone downstairs, and had wanted her reassurance that she had suffered no after-effects of her fall, she had left him in no doubt as to her feelings. Although it had been difficult to speak to him in his parents' company, her accusing eyes, and the determined way she had shaken off his hand, when he'd attempted to escort her into dinner, had been pointed enough; and Jake was no innocent. He knew exactly what was wrong with her, and during the meal that followed his manner had grown increasingly withdrawn. Only when he'd met her gaze across the table, had she glimpsed a little of what he was feeling, but she had refused to be distracted by his brooding contemplation. It was all his fault, she told herself tensely. He had tricked her into coming here, and now he had to face the consequences.

All the same, she couldn't entirely exclude herself from all responsibility. As she lay there, watching the curtains moving in the draught from the balcony doors, which she had left slightly ajar, she had to admit that she hadn't offered much resistance, when Jake had told her that Julie wasn't coming with them. She could have insisted on spending the night in London, and waiting until her daughter was able to accompany her, but she hadn't. And if she was perfectly honest, she would have to say that she had given in, as much because of her own guilty attraction to Jake as in response to his persuasion.

She sniffed, and rolled on to her side, as a fat tear overspilled her eye, and dropped on to the pillow. It was such a beautiful night, the moonlight shining through the crack in the curtains, giving the room a pearly luminescence. It was a night for love, she thought unhappily. And wasn't it a pity that the only man she might have loved was too young, too rich—and involved with her own daughter...?

She thought at first she was dreaming. When she felt the depression of the mattress, and a warm body curled, sensually, about her own, she responded with instinctive willingness. She had been thinking about Jake, and it wasn't the first time she had had dreams of this sort. Indeed, she seldom slept without dreaming about Jake these days, and, although in daylight it might seem pathetic, at night she was incapable of denying her fantasies.

But this was different. As she turned in his arms, and felt the heat of his naked body, she was puzzled. The strength of his embrace was so real, so physical, that she could actually feel the taut muscles that covered his belly, could even smell the musky scent of his skin. Always before, the dream had given way to substance; when she'd reached for him, he had melted; when she'd tried to hold on to him, he'd been gone. That was why she had always awakened, hot and frustrated, torn by emotions she had had no hope of fulfilling.

But not now. Now, she could wind her arms around him. She could press herself against him, and feel the instantaneous response of his body in return. Oh, God, she thought wildly, was she going mad? Was his arousal of her body the previous day responsible for this change in her perception?

But when his lips found hers, any previous perceptions fled. This was no dream, she realised, even while her mouth opened helplessly beneath the hungry possession of his. This was real. This was actually happening. Jake was in her bed, as naked as the day he was born, and she was coiled about him, as if she never wanted to let him go.

Reason was slow in coming, but, when it did, she fought to get free. Even though, seconds before, she had let him thrust his wet tongue into her mouth, she beat at him now with her fists, until he was forced to lift his head.

'Let go of me!' she choked, trying to wriggle away from him. 'You have no right to do this!'

'No?' Jake resisted her attempts to escape him without too much effort. 'I rather thought you were glad to see me.'

'Me?' Laura panted. 'You're crazy!'

'Well, a few moments ago——'

'A few moments ago, I was asleep,' she retorted, aware that her struggles had driven her nightshirt up above her thighs. 'Jake, let go of me. Please.'

Jake shifted, but he didn't release her. He simply drew her closer, opening his legs and trapping her between them. It enabled him to free one hand to smooth the tumbled hair back from her temple, to brush her quivering lips with his thumb, and scrape his nail against her teeth.

'Keep still,' he said, and in the moonlight she could see the sensual twist of his lips, as he took every conceivable liberty with her body. Ignoring her frustrated efforts to fight him, he allowed his hand to trail down over her breasts, and her uncontrollable response made him smile.

'This—this is—unforgivable,' she gulped, using her anger to sustain her. But she knew that the longer he held her, the longer he played with her treacherous emotions, the less likely it was that she would win this unequal contest. One hand in the small of her back was urging her against his tumescent maleness, and the heat of him against her groin was driving all coherent thoughts out of her head.

'You want me,' he said, inching the nightshirt over her midriff.

'No——'

'Yes.' He sighed with satisfaction as the offending garment flipped over her breasts, and their fullness was exposed to his hungry gaze. He took the swollen globes into his hands, and squeezed them sensuously. 'Now, tell me about it,' he breathed, stroking their proud crests with his thumb. *'Ah, cara, sono belli, vero?'*

'I don't know—I don't know what you're saying,' protested Laura fretfully, but the possessive touch of his hands on her body was rapidly making everything else of little importance. He had removed the nightshirt completely now, and the fine dark hair that filmed his chest was disturbingly pleasurable against her skin. It arrowed down below his navel to the cluster of rough curls that cradled his sex. And as he moved, she involuntarily arched against him.

'I was only telling you you're beautiful,' he whispered huskily, taking one of her fluttering hands, and pressing it over his pulsating shaft. He groaned. *'Molta bella,'* he got out thickly. 'I want to be a part of you.'

'Oh, Jake,' she breathed unsteadily, but it was no longer an objection. The silky heat of his arousal against her hand had banished any lingering thought of resisting him. When his hand slid between her legs, she didn't try to stop him. She wanted him to touch her there. Her flesh was crying out for the quivering release he had given her the day before. But when his lips slanted over hers, and his tongue plunged aggressively into her mouth, she knew she wanted more. She could smell him; she could taste him; the musky male scent of his body was driving her insane. She could feel her readiness on his hands—readiness for him.

She wasn't aware of making any sound, but when Jake removed his hand she must have done, because he soothed her with a kiss. 'Be patient, *amorissima*' he said, though his own voice was far from controlled. He parted her legs with one hairy thigh, and moved until the throbbing pulse of his manhood was nudging her tight core. 'Let me love you,' he added hoarsely, and unable to restrain himself any longer, he thrust urgently inside her.

Laura gasped. She couldn't help herself. It was so long since she had known a man's body, so long since Keith had taken her virginity. It was as if she had never known a man before, and Jake was so big that he couldn't help bruising her.

'Laura! *Cara!*' he exclaimed, covering her hot face with kisses. '*Mi dispiace*, I am sorry! Did I hurt you?'

But Laura was finding that any pain she had felt was disappearing beneath the overwhelming pleasure of feeling his taut strength stretching the yielding source of her femininity. 'Oh, no,' she breathed, hardly aware of saying anything, as his body moved and swelled inside her. 'Oh, no, you're not hurting me,' she added, as her long legs curled about his hips. 'Oh, God, that feels so good! Jake—please! Don't stop now.'

It was as if she had been sleeping, as if every dormant nerve was awakening to the amazing awareness of her own sexuality. She had never felt like this before, never imagined she could feel such a tumult of emotion. She wound herself about him, meeting his invasion with an eagerness she simply couldn't deny. She no longer thought about who he was, or where they were, or anything outside this room, and this bed, and the satisfying thrust of Jake's hard body...

Of course, she had to think eventually. No matter how dramatic her personal fulfilment might have been, sooner or later, reality had to raise its ugly head. And it was ugly, she thought dully, as the wild heights of enchantment Jake had lifted her to, dropped back into a well of despair.

Oh, it was easy to be wise after the event, easy to berate herself for allowing it to happen, for letting Jake do what she had sworn he never would. But, the truth was, she was far too vulnerable where he was concerned, and he had known that, and used it to his own advantage.

And, as the ripples of delight faded away, and were replaced by increasing waves of remorse, a chilling self-abasement sowed the seeds of disenchantment. What had she done? she asked herself bitterly. What kind of a woman was she? What kind of a mother, to make love with her daughter's lover!

A groan of nausea rose inside her, and, half afraid she might lose control of her stomach, as well as everything else, she struggled to get free of him. But Jake was a solid weight on top of her. Lying between her splayed legs, with his face buried in the moist hollow between her breasts, he was apparently quite content to prolong his pleasure in the moment. However, when she began to shift beneath him, she distinctly felt his immediate arousal.

'God—*no*!' she choked, as her own body quickened in response. Not again. But she realised she had to get away from him, and quickly, before he used her own weakness against her.

'*Basta! Cosa fai?*' he protested sleepily, as she made a superhuman effort to wriggle off the bed, and she wondered, somewhat painfully, if he was confusing her with someone else. Did he sleep with so many women that he couldn't keep track of their nationality? Dear God, this was a nightmare! If only she could wake up.

But when Jake lifted his head and saw her, there was only satisfaction in the dark sensual gaze he bestowed upon her. '*Bella Laura,*' he said, confounding all her fears about identity. '*Mi amore, ti voglio*——'

Laura's heart pounded. She would not have been human if she had not felt some response to the husky resonance of his words. When his mouth brushed her temples, his tongue feathering over her eyelids, they fluttered closed. And she could feel herself beginning to drift, the sensuous touch of his lips and hands a mindless provocation. Where was the harm? her senses cried. Why shouldn't she just give in?

Not again!

Forcing her eyes open, Laura turned her head away from Jake's questing tongue. 'No,' she said harshly. 'No, don't touch me! How—how can you do this? You're going to marry—Julie!'

'*Che?*' Jake's reaction was vehement, and he came up on his elbows, to glare down at her accusingly. 'What are you saying?' he demanded, and when she would have used the freedom he had given her to put the width of the bed between them he straddled her with his knees. Then, imprisoning her between his strong thighs, he said savagely, 'No!' And, although the word sounded more Italian than English, its meaning was unmistakable. 'No, I am not going to marry Julie,' he repeated emphatically. 'I do not know where in hell you got that from, but believe me, it is not going to happen!'

The postcard was lying face-up on the mat, when Laura opened the cottage door. It was a colourful postcard, the picture showing a view of the Hollywood hills, with the famous HOLLYWOOD sign, depicting the movie capital of the world, in the foreground.

It was from Julie, of course, thought Laura tensely, bending unwillingly to pick up the card. And she ought to be flattered that, even on such an exciting mission, her daughter hadn't forgotten her.

But, it was the last thing she needed at this moment. A reminder of where her daughter was, and what she was doing, and why she hadn't spent the weekend at Castellombardi.

Now Laura lifted her case into the tiny hallway, and inched herself round it, so that she could close the door. Then, she collapsed somewhat tearfully back against it, allowing the pent-up emotions of the past twenty-four hours to have their way. It was so good to be back in her own home again, and without the postcard in her hand she could almost have convinced herself she was content.

But the postcard had changed things. No matter how unwelcome it might be, it had served to bring reality back into focus. She couldn't escape what she had done. She couldn't erase the events of the past forty-eight hours. What had happened, had happened, and she was going to have to live with it.

She closed her eyes, as a wave of weariness swept over her. She was tired, so tired. And it wasn't because Jake had exhausted her—not directly, anyway. She sighed, remembering the terrible row they had had over Julie. Whatever feelings Jake might have had for her, the bitterness of the words they had exchanged must have changed that, too. He hadn't appeared at breakfast. He hadn't driven her to the airport in Pisa. Indeed, she hadn't seen him since he'd stormed out of the bedroom the night before.

God! She pushed herself away from the door, and walked heavily into the cold living-room. While she was away, she had turned the heating off, and although it should have been warm enough she felt chilled right through. But she had the feeling that the coldness she felt came from within, not without, and no crackling fire or clunking radiators would make a scrap of difference.

She looked at the postcard again. She supposed she ought to see what Julie had to say, but she was loath to look at her daughter's handwriting. Not yet, she thought tightly, setting the postcard down on the mantelshelf. She needed a hot drink, before she could face that.

She took some time, watering her plants, and washing the coffee-cup she had used early on Saturday morning. Even that reminded her of the excitement she had felt when the chauffeur-driven limousine had called for her, and it took the utmost effort not to give in to tears again. She felt so lost, so empty; and she thought how naïve she had been to think that what she had felt when Keith had left her had meant anything at all. Then, she had been more concerned about what her friends would say, and learning she was pregnant had aroused feelings of panic, not unrequited love.

But this was different, *so* different. Now, the idea that she might never see Jake again filled her with despair, and she didn't know how she was going to survive it. There were times when she actually wondered whether it wouldn't have been better to know that Jake was going to marry Julie. At least, then, she would have stood a chance of seeing him again. And, although that might sound like the ravings of a madwoman, desperation came in many guises.

If only they could have met one another, without Julie's being involved, she thought now, filling the kettle, and plugging it in. Only, of course, there was no way someone like her would ever have encountered a man like him. It simply didn't happen. She was a north-country school-teacher, whose only claim to fame was that the children seemed to like her. Well, other people's children, she acknowledged ruefully. She hadn't had such success with her own.

Nevertheless, the chances of a middle-aged teacher meeting a man like Giacomo Lombardi were virtually non-existent. She simply didn't move in the same kind of social circles, and without Julie's intervention their paths would never have crossed.

But they had, and, according to Jake, he had been attracted to her from the very beginning. Laura shook her head, scrubbing an errant tear from her cheek. Well, that was easy for him to say, she thought bitterly. How could he say anything else, when he'd just spent the last half-hour seducing the woman he was expressing his feelings to? And a man like him could be attracted to any number of women. It didn't mean anything. Not really. It was gratifying; flattering even; but it was just empty talk.

And she hadn't taken him seriously, she told herself firmly. She had known all along that any relationship between them couldn't last. Aside from everything else, there was Julie to consider, and Laura would do nothing to hurt her daughter.

Which was the reason she and Jake had had that almighty row, she remembered, with a shiver of dismay. So far as he was concerned, she was just using her daughter as a reason for denying what was between them. She didn't really care about Julie, Jake had told her contemptuously. She was just afraid of life, and Julie was a convenient scapegoat.

Of course, Laura had denied it. She had told him what Julie had told her, and, even if he hadn't believed her, it had opened up an unbreachable gulf between them. Besides, she wasn't sure she wanted the kind of relationship he had been talking about anyway. She was a conventional woman, with conventional needs. She simply wasn't the type to exist in that surreal world between what she knew and what she didn't.

Oh, he had told her he loved her. While he was making love to her, he had told her so in his own language, and, although Laura was no linguist, some words were unmistakable. But it meant nothing. In the throes of sexual release, people said lots of things they didn't mean. She had done it herself. Although what she actually had said, when

he had driven her to clutch at his hips and cry out in ecstasy, she would rather not remember. Suffice it to say, she
had betrayed everything she had ever believed in. She had
given herself to Jake, wantonly and shamefully, and he had
been angry because she had fallen back on the precepts of
a childhood she had lived with for almost forty years.

The kettle boiled, and she made herself a cup of instant
coffee. Then, after giving the garden an uninterested glance,
she carried her cup into the living-room. It was strange,
she thought, settling herself in an armchair beside the fireplace. In just three days, everything looked totally different
to her. The cottage; the garden; even this room—which used
to be so familiar to her—had lost its appeal. She felt like
a stranger in her own home. Well, she was a stranger, she
reflected painfully. A stranger to herself at least.

But it was no use, she rebuked herself impatiently. This
was where she lived, where she belonged. Meeting Jake—
even *sleeping* with Jake—had only been a minor deviation.
It wasn't as if he wanted to marry her, or anything old-
fashioned like that. The way he had reacted, when she had
suggested that Julie wanted to marry him, had convinced
her of that. An affair, yes. That was something else. But
how could she have an affair with him, knowing that when
it was over she would be left to pick up the pieces of her
life *alone*?

The postcard mocked her from its position on the man-
telpiece, and, pushing herself up from the chair, she took
it down. Hollywood, she thought ruefully. What must the
postman have thought?

Turning it over, she checked that it was addressed to her.
Yes, there was her name, and there was Julie's signature.
There was no mistake. The card was for her. So why not
read it? She was going to have to eventually.

She frowned.

Hi Mum. Here I am in Beverly Hills, and loving every
minute of it. The weather's great, the hotel's fantastic,
and I've met so many gorgeous men that I've lost count.
David—that's David Conti, the producer—he's been ter-
rific. He's introduced me to ever so many important
people—and he's single! He thinks I should stay out here,
and I'm really considering it. Sorry about the Italian trip,

and all that, but I don't suppose you were too disappointed. You didn't want to go anyway, and I'm sure
Jake let you down lightly. Will write when I have time...

Julie's signature was squeezed at the bottom, and Laura
bent her head towards the card to make sure it was her
daughter's name that was signed there. Of course it was.
Who else was likely to write to her from Hollywood?
Besides, it all fitted—except the bit about the trip. She
swallowed. Good lord, didn't Julie know she had gone to
Italy without her? Had Jake been expected to cancel the
arrangements?

Julie hadn't put a date on the card, but as another thought
occurred to her Laura tried to decipher the postmark. After
all, the card had travelled all the way from California. For
it to be lying on her mat, it had to have been posted several
days ago. But how many days?

After coping with the fact that the United States reversed
the date and the month of the year, Laura eventually worked
out that the card had been posted in Los Angeles more than
ten days ago. Which probably meant Julie had left for the
States before Jake had telephoned her.

She breathed a little faster. So he had been expected to
tell her the trip was off. So far as Julie was concerned, it
hadn't happened. But, could she seriously be considering
staying in California? What about her career? What about—
Jake?

CHAPTER THIRTEEN

THAT question haunted Laura in the days to come, days
that dragged interminably, until it was time to go back to
school. There was no one she could discuss it with, no one
she could confide in. Even Jess was unavailable, having
taken advantage of the mid-term break to have a short
holiday with her husband.

Not that Laura was convinced she would have confided
in Jess anyway. After all, she had only told her friend she
was accompanying Julie on a visit to her proposed in-laws.
She had said virtually nothing about the fact that Jake was
going with them. Oh, it had probably been taken for

granted, she realised that, but what would Jess think if she told her she'd gone with him alone?

Well, she could imagine what Jess would think, Laura conceded. What anyone would think, given the circumstances. That she was desperate for a man, she acknowledged glumly. That even though she had known her daughter was away, she had jumped at the chance to take her place.

She refused to consider why Jake had chosen to deceive her. It seemed fairly obvious to her. After his abortive trip to the cottage, he had obviously given up the idea of seeing her again, but this opportunity had been too good to miss. And she had made it so easy for him—believing his ready lies, and saying nothing to embarrass his parents...

Back at school, it was easier to pretend that nothing had changed. There, no one but Mark knew she had spent a weekend away. And he didn't know all the details. She had simply said she was going to stay with Julie.

Nevertheless, he did ask her about her trip when he caught her in the staff-room one morning. 'I hope you didn't spend the whole weekend running after Julie,' he said, risking another rebuff, but for once Laura couldn't meet his eyes.

'No. No, I didn't,' she said, gathering her books together, and preparing to depart. 'It—er—it was very pleasant actually. A nice—break.'

'Well, good.' To her dismay, Mark accompanied her out of the door. 'It's about time she started looking after you for a change. Does this mean you'll be seeing more of one another from now on? I must say Mother thinks you should.'

Laura couldn't prevent a spurt of irritation that Mark should have been discussing her and Julie with his mother, but it didn't last. If that was all that he had to talk about, why get annoyed about it? They probably had her best interests at heart. Or Mark did, anyway. She wasn't so sure about Mrs Leith.

'As—as a matter of fact, Julie may be going to work in California,' she admitted, not knowing exactly why she should want to tell him that, and Mark frowned.

'You mean—on a modelling assignment?'

'Well—no.' Laura wondered if she simply wanted to say it out loud, to prove it to herself. 'I think she'd like to become an actress. You know: films and all that.'

Mark stared at her. 'You mean, she's going out to California on the off chance that she might——?'

'No.' Laura sighed, wishing now that she hadn't confided in him. 'Not on the off chance. She's been invited to have a screen test. Apparently David Conti——'

'David Conti?' Mark arched his sandy eyebrows. 'She knows David Conti?'

Laura could feel the beginning of a headache starting in her temples. 'Yes,' she said wearily. 'I believe she was introduced to him in London. But now, I'll——'

'David Conti!' Mark said the name again and shook his head. 'My God! I wonder how she met him.'

Laura knew she should just leave it there. She wasn't in the mood for long discussions, but unwillingly Mark had piqued her interest. 'Why?' she asked, giving in to the curiosity he had kindled. 'Who is David Conti? I don't think I've heard of him.'

'Of course you have.' Mark frowned now, evidently trying to think of a way to spark her memory. 'That film we saw at the Gallery, about six months ago. You remember? God, I can't recall what it was called, but it had won an award at Cannes. A black comedy, about eastern European rapprochement. Very topical, as it's turned out. Damn, what was it called?'

'*Social Graces?*' suggested Laura doubtfully, and Mark pounced on her words.

'Yes. That was it. *Social Graces*. Well, Conti produced that film—and many others, of course. He's an Italian, I believe, though he spends most of his time in the United States.'

Laura's mouth went dry. 'An Italian?'

'Yes.' Mark nodded. 'Why? Did you meet him?'

'Heavens, no.' But Laura could feel the betraying colour deepening in her cheeks. 'I—was just surprised, that's all. Julie didn't mention that he was an Italian.'

'Is it important?' Mark was curious now, but Laura decided she had said enough.

'Only to Julie,' she managed lightly, pretending to straighten the pile of exercise books in her hands. 'Now, I really must go. My third-years will be climbing the walls!'

'Will I see you this week?' Mark called, as she started down the corridor, and Laura turned back rather reluctantly.

'Maybe—maybe next week,' she said, forcing an apologetic smile. 'With being away, I seem to have such a lot to catch up on at home. And you know how tiring housework can be.'

Nevertheless, she half wished she had agreed to go out with Mark when she got up on Saturday morning. The weekend stretched ahead of her, stark and uninspiring, and tackling household chores seemed the least attractive part of it.

Not that they took long. Despite what she had said to Mark, since her return from Italy she had had plenty of time to clean the house. Until she started back at school, it had been one way to fill all the hours in the day. He couldn't know that the last two weeks had seemed the longest two weeks in her life. It was hard to believe it was only fourteen days since she had left the cottage to go to the airport, in the limousine that had been hired for her. So much seemed to have happened in that time, and falling in love with Jake was no small part of it.

She was working in the garden, when she heard footsteps coming along the path that ran along the side of the cottage. She wasn't expecting anybody. She had even refrained from ringing Jess, because she hadn't wanted to get involved in awkward explanations. She assumed she would have to tell her friend one day. But, hopefully, not yet.

Now, however, she got up from her weeding, and looked rather apprehensively towards the sound of the footsteps. Her heart leapt briefly at the memory of another Saturday, when Jake had arrived so unexpectedly, but somehow she knew her visitor wasn't him. The footsteps sounded too feminine, she thought uneasily. And although it might be Mrs Forrest, she wasn't really convinced.

Even so, she still felt a sense of shock, when Julie appeared around the corner of the house. The suspicion that it might be her daughter had already occurred to her but,

nevertheless, seeing her doubts realised still caused a flutter
of panic.

Not that Julie seemed at all unfriendly, as she came to
the edge of the small sunlit patio, and subjected her mother
to a resigned stare. On the contrary, she looked rather
pleased with herself, and her attitude towards Laura was
as patronising as ever.

'Whatever do you look like?' she exclaimed, making the
older woman instantly aware of her mud-smeared
dungarees, and sweat-streaked face. 'Don't you ever feel
like wearing something—attractive?'

Laura stiffened. 'Sometimes,' she said, her own guilt not
quite sufficient to quell her indignation. 'I'm gardening,
Julie. You don't get dressed up to do gardening. You should
try it yourself and see.'

'No, thanks.' Julie changed the green suede bag she was
carrying from one shoulder to the other, and grimaced. She
flicked an insect from the skirt of her striped crêpe suit,
and visibly preened at the satisfying length of shapely leg
below its short hem. 'I've got much better things to do.'

'Really?'

Laura found she couldn't keep the cynicism out of her
voice, and Julie's expression hardened. 'Yes, really,' she
said, tapping an annoyed foot. 'So—are you going to come
indoors and offer me a cup of tea, or what? This is just a
flying visit, I'm afraid. I've got to be back in London tomorrow morning. But I thought I ought to see you, before
I go.'

'Go?' Laura blinked. 'Go where?'

'Back to Los Angeles, of course!' exclaimed Julie,
glancing impatiently up at the sun, and then backing into
the shade of the cottage doorway. 'Didn't you get my card?'

'Your card?' Laura stared blankly at her daughter, and
then gathered herself sufficiently to follow her into the
kitchen. 'Well—yes. Yes, I got your card.' She moistened
her dry lips. 'But I didn't—you didn't——'

'I did tell you about David, didn't I?' Julie broke in,
somewhat irritably. 'David Conti? The producer?' she
added, emphasising the words, as she would to a rather
backward child. 'I know I told you about having a screen
test, when I phoned you about going to Italy. Oh—sorry

about that, by the way.' She pulled a wry face. 'Still, I don't think I was cut out to be a *contessa*!'

Laura reached for the kettle, but it was an automatic action. She was hardly aware of what she was doing, and only when it started to hiss did she realise she hadn't filled it with water before plugging it in.

But had Julie really said she wasn't going to marry Jake? she wondered distractedly, almost scalding her hand as she took off the lid to fill the kettle. It certainly sounded that way, but she had been wrong before.

'Are you listening to me?'

Julie's complaining tone reminded Laura that she had indeed been allowing her mind to wander, and swallowing her confusion, she managed to shake her head. 'I'm sorry,' she said, steadying the rattle of the cups, as she took them out of the cupboard. 'I was just—so surprised, when you said you'd—changed your mind.'

'Changed my mind?' Julie frowned now, and Laura expelled the breath she had been holding rather quickly.

'Well—yes,' she said, feeling the heat invading her throat. 'I mean—you did say you wanted to marry Jake, didn't you?'

Julie sniffed. 'Oh, him!' She lifted her slim shoulders. 'I haven't seen him since before I left for the States.'

'No, but——'

'Oh, *Mum*!' Julie looked angry now. 'I'd rather not talk about Jake Lombardi, if you don't mind. Let's just say he and I have very little in common. I was wrong. I admit it. Let that be an end to it.'

Laura drew her lower lip between her teeth. 'But—I don't understand. I thought—I mean, you said he was the one!'

'Oh, God!' Julie groaned. 'Haven't you ever made a mistake?' Then her eyes glinted. 'Of course you have. How could we forget?'

'Julie——'

'All right, all right. That was below the belt. I'm sorry. But talking about Jake Lombardi brings out the worst in me. I thought he was in love with me, if you must know. But he wasn't. End of story.'

'He *wasn't*?' Laura knew she was risking a row with her daughter, but she had to pursue it. 'But—he did invite you to go to Italy with him.'

'Did he?' Julie didn't sound convinced. 'I suspect that invitation emanated from his parents. In any event, I don't think he had any intention of following it through.'

'You don't?' Laura could hear the kettle starting to boil behind her, but she paid it no heed.

'No.' Julie flung herself into a chair at the table, and propped her photogenic features on her knuckles. 'You see, it turns out that David is Jake's second cousin, or some distant relation like that. My guess is that Jake used that connection to get me off his back.'

'I see.'

Laura at last heard the kettle boiling, and turned to make the tea. It was quite a relief to do so, although her mind was still buzzing with what she had heard. Had Jake really arranged for Julie to have a screen test? Was the invitation to Italy intended for her all along?

'He was too old for me anyway,' Julie said, behind her, and Laura turned. 'He was,' Julie added broodingly, tracing the grain of the pinewood table with a crimson fingernail. 'I mean, you must have noticed what he was like, when he was here. Telling me what I should or shouldn't do. Trailing me round all those ancient monuments!'

Laura filled the teapot, and set it on its stand. 'You—you did say he was—old-fashioned,' she ventured. 'When—when you rang to say he wanted to—to meet me——'

'Oh, that was all my idea,' retorted Julie carelessly, helping herself to the milk. 'I mean—he was the most attractive man I'd ever met. And the richest, if it comes to that. And I'd heard that Italians place a lot of importance on the family. So—knowing what a homely little person you are, I thought for once I'd take advantage of the fact. But—it didn't work.'

Laura was staggered. 'You mean—it wasn't Jake's idea to meet me? You weren't on the point of getting engaged, or anything?'

'I never said we were.' Viewing her mother's shocked face, Julie shifted a little resentfully. 'I might have implied . . .'

Her voice trailed away. 'Anyway, I don't see that it matters. It's not you who's been dumped, is it?'

Laura couldn't take it in. 'Are you saying that when you brought Jake here, you weren't already lovers?'

'Lovers?' Julie scoffed. 'What dear old-fashioned words you use, Mum! We weren't sleeping together, if that's what you want to know. Though I don't see why you're asking. It's nothing to do with you, is it?'

Laura sat down rather abruptly. It was all too much to take. Suddenly, the things Jake had said made sense, and she felt a searing pain for her own stupidity. Yet how could she have known he was telling the truth? She was Julie's mother. It was only natural that she should have believed her daughter. But that didn't alter the fact that she had probably hurt him deeply. That, whatever his intentions, it was her he had wanted.

'Are you all right?'

Julie was gazing at her a little curiously now, and Laura realised her feelings must be showing. But what could she expect, when her whole world had been turned upside-down? she thought bleakly. Oh, God! If only she'd known!

'You look awfully pale,' Julie continued, though the concern was tinged with impatience now. 'I expect it's with working outside, in that hot sun. You'd better start looking after yourself, you know. You're not as young as you used to be.'

Laura expelled a trembling breath. 'I'm all right.'

'Oh, well...' Julie was easily convinced. 'As long as you know what you're doing. So—aren't you going to ask me why I'm going back to California? You seem more concerned with Jake than how successful my screen test was.'

Laura's fists clenched on the table. The temptation to tell her daughter why that should be so was almost irresistible. But old habits died hard, and Laura still had no wish to hurt her. Besides, it was too late now to regret the past. That interlude at Castellombardi would remain her secret. Not a guilty one any more, just a poignant memory...

Almost a week later, Laura found Mrs Forrest waiting for her when she got home from school.

It had been another long week, enlivened only by the fact
that it was one week nearer the summer holidays. And,
from Laura's point of view, the holidays themselves would
give her far too much time to brood about her mistakes.
But she was hoping to get away for a couple of weeks at
least, and she was clinging to the belief that time would
heal all wounds.

However, finding Mrs Forrest sitting in her living-room,
when she opened the cottage door, dispelled any personal
considerations. Something was wrong, she thought. She
knew it. Mrs Forrest's anxious expression, as she got to her
feet, convinced her of that.

'Is it Julie?' she asked, dry-mouthed, only capable of
one conclusion. Something must have happened to her
daughter. She had no one else.

'No——' Mrs Forrest put down the handbag she had been
clutching on her knee, and took an involuntary step towards her. 'There was a phone call, Mrs Fox. From—er—
from Italy. The caller asked if I would deliver the message
personally.'

Laura's knees sagged, and she reached for the back of a
chair to support herself. 'From—Italy?' she got out
unevenly. 'But—I—who——?'

'It was a lady, Mrs Fox,' said the cleaning woman eagerly.
'I think she said her name was Lombardy, is that right?
Anyway, she said you'd know who it was. She wants you
to call her back. Straight away.'

Laura caught her breath. 'Are you sure?'

'Oh, yes.' Mrs Forrest nodded. 'She said immediately.
That was the word she used—immediately.'

'No. I mean—about the name? Are you sure it was
Lombardi?' Laura stared at her.

'Oh, yes.' Mrs Forrest was adamant. 'That was the name
all right. You said it just like she did.' She bent and picked
up the pad beside the phone. 'Look, here's her number. I
jotted it down ever so carefully. She said you can dial it
direct. Marvellous, isn't it? Being able to call somebody all
those miles away.'

Laura nodded now, her mind busy with wondering why
Jake's mother should be calling her. For it had to be Sophia

Lombardi. She was the only female Lombardi she knew—apart from Luci, of course.

Pressing her lips together, she tried to adopt what she hoped was a casual expression. 'Well—thank you, Mrs Forrest,' she murmured, glancing uneasily towards the phone. 'I—er—I'll call her right away.'

'Oh...' Mrs Forrest looked a little disappointed now. Clearly she had hoped Laura would be so anxious to make the call that she might forget she was there. 'Then I'd better go, hadn't I?'

Laura managed a smile. 'I do appreciate your staying. To deliver the message, I mean.'

'You wouldn't like me to stay on?' suggested Mrs Forrest hopefully. 'If it's bad news...'

'I'm sure it won't be,' said Laura, more confidently than she felt. 'But thank you anyway.'

With the door closed behind the cleaning woman, Laura was able to breathe a little more easily. But not for long. Whatever reason the Contessa had for ringing her, she would not have done so unless it was something important. But what? Laura's brain simply refused to work.

A maid answered the phone to Laura's ring, and, although the woman's English was poor, a mention of the Contessa's name soon brought Sophia Lombardi to the phone.

'Laura?' she exclaimed, and hearing the relief in her voice, Laura's knees gave out on her. 'I'm so glad you felt able to return my call.'

'Um—not at all.' Laura sank down on to the arm of the chair. 'I—er—what can I do for you?'

'You did not mind me ringing?' the Contessa persisted anxiously. 'I realise it is something of an imposition, but I did not know what else to do.'

'No?' Laura shook her head bewilderedly. 'Really—it's not a problem.'

'You're very kind.' The Contessa let out her breath on a wispy sigh. 'But, even so, I am not sure I have done the right thing in calling you.'

Laura tried to contain her impatience. 'Why?' she asked, as a thousand different reasons presented themselves. 'I—please—is something wrong?'

'You could say that.' The Italian woman sounded rueful now. 'I—it's Jake, you see. He's—had an accident——'

'An accident!'

'—and I'm very much afraid he doesn't want to get better.'

CHAPTER FOURTEEN

LAURA came out of the airport at Pisa to find the Count's chauffeur waiting for her. She recognised the man immediately, not least because of his distinctive livery, though his good-humoured features and luxuriant moustache were surprisingly familiar. Probably because it was he who had brought her back to the airport after the shattering weekend at Castellombardi, Laura reflected tensely. There was nothing about that weekend she could forget.

'*Signora,*' he greeted her politely, installing her in the back of the limousine, as before, and depositing her single suitcase in the car's huge boot. '*Come sta?*'

'Oh...' Laura knew what that meant. 'Er—*bene,*' she murmured awkwardly. And then, with a tight smile, '*Grazie.*'

Nevertheless, she hoped the man wouldn't imagine she had taken a crash course in Italian. The few words she did understand had mostly been picked up from Jake, and in her present state of nerves it was difficult enough to remember her own language, let alone his.

However, after ensuring that his passenger was comfortable, the chauffeur seemed more concerned with negotiating the traffic around the airport than in conducting a conversation, and Laura was able to relax. Or at least try to, she amended, torturing the strap of the handbag in her lap. But, for the first time since speaking to Jake's mother, she felt she was actually making some progress towards her destination, and she forced herself to accept that for the moment there was nothing more she could do.

But it had been a terrible twenty-four hours since the Contessa's call. For the first time in her life, Laura had regretted the fact that she lived in the north-east of England.

It had been impossible for her to get a flight to London the night before, and although she had caught the first available plane this morning she had still had problems about getting on a flight to Pisa. It was Saturday, and approaching the height of the tourist season, and all morning flights were full. In consequence, she had had to wait until the middle of the afternoon before she'd been able to continue her journey, and the flight to Pisa had seemed the longest flight of her life.

But she was here now, she told herself steadyingly, feeling the coolness of the leather squabs against her back. Until they arrived at Castellombardi, there was nothing she could do, so she might as well try and rest, and enjoy the journey.

Which was something she hadn't been able to do since she'd made that call to the Contessa, she admitted drily. But how was she supposed to react, after learning that Jake had suffered some kind of mental breakdown? she wondered. It was hard enough to cope with the reality of what Sophia Lombardi had told her. To believe that she herself might play some part in his trauma was sufficient to convince her she might never rest again.

She turned her face against the cool upholstery, and tried to stem the ready tears that burned behind her eyes. It was unbelievable. Things like this didn't happen to people like her. For nearly forty years she had lived a fairly conventional existence. Even having Julie was not such a remarkable event, and the problems they had had were common enough, even in families where there were two parents. She had been quite content to believe that that was all there was. Until Jake Lombardi had come into her life...

She stifled a sigh. What had his mother said exactly? That Jake had had a fall from his horse? Yes, that was it. He had been missing for almost eight hours, and when the search party had found him he had been unconscious.

God! Laura shivered, even though the air outside the car hovered somewhere in the high seventies. According to Sophia Lombardi, he had been found near the foot of the ravine, and, remembering the morning she had sat on Caesar's back looking down into the valley, Laura could only marvel that he hadn't broken his neck.

In fact, Sophia had said, no bones had been broken. He had had concussion, and multiple bruising, but somehow he had survived any serious injury. Of a physical kind, anyway, Laura conceded, remembering what else his mother had said. The accident had apparently happened the day after Laura had flown back to England, and since then Jake's mental condition had deteriorated rapidly. His family had thought at first that it was simply the after-effects of his concussion, but, as time went by, they began to realise that something more serious was wrong.

'That was when my husband began to suspect that Giacomo's accident might not have been an accident,' Sophia had explained unevenly. 'He is—he has always been—an expert horseman, and although at the time our relief at finding him alive, and apparently unharmed, blinded us to other considerations, it soon became apparent that all was not well.'

'Even so——'

'Even so, nothing.' Laura's shocked protest had been swiftly swept aside. 'You have not seen him, *signora*. Believe me, he is not the man you knew—or the son I believed I did. I—we—are seriously worried about him.'

Laura had persisted even then. 'But—what do you think I can do?' she demurred. 'I mean, I——'

'I do not know if there is anything you can do,' Sophia had responded honestly. 'But—and it is a faint hope on our part—Giacomo did mention your name, while he was unconscious. When—when my husband found him, he said something, which we are now convinced was "Laura". Although I must also tell you that, since he has regained consciousness, your name has never been mentioned.'

A faint hope indeed, thought Laura now, pressing her face against the soft leather. But one which she, no less than his parents, could not ignore. According to the Contessa, Jake's withdrawal had begun the day she'd flown back to London, but whether that belief was based on truth, or a simple desire to manipulate the facts, Laura couldn't be sure. All she could be sure of was that Jake had told his parents he was bringing someone to meet them, whom he cared about. But in what context, and how deeply, only Jake knew.

She pulled a tissue out of her bag, and blew her nose. She would soon find out, she thought bleakly. Again, according to the Contessa, Jake had become virtually a recluse. He seldom left his apartments. When he did, it was always at night. He seldom spoke. Even Luci couldn't penetrate the wall of indifference he had built around himself.

Needless to say, he had lost weight, Sophia had continued. As no one seemed capable of persuading him to eat, the food prepared for him was returned to the kitchen untouched. He was simply not interested in anything, and, although it was obvious the Contessa was not happy about contacting Laura, she had felt she had no other option.

No doubt his parents blamed her for what had happened, Laura conceded tightly. They needed someone to blame, and she was vulnerable. Not that she resented it. It must be hell, when someone you loved wouldn't let you help them. It was hell even contemplating how she would feel if they were wrong...

It was almost dark when they reached Valle di Lupo. But the scent of the pine-strewn hillside was unmistakable, and as they drove down the steep track into the valley Laura tried to calm her suddenly fluttering nerves. What if Jake refused to see her? she fretted uneasily. What if he resented his mother's intervention? What if he simply insisted she turn around and go back home again?'

She closed her eyes against that possibility. What would she do if he did send her away? How would she cope, not knowing if he was alive or dead? Dear God, ever since she had spoken to Julie, and learned of the deception her daughter had practised, she had dreamed of seeing Jake again. How unbearable it would be if, having been given this chance, she was not allowed to tell him.

The huge limousine crunched over the gravelled forecourt in front of the house, and her nails curled into her palms. She was here. The time for uncertainty was over. Already the heavy doors of the *castello* were opening, and the Count's servants were coming out to meet them. She had to get out of the car and behave as if her arrival here was the most natural thing in the world, and not the single most important event in her whole life.

She was ushered into the huge baronial hall, just as she had been before, only then Jake had been with her, she remembered tensely. Now, she was on her own, and, in spite of her eagerness to get here, a timid sense of reluctance reared its cowardly head. Where was Jake's mother? Where was the Count? Suddenly the house seemed too big, too alien, for her limited ambitions. How could she presume on what had been, at best, a fleeting attraction? The Contessa must be wrong. If Jake was ill, it was nothing to do with her.

'*Signora!*'

A man, whom Laura vaguely recognised from her previous visit, was crossing the vast hall to greet her. She seemed to recall he was the Count's major-domo, or some equally archaic factotum, and her lips twisted as he came to a halt in front of her. Apparently she didn't warrant a personal welcome from Jake's parents, she thought bitterly. Whatever the Contessa had said on the phone, she was evidently not considered of sufficient importance to be granted a private reception.

But that wasn't this man's fault, and Laura responded to his greeting with a polite, '*Buona sera.*' It was all very formal and respectful, and, although she was grateful he didn't pursue a lengthy diatribe that she would not have been able to understand, she allowed him to escort her to the rooms she had occupied before with definite misgivings. What was she supposed to do? Behave as if everything was as it should be, and after a suitable interval go down to dinner, just as she had on that other memorable occasion? Without an alternative, what choice did she have?

By the time she had taken a quick shower, and refreshed her make-up, her nerves were as taut as violin strings. No one had come to inform her of the evening's arrangements, and, while she was fairly sure she was expected to join the family for dinner, she would have appreciated the confirmation. As it was, she had no idea how formal an occasion it was likely to be, and, remembering how elegant Jake's mother always appeared, she wished she had taken the trouble to pack an evening dress. But, when she'd been filling the one small suitcase she had brought with her, evening dresses had not been high on her agenda, and now

her choice was limited to the cotton suit she had travelled
in, and a simple linen tunic, packed more for its coolness
than its style.

She eventually chose the coffee-coloured tunic. In spite
of the sense of chill that emanated from some place deep
inside her, her head felt hot, her hands clammy. She
probably looked as if she was suffering from a fever, she
thought unhappily, pressing the backs of her hands against
her cheeks. If only she could be as cool and composed as
the Contessa. Although, she had to admit, the Contessa
had not been particularly composed the previous afternoon.

At eight o'clock, wanting any alternative, Laura left her
room, and made her way downstairs. The house was quiet,
unnaturally so, she reflected, remembering the buzz of conversation that had greeted her first appearance for dinner
in the *castello*. But then there had been a dozen guests or
more thronging the exquisitely appointed elegance of the
library. Now, as she paused in the open doorway, she found
she was the only occupant, the tray of drinks on a central
table mocking her solitary attendance.

She frowned. This was ridiculous, she thought tensely,
trying to summon anger as a counterpoint to panic. Where
was everybody? Why had she been brought here, if she was
to be abandoned to her fate? Dear God! A quiver of something approaching fear brushed the bare skin of her arms.
It was almost as if she was a prisoner here. If she didn't
hang on to her sanity, she would start believing Jake had
planned the whole thing...

She glanced behind her, but there was no one there. No
one to prevent her from leaving the *castello* now, if she
chose to do so. Except that she was at least a hundred kilo-
metres from the airport, she reminded herself bleakly. With
no obvious means of transport at her disposal.

Feeling in need of something to bolster her crumbling
confidence, Laura entered the library on tentative feet.
There was Scotch on the tray, as well as gin, and Campari,
and a dozen different liqueurs and mixers. Steeling herself
for discovery, she lifted the whisky decanter, and poured
herself a generous measure. Then, after ensuring that her
audacity was unobserved, she swallowed a mouthful of the
spirit, undiluted.

She was choking as the raw alcohol tore at her throat, when she sensed she was no longer alone. She turned, and through streaming eyes, she saw the shadowy figure standing in the doorway. Typical, she thought tearfully, dashing away the tears that caused her lack of clear perception. Whoever it was was seeing her at her worst, which was probably what they had intended.

'*Dio mio*, I should have guessed!'

Jake's hoarse exclamation was overlaid with tiers of self-derision, and while Laura tried, rather ineffectually, to regain her shattered composure, he turned sideways, and propped his shoulders against the door-frame.

'I—beg your pardon,' she got out at last, coughing to clear her throat of the constriction, which had little to do with the Scotch she had swallowed. 'Um—didn't you know I was coming?'

Jake rolled his head sideways and looked at her, his eyes dark with unconcealed irritation. 'Did you really think I did?' he queried, and, unable to sustain that cool, faintly mocking gaze, Laura's eyes flickered down over the lean contours of his body. Not that this exercise afforded her much satisfaction, she acknowledged ruefully. In spite of the earliness of the hour, Jake was apparently dressed for bed, his uncompromisingly black silk dressing-gown relieved only by the comparative paleness of his bare calves beneath.

'I—where is your mother?' she asked, instead of answering him, forcing herself to look into his face again. He certainly didn't look well, she thought, almost inconsequentially. But even now, here, faced with the undeniable evidence of what the Contessa had said, Laura still couldn't believe she was in any way responsible for his condition. Even though her heart palpitated at the thought that he might be suffering some inner mental torment, she couldn't bring herself to speak the words that might unlock his anguish. His mother could be wrong...

'Don't you know?' Jake responded now, his voice entirely without expression, and, realising she had to take the initiative here, Laura shook her head.

'Why should I?'

Jake studied her still-flushed face for a few seconds, and then straightened away from the frame. 'But it was she who invited you here, was it not?' he enquired flatly. 'I should have suspected something was going on, when she told me she was leaving——'

'Leaving?'

Laura was aghast, and Jake's mouth assumed a cynical slant. 'Yes, leaving,' he repeated, with the first trace of satisfaction in his tones. 'She and my father are spending the weekend in Rome—with Luci.'

Laura caught her lower lip between her teeth. 'I see.'

'Do you?' Jake's dark brows arched over eyes that had never looked more bleak. 'Well, I do not.' He raked a hand through his already tumbled hair, and, in spite of her anxiety about him, Laura found the fact that it trembled slightly gave her more hope, not less. 'Ever since—well, ever since I had a slight accident, a fall from my horse, nothing more— my mother has scarcely let me out of her sight. Then, sud-denly, this morning, she announces she is desperate for en-tertainment. She says she has things to buy, people to see, a desire to visit the opera. All of which necessitate a visit to the city.' He made a gesture of impatience. 'I should have realised it was out of character. After all that had gone before, I should have known she would not leave, unless——'

He broke off then, and in spite of her own misgivings Laura guessed he was already regretting saying what he had. In a few words, he had endorsed most of what the Contessa had told her, and, although it was a long way from the interpretation his mother had put upon it, nevertheless, it gave Laura the opportunity she needed.

'Yes,' she ventured carefully. 'Your mother—did tell me you'd had a fall——'

'Really?'

The sarcasm in his voice was unmistakable, but Laura refused to be deterred. 'Yes,' she said again, smoothing her damp palms down the seams of the cotton tunic. 'She— also said you were unconscious when they found you.'

'All right.' Jake's fists balled in the pockets of his dressing-gown. 'So, I knocked myself out, when I fell. *Basta cosi!*'

Laura pressed her lips together for a moment. 'How—
how far did you fall? The Contessa said you were found
near the foot of—of the ravine.'

Jake's mouth hardened. 'Does it matter? As you can see,
I am quite recovered.'

Laura trembled. 'I—don't think so.'

'What? You don't think it matters? My sentiments
exactly.'

Laura tensed, but his derisive words did not deter her.
'No,' she said steadily, 'that's not what I meant, and you
know it. I—I don't think you have recovered. And—and
nor does your mother.'

'Ah.' Jake's lips twisted, and, leaving the door, he walked
heavily across to where the tray of drinks was waiting. For
a moment, Laura half thought he was coming towards her,
and her pulse faltered in its mad tattoo. But then, as his
real destination was revealed, her heart picked itself up
again, battering away at her chest, as if it were some im-
prisoned creature, desperate to escape. 'Now, we come to
the crux of the matter, do we not?' he remarked, pouring
himself a generous measure of the spirit that had caused
Laura so much discomfort earlier. 'My mother's opinion
is of the essence, *no*? The only opinion worthy of any value.'

'What do you mean?'

Laura was troubled, not least by the way he was swallowing the whisky. Should someone in his condition be
drinking alcohol? she wondered. But then, she chided
herself, she didn't really know what condition that was.

'I mean,' he responded, after pouring himself another
measure, 'were it not for my mother, you would not be
here.' He studied the contents of the glass with bitter intensity. 'Still, that is not entirely your fault. I know how
persuasive my Mama can be. Were it not for her silver
tongue, I would never have attended the charity function
in Rome, where I met your most estimable daughter. Ergo,
we would never have met.' He raised his glass in mock salute.
'Like me, I expect you are wishing now we never had.'

'*No!*'

Laura's response was vehement. She could never wish
that. Even though there had been times when she had wished
for the ignorance of not knowing the torment Jake had

brought her, deep inside her she knew it was a torment she would willingly face again, if it was a choice between her and Jake's happiness.

'No?' he echoed now, and, although the word was innocent enough, its enunciation wasn't. 'No, don't tell me. You've suddenly realised I'm the single most important thing in your life, and you were just waiting for my mother's call to fly here and tell me so!'

Laura hesitated, and then, realising he deserved nothing less than the truth, she nodded. 'Yes.'

'*Dio*!' The expletive that followed his curse was every bit as contemptuous as she had expected. 'I thought better of you, Laura. *Bene*, you have come here—at my mother's request, you have virtually admitted as much—and now, because you find my parents are not here, you think you can stand there and tell me you came because I needed you!' He swore again. 'What is going on? Are they *paying* you to say these things to me?'

Laura was appalled at the depths of his cynicism. Dear God, had she done this to him, as his mother had implied? Was she to blame for the bitter, world-weary lines that scored his face? He had lost weight. She had noticed that at once. But now she noticed how his bones bulged from the shoulders of his dressing-gown; how thin and angular were the hands that gripped his glass. The Contessa had not been exaggerating, she saw. Whatever the reason for Jake's malaise, something was tearing him to pieces from the inside out, and she knew she couldn't leave here without discovering what it was.

'No one's paying me,' she said now, bringing her hands together, and slotting her fingers. 'I admit it—I did come because your mother asked me to. But—but that doesn't mean I didn't want to come anyway. I—I did. I just didn't know how.'

'Liar!'

'I'm not lying.' Moistening her lips with a nervous tongue, Laura moved a step nearer to him. 'I—I did want to see you again——'

'To *see* me.'

'Yes, I did. But—how could I?'

'Is that supposed to be a serious question?'

'Yes.' She swallowed. 'You forget—I don't know where you live either in Rome or—or that place near Viareggio you spoke about. I don't even have your telephone number.'

'Julie would have told you.'

Jake was dispassionate, but Laura was glad he had mentioned her daughter's name. It gave her the opportunity to tell him what had happened. She doubted he knew. His mother had said he had refused to take any calls.

'I—didn't want to ask Julie,' she said, and, although it was the truth, its connotations were ambiguous, to say the least, and Jake knew it.

'No,' he conceded, agreeing with her when she least wanted him to. He swallowed the remainder of the whisky in his glass, and, to her dismay, poured himself another. 'We must not upset Julie, must we? Never let it be said that her happiness should take anything but prime position in your life. To hell with everyone else's happiness—even your own. So long as we ensure that dear little Julie gets everything she wants.'

'It's not like that!' Laura caught her breath despairingly. 'Please——' as he gave her a scornful look '—it's not! I—didn't understand before. Now, I do.'

'Do you?' Jake gave her a weary look. 'Or has Julie told you she is giving up her modelling career, in favour of an acting one, and you no longer feel the need to worry about her?'

Laura stared at him. 'Yes. No.' She blinked. 'How did you know about—about——?'

'Her acting career?' Jake's lips twisted. 'Didn't she tell you I introduced her to David Conti?'

Laura tried to absorb what he was saying. 'You mean—it was because of you, that—that——?'

'That he offered her a screen test?' Jake put down his glass, and wedged his hips against the edge of the table. Folding his arms across the parting lapels of his dressing-gown, he regarded her pityingly. 'You didn't honestly believe that a man like Conti would fly her out to Los Angeles, just to have a screen test, without some incentive!' He shook his head. 'She could have been tested equally well in London. And besides, the odds against someone like Julie, with no acting experience, and fairly average looks, at-

tracting the attention of a well-known film producer, must
be astronomical!'

Laura stiffened. 'Julie is a beautiful girl!' she exclaimed
defensively, but Jake's mouth only took on an even deeper
curl of derision.

'David knows hundreds of beautiful women,' he assured
her flatly. 'Los Angeles—*California*—is full of them!'

'But—she says—he—*likes* her.'

'He does.' Jake shrugged. 'For some reason, best known
to himself, he is attracted to her. But do not go imagining
that gold rings and orange blossom are on the horizon. They
are not.'

'As I did with you, you mean?' Laura countered quickly,
and Jake's mouth hardened.

'There was never any question of my association with
your daughter ending in marriage,' he told her harshly. 'If
she told you there was, she lied.'

'Yes.' Laura's head dipped up and down. 'Yes, I know
that now.'

'Because she told you so?' Jake regarded her coldly. 'So—
you believe her, but not me.'

'I wanted to believe you——'

'But you did not,' retorted Jake, his lean face contorted
with emotion. 'What kind of man did you think I was? Did
you really believe I could sleep with Julie one week, and
her mother the next?'

Laura shifted unhappily. 'I—I didn't know what to think.'

'Oh, no!' Jake wouldn't have that. 'I will not accept that
even you were that naïve!'

Laura bent her head. 'And if I was?'

'It's not relevant.'

'It is relevant.' She lifted her gaze to his, her eyes seeking
some minute trace of weakening in his contemptuous face
'You—you have to understand, my—my sexual experience
began and ended when I was sixteen. Oh, I know it sounds
incredible, but it's true. Keith—that was Julie's father's
name—he—he taught me everything I knew. And that was
precious little, as—as you must have realised for yourself.
You see, sex—sex with him was something—furtive; a for-
bidden experience, that I imagined would be—romantic.
Only, of course, it wasn't. It—it only happened one time.

As soon as he discovered I was a—that I had never been with a man before, he ended the relationship. By the time I realised I was pregnant, he had left town. I never saw h:.n again.'

Jake's face was expressionless, and when he didn't say anything Laura hurried on, before her courage abandoned her completely.

'He was married, you see,' she added, biting her lips. 'I didn't know that, of course. And I don't think he ever intended his association with me to go as far as it did. It—it was my fault, for assuming—for assuming—well, for thinking he meant the things—the things he said.'

There was silence after she had finished. Jake still said nothing, and, had it not been for the fact that he had watched her intently throughout her fumbled explanations, Laura thought she would not have been unjustified in wondering whether he had actually heard a word she said. Or perhaps he had heard, but he still didn't believe her, she conceded wretchedly. And why should he, after all? It was a pathetic admission to make.

'So—so you see,' she appended at last, when the unnatural stillness was beginning to shred her already screaming nerves, 'you—you have to make allowances for my—my ignorance. I—I'm not like—not like the women you're used to—to dealing with.' A faintly hysterical laugh escaped her. 'I think—I think even you have—have to admit that.'

Jake moved then, and Laura jumped, but he only lifted his hand to massage the muscles at the back of his neck. She stood there numbly, while his fingers kneaded the taut flesh, and the lapels of his robe pulled apart and came together again in unison.

The action was magnetic. Laura tried to look away, but her eyes were drawn to that tantalising opening. All of a sudden, she was remembering the feel of his satin-smooth skin against her cheek. She was recalling how it had felt, when he had rubbed himself against her, and when she caught a glimpse of the disc of dark flesh that surrounded his nipple, she wanted to go to him, and take it into her mouth . . .

Her head spun, and, realising that if she stayed here any longer she was likely to do exactly as she was fantasising, Laura forced herself to look elsewhere. Her hands provided a satisfactory alternative, the knuckles white, as she dug her nails into her palms. She had to get out of here, she thought. She had to make a dignified exit. But how did one make any kind of exit in circumstances like these?

'Do you want to go to bed with me?'

The dispassionately spoken invitation stilled the madly churning turmoil of her thoughts, and Laura's eyes jerked to his in horrified comprehension.

'I—what did you say?'

'I said—do you want to go to bed with me?' Jake repeated, with a callous lack of delicacy, and Laura's control shattered into a thousand jagged pieces.

'You—you—how dare you?' she got out at last, all thoughts of humouring him swept away on the tide of humiliation that poured over her. 'What—what do you think I am?'

'That is what you came for, is it not?' he taunted, not a whit daunted by her feeble surge of indignation. '*Perche?* Did you find you liked it, after all? Or did your current partner not come up to your expectations?'

'I—I don't have a—a current partner,' Laura protested in a choked voice, and then, realising what she was doing, she said no more. She had no need to justify herself to him, she thought painfully. He had no right to say these things to her. Just because his mother had asked her to come here, and she had done so, did not give him licence to treat her like some kind of high-priced whore. It was sickening. It was obscene. And she had no intention of pandering to his perversions.

The door was still open, and she headed towards it. The Contessa was wrong, she thought, blinking back tears. Jake didn't care about her. He only wanted to destroy her. And she had given him the weapons to do it quite successfully...

CHAPTER FIFTEEN

LAURA was pushing her belongings back into her suitcase, without much regard for their well-being, when someone knocked at her sitting-room door.

She was tempted to ignore it. It was probably one of the servants, she thought, come to see if she wanted anything to eat, but even the possibility that it might be Jake did not arouse any feelings of anticipation inside her. If it was him, he had probably come to finish what he had started downstairs, she thought bitterly, and she knew she wasn't strong enough to take any more of his accusations. Besides, he was right. If she was totally honest with herself, she would admit that she had come here to go to bed with him. But what he didn't know, and what he had completely failed to understand, was why.

The knock came again, and, although she was reluctant to waste any more time, courtesy demanded that she answer it. Crossing the floor, she paused to school her features into a mask of politeness, and then pulled open the door.

It was Jake, and even though none of her feelings showed in her face Laura realised she had known it all along. She was so deeply attuned to his mind that she had sensed that, however painful it might be, their involvement with one another was not over yet. But what she had not been prepared for was the fact that he had taken the time to put on a shirt and a pair of black trousers, and although his feet were still bare he looked more civilised.

'I'm sorry,' he said simply, and, because it was the very last thing she had expected him to say, Laura was briefly speechless.

Then, because something was obviously expected of her, she managed to shake her head. 'Are you?' she asked, in a tight, brittle, little voice. 'For what?'

'For this,' said Jake softly, putting out his hand, and wiping an errant tear from her cheek. 'For everything. Will you forgive me?'

Laura stared at him, her eyes burning with tears as yet unshed. 'I'm—I'm packing,' she blurted, glancing behind her at the clothes tumbling from the suitcase, clearly visible on the bed in the adjoining room.

'Then unpack,' Jake advised her huskily, stepping forward, so that she was obliged to move aside. 'I'll help you.'

Laura didn't know what to do. She glanced from him to the open door, and back again, and then, pressing her palms on top of one another over her midriff, she said unsteadily, 'I—I won't go to bed with you. Whatever you say, I—I won't be—used.'

'Who's using whom?' murmured Jake drily, and there was a wealth of self-derision in his tone. Then, as if losing patience with this stilted little conversation, he reached for her, his hands at the nape of her neck leaving no room for deviation. With grim determination, his mouth found hers, and the hungry urgency of his kiss drove all sane thoughts from her head.

He kissed her as if he was desperate to assuage all the pain and torment he had inflicted by his cold indifference. The heat and anguish of the words he muttered as he devoured her lips ignited a warming flame inside her, and the invading possession of his tongue incited an answering hunger.

Abandoning all hope of retaining any self-restraint with him, Laura wrapped her arms around his narrow waist, and pressed herself against him. This was what she wanted, she acknowledged raggedly. This was where she wanted to be. If he was only using her, then so be it. If he was taking advantage of the feelings only he could arouse inside her, then that was the way it had to be. She couldn't hold out any longer. Dear God, she loved him!

The intensity of the emotions they had unleashed made any kind of withdrawal impossible. With their mouths still melded together, Jake swung her up in his arms, and carried her to the bed, carelessly overturning her suitcase on to the floor, before collapsing on the mattress with her.

Then, holding her on his knee, he covered her face with kisses, murmuring to her in his own language, as he nibbled at her ear, deposited light caresses on her eyes, bit the quivering fullness of her lower lip. His hands cradled her cheeks, explored the sensitive hollows behind her ears, invading the scooped-out neckline of her tunic.

And while he brought every nerve and sinew of her body to shuddering awareness, he encouraged her to do the same. And she needed no second invitation. Already, her fingers were deep in the thick, silky hair that he had neglected, just like the rest of him. Her nails had grazed his scalp, before exploring the shape of his head, the size of his ears, the vulnerable curve of his neck.

The zip of her tunic was quickly dealt with, and she obediently withdrew her arms when Jake pressed it down to her waist. Her bra proved even less of a hazard, and then he was burying his face in the hollow between her breasts, and she could feel the heat of his tongue tasting her flesh.

For her part, she contented herself with unbuttoning his shirt, and as she eased its folds from his shoulders she caught her breath at the taut skin she had exposed. There was not an ounce of flesh on his shoulders, and if nothing else, it convinced her that she must have played some part in his breakdown.

Jake's mouth sought hers again, and his exploration of her body reached her knees, suddenly clamped tight together in his lap. With painstaking insistence, he massaged the taut bones that blocked his further invasion, and then, as the limbs weakened beneath his patient ministrations, he slid his hand along her thigh, to the throbbing junction of her legs.

Laura's senses rioted. Every part of her was awakening and expanding to the seductive pressure of his touch, and, between her legs, she was flooded with the proof of her need for him. With a helpless little moan, she wound her arms around his neck and pressed her tongue into his mouth, and his immediate response was both urgent and satisfyingly thorough.

Rolling her on to the bed beside him, he quickly disposed of the rolled-up tunic, and then startled her by bending to press his face against the dark triangle clearly visible through her lacy bikini briefs.

'*Mi bella Laurissima,*' he whispered, his voice ragged with emotion, and she was no longer in any doubt as to his need for her.

She helped him undress, smiling when she found he wasn't wearing any underwear. 'Well,' he said huskily, as his trousers joined his shirt on the floor, 'I hoped I wouldn't need them.'

'You don't,' she assured him unsteadily, winding her legs around him. 'Oh, God, Jake, I want you!'

'I want you, too,' he told her, equally emotionally, 'and I really don't think I can wait any longer...'

Hours later, Laura discovered that the huge porcelain tub was quite big enough for two people. Sitting between Jake's legs, there was plenty of room to enjoy the frothy depths of the water, and Jake assured her that he had no objections to assisting her with her ablutions. On the contrary, he seemed to take a definite pleasure in soaping her rosy skin, and if his hand sometimes took the place of the sponge Laura didn't care. The eroticism of his caresses made a dizzying delight of this simplest of tasks, and when she began to emulate his actions he scooped her out of the water, wrapped her in a towel, and carried her back to bed.

'Couldn't we——?' she began regretfully, looking back over his shoulder at the bath, and Jake's lean mouth curved into a sensual smile.

'I didn't want to shock you,' he remarked, lowering her on to the bed, and beginning to towel her limbs dry, but Laura merely pulled him down on top of her.

'You can do anything you like to me,' she breathed, circling his lips with her tongue, and Jake needed no second bidding. With the ease of growing familiarity, his body slid slickly into hers, and the urgent lovemaking that followed left no room for any coherent conversation.

But later, after Jake had fetched a bottle of champagne from the cellar, and they were sharing a toast, he said huskily, 'Anything?'

Laura frowned then, not understanding what he meant, and Jake prompted softly, 'You said I could do anything I liked to you.'

'Oh!' Jake was enchanted to see that she was blushing, her cheeks pink in the lamplight. 'Well—yes. Of course I meant it.'

'All right.' He nodded. 'Then that must include marrying you.'

Laura caught her breath. 'Marrying me?'

Jake's expression tensed, just slightly. 'Doesn't it?'

'Doesn't it—what?'

'Include marrying you?' said Jake, a little tersely. He looked down at the sparkling liquid in his glass. 'It's what I want. It's what I've wanted ever since I met you on the stairs at the cottage. And—I'd begun to believe you might want it, too. Was I wrong?'

'Oh, no!' Laura couldn't let him think that, and the tension in his face eased considerably. 'You know I love you. I never want to leave you. But——'

'But—what?'

'Oh——' Laura lifted her slim shoulders, unaware that when she did so the peaks of her breasts bobbed enticingly. 'What are your parents going to say? I am years older than you are.'

'You don't look it,' declared Jake thickly, leaning forward to brush his lips against those dusky peaks. 'And besides, I should think my father and mother can be left in no doubt as to what I want. You don't suppose they took themselves off to Rome, without anticipating what was likely to happen in their absence?'

'Even so...'

'Look!' Jake took her chin in his hand and turned her face to his. 'I love you. I want you. What else matters?'

'But Luci——'

'I'm tempted to say I don't give a damn what anyone thinks, including my daughter,' declared Jake wryly. 'Anyway, Luci likes you. She never knew her own mother, so she doesn't know what having a mother is like.'

'All the same...'

Jake sighed. 'What else is there?'

'I just think your parents would have wanted you to marry someone else.'

'Really?' Jake shook his head. 'I think my parents will be incredibly relieved to know that they can stop worrying about us.'

'About you, you mean,' ventured Laura, regarding him anxiously. 'Did you—did you really miss me that much?'

'Stop fishing,' ordered Jake drily, but his eyes were eloquent with feeling. 'Of course, I missed you. *Dio*—when you walked out of here——'

He broke off abruptly, and Laura rubbed her cheek against his fingers, realising there was plenty of time to convince him he didn't have to miss her any more.

The moment was taut with emotion, and in an effort to restore their earlier inconsequence Laura said, 'Nevertheless, I'm sure your mother would prefer you to marry someone more—chic. More—sophisticated.'

'Which brings us back to rich again, doesn't it?' remarked Jake humorously, taking the point. He bore her back against the pillows, and pressed his face into her neck. '*Cara*, I married someone chic and sophisticated when I married Isabella. And it wasn't like this.'

Laura's eyebrows arched. 'Wasn't it?'

'No.' Jake bit her ear reprovingly. 'I told you before. I've never loved anyone as I love you.'

Laura shifted with sensuous grace. 'But what will your friends——?'

'My friends will envy me,' declared Jake huskily, and, losing patience with her questions, he found her mouth in a long drugging kiss.

But then, just as Laura was sinking into a deliciously erotic state of lethargy, he jerked back, cursing roundly. 'Damn,' he said, and when she gazed up at him uncomprehendingly, he pulled a wry face. 'I've spilled the champagne!'

Laura started to giggle, but she sobered somewhat when Jake pushed himself up to sit on the side of the bed. 'OK,' he said. 'I think the time has come to go back to my own bed.'

'No——'

Laura came up now, her eyes wide with apprehension, but Jake only regarded her with cool indifference. 'Yes,' he said, and then, as her expression grew anxious, he got

up, and pulled her up into his arms. 'You didn't think I
was going to leave you behind, did you?' he asked teas-
ingly, his grin pure devilment. 'Oh, *mi amore*, what I have,
I keep.'

Some time later, after they had transferred to the masculine austerity of Jake's suite of rooms, Laura brought up
the one subject they had not discussed so far: Julie.

· 'I don't know what she's going to say,' she murmured
sleepily, although the problem of her daughter seemed very
far away at this moment. 'When she came to see me, before
she left for California, I didn't even tell her I'd been here.'

'I shouldn't worry about it.' Jake was philosophical. 'You
can invite her to the wedding.'

'Do you think she'll be very unhappy about it?'

'Unhappy?' Jake uttered a short laugh. 'Oh, *mi cara*,
when has Julie ever cared about *your* happiness? Did it
ever occur to her that you might need a life outside that
existence you've been living for the last twenty years?'

'No, but——'

'No more buts,' said Jake flatly. 'From now on, we're
just going to look to the future, not the past.' He smiled.
'Now—do you know what? I am hungry. How does a midnight feast sound to you?'

David Conti's house at Malibu was right on the beach, with
a huge sun-deck opening off the spacious family room.
According to Julie, the house was usually full at weekends,
with friends of David's and their families, mingling happily
with David's own children from his three previous
marriages.

Julie, herself, seemed happy, Laura thought, watching
her daughter from her position on the sun-deck. In the year
since she had come to California, Julie had lost a lot of
the brittleness she had had when she'd worked in London,
and although she and David were not married yet Laura
thought it was a distinct possibility, whatever Jake said.

Her daughter had taken the news of her and Jake's marriage with some belligerence at first, and their first meeting
after the engagement was announced had not been entirely
friendly. But Julie was like that, Jake told her. She would
always seek to dominate her mother. She had done it for

so long. But now, Laura had Jake to back her up, and what might have been awkward had quickly been defused. Besides, even Julie had been unable to ignore their obvious happiness together, and perhaps she had realised she was in danger of losing more than she gained.

In any event, the idea of being related to the Lombardis, if only by marriage, seemed to have persuaded Julie of its many advantages. It made her association with David Conti that much more serious. She was now *family*, after all. And she did have a pleasant life in Los Angeles.

This was Jake's and Laura's first trip to the United States since their marriage. Although it was almost ten months since that event had taken place, three months ago Laura had had a baby son, and during her pregnancy she hadn't wanted to travel so far. Besides, Jake had insisted she do nothing to upset either her, or the baby, and Laura had been quite content to enjoy his undivided attention.

It had also given her the chance to get to know her step-daughter. Luci had been surprisingly eager to welcome her into the family, and it was not until the little girl had confided why that Laura had begun to understand her feelings.

Because her own mother had died before she was old enough to understand, Luci had spent most of her time with her grandparents, and although she loved them dearly, she loved her father best. But Jake had spent very little time with his daughter. He worked with his father, and because he'd had no wife to restrict his movements Count Lombardi had relied on Jake to accomplish most of their overseas business. In consequence, although Jake cared about his daughter, he had never been a proper father to her.

Now, it was different, Luci confided. Now they were a proper family, and whenever Jake travelled abroad he took his family with him. Especially Luci, Laura insisted, on those occasions when Jake would have preferred to have his wife to himself. She wanted the little girl to know she was just as important to them as the new baby. There would be no misunderstandings this time, she said.

Of course, they had a nanny for the children, and now, looking towards the ocean, Laura could see Miss Frobisher, tagging along behind Jake, Luci and David. Jake was carrying Carlo, their baby son, and the dapper little English nanny was trying valiantly to keep up with their easy strides.

As if sensing her eyes upon him, Jake looked back then, and waved, and Laura's heart turned over. It still seemed incredible that it should be she whom Jake loved, but he had proved it to her, over and over, in a million different ways.

His parents had been amazingly supportive, too. But then, no one could deny how good Laura was for Jake. He had never looked fitter, so relaxed and handsome, and when they were together their happiness was infectious.

Now, Laura waved back, aware, as she did so, how much she had changed, too, in the last year. Once, the idea of sitting on a sun-deck in a bikini, sunning herself in front of a crowd of strangers, would have sounded totally daunting. But Jake's love had made her confident. Because he thought she was beautiful, she felt beautiful, too.

'You have a super tan,' remarked Julie suddenly, coming to take the cushioned chair beside her. 'I suppose you spend a lot of time outdoors.'

Laura nodded. 'I suppose we do. We—er—we've been staying at Marina di Salvo since Carlo was born, and the sea air——' She shrugged. 'You know what it's like.'

'Hmm.' Julie swung her long legs on to the lounger, and adjusted her dark glasses. 'Marina di Salvo? Where's that?'

'Near Viareggio. Jake—that is, *we* have an apartment there.'

'Nice.' Julie closed her eyes. 'I guess it all worked out for you, didn't it?'

Laura sighed, wishing Jake were there to support her. But then, she rallied. She wasn't a silly spinster any more. She was Jake's wife, and whatever Julie said, she couldn't really hurt her.

So, 'Yes,' she said, in answer to her daughter's question. 'It did.'

'I'm glad.'

Nothing Julie said could have surprised her more, but Laura was sensible enough to be cautious. 'You are?' she ventured swiftly.

'Hmm.' Julie nodded. 'I guess I'd forgotten how young you really are. I'd gotten so used to seeing you as "my mother'', in quotes. The schoolmistress! It's easy to be selfish, if you never look beneath the label.'

Laura expelled her breath slowly. 'I see.'

'I hope you do.' Julie opened her eyes again, and turned to look at her mother somewhat ruefully. 'I've been a bitch. I know it. And when you said you and Jake—well, I could have scratched your eyes out then.' She grimaced. 'But recently—well, I guess you could say I'm getting softer in my old age. It's obvious Jake is crazy about you, and I'd be a fool to deny myself the only family I've got.'

Laura's lips parted. 'Oh, Julie!' she exclaimed, and she had hardly time to squeeze her daughter's hand before her stepdaughter came dancing across the deck.

And Luci wasn't alone. Jake, and Carlo, were right behind her, her husband's sable eyes dark and expressive, as they took in the scene they had interrupted.

'Are you all right, *cara*?' he asked, squatting down beside her, and giving Julie a wary look, and Laura smiled.

'Perfectly,' she said, taking their baby son, and tipping him over her shoulder. 'Julie was just complimenting me on my tan.'

'Really?' Jake didn't sound convinced, and Julie shook her head.

'Yes, really,' she declared, swinging her legs to the deck and getting to her feet. 'But don't say I don't know when I'm not wanted,' she added. 'Here—*Daddy*—you can have my chair. And stop looking at her like that. This is a respectable household.'

Jake grinned then, but he didn't argue, and after she had gone he lowered himself into the chair beside his wife. 'No problems?' he asked, linking his fingers with hers, and Laura felt almost too overwhelmed with happiness to speak.

'No problems,' she agreed huskily, and Jake gave a suitably contented sigh.

Next month's Romances

Each month, you can choose from a world of variety in romance with Mills & Boon. These are the new titles to look out for next month.

THE GOLDEN MASK ROBYN DONALD
THE PERFECT SOLUTION CATHERINE GEORGE
A DATE WITH DESTINY MIRANDA LEE
THE JILTED BRIDEGROOM CAROLE MORTIMER
SPIRIT OF LOVE EMMA GOLDRICK
LEFT IN TRUST KAY THORPE
UNCHAIN MY HEART STEPHANIE HOWARD
RELUCTANT HOSTAGE MARGARET MAYO
TWO-TIMING LOVE KATE PROCTOR
NATURALLY LOVING CATHERINE SPENCER
THE DEVIL YOU KNOW HELEN BROOKS
WHISPERING VINES ELIZABETH DUKE
DENIAL OF LOVE SHIRLEY KEMP
PASSING STRANGERS MARGARET CALLAGHAN
TAME A PROUD HEART JENETH MURREY

STARSIGN
GEMINI GIRL LIZA GOODMAN

Available from Boots, Martins, John Menzies, W.H. Smith, most supermarkets and other paperback stockists.

Also available from Mills & Boon Reader Service, P.O. Box 236, Thornton Road, Croydon, Surrey CR9 3RU.

An irresistible offer from Mills & Boon

Here's a personal invitation from Mills & Boon Reader Service, to become a regular reader of Romances. To welcome you, we'd like you to have 4 books, a CUDDLY TEDDY and a special MYSTERY GIFT absolutely FREE.

Then you could look forward each month to receiving 6 brand new Romances, delivered to your door, postage and packing free! Plus our free newsletter featuring author news, competitions, special offers and much more.

This invitation comes with no strings attached. You may cancel or suspend your subscription at any time, and still keep your free books and gifts.

It's so easy. Send no money now. Simply fill in the coupon below and post it to -

Reader Service, FREEPOST, PO Box 236, Croydon, Surrey CR9 9EL.

- - - - - - - - - - - - - - NO STAMP REQUIRED - - - - - - - - - - - - -

Free Books Coupon

Yes! Please rush me my 4 free Romances and 2 free gifts! Please also reserve me a Reader Service subscription. If I decide to subscribe I can look forward to receiving 6 brand new Romances each month for just £9.60, postage and packing free. If I choose not to subscribe I shall write to you within 10 days - I can keep the books and gifts whatever I decide. I may cancel or suspend my subscription at any time. I am over 18 years of age.

Name Mrs/Miss/Ms/Mr _____ EP18R

Address _____

_____

Postcode_____ Signature _____